y
g
r,

o

d
l-

of
n
e

Also by Christine Kling

CROSS CURRENT
SURFACE TENSION
WRECKERS' KEY

BITTER END

A Novel of Suspense

Christine Kling

BALLANTINE BOOKS • NEW YORK

2007 Ballantine Books Mass Market Edition

Copyright © 2005 by Christine Kling
Excerpt from *Wreckers' Key* copyright © 2007 by Christine Kling

Published in the United States by Ballantine Books, an imprint of The Random House Publishing Group, a division of Random House, Inc., New York.

BALLANTINE and colophon are registered trademarks of Random House, Inc.

This book contains an excerpt from the forthcoming book *Wreckers' Key* by Christine Kling. This excerpt has been set for this edition only and may not reflect the final content of the forthcoming edition.

Originally published in hardcover in the United States by Ballantine Books, an imprint of The Random House Publishing Group, a division of Random House, Inc., in 2005.

ISBN 978-0-345-47904-4

Cover photograph: © Alamy

Printed in the United States of America

www.ballantinebooks.com

OPM 9 8 7 6 5 4 3 2 1

for Tim
who's been there

The bitterest tears shed over graves are for
words left unsaid and deeds left undone.

—HARRIET BEECHER STOWE

ACKNOWLEDGMENTS

I would like to thank the following people:

My editor, Mark Tavani, my agent, Judith Weber, my sailing friends, Ken Bloemker, DEA retired, captain of the sailing yacht *Thalia,* and Michael Lyon, captain of the sailing yacht *Bossa Nova*. Officers Chris Reyes and Rich Love, Fort Lauderdale Police Department, my friends who let me bounce ideas off them, Kathleen Ginestra, LaShon Thompson, Fred Rea, Michael Black, David Raterman, Neil Plakcy, Laurie Foster, and Barbara Lichter, and finally my parents, brother, sister, and son who have always shown me their unwavering support.

I.

THE sun wasn't up yet when I rounded the bend in the river and came upon the fifty-foot Hatteras *Mykonos,* the yacht that belonged to the ex-husband of my ex–best friend, idling in front of the Andrews Avenue Bridge. The sky was a pale, washed-out blue, cloudless, promising a warmer day once the sun rose. But at that hour the morning was cold enough that wisps of steam rose off the surface of the dark river. Nikolas Pontus, the ex-husband himself, was up on the motor yacht's flybridge. He was alone, which surprised me, because now that he was a gazillionaire, I didn't think he ever did anything for or by himself. I pulled the hood of my sweatshirt up over my ponytail to drive off the chill that suddenly danced along the back of my neck.

Up on the Andrews Bridge, the bells were ringing and the bridge tender had started lowering the traffic gates. I shifted into neutral, not wanting to get too close to Nick or his boat and hoping the bridge would open soon so the *Mykonos* could disappear upriver, out of my way and out of my life. Nick was the reason my friendship with Molly had come to an end, and a thing like that you can't ever forgive.

It was quiet on the avenue for a Monday morning, especially compared to what it would be like an hour from now when the worker bees started filing over the bridge on their way to the courthouse. On the south bank of the river, the Downtowner, my favorite Fort Lauderdale restaurant and bar, stood silent and shuttered. Several white plastic beer glasses littered the tables out front, leftovers from those who had partied past closing last night.

An old woman pushing a baby stroller full of clothing and plastic trash bags emerged from the courtyard next to the restaurant and, after studying my boat for several seconds, turned away from me, passing under the bridge. I often saw her bent body walking the streets downtown, especially along the riverfront, her bones showing through the thin cotton of the plain white blouse she always wore, her white hair neatly pinned up off her neck. This morning, she hugged the ends of a bright red shawl wrapped tight round her shoulders. Beneath her skirt, her bare ankles looked frail above her dirty sneakers, and I wondered where she'd slept during the night.

I was traveling up the river onboard my forty-foot salvage tug, *Gorda*, bound for Summerfield Boatworks, where I had a 7:00 a.m. appointment to pick up a jittery new boat owner and his recently purchased fifty-seven-foot ketch. The job was a referral from George Rice, a broker friend of mine, who had called and pleaded with me, saying, "Seychelle darling, this is such a goddamn beautiful boat, and this buyer has never even driven a dinghy. The owner says he feels like he's turning his sixteen-year-old daughter over to a Hell's Angel, for God's sake, and he's refusing to sign unless this newbie gets help getting down the river." I'd quoted them a ridiculous price, and when they'd said okay, I couldn't turn it down.

Up ahead, the bridge span began its slow climb. The *Mykonos* had drifted side-on to the bridge, and Nick began trying to horse her around with alternating heavy-handed squirts to the big twin diesels. He was a lousy boat handler and, to my mind, an even worse human being. I wondered how such a creep could have made it so big in so short a time. When he'd married seventeen-year-old Molly and taken her out of our lives, he'd owned a greasy Greek sub and gyro take-out place on the boardwalk on Hollywood Beach. Now, he was the owner of a chain of high-end restaurants as well as a fleet of casino gambling boats. I watched as he finally got his yacht lined up with the bridge opening, then gave her too much throttle and flew through the gap on the rising tide. Money hasn't changed much, I thought. He's still a jerk.

The *Mykonos* had just cleared the far side of the bridge and I was just starting my approach when I heard a loud crack that echoed off the tall high-rises on either side of the river. That was followed by another crack; then from up on the Andrews Bridge came the sound of squealing tires. I caught a quick glimpse of the top of a black car headed north, down off the bridge, and it wasn't until later that I realized it must have made a U-turn up by the gates. My attention had been drawn to the sight of Nick Pontus slumped forward over the controls.

Nick wasn't moving, but his boat sure was. My God, I thought, he must have pushed the throttles forward when he fell. The big white sport fisherman's stern was starting to squat, and her wake frothed as she churned upriver past the shops and restaurants of the Riverfront development, where early-morning employees had stopped what they were doing to stare as the big yacht steamed past the docks, headed for the narrow opening at the railroad bridge.

I jammed the throttle forward on *Gorda* without thinking. Shit! On smooth water like this, that boat would pick up speed like a Porsche. There was no way my little tug could catch a Hatteras with her cruising speed of over thirty knots, but my years as a beach lifeguard and as a salvage operator had left me with certain reflex reactions to the sight of a person or boat in peril—even if that person was Nick Pontus.

The unmanned railroad bridge always remained in an upright position until a train was approaching. Then a buzzer went off, and a large digital clock told boaters they had five minutes to get clear before the bridge would automatically lower. Fortunately, the bridge was up, and there were no numbers on the clock, but the opening still looked mighty narrow for that Hatteras's sixteen-foot beam. From my angle, she looked to be lined up pretty square with the opening, but the slightest gust of wind, the smallest wave, or even a shifting of the weight onboard the boat would turn her aside and slam her into either side of that bridge trestle.

None of that happened. Breath exploded from my mouth. Nick still hadn't moved, and the boat slipped between the arms of the tracks, plowing on toward the huge oaks and quaint historical buildings of Riverwalk. While the boat had not hit either side of the railroad bridge, she was now headed dead-on for the boulders that made up the riprap that rimmed the park in front of the Old River Inn. The converted hundred-year-old pioneer home was Nick's flagship restaurant, his baby, the last place on earth Nick Pontus would want to crash and burn.

I leaned forward over *Gorda*'s controls, urging more speed out of the little tug. I had no idea if Nick was still alive, but I just kept thinking of all the fuel that boat must have in her tanks as she drove on, seeming to split the river with her wake.

Again, the boat's course never wavered. I gritted my teeth and felt every muscle tighten as I anticipated the impact. The *Mykonos* must have been traveling at better than fifteen knots when she hit the rocks.

I expected an explosion like something out of the movies. Instead, the big white yacht reared up out of the water like a humpback whale breaching in the deep waters far offshore. The thunder shattered the city's quiet as the fiberglass slid up onto the rocks and the diesels screamed out of control. I thought she was going to drive right across the twenty feet of lawn and into the Old River Inn's bar. The sight of that boat climbing skyward, her long bow and red bottom paint canted at a surreal angle, was something I had trouble wrapping my mind around. She looked like she was trying to fly. With half her hull clear of the water, the noise of the engines sounded louder than the night freights that crossed the bridge past midnight. Then, her screws must have hit stone, and she found the apex of her climb. Both engines stopped abruptly, and she began a slow, screeching, scraping slide back into the river.

The first thing I saw when I pulled alongside the yacht's port side was the blood splatter on the inside of the clear plastic enclosure surrounding the flybridge. Then I saw Nick's face. He'd slumped forward in the helmsman's chair, his head resting on its side on the steering wheel. His eyes were fixed open, dull as glass eyes from the taxidermist, and there was a gaping hole where his forehead should have been.

I closed my eyes and turned away, hand over my mouth, throat fighting to hold down the bile. Not even Nick deserved that. I blinked, felt the dampness on my lashes, and struggled for control.

Sirens. I probably should have called someone on the VHF, but the cops would make it here before the Coast Guard. The bridge tender must have called 911 as soon as he realized Nick had been shot. I heard them making their way across the quiet morning city. Police, ambulances, paramedics. Too late for Nick. The *Mykonos,* his million-dollar play toy, had become a crime scene.

The yacht's waterline was already several inches underwater, her blue boot stripe completely submerged. She'd come loose from where she'd lodged on the rocks and was starting to drift back out into the river. I could hear the whine of her working pumps, but the water was going in faster than it was going out. I didn't know how badly she was holed, but one thing was clear: the *Mykonos* was soon going to be on the bottom of the New River.

I guess you could say that's how I justified it. Taking her under tow, I mean. The cops wouldn't get it. Once they got here, they'd just string up their yellow tape and watch her go down. It also occurred to me that the insurance company would be more than a little pleased if I could get this damaged vessel to the boatyard before she sank.

It didn't take more than a couple of minutes to lash *Gorda* alongside the big yacht's aft quarter so I could climb aboard. I grabbed a couple of thick hawsers I'd already set out on deck for towing the ketch, and I tossed them into the yacht's cockpit. While aboard, I worked swiftly, dragging the lines forward and tying them to the windlass and cleats on the bow. I avoided looking up at the flybridge.

I leaped over the gunwales back into *Gorda*'s cockpit and threw off the lines that bound the two vessels amidships. Back in the wheelhouse, I backed off, then eased ahead slow, so that the towlines wouldn't drop off my decks until the lines grew tight. I glanced downriver toward the Allied Marine Yard. They had a big seventy-five footer in the slings already. I'd do better heading upriver for boatyard row. Increasing the power slowly, I straightened out the two boats and got us on course for the Seventh Avenue Bridge. I was determined not to slow or stop, so I reached for the mike and called the bridge tender.

"Securité, securité, this is the tug *Gorda* calling the Seventh Avenue Bridge, requesting an emergency opening."

Onshore I saw flashing blue lights in front of the Broward Center for the Performing Arts, and a couple of cops trotted across the lawn toward the river, waving their arms at me, stunned looks on their faces as I pulled away from their location. I called the bridge again as I nudged the throttles forward. "Securité, securité, tug *Gorda* calling the Seventh Avenue Bridge, requesting an emergency opening. My tow is sinking."

The bridge was about twelve hundred yards off, and I didn't hear any bells or see any movement in the bridge tender's tower. I reached for the tug's horn and blew five short blasts, waited about five seconds, and blew another five.

Gorda had plenty of clearance without a bridge opening, but the Hatteras stood tall. I looked back at her and reckoned that, at worst, she'd lose the hard top over the flybridge, and that was an acceptable loss. If we stopped now, I thought, as I checked *Gorda*'s gauges, we'd lose the whole vessel.

At last, bells started ringing, the traffic gates went down, and the bridge had just started to open when *Gorda* slid under. By the time the Hatteras slipped through, she cleared by mere inches. I doubt she would have made it if she hadn't already been a foot down on her lines.

As we plowed our way up the New River, past Sailboat Bend, under the Davie Bridge, and through the Citrus Isles canals, we were throwing up an atrocious wake.

Waterlogged as that fifty-footer was, I was still pulling her at better than six knots, though I had to slow her down some as we rounded the hairpin bend at Little Florida. Masts danced and lines groaned as the boats tied up in front of the luxury homes bucked and rolled. One fellow ran out across his pool deck, coffee mug in hand, shaking his fist at me and screaming curses. I knew I'd be responsible for any damage I caused, but I also knew that the Hatteras was sinking fast, and I had only minutes to get her to the slip.

I switched channels and tried to hail River Bend Marine, hoping like hell that someone was in the office at this early hour and had turned on the radio. No luck. After calling three times, I switched to channel 16, the emergency and hailing frequency, and began calling any vessel in River Bend Marine. I finally got an answer from a cruiser, an older fellow who told me after we'd switched frequencies that he'd round up some yard guys and they'd be waiting with the Travel Lift when I got there. I thanked him, and as we ended our conversation, the Fort Lauderdale Marine Patrol broke in, calling *Gorda*. I glanced back at my tow as she swung to starboard, and I tried to correct. The radio crackled again, the officer's irritation growing more apparent. I didn't have time to deal with them. I switched off the VHF and got back to the business of trying to keep my tug and waterlogged tow under control as we steamed upriver at a speed that made control purely an illusion.

As I swung round the bend and headed into boatyard row, it looked like an entire fleet of small vessels was there to greet me. Every yachtie in the area who had been listening in on channel 16 had jumped into his dinghy and come out to assist in getting the sinking yacht into the slipway. Charlie, the boatyard foreman, was in the yard launch, and he pulled alongside the aft port quarter of the wallowing sport fisherman to help slow her down. In the basin off the slipway, out of the current, I shortened up my towlines, got *Gorda* back off the starboard quarter, and, together, we eased *Mykonos* into the slings that dangled deep in the slip. The Travel Lift engine blew off a puff of exhaust and the slings tightened under the Hatteras just as the Fort Lauderdale Marine Patrol boat came screaming around the bend, blue lights flashing in the gilded morning light.

II.

"**W**HAT the hell did you think you were doing, Sullivan?"

Skip Robinson, Fort Lauderdale Marine Patrol officer, was standing on the wood dock next to *Gorda*, legs spread slightly apart, hands on his hips, his face redder than a Canadian's who fell asleep his first day on the beach. I'd docked my boat at the river end of the seawall that led to the slipway, and I'd sat perched on the bulwark, watching as Skip arrived and established a perimeter around the *Mykonos*.

"I was doing what I could to preserve your crime scene."

He let out a dry bark that was supposed to resemble a laugh. "Right. If that was all you wanted, you could have just left that Hatteras on the rocks where she was, and *my* crime scene *would have* been intact."

"I'm not going to argue with you, Skip. Arrest me if you want. Fact is, she hit in a spot where the riprap was so perfectly sloped she just slid straight up out of the water, and then straight back in." I shook my head, as I still had trouble believing it. "It was something to see. Anyway, there was nothing for it to hang up on."

Emergency vehicles began pouring into the boatyard: several police cars, an ambulance, even a fire truck that barely squeezed through the gate. I imagined the pack of them wandering all over town, not knowing where their crime scene had gone.

"But you took the victim away from medical assistance," Skip said.

I watched as the paramedics climbed first onto the boat. Two guys in blue jumpsuits from the Fort Lauderdale Fire Department climbed up the stainless ladder to the flybridge. "Come on Skip, look at him. It doesn't take a medical professional to see the guy's way beyond medical assistance." The two medics were already climbing back down off the bridge. It had taken them less than fifteen seconds to come to the same conclusion.

"Just don't go anywhere, Sullivan," Skip said, turning and walking away. Over his shoulder, he added, "You're not off the hook yet."

As I set about coiling the lines on deck and calling Summerfield Boatworks on the VHF to tell them why I'd been delayed, my brain kept playing short flashbacks from the good times, when we were kids, when Molly and I had lived inside that secret world of childhood best friends. We'd met in Ms. Winnick's kindergarten class and discovered that we lived only one house apart. Her family had just moved in the week before school started. For the next twelve years, when it came to female friends, we were it for each other. Molly and I didn't get along with most of the other girls—the giggly, silly ones who teased the quiet kids and always talked about clothes and TV and things that mattered little in our world. We were essentially both loners, a couple of the peculiar children who are always standing apart from the crowd, and we struck up a friendship out there on the perimeter.

By high school, we certainly made an odd couple when we hung out together. Molly, standing a petite five-foot-two, had flashing dark eyes and long ink-black hair inherited from her Seminole grandmother. She had her own artsy style of dress, and the boys were starting to take notice of her curvaceous shape, while at five-foot-ten, I was a giant gawky tomboy who kept my budding curves well hidden under my constant wardrobe of jeans and baggy T-shirts. She had her passion for drawing nature and always carried her sketchbook as I dragged her along to follow my enthusiasm for boats and the river.

It was in the fall of his senior year that my brother Pit, who had always been far more interested in surfing than girls, fell hard for Molly. As kids, the three of us had often played together, since Molly and I were only a year younger than Pit. He got along with us better than he did with my other older brother, Maddy. We'd be fishing off our seawall, taking the dinghy up Mosquito Creek, and playing pirates or catching pollywogs. It was my junior year when Pit and Molly started dating, and while at first I was a little jealous of the secrets they shared, eventually I realized they weren't going to shut me out, and I could be happy for the two people I loved most in my teenage world.

Throughout the last thirteen years, ever since she'd dumped Pit just before his senior prom and run off and married Nick Pontus, Molly and I had not spoken a single word to each other. She disappeared from my life without a word, without even telling me that she was getting married or moving out of her parents' home. We were supposed to be *best friends,* and one day she was there at school, talking about the big dance, then she was gone, married and living in a little Hollywood Beach apartment with her new husband, working behind the counter in his take-out joint. And my sweet brother Pit, the most gentle, sensitive one of us three kids, had his big heart ripped out. He didn't talk to anybody for a week. Every day he'd head straight to the beach after school and surf until it was too dark to see. Then he'd come home, go into his room, and close the door quietly. He stayed behind that door the night of the prom, playing loud music full of crashing guitars. I waited for her to call me, to apologize, to explain how and why she could have done this to both me and Pit. But that call never came, and I promised myself I would never be the first to make a move.

Over the years, I'd seen her picture sometimes in the papers or on the news as her art career took off and Nick became first the town's darling as a restaurant mogul, then the demon himself when he brought casino gambling boats to South Florida.

"Miss Sullivan?"

I'd been sitting on the bunk in the wheelhouse, daydreaming, purposely not watching what was going on around the *Mykonos*. I stepped out through the companionway door and checked out the fellow standing on the dock next to my boat. He was wearing a yellow knit sport shirt and light brown Polo chino slacks. He stood about five-foot-six and couldn't have weighed more than 135 pounds. His hair was bleached white blond and stood up straight in a tall, flattop crew cut. His smile was so white for a man clearly in his forties, I wondered if his teeth had all been capped.

"What can I do for you?" I asked.

He bent down and held out a card for me. "I'm Detective Rich Amoretti." He flashed me that mouth full of Chiclets again. "Mind if I come aboard?"

I shrugged. "Be my guest." I took his card as he climbed down onto the afterdeck, and I examined it. "This says Special Investigations Unit/Vice Squad." I pointed toward the *Mykonos*. "Isn't this a homicide?"

He glanced over at the Hatteras and all the men and women working on and around the boat. "Yeah, you're right." He sat down on the aluminum bulwark around *Gorda*'s stern and crossed his straight legs at the ankles. The contrast between his bleached hair and dark tan told me he'd spent some time this winter in a tanning booth. Nobody who was a permanent resident here looked that color from the sun in February. "But you see, Miss Sullivan, Nick Pontus and his casino gambling boats have been an interest of mine for over two years. I'll be assisting the homicide detectives in coming up with a list of suspects."

"A list of people who wanted to kill Nick? Seems to me that would be a mighty long list."

He laughed, and then proceeded to grill me for details about the shooting, focusing especially on the glimpse I'd had of the black car. Because I was approaching the bridge, I told him, I really couldn't see anything more than the top of the car. I had no idea what the make of the car might be. I advised him to talk to the bridge tender. I told Detective Amoretti that I suspected the shooter would have had to exit his vehicle to get that shot off, and even at that hour of the morning, someone must have seen something.

"We have officers interviewing the bridge tender and canvassing the area for any other witnesses. You do understand you're going to have to come down to the station? It was a pretty stupid stunt you pulled this morning. You pissed off some people moving that boat like that."

I lifted my shoulders. "Yeah, I guess I probably did. You know anything about the salvage business, Detective Amoretti?"

"Not a thing," he said, crossing his arms and raising his almost invisible blond eyebrows.

"For starters, there are no set fees for services in this business. For towing, yes, but not for salvage. The marine salvage laws go back a couple hundred years, and they were meant to encourage good Samaritans to volunteer to *help* another vessel in peril rather than just pillage it. Today, we call this 'no cure–no pay' salvage. When it's successful, the salver is rewarded a percentage of the value of the boat he saves. This morning, before the shooting, that three-year-old Hatteras over there was worth well over a million dollars. Now she's busted up her screws, maybe ruined the engines when she nearly sank, definitely holed her hull, but she's still gonna be worth a lot more than you or I make in a year. In addition, if she had sunk with full fuel tanks in the middle of the New River, it would have been an environmental disaster as well as a hazard to navigation. The owner and his insurance company could have been held responsible for all that. Eventually, if we can't agree on a sum, it could go to arbitration, and they'll figure how much I risked and then award me somewhere in the vicinity of ten to thirty percent of the value of that boat as she sits right now. Now, I ask you, Detective, would you have let her sink?"

He flashed me his too-perfect teeth. "I see your point."

I rode over to the Fort Lauderdale police station with Detective Amoretti in his bright red Corvette. He had a tendency to speed, a habit I'd noticed most cops shared. I hung on to the armrest with both hands when he accelerated.

On the way, he told me something about Nick Pontus that I did not know. He said it had been reported widely in the news, but I hated to admit that, though I loved to read the newspapers when I had the time, there were days, sometimes weeks, when I rarely heard any news other than the fish or weather reports I caught on the VHF. He said that a little over six months before, Nick had sold his whole TropiCruz Casino Line to a group of partners headed up by some guy named Ari Kagan, but that the new guy had had a falling out with Nick. They had each accused the other of cheating, stealing, and lying, and it had got so bad, they each had a restraining order out on the other. Nick had been in the process of taking Kagan to court to get the business back.

"This guy Kagan is American, but he's linked in business and social circles to some heavy Russian guys who don't always play nice," Amoretti said. "It looks like Nick may have gotten in over his head, messed with the wrong people."

"Are you saying Nick was mixed up with the Russian mafia? That they killed him?" I'd heard scuttlebutt at the Downtowner about how the Russians were making big inroads into prostitution and the drug trade in South Florida. When I didn't have time for the papers, the Downtowner was my other source of news and local gossip.

The detective smiled as he burned rubber on a turn into the residential neighborhood behind the police station. "I didn't say that, now did I?"

Inside the station, Detective Amoretti left me with an efficient young woman who typed my statement into a computer as fast as I could tell it. After she'd printed it out and I'd signed it, I asked her if I could use her phone to call a friend for a ride back to the boatyard. I didn't tell her that my friend is also my attorney. She agreed, but insisted on dialing the number herself.

"Hey, Jeannie, it's me," I said after the young woman handed me the receiver. "I'm at the Fort Lauderdale police station, and I need a ride."

I braced myself for the harangue I knew was coming. Since I'd recently had some difficulties with the police,

Jeannie insisted that she be present anytime I dealt with them. I'd already violated that rule.

"Seychelle Sullivan, what have you got yourself into this time?" she asked.

I told her about the shooting, and as soon as she heard Nick's name, she turned very serious and told me not to say one more word. She was on her way.

AMORETTI must have been hanging nearby, because as soon as I hung up the phone, he reappeared and took me upstairs to the detectives' bull pen, a large space broken up by individual desks and office cubicles.

"Don't tell me," I said. "You're taking me to Detective Collazo?"

"Vic? Nah, he works the four to midnight now. You won't find him in here in the mornings."

That threw me. I'd never thought about Collazo working a shift or adhering to hours. He was just always there. Much as he and I had banged heads in the past, Collazo was a known quantity. I knew where I stood with the man.

Amoretti led me over to a metal desk occupied by a large dark-haired man wearing a brown suit. As excessively polished, tanned, toothed, and coifed as Amoretti was, this man was the exact opposite. His suit, shirt, and tie looked as though they had been selected randomly, not taking into account color or print. A splotch of something that looked like dried egg was stuck on his paisley tie, and his multiple chins were darkened by a day's growth of beard. Rose-colored pouches hung beneath his green eyes, and when he stood, smiled, and extended his hand, his belly hung over his belt, straining the buttons on his wrinkled shirt. Due to the nicotine stains on both his teeth and fingers, I kept the handshake brief.

"Detective Clayton Mabry," he said. "Pleased to meet you, ma'am."

Ma'am? Seeing as it was less than a week until my thirtieth birthday, I was sensitive to things like that. It was the first time I remembered anyone calling me "Ma'am"—before that, I'd always been "Miss," and somehow, hearing it in that good ol' boy accent made it seem even worse. Hell, thirty wasn't that old—was it?

Detective Mabry pointed to the chair on the opposite side of his desk and offered me the pink box of Good & Plenty he held in his hand.

"Want some?"

I held out my hand as he shook some candies out of the box, then completely ignored Jeannie's advice and began to talk to him. The thing was, you felt sorry for him. The man looked like such a mess, and he sounded like he was an oar short of a pair. I couldn't imagine him ever solving a case, and I felt like any little bit I could do to help him out would be a kindness. Detective Amoretti slouched into a chair at an adjacent desk, pulled out his cell phone, and began playing with the numbers on the phone's face.

Mabry interrupted my retelling of the morning events. "When you say Nick Pontus's name, honey, you flinch. You got history with him?"

I exhaled loudly to buy some time. Maybe he was more perceptive than I thought. I really didn't want to talk about this. "History. I guess that's one way to put it."

He extended the box with raised eyebrows and then poured a few more pink and white candies into my hand.

"Go ahead," he said. "Tell me about it."

I chewed the licorice-flavored candies slowly, trying to think of some way to get out of telling the whole story.

It was impossible. The way his eyes were fastened on my face, he wasn't going to let me dance around. I swallowed and started. "Back when I was in high school, eleventh grade, Nick dated a friend of mine. My best friend, actually. He was older than her by about five years, which is a lot for kids that age, and even back then he was into flash. It was one of those whirlwind courtships they talk about. I tried to warn her off him, but she found something fascinating about him. Basically, he bought her affections, got her pregnant, then married her. She quit school. I haven't spoken to either one of them since."

"That's it? You didn't get an invite to the wedding so you dumped your best friend?"

I didn't want to look away, but his eyes cut into me like serrated jade. "It's complicated," I said to the ceiling. "You wouldn't understand." I didn't see how dredging up any of this would help them find Nick's killer. I crossed my arms over my chest and slumped in my chair.

He slowly shook his head as he wrote something down in his notebook. Then he asked, "You sure the shots came from up on the bridge?"

I bounced my shoulders once. I knew I was acting like a bratty kid, but I couldn't help it. "Not really. I guess I just assumed that from the way the car peeled out, you know, made a U-turn and burned rubber."

"Hmm. And you said you couldn't see the driver at all."

"I barely saw the roof of the car. What I could see of it was black, though, and shiny—not a convertible. There are low concrete barriers along the sides of the bridge. Come to think of it, I can see over those walls with no problem when I'm driving my Jeep, so I guess it must have been more like a sports car. Something fairly low."

He wrote at length in his notebook, without looking up at me. I glanced over at Detective Amoretti. He still seemed engrossed in his cell phone.

"Detective Mabry," I said, "do you think the killers were Russian mafia?"

"Whoa, darlin'." He shot a quick look at Amoretti. "Don't know where you got that idea." He shook his head. "Fact is, most folks are murdered by somebody close—family members, upset lovers, that kind of thing."

"Yeah, but you've got to admit, this one does look like a professional hit."

"Seychelle, that's enough," Jeannie said, sweeping into the room wearing one of her voluminous tropical print muumuus, flip-flops slapping the linoleum as she crossed the room. There were too many desks crammed into that office, and the space between them was scant. At nearly three hundred pounds, Jeannie was a substantial woman, and as she approached the chair where Amoretti slouched, he leaped to his feet and pushed the chair under the desk, clearing the way so she could pass. She produced business cards and handed them to both Mabry and Amoretti. "I'm Jeannie Black, Miss Sullivan's attorney."

Detective Rich Amoretti took her card, sucked his teeth, and rolled his eyes. My immediate reaction was pity. Not for Jeannie, mind you, but for Amoretti. As a vice cop, he undoubtedly spent lots of time dealing with hookers and strippers, and considered himself an expert on tough women.

Jeannie went easy on him and just cast him a withering look as she took my forearm. "Come on, Seychelle, we're leaving."

Amoretti stepped in front of her, resting his thumbs on the fabric belt that encircled his twenty-nine-inch waist.

"We aren't finished questioning this witness," he said, looking up at Jeannie.

Her laugh filled the room. "Honey, oh, yes you are." She pulled me to my feet and turned back to Amoretti, looking him up and down. "They must have made you a detective because they don't make patrol uniforms in boys' sizes."

For the first time, I saw the grin fade off Amoretti's face. "Very funny," he said.

"Detective, have you charged my client with a crime?"

Not sure I wanted to hear the answer to that one, I glanced back at Mabry. He had rocked back, balancing his chair on two legs, his fingers laced across his belly and his eyes shining as he watched the exchange between Jeannie and the vice detective.

Amoretti started to speak. "No, but—"

"Then there is no reason for her to stay. I understand she has already voluntarily given and signed a statement downstairs. Good day, gentlemen."

Detective Mabry pushed back his chair and stood up, nodding and grinning at Jeannie like a schoolboy with a crush. "Been a pleasure doing bidness with you, ladies. Hope to see you again real soon."

Jeannie pushed me ahead of her and we walked out into the hall, turning toward the elevator. We didn't say a word until we were in her van and pulling out of the police department parking lot.

"Just take me back to the River Bend Boatyard, okay? *Gorda*'s there, and I've got a job to do," I said.

"I don't think so."

I turned to face her, surprised by her hard tone of voice. "Why not? Are the boys home?" Jeannie was the single mom of twin ten-year-old boys.

"No, they'd just left for the bus stop about the time

you called. We've got to stop off and see a client of mine."

I slumped in my seat. "Oh, geez." Jeannie's clients were usually women divorcing scumbag men, and they needed to vent at length about their soon-to-be-ex's various affairs. "Jeannie, I've got to catch the tide."

She ignored me. "I handled this client's divorce about a year and a half ago. Her husband had cheated on her with a woman who worked for him, and he intended to marry the younger woman as soon as possible. He was a very wealthy man, and she was agreeing to take almost no money, on the condition that he have a prenuptial agreement with the new wife protecting his assets for their son."

I stared out the window, barely listening. I had more to worry about than marriages with ugly endings.

"This morning's events will bring those documents into effect."

I had let my mind start wandering, but those last words of hers brought me right back. "Oh my God." I sat up straight and looked at her. "Jeannie, you're Molly's attorney?" I unfastened my seat belt and reached for the door handle. "Oh, no you don't. I can't go over there. Stop the van. Let me out right here. Jeannie, I mean it. I'll walk back to River Bend."

"Shut up and get your hand off that door handle." She shifted her bulk sideways so that she could face me as she drove. We were crossing the Seventh Avenue Bridge, and I looked nervously out the windshield. I wished she'd watch the road. Her van had electric windows, and I considered rolling mine down just in case— so I could swim out when the van went into the river.

"Molly Pontus asked me to handle her divorce because she had seen an article about you and me in the paper after you inherited your dad's business. She told me she figured if you thought I was a good lawyer, then that was recommendation enough for her."

"Geez, Jeannie, would you watch the road? Okay, already."

Her words surprised me. I had watched Molly from afar, reading everything about her I could find. It had never occurred to me she might be doing the same with me.

"Molly also told me about this feud between the two of you—that you used to be best friends before both of you'all's pride got in the way. Seychelle, this gal's gonna need friends in the next few days. You need to get over it."

"Ha! Just like that. You think it's that easy, Jeannie? When two people haven't talked in over thirteen years? She's the one who walked away from me."

"You better *make it* that easy. She had her reasons back then. Besides, all these years, your hand's been broke? You could've picked up the phone and called her, you know."

"Like hell."

"You do know she's got a son." Jeannie chuckled. "Kid's name is Zale."

"Yeah, I know," I said, deliberately not joining in her laughter. "Only Molly would saddle a kid with a name like that."

Jeannie looked at me again, not just a driver's glance, but a long stare.

"Would you keep your eyes on the road, dammit?"

"For a person with brothers named Pitcairn and Madagascar," she said, "you've got lots of nerve talking about weird names."

"So my parents had a thing about islands. Look, I know what it's like to go through life with an odd name. Poor kid." I turned from Jeannie and stared out the window again. "Molly always was the artsy type. Zale," I said, exhaling so sharply that my breath made a faint fog on the van's window.

She turned on Davie Boulevard and headed for the bridge.

I thought about that morning, going through the bridge towing Nick's body on the *Mykonos,* and I remembered the first time I met him. Molly and I had skipped school that day at Stranahan High. She had an old Volkswagen convertible, her first car, and we'd put the top down and headed to A1A to cruise the beach. Nick Pontus had driven his Tropi-Subs & Gyros delivery van to Fort Lauderdale Beach that same afternoon, and we parked next to each other north of Sunrise Boulevard. He looked so mature, so unlike the teenage boys we knew, with his thick, brown, wavy hair, black T-shirt, and sockless canvas shoes, leaning against the side of the van smoking a cigarette, staring at the ocean through squinted eyes. He was so different, so exotic, still with the trace of a Greek accent, though he had come to this country ten years before. We struck up a conversation, and when he spoke my name he put the accent on the first syllable instead of the second, and I thought it sounded sexy and exciting. I felt something stir in me that I'd never felt with the boys at school, but when we said our good-byes that afternoon, it was Molly's number he asked for.

Jeannie turned left into Shady Banks, my old neighborhood. She said, "Did you know Molly lives in her parents' old house now? She bought it from them when they divorced not too long after she did."

"I didn't know they'd divorced," I said, looking out the window at the familiar little fifties-era tile-roofed bungalows. Molly's parents were alcoholics who used to fight in screaming, cursing voices that often drove their daughter to sleep on the floor in my room. But when they were sober, they laughed and joked and seemed to get along just great. In spite of their drinking, it was hard to imagine them getting divorced. It must have happened right around the time my father, Red, died, when my brothers and I sold the house on the cul-de-sac to pay off Red's medical bills. I'd been too wrapped up in my own pain to notice any changes over at Molly's house.

Jeannie pulled to the curb in front of an immaculate bright yellow house with a tea-green door. I knew my old family home was just down the street, but I didn't want to look. "Let's go," she said, swinging open her door.

The colors and the landscaping at the house were different, but I would have recognized her house all the same. I'd spent part of nearly every week of my childhood crossing the yard to that door. Jeannie stepped up onto the porch to ring the bell, and I positioned myself behind her so that her large frame hid me. I pretended to look around the old neighborhood, pretended that I wasn't hiding, while doing everything possible to postpone having to look at Molly.

The door opened. "Hi, Jeannie. What brings you around here?"

The voice was so familiar, and yet strange at the same time. Our friendship had been marked in large part by our ability to *not* have to say things, our intuition into each other's emotional state. When my mother had locked herself in her room in one of her "moods," Molly knew without my having to tell her. And now hearing those few words this morning, I knew—even after all these years—that she didn't know yet.

"I just wanted to stop by and see how you were managing. See if there is anything I can do to help," Jeannie said.

"Help with what? Why would I need help?" Molly asked.

"You haven't heard? Oh, shit. Molly, can we come in?"

"We?"

Jeannie turned to her side to look for me, and even in profile, I saw the expression of puzzlement on her face when she didn't see me. I turned my head away and tried to look very interested in the Haitian gardener with the hedge clippers across the street. Jeannie grabbed me by the back of my sweatshirt and yanked me up onto the porch. "Yeah, we. Me and Seychelle."

I stood not three feet from her, so I saw her body stiffen, saw her start to turn aside, to go back into the house, and leave me standing out there, rejected. I couldn't take that one more time. I said the only thing that I knew would change everything between us.

"Molly, Nick's dead."

III.

MOLLY staggered back a step as though I had struck a blow to her body. She raised a hand to her cheek and looked at Jeannie, opening her mouth like an exotic tropical fish.

"Let's go inside," Jeannie said.

"What?" She stood her ground in the doorway, trying to get the words out. "Is she—this—" She turned to Jeannie. "Is this some kind of joke?"

When we were little girls and the other girls walked around holding hands or with their arms around each other's shoulders, we had laughed at them and thought them silly. Molly and I had never been very touchy-feely, probably a result of the mothers we had. So, I surprised her when I stepped forward and put my arms around her, and she knew absolutely in that moment that this was no joke—Nick was dead.

"I saw it happen, Molly," I whispered into her dark hair, knowing that I was breaking that long-ago promise never to make the first move. "This morning. He was shot."

I nearly had to carry her inside. Her breathing changed to quiet, ragged sobs, and she buried her face in my shoulder as her legs sagged beneath her. I got one of my arms under hers and, once in the living room, lowered her to the couch. I heard Jeannie head for the kitchen, probably after tea or coffee or, I hoped, something stronger.

Through the soft blue sweater Molly was wearing, I could feel her bones just beneath the skin. I'd never known her to be so thin. Her jeans were bunched at the waist where her belt fought to keep them up. The divorce must have been hard on her, and I wondered all over again how she could have loved him that way, how she could have chosen him over Pit—and me. As I sat next to her on the couch and held her and let her cry it all out, I was amazed that she could feel sadness over losing that man all over again.

We'd been sitting like that, my arm around her and Molly's body shaking with silent sobs, for what seemed like hours when we were startled by a voice from the dark hallway.

"Mom?"

Molly pushed herself into a sitting position, rubbed at her eyes with the backs of her hands, and stared at her son. Other than in pictures, I'd never seen him before. I knew he had to be about thirteen, but he looked small for his age, his narrow shoulders in a thin T-shirt with a picture of Batman on the front. His hair was fine, dark blond, and behind his round, wire-rimmed glasses, he had eyes the color of the sky at dusk. I couldn't put into words what aspect of his face resembled his mother's, but I felt transported back to our childhood, a sense of déjà vu when I looked at him.

"Come here, Zale." She patted the couch next to her and said, "Sit down, honey." When he sat, she took him in her arms.

"Mom? What's wrong? Why are you crying?"

From the surprise in his voice and what I knew of his mother, I imagined this was the first time he had ever seen her cry.

"Something terrible's happened." She hugged him tight, then pushed back so she could look into his face. She held both his hands on her lap. "Your dad's been killed."

He shook his hands free from hers and slid back away from her. "What? No way."

"Zale—"

"No. That can't be right. Dad's got bodyguards. He told me. He was just gonna go to the boatyard today."

Molly reached her arms out to her son. "Zale," she said again, her voice breaking.

"You're right, Zale," I said, leaning out to look at the boy on the other end of the couch. "Your dad was on his boat going up the river. But he was alone. I was on my boat behind him, and I saw it happen. Someone up on the Andrews Bridge had a gun."

The boy looked up at his mother's face. "Mom?" His face said she was the one person who had always been able to restore order in his world. "It's not true, is it?" He was shaking his head, back and forth, faster and faster. "She made a mistake, right? Tell me, Mom, it's not Dad."

"No, honey. It's no mistake." She whispered the words.

The boy jumped up off the couch and let loose an animal-like sound, somewhere between a cry and a retch, and he fled down the hall to Molly's old room. She stood and followed him, stopping only long enough to give me a look with a face so contorted that for the first time that morning I felt tears wet my cheeks. Not for Nick Pontus or even for the long years I'd wasted away from my friend, but because I knew what it was like to be a kid and learn that one of your parents was dead.

I felt the little projector fire up in the back of my head, the one that replayed the scene over and over whether I wanted to watch or not. I saw the three of us, me, Molly, and Pit, playing together, starting to pack our things into Pit's skiff for another of our adventures on the river. Then my mother, who had been locked in her room, the curtains drawn, all morning, was there, dragging me away, insisting that I accompany her to the beach, and I saw the lipless line formed by my mouth as I stared out the backseat car window, my arms crossed tight on my chest.

The sound track plays my silence louder every time I have to watch. I see my mother's face, the way her mouth turned up on one side in a mirthless little half smile. And every time she asks me her question, asks if I will ever forgive her, I speak the one word I spoke to her that whole afternoon, and my "No" is louder and more resounding and more full of condemnation each time. The scene jumps then to me going through the crowd on the beach and seeing my mother's white foot in her purple beach shoe. The color of her skin is wrong, as is the color of her lips where the lifeguard labors, trying to blow life back into her body. Unlike Molly's son, I never went through any denial. From the moment I saw that foot, I knew she was dead.

Jeannie came in from the kitchen with ceramic mugs and a bottle of rum on a tray. She lifted her eyebrows.

"I take it you heard," I said. I knew how sound carried in that little house.

"Yeah, that's tough," she said. "Even though everyone else in the world thinks Nick was pretty much of a shit, to that kid, he was still dad."

Molly came back into the living room and collapsed on the far end of the couch. "He says he just wants me to leave him alone for a while. He won't even let me in." She leaned forward, resting her elbows on her knees, and ran her fingers through her hair. "I can't believe this is happening."

Jeannie placed a steaming mug on the coffee table in front of her and offered her the bottle of rum and a box of tissues. Molly nodded and blew her nose while Jeannie poured a good slug of liquor into all three mugs.

"So, what do you think's going on, Molly?" Jeannie said. She settled onto the large ottoman on the far side of the coffee table. "Any idea why nobody's called you yet?"

"It's *her*. You know that." I looked back and forth between them, not getting it, missing the inside scoop. Molly put her face in one hand and rubbed her forehead just above her brows. It looked like she was trying to make a pain go away. When I caught Jeannie's attention, she rolled her eyes and shook her head.

Molly continued. "She's the next of kin now. Not me. I'm sure they've contacted *her*."

"Molly, it's probably just an oversight. Don't go reading something more into it," Jeannie said.

"You don't know her like I do, Jeannie. I keep telling you that. You only see the public side of her. Inside she's mean and nasty. She'd do anything to keep me out of their lives." She drew in a quick gasp of breath and sat up straight. "Oh my God." She put her face in both her hands and mumbled something under her breath that sounded like the word "stupid."

"What is it? What did you just think about?"

"I was going to call you, Jeannie," Molly said without lifting her head. "Something happened last Friday night when I dropped Zale off at Nick's for the weekend." She sat up and began pounding her fists on her legs, saying, "Shit, shit, shit."

"Molly," Jeannie said. "Calm down. Start at the beginning. Tell me what happened."

I saw her chin tremble as she struggled for control. The whites of her eyes flashed brightly as she searched around the room, and I remembered what it was like the first time we went back to her house after a movie and found her parents in the kitchen, passed out in the middle of broken glass, spilled vodka, and blood. She'd looked at me then trying to find the words to explain how that was just a part of her world. In the morning, they had smiles and Band-Aids on their faces and life went on.

I took her hand. "You took your son to Nick's house," I said. "Then what happened?"

"His new wife, Janet. She hates me. I don't know why, except that Nick and I are still friends. We talk about Zale."

I noticed she was still referring to Nick in the present tense.

"Anyway, she'd do anything to hurt my feelings. And she leads Nick around like she owns him, like he's her pet dog. She'd talked him into going after full custody of Zale. I don't know why, because she never really seemed to like having him over there. When I went to the house Friday, Nick invited me in. He never does that. Zale went upstairs to his bedroom. He and I'd had a fight, too. He didn't want to go to his dad's, and I had to make him go. Zale's crazy about his dad, but he can't stand it when she tries to play stepmom."

"Okay, so what happened then?"

"Nick took me into the living room, poured me a glass of wine, and told me he thought Zale should live with him full-time and visit me only on the weekends. I was stunned. This came totally out of nowhere. Then she came in with that brother of hers, Richard. He was one of Nick's charity cases. He's kinda' pathetic. Thinks he's gonna make it big someday as a Christian country

singer. Nick hired him when he was a drunk homeless
vet living on the street, got him to AA, and the guy
worked his way up through the ranks. Now he captains
the TropiCruz boat that runs out of Hollywood. Anyway, whatever happened overseas, the whole Desert
Storm thing really messed him up. I hate to send Zale to
their house when Richard's there. He's always falling off
the wagon."

I'd forgotten how crazy she used to make me with
these long-winded stories of hers. "Molly, get to the
point."

She waved her hands in the air in a gesture that suggested she was either surrendering or parking a jet. "It
was like they were ganging up on me, all three of them.
They said they could provide him with a much better life
than I could, that I was too *eccentric*. They disapprove
of my lifestyle, of my homeschooling Zale. They say he's
suffering here because I don't allow him to have a TV or
play video games."

I shook my head. "Geez, Molly. You're still into all
that? You probably make him eat natural foods, too—
no McDonald's or anything?"

"What's wrong with wanting to raise a healthy child?"

Jeannie said, "Is that the only reason you're so upset?
That's it? So you argued the last time you saw Nick
alive. Honey, after the way that bastard treated you, you
should have threatened to hack his balls off."

"It was more than just an argument." She looked at
me, then back to Jeannie. "You know how crazy they
make me."

Jeannie set her mug down on the table. "What did
you do?"

Molly hung her head between her hunched shoulders
and stared at the floor for several seconds before she
continued. "Well, when Janet started telling me that

Nick was going to go to court to prove I was an unfit mother, I just lost it." She looked up and fixed her eyes on mine. "Here's this twenty-five-year-old blackjack bimbo telling me how to raise my child, and there's my son's idiot father going right along with it, hanging on every word she's saying. I just blew. I threw my glass of wine at him and ran out into his driveway. I yelled so loud, I'll bet even his neighbors heard."

"What did you say, Molly?"

"I didn't really mean it."

Jeannie looked away. "Oh shit, what did you say to him?"

"I told him if he tried to take my son away from me, I'd kill him."

IV.

NOBODY said anything at first. I kept hearing her voice echoing in my head, so the silence didn't weigh on me. When we finally started talking, we took Molly's words and tossed them this way and that, discussed what she'd said, offered up different ways of looking at it, and after about fifteen minutes we were all exhausted, and still hadn't found a way to put a positive spin on it. First of all, there was no way to keep it quiet. According to Molly's version, Janet hated Molly so much, she would never consider keeping such a thing to herself. Jeannie downplayed the issue of animosity from Janet, but pointed out that the homes in that neighborhood are very close together, and, by her own admission, Molly had screamed at Nick. Someone else certainly heard, and the police would talk to the neighbors. And second, even without having made a threat, it was like Detective Mabry said, the family was the first place they would look for suspects.

I stood up and began to pace the floor in front of the coffee table. "Jeannie, look at her. Come on. How bad can this be? What is she, five-two? A hundred pounds? Does she look like she could even *lift* a gun? Let's get real. Could anybody suspect Molly of being a sniper?"

The words had barely cleared my lips when Molly's doorbell rang.

"We're about to find out," Jeannie said.

I was the first to the door, but Jeannie was right behind me. And she was right about finding out, too. Detective Mabry was standing outside on the porch, and his stern face brightened considerably when he looked past my shoulder.

"Good afternoon, ma'am. Sure is a pleasure to see you again."

He wasn't speaking to me.

"Can't say as the feeling is mutual, Detective," Jeannie said.

Mabry lowered his eyes and his tongue seemed to be fishing out a piece of food in one of his back molars, stretching the skin of his cheek. When he looked up again, he said, "Is Ms. Pontus home? I'm afraid I need to speak to her."

"Molly Pontus is resting at the moment, Detective. She's just learned of the death of her husband of eleven years, the father of her son."

"I can understand she's upset, ma'am, but this is a murder investigation. I will need to speak to her. And by the way, he was her *ex*-husband."

From the living room Molly called out, "Hell, Jeannie, let the man in."

My opinion of Detective Mabry slid up a couple of notches over the next thirty minutes as he questioned Molly concerning her whereabouts over the last twenty-four hours. His questions were direct and yet showed a certain amount of sensitivity. Molly and Zale had gone to bed around 10:30, she told him, and Zale had gotten up at 8:30, when Molly woke him. As a young teen, he would sleep until noon if she didn't wake him to do his schoolwork. She explained to the detective that she homeschooled her son, and he had been in his room

working on a research project on his computer when
Seychelle and Jeannie had arrived.

"So, just for argument's sake, ma'am, it would have
been possible for you to leave the house, say between
6:00 and 7:30 in the morning, and drive over to the Andrews Bridge, and your son would not even have been
aware of it."

"Yes, I suppose it is possible, but it didn't happen. I
didn't leave the house this morning. And I certainly
didn't kill Nick. Ask any of the neighbors—they're all
snoopy enough."

"I'll do that, ma'am. I surely will." Mabry dropped
his notebook and pen into his lap and looked around
like he was startled. "You know, I didn't notice when I
walked up to your front door. What kind of car do you
drive, Ms. Pontus?"

"A Mustang."

Mabry's head jerked back. "A little thing like you?
Now that's a nice car. I didn't see it out front. You got a
garage?"

"Yeah, it's an addition. My parents had it set back
along the side of the house."

"Mind if I take a look?"

Molly stood up. "Come on."

When the two of them had gone out the front door,
Jeannie heaved herself up and started after them.

I began cleaning up the tea fixings, then called out to
Jeannie, "Hey, please, tell me her Mustang isn't black."

She shook her head. "Sorry."

WHEN the three of them returned, Mabry was telling
Molly that she would need to go down to the station
to give a formal statement, the sooner the better. He
wanted one from Zale, too, but he said it could wait a
day or two. The detective was smiling at both of them,

so it appeared that things hadn't gone too badly out in the garage.

Jeannie said, "I'll drive you to the police station right now if you want, Molly. I think it would be best to get it over with."

Molly nodded and headed down the hall toward her son's bedroom. She mumbled "I can't leave him alone" before she disappeared from view.

"Well, ladies," Detective Mabry said, nodding to each of us in turn, "I expect I'll be seeing you later this afternoon, then." He looked straight at Jeannie and smiled. "Thank you for your time," he said, letting himself out the front door.

"I think he likes you, Jeannie," I said.

"Me?" she said, her eyebrows forming an upside-down V. "Yeah, right."

"Well, look, much as I love hanging out at the police station, I've got work to do. I need to file a salvage claim on the *Mykonos,* and," I said, glancing at the dive watch on my wrist, "I'd like to catch the tide this afternoon to bring my tow down to Bahia Mar. Can you drop me off at my place first?"

"Sure."

Mc'ly and Zale emerged from the dark hall. She had her arm around the boy, but the way his shoulders were rounded, he looked like he was trying to fold himself in two.

Jeannie jingled her keys. "Okay, gang, let's go."

When Jeannie told Molly in the car that they were dropping me off first, Molly said, "Sey?"

I swung around to look at her sitting next to her son on the backseat. "Yeah?"

Her eyes were on her lap where her hands clasped her son's, and she faltered as though she were afraid to speak. "Could—could you do something for me?" She looked up. "I know I have no right to ask after—"

For years, I had imagined this moment. How I would turn away and make her suffer as I had suffered. Now, all I could think of was how I could make the pain in her eyes go away.

"What do you want me to do?"

"Could you take Zale with you today? I don't want him to have to talk to the cops just yet."

"No problem. I've got a sailboat to get downriver, and from what I hear he's pretty good around sailboats." That comment won me a weak smile from the boy. I'd often read about Zale's big wins in the youth sailing division at the fancy Lauderdale Yacht Club. He was making a name for himself, and I'd even heard talk about Olympic hopes for the kid.

"Is he going to be okay going by his dad's office?"

Molly turned to look at the boy and he nodded his head once without looking up.

She turned to me, her once lush lips now compressed into two thin lines. "Thanks," she said, and I turned around in the front seat and watched the streets of my city go by. There was still so much we were leaving unsaid. But this was a start.

ABACO, my black Lab, jumped up, put her paws on the kid's chest, and gave him a doggy kiss as soon as we came through the side gate after Jeannie had dropped us off on my tree-shaded street in the Rio Vista neighborhood where I lived.

"Abaco, down girl," I said, and she jumped off him and did a neat one-eighty in midair. She landed facing the river and dashed down the walk ahead of us.

"I grew up on the same street where you and your mom live," I continued telling the boy, "and when we sold my dad's house, I moved in here." We had arrived in front of my riverfront cottage, and I pointed back at the tall sprawling house set back on the lot. "The Larsens own that house. It's something, isn't it?"

I wasn't sure how much of what I was saying was sinking through the haze of grief that was wrapped around him. I remembered what it was like, but I just kept talking. "This is one of three or four houses they own all over the States. They knew my dad before he died, and they invited me to live here for incredibly cheap rent in return for keeping an eye on the place when they're not here—which is pretty much all the time. There's no other way I could afford to live in this neighborhood. It's been a really good deal for me."

Zale was still looking back at the main house, his hand shading his eyes as he looked up at the sand-colored stucco and red-tiled monstrosity with its various towers and turrets. "It looks kinda spooky," he said.

"Yeah, I guess it does. But no ghosts, as far as I know. The main house was built a long time ago, though, back in the 1930s, and it's had lots of different owners. Each one had to remodel and put on a new addition or add another tower, and they all *sorta* kept to that old-Spanish style. That's why it looks so weird. Like nothing fits or goes together. But check this out. This is where I live." We were standing at the fork in the brick path—one way led to my front door, the other to the wood dock where *Gorda* was normally tied up. I held my arm out to display the squat stucco structure with a red tile roof. "This is my cottage. It used to be a boathouse. They could drive powerboats right into the slip under the roof. Back in the sixties, someone decked over the slip and turned the place into a cottage. Sometimes when a boat makes a big wake, I can even hear the water sloshing under my living room."

"Cool," he said as I unlocked the door and we walked in. I took that as high praise from a thirteen-year-old.

"It's not very big, but I like it. I've got the best river view, and I can dock my boat practically right outside my door." I waved my hand toward the couch. "Make yourself at home. I've just got to grab some paperwork for the salvage claim on the *Mykonos*." I opened the window to let in some air, then pulled a standard form salvage contract out of the file cabinet I used as an end table, sat down at the kitchen table, and started to fill it out. Even though I would be able to make a salvage claim against the *Mykonos* without a signed contract, and the form was usually signed before the salvage was performed, getting a contract after the services have been rendered would give both parties more protection under the law.

Out in the yard, Abaco began barking and yelping her happy bark. Zale went to the door, looked out, and said, "There's a man out there playing with your dog."

"Yup. And I can tell from her bark who it is. Hey B. J.," I hollered. "Come here a sec."

Zale stepped back, his mouth open as B. J. came trotting through the open door, then jumped, spun in midair like a quarterback, and hurled the bright green tennis ball back out into the yard.

"Close the door before she brings that slobbery ball into my house," I said.

B. J. ignored my request and instead came up behind my chair, slid his arms around me in a quick hug, and kissed me on top of the head. "Good morning, Captain," he said.

I heard the front door close, and I figured Zale was much better at following orders than B. J. Without looking up from my paperwork, I said, "B. J., I'd like you to meet Zale Pontus. Zale, this is B. J. Moana, my good friend and sometime first mate on the *Gorda*." I could have said my sometime bedmate as well, but that was more than the kid needed to know, and it certainly didn't do justice to our friendship. Or relationship. Or whatever you wanted to call it. It was the problem I always had when introducing B. J. to people. I loathe the word "boyfriend" to describe a grown man. Besides, it implies a permanency that I don't feel. These days, B. J. and I were taking things one day at a time.

When he let go of me and crossed to Zale, I took a sneak peek at the two of them shaking hands. B. J. was wearing a beige long-sleeved T-shirt with some surfboard company logo on the back and a pair of cargo pants. He was the only person I knew who still wore his Birkenstocks without socks on cold mornings like this. That was the Pacific Islander in him. B. J.'s mother was mostly Samoan, his father mostly Japanese/American, and the combination had produced this man with skin the color of oiled teak, straight black hair that he wore pulled back with a rubber band, and torpedo-shaped brown eyes—a man who would go barefoot in a snowstorm rather than wear shoes and socks.

B. J. stepped back from the boy and looked him up and down. "Aren't you that hotshot sailor kid? I read about you."

Zale blushed, his mouth turning up in a hint of a smile, and he nodded. "I'm not really that good yet."

"That's not what I hear," B. J. continued. "People are saying they've never seen anyone your age with that kind of instinct, helmsmanship ability, and logistical intuition. Didn't you take the state championship title last year?"

"Yeah, that was in the Optimist, though. I've been racing Lasers this year, and I'm not doing as well."

"I'd say you will, once you grow a little more and gain about thirty pounds." B. J. touched the boy lightly on the side of his head. "What matters most is that you've got what it takes up here and," with three fingers he pushed on the left side of Zale's chest, "in here."

"Hey guys," I said, slipping the salvage paperwork into a manila envelope, "I love the sailing chitchat, but I've got a living to make." I picked up my shoulder bag and got the keys to my Jeep out of the side pocket.

"Listen, you two want a chauffeur this afternoon?" B. J. asked, and then he turned to Zale and said, "Trust me when I tell you, you'd rather ride in my truck in this weather. Her Wrangler is ancient. Feels like a wind tunnel and sounds like a locomotive." B. J. imitated the rumbling made by the Jeep's engine and the boy laughed.

"Leave Ol' Lightnin' alone," I said. "She's been good transportation, and she starts when I turn the key."

When I passed in front of Zale to reach for the doorknob, I saw the color of his skin fade to pale. Tears began to pool in his eyes, and in a barely audible voice, he said, "I forgot."

"Forgot what?" I asked, thinking at first that he needed something from Molly's house.

The skin sagged on the bones of his face as though it were melting. "I was laughing," he said, choking on the words.

I reached out for him, and he collapsed in my arms. He pressed his face into my shoulder, pinching my skin with the metal frame of his glasses. With B. J.'s help, I got him to the couch, and we sat on either side of him while his torso shook and convulsed. It was as though the grief he'd held inside just this past hour had already grown too big to be contained in such a small body. I wasn't sure if B. J. knew what had happened that morning, so I said, "His father was Nick Pontus, and—"

"I know," B. J. said before I could go any further. He closed his eyes for a few seconds as though forcing something down, back inside himself, then he reached out to rub the boy's back. "I heard."

V.

ZALE sat between us on the front seat of B. J.'s 1978 black El Camino pickup as we drove out of the Rio Vista neighborhood. He was quiet now, sitting very still with his hands resting on his thighs, staring out the front window of the truck, but I had the feeling he wasn't seeing any of the tree-lined streets we drove through.

Zale had told us that the Pontus Enterprises offices were on the far side of the Seventeeth Street Causeway Bridge, and that I would need to speak to Leon Quinn, his father's partner and lawyer. After he had stopped crying, he answered my questions in a monotone voice, then he had grown quiet and still like he was now. I was worried about him. I knew he was still in shock, and I also knew that there was no right thing to do at times like this. No matter what you did, there would be moments when you would feel guilty for still being alive when someone you loved was dead. But you can't just cry for days at a time, either. The afternoon after my mother died, I remembered going back to the house and sitting on the bed in my room and thinking about opening a book, turning on the TV, playing a game, wanting to do something to get my mind off what had happened, but feeling that anything I might do would be somehow disrespectful to her, to her death. So, I sat there on my bed in a pose very similar to Zale's. And even when my family came in and tried to talk to me, I couldn't, or wouldn't, answer them. At least Zale was talking. I didn't talk for months after my mother killed herself. I was so afraid to open my mouth for fear I would say something that would give me away, that would reveal to them that it was my fault, that I was the one who had driven her into the sea that day.

"What have we here?" B. J. said as we pulled off the Seventeenth Street Causeway Bridge into the parking lot where Pontus had its offices.

Out front along the Intracoastal Waterway was an aging motel, behind which was a little shopping center with offices and kitschy tourist shops selling beach towels, T-shirts, and rubber alligators. A few upscale boutiques were attempting to turn things around for the overlooked strip mall, but the dark windows with the red-lettered FOR LEASE signs told the real story.

Pontus Enterprises' office was not very big, given the financial resources of the company and the fact that they owned the entire piece of property, motel and all. I'd heard that their plan was to raze everything on the site and start anew with a thirty-story condo/hotel, with shops and offices on the first floors, a multistory parking garage, and a nice new dock out front for the gambling boats. The homes in the Harbor Isles neighborhood behind the shopping center were mostly lush, upscale million-dollar homes with a smattering of little old Florida homes owned by folks who resisted the dollars of the tear-down entrepreneurs. Most of the locals who lived out on the barrier island were tired of the traffic and the tourists and the way the beach was changing into another South Florida condo canyon. Several dozen of them, a mixture of housewives, retirees, and hippies, were milling around in front of the Pontus offices carrying picket signs with sayings like SAY NO TO TROPITOWERS and NO DICE IN PARADISE when we drove up.

"Looks like your dad's latest project isn't all that popular," B. J. said as he pulled the El Camino into a parking space directly in front of the Pontus office's door.

"Yeah, I know." There was something about the way Zale said it that made me think he might have had to spend a lot of his time defending his dad at places like the Lauderdale Yacht Club.

I gathered my shoulder bag and the envelope with my papers from the floor of the truck and prepared to walk through the crowd where the picketers had started eyeing us. I asked B. J., "You coming?"

"No, I think I'll let the two of you handle this on your own." There was a glint of light in B. J.'s eyes that told me he was going to enjoy watching me cross the picket line.

"Thanks," I said, as I swung open the passenger-side door.

It was as though someone had run a current of electricity through the group of protesters. No sooner had Zale and I slid out of the car than we found ourselves surrounded by bobbing signs and angry faces. They were chanting slogans like "Hell no, Pontus must go" and "Plant flowers, not Towers." I hoped no one in the crowd would recognize Zale.

Most of the protesters stepped aside as we passed through them, but right in front of the office door, an older woman held her ground. There was something about her pinned-up hair and white blouse that looked familiar, but I couldn't place where I'd seen her before.

"Excuse me," I said. Her icy blue eyes locked on mine. I wanted to speak to her, to explain that I felt as she did. I didn't want to see any more development on this beach, either. I hated the traffic and the high-rises. And the kind of people who were attracted to casino gambling boats weren't always the kind I wanted driving through my neighborhood. I wanted to tell her that I considered this my neighborhood, too. But there was something unapproachable about her. More than unapproachable, she scared me. Her stare seemed to burn right through me. I couldn't open my mouth to speak. Then, without a word, and without breaking her stare, she slowly stepped aside. I pushed the glass door open and hurried Zale into the office.

The woman sitting on the far side of the reception desk had brassy blond hair and glasses with bright red frames. It was clear from the splotches of color on her skin and the mascara on her cheeks that she had been crying, and as soon as she spotted Zale, she burst into fresh sobs and hurried off into a back room.

"That was Roma," Zale said. "She's worked for my dad since before he met mom."

I put my arm around the boy's shoulders. I was still feeling shaken up by that strange woman outside, but I willed myself to concentrate on the matter at hand. "I guess the news travels fast in this town." Speaking softly, I said, "You're going to be seeing a lot of that. Are you sure you're okay with being here?"

He swallowed and bobbed his head up and down a couple of times.

I stepped over to a Plexiglas-covered box that sheltered a mock-up model of the proposed hotel, restaurant, and dock project. The paper taped to the inside of the glass read, "TropiTowers will offer the finest in luxurious hotel accommodations in these stylish twin thirty-story towers. The first two floors will feature retail shops, a day spa, and restaurants, all overlooking the docks and the thrilling views of Port Everglades."

The model showed a pair of ultramodern towers, a pool deck between them, and, adjacent to them, a huge gray multistory parking garage with tennis courts on the roof. At thirty stories, they would tower over the seventeen-story Pier Sixty-six across the street. Not a piece of it belonged in this neighborhood.

"All right," I said, tapping my fingers on the Plexiglas. "I guess we find our own way to this Leon Quinn, then. Lead on, buddy."

Zale threaded his way through a couple of empty desks, and I followed. He stopped in front of a closed door at the end of a long hallway. The brass plate on the door read LEON QUINN, EXECUTIVE VICE PRESIDENT. I lifted my hand to knock, but Zale grabbed the doorknob and swung the door open.

The man sitting behind the desk would have looked equally at home on a café terrace overlooking the Aegean as he did sitting amidst the trappings of a power office. His thick, dark hair and full moustache framed deep-set eyes, and as he stood, I saw that he moved with the grace of a man who knew the effect his Mediterranean looks had on women.

"Uncle Leo, I want to introduce you . . ." Zale started, but before he could get any further, Leon Quinn bounded around the desk and embraced Zale in a hug that literally lifted the boy off his feet.

"Son," he said in his deep, accented voice, "I am so sorry about your father." When he set Zale down again, he took the youngster's face between his hands, kissed him by each ear, then patted his cheek. "Such a terrible thing. How could they do this to him? Russian bastards. How is your mother taking it?"

"She's okay, Uncle Leo. She's pretty sad, but she's gonna be okay, I think."

"You gotta step up now, Zale. You gotta be a man for

your mother. She's gonna need you. A lot's gonna fall on your shoulders, son. And you know, you need anything," he said as he patted the boy's cheek again, "*anything*, you just come ask your Uncle Leo."

Quinn's face was very animated as he spoke, and I found myself staring at the moustache as it jerked and danced on his face.

"Uncle Leo," Zale said, turning and twisting his face out of the older man's grasp. "This is Seychelle Sullivan. She's a friend of Mom's, and she's the one who was there this morning. She saw—"

I stepped forward with my hand outstretched so Zale wouldn't have to finish the sentence. "Mr. Quinn, I run the salvage tug *Gorda,* and I towed the *Mykonos* up to River Bend Boatyard this morning. I'm here to inform you of my intent to file a salvage claim against the vessel." I slid the papers out of the envelope and handed him the open form documents. "I'd also like to express my condolences. I understand you and Nick were close."

"Salvage claim?" His eyes bounced back and forth as he read through the document. He looked up at Zale. "What the hell? This is a lot of money."

"Mr. Quinn, please look over the documents. I have proposed a fee for my services there, but that is open to negotiation. I'm sure the insurance company will take care of this. I don't know anything about Mr. Pontus's estate, or whether the *Mykonos* was owned by him personally or by the company, but I was told you are his personal attorney, so I am bringing these documents to you. You'll find the numbers listed there for my attorney, as well as my home phone. If you have any questions, give us a call."

I turned and reached for the office door, but Quinn stepped over to me and put his hand on my arm.

"Miss Sullivan, I apologize for my lack of manners. Please, sit down for a few minutes before you have to go back outside and face those terrible people." He steered me to an antique chair on the opposite side of his heavy wood desk. Zale sat in the chair's twin, and Leon Quinn settled himself behind his desk.

"Zale said you are a friend of his mother's?"

I didn't see any sense in trying to explain the real state of our relationship. Not even Zale would fully understand that. "Yes, we grew up together."

"Ah, friendship that stands the test of time. That is real friendship."

I forced a smile at Quinn and nodded, then diverted my eyes so as not to have to meet his. I was certain he would see what a liar I was. On the shelves behind his desk were half a dozen framed snapshots of Nick and him catching a marlin onboard a sport fisherman, wearing yellow construction hats at a groundbreaking ceremony, slapping each other on the back while wearing identical tuxedos, that sort of thing.

Quinn followed my eyes to the photos. "Nick Pontus was an extraordinary man." His voice cracked and he paused, cleared his throat, then continued. "I was more than fifteen years his senior, but I was one of the first people he hired when he started his TropiSubs down on Hollywood Beach. I was struggling to pay my way through law school, and I worked nights and weekends for Nick. He was just this brash kid determined to make a place for himself in this country. I guess you could say we grew up together, too."

"I knew Nick over ten years ago, back when he and Molly first met. You're certainly right when you describe him as brash."

"Yeah, he did things his own way." Quinn smiled.

"*Regardless*. And that seemed to work okay for him until he met Ari Kagan and sold TropiCruz to him and his syndicate. Bastards. But I never thought it would come to this."

"You seem certain that they're responsible."

"Who else?" He spread his big hands wide in front of him. Then his eyes lit on Zale. "Sorry, kid, but you're gonna be hearing this all over town. These assholes killed your dad to screw him outta a few million bucks." He shook his head and turned to me. "See, Nicky decided to sell the casino cruise line because he was getting into hotels in a big way. Besides, he was tired of it. He gets bored easy. But he retained ten percent of Tropi-Cruz—like a silent partner, see? And the new resorts, like the one he's building here, were going up just to service the gamblers coming here to Lauderdale to go out on the boats. That asswipe Kagan owed Nick millions from cash that was on the boats at the time of the sale and payments he stiffed us on. This is no secret. It's been all over the papers. Nicky wasn't letting Kagan get away with it. We just went to court last week to start the process to get the boats back." He shook his head. "Fuckin' Russians are animals."

The secretary, Roma, appeared at the door, her face still blotchy and her chin quivering. "Mr. Quinn, pardon me, but there is a police detective on the line for you."

"Look," I said, rising out of the chair, "we've got to go. Thanks for your time, Mr. Quinn."

He came around the desk once again and smothered Zale in another of those hugs. "Anything," he said. "Remember, there is *anything* I can do, you call, right?"

Zale nodded and backed away from him. As we headed back out toward the front door, I said in a low voice, "I think I'd rather face the protesters out there than get a hug from Uncle Leo."

The corner of Zale's mouth twitched a little, and I figured that a few hours after his dad's death, that was about the best I should expect.

VI.

THE protesters chanted and waved their placards with renewed vigor the minute we exited the building, but I didn't see the old woman. There were only about fifteen to twenty people in the crowd, and they closed in around us as we tried to make our way to the El Camino. I wanted another look at the woman, just to try to nudge the memory out, to figure out where I had seen her before, but she was gone.

B. J. leaned across the seat and opened the passenger-side door from the inside. Strains of airy flute music wafted out of the truck's interior as I waved the protesters back so that I could open the door wide enough for Zale to get in.

"Let's get out of here," I said. "We need to go pick up *Gorda* at River Bend."

Zale slid into the middle, and once I'd squeezed in and slammed the door, B. J. sat a moment longer, listening to the final notes of the music, his eyes closed.

"What is that?" Zale asked when the song ended and B. J. switched on the ignition.

"James Galway on the flute. The song's called 'Smoke Gets in Your Eyes.' "

Zale's eyebrows drew together, wrinkling his forehead, and he stared at the CD player. When the next song started, and the simple, clear guitar notes floated out of the sound system, the boy looked up and nodded at B. J. "Red Hot Chili Peppers," he said as he started bouncing his index finger on his jeans-covered leg. Then he lifted his hand and pointed at the CD player. " 'Under the Bridge,' " he said just before the vocals started.

B. J. nodded and the two of them sat there, eyes narrowed and heads barely bobbing as we drove the new high span over the Seventeenth Street Causeway that gave us a view of the growing high-rises over in the city's center. I could count seven construction cranes on the horizon. The makeshift offices had been the first little boxes to go up on the construction sites behind the big signs, artists' renderings of condos with a river view starting at $700,000.00. Where did they expect to find the people to fill these steel towers? I thought of the Pontus offices, their model tower project encased in Plexiglas, and the protesters down below us. Now with Nick gone, would the momentum still be there to add two more? The Chili Peppers sang of loneliness in the city, and I wondered if each of us was hearing a different song.

THE crunching sound of tires on stone woke me from a daydream. The three of us in B. J.'s truck had not spoken a word on the drive across town to River Bend Boatyard. I'd been thinking about the time I had tried to teach Molly how to row a dinghy. We were probably no more than seven years old, and we'd taken my dad's pram out into the middle of the canal. I was crouched in the stern and Molly was on the seat at the oars, but she couldn't get them both to bite at the same time and we were going in circles. I couldn't help laughing, and she was getting furious with me. She splashed me with an oar, then I picked up the old milk-jug bailer and soaked her a good one in return. Soon we were giggling so hard

Molly fell off the thwart seat, and we both kicked our feet up in the air. At that point Red looked out the window to check on us in the canal and saw a dinghy with two pairs of waggling legs. He came roaring out to see what all the foolishness was about, made us tie the dinghy up properly, and beached me for a week. That's what he called it when I wasn't allowed aboard any boats, and it was punishment in the extreme.

"Time to get to work," B. J. said when he'd parked the El Camino in front of the boatyard office.

As we walked through the dozens of boats propped up in the yard, I hoped we could avoid seeing the *Mykonos*, but when *Gorda* came into view, right where I'd left her on the outside dock, I saw the fat stern of the Hatteras between us and her. Rather than move her around the basin to the other side where the long-term jobs were stored, they'd propped her up right outside the big work shed, between two large sailboats. I felt Zale stiffen beside me, and I knew he had seen her, too. Both props and shafts had already been removed. But even from this distance, I could see the dark shadow on the enclosure around the flybridge. No one had bothered to clean off the plastic—or maybe they weren't allowed to go up on the bridge, as the boat and her decks were still draped with yellow crime scene tape.

I made a show of looking at my watch. "Hey, we'd better get a move on," I said. "The tide's turned, and I'd like to get this ketch downriver before dark. Come on, guys."

Zale looked back over his shoulder once, just before climbing aboard *Gorda*. He was a smart kid. I figured he knew what he was looking at.

ONE of the things about B. J. and me is that we've worked together so long we hardly have to say anything on a

job. Which is a good thing because on that chilly afternoon, none of us felt like talking. We ran *Gorda* across
the river from one boatyard to the other and docked at
Summerfield. I went up to the office to do the paperwork, and B. J. stayed back to rig the ketch and get her
ready for the trip downriver. Once we got under way,
Zale positioned himself up on the bow of the tug. B. J.
was aboard our tow, and I was stuck in the wheelhouse.
In the twisting confines of the New River, I couldn't
leave the helm for a minute.

The trip down the New River from Summerfield Boatworks to Bahia Mar Marina generally took less than an
hour, but this afternoon it felt much longer. Though the
day had grown warmer around midday, as the sun
dipped low in the west at only 5:00 on this February afternoon, the wind blowing off the water seemed to bite
right through our clothes.

Just past the high-rise condo canyon that downtown
Fort Lauderdale had become, we entered the section of
river with the really pricey waterfront homes. Many
of the original homes had been built between 1920 and
1950, and they were small Florida bungalows with
barrel-tile roofs and jalousie windows. In the past decade
the nouveau riche stars and dot-commers had started
buying them up, tearing them down, and building mini-
mansions in their places, with faux Spanish styling or
cheesy attempts at New England–style architecture complete with widow's walks. Amid the new construction,
you could still spot the well-maintained older homes
nestled back amid oak trees older than the town, homes
that maintained the old Florida charm with porches and
little chimneys that often puffed wood smoke on cold
winter days like this.

Just as interesting as the homes were the boats docked
along the riverbanks. From hailing ports like Cannes,

Grand Cayman, and Recife, most of the yachts were huge custom powerboats valued in the millions. One of my favorites, though, was a perfectly maintained 1920s yawl with a white trunk cabin and gleaming varnished masts. She was docked in front of a house of the same vintage. The boat's name, *Annie,* my mother's name, was stenciled in graceful black paint and gold leaf on her stern. I always admired it when I passed. Though the boat was in far better condition than the home, neither seemed to have been updated or changed from its original designs.

As we went by the Larsens' place, Abaco recognized the sound of my tug's engine, crawled out from under her favorite bougainvillea bush, and jumped around barking at us. When Zale turned his face to look back at the begging dog, I saw that his cheeks and nose were glowing bright red from the cold. I waved him into the deckhouse.

"You look like you're freezing out there. Why don't you come in here and warm up?"

The noise of the tug's Caterpillar engine made conversation difficult, but you could hear as long as the other person was willing to shout.

"I like it out there on the bow. It's always my favorite spot on a boat."

"Me, too," I said. "It's a good place to go to feel alone. A good place to think."

He nodded, but didn't go back out to his post on the bow. It was not until we were entering the Intracoastal Waterway at the mouth of the New River and turning northeast toward Bahia Mar that he spoke again. I'd idled the engine down a bit and the noise level was kinder to conversation.

"Are you religious?" he asked.

I had been reaching for the VHF microphone to hail

the harbormaster at Bahia Mar, but I paused with my arm in the air and stared at him for a second. "Not in the sense of any kind of organized religion," I said, dodging the real question as I usually did, and lifting the microphone out of its holder. "Why do you ask?"

"Well, you know my mom," he said, climbing onto the wheelhouse bunk and crossing his legs Indian-style. Sitting like that, he looked even younger. Much too young to be juggling these issues. "She never really took me to any church when I was growing up. The only one who ever talked to me about stuff like that was my great-grandmother."

I hailed the harbormaster to ask where he wanted us to dock, then said, "I remember meeting Molly's grandmother. She's quite a character."

"Yeah? You know Gramma Josie?"

"When I was little she used to scare me."

"How come?"

"She was so different, so foreign. Molly's mom, your grandmother, she grew up on the Seminole reservation, but she never really wanted to talk about Indian stuff. But when Gramma Josie came, that was *all* she talked about. I guess I'd seen too many movies where Indians were bad guys."

"Nah, Gramma Josie's cool. She lives in this neat house out at Big Cypress, in the Everglades. Mom and I used to go out there for the weekend sometimes and stay with her. It was fun. When I'd go outside and play with other kids out there, they always thought it was a big deal that my gramma was Josie Tigertail. I guess she's like an old medicine woman in the tribe or something. She's kinda' hard to understand because she doesn't speak English too good. She says her language is called Creek. She used to tell me these stories about animals and stuff, and they would, like, have secret meanings to teach kids to be good and all."

"Do you remember any of them?"

"Sure. Mostly, though, I was thinking about when she used to talk about God and heaven. She called God the Breath Maker, and she said when people died they went to a place called Skyland."

"I don't ever remember her talking about that to your mom and me."

"Gramma Josie calls me an 'old soul.' She says I'm too serious for a kid my age. I can't help it. I'm interested in stuff like that. I read a lot. She once told me that the Seminoles believed that they had to leave a place if a person died there because their spirit would haunt that place. Then, the spirit wouldn't go on to join the Breath Maker. And she said when you buried someone, you always had to bury their possessions with them so they could use them in the afterlife."

I nodded. I wanted to comfort him, to tell him that I was sure his dad was happily residing up in Skyland, but I had too many of my own questions on that count. Besides, even if I believed in heaven, I thought it might be a stretch to think they'd let Nick in.

It was dark by the time we started back up the river in *Gorda* after docking the ketch at Bahia Mar and turning the keys and the responsibility over to her new owner. The guy had looked ashen-faced after Zale and I had thrown off the towlines, setting B. J. and the new ketch adrift. I'd docked *Gorda* on the T-pier, and then he'd watched as B. J. started the engine and brought his fifty-seven-footer in so easily that Zale and I were able to reach up and grab the dock lines neatly coiled on her bow.

The three of us were huddled in *Gorda*'s deckhouse now, headed home, just waiting for the warm lights of the Larsens' place to appear around the next bend. B. J. came up behind me and reached around to put his hands in the pockets of my sweatshirt. I leaned back into his chest, rested my head in the hollow of his neck, and pressed my butt against him. The instant rise in my temperature was due more to the thrumming I felt inside than to the mere combination of our body heat. With his hands still inside my sweatshirt pockets, he began tracing small circles on the front of my jeans. We had a couple hundred feet of clear water between us and the next channel marker, so I let go of the wheel and turned into his arms. Over his shoulder, I saw Zale sitting on the wheelhouse bunk, wrapped in a blanket, his head lowered, and I heard him sniffling in the darkness. I nodded my head and B. J. looked over, too. I didn't know if it was the cold making the kid's nose run or if he was crying again. I saw in B. J.'s eyes that he felt as I did—either way, we were helpless to cure it.

Once we'd tied up the tug at my dock and I'd shut down the engine, the night seemed eerily quiet. As is typical the day after a cold front comes through, the night was dry and cold, with temperatures in the forties already and headed for the thirties by morning. The unusual lack of humidity made the night air crisp and clear, and the stars and the lights of the city all seemed to pierce the black night with uncharacteristic clarity.

As the three of us walked up the path toward my cottage with Abaco bounding ahead, Zale stopped dead, staring upward. Without looking at me or B. J., he asked, "Where do you think he is right now?"

I didn't know what to say to that. I tried not to let on how often I wondered that same question about all the people I'd loved and lost.

"Do you think he still *is*?" He looked at me, the starlight reflecting off his wire-rimmed glasses. "I mean, is my dad up there somewhere in the heavens—like Gramma Josie says, in Skyland—watching me? Is he still, you know, my dad?"

B. J. slid in between us and put his arms over both our shoulders. He hugged Zale especially tight. "Hey kid, there's no way we can really know for sure about that, is there? We humans are always asking that question, the question of another life, of whether there is such a thing as an afterlife. But you know what I think? You know that feeling inside you right now? That hurt, that sense of loss?"

Zale nodded.

"That's your dad settling in right here." He took the arm off my shoulder and patted Zale on the belly. "You'll always have that feeling there when you think about him. You'll always carry that part of him with you."

"I miss him so much already," he said in a choked whisper. Then he wrapped his thin arms around his midsection, shrugged off B. J.'s embrace, and stepped off the path. He swung his torso back and forth as though he were suffering from a bellyache. Then, turning to us, he asked, "Why?" The tears rushed back and his voice cracked with emotion as he struggled to say between sobs, "Why would somebody shoot my dad?"

VII.

WHEN I pulled my Jeep to the curb in front of Molly's house, I thought at first that she wasn't home. The house looked dark and there wasn't any sign of a car parked in the drive. We climbed out and B. J. lifted the seat so that Zale could get out of the Jeep's backseat, and as soon as the kid's sneakers hit the pavement, he trotted up the walk, opened the front door, and disappeared inside. He'd left the front door standing open, and from inside I could hear faint strains of Norah Jones's voice coming from the stereo. I recognized the song "I Don't Know Why."

I looked at B. J. "Think we ought to go in?"

"Yeah, just to make sure his mom's there and the kid's safe. And to close the front door, anyway."

"She's there. You could go close the door."

"Sey, what's the matter with you?"

"B. J., I don't have time to tell you the whole story right now, but Molly and I used to be friends. Best friends. And then it ended."

"So, that was then and this is now. Now we need to get in there and make sure the two of them are okay. It's about basic human decency, Seychelle. It's what we're going to do."

It was only when we got to the front door that we saw the light from the single candle burning on the coffee table. Molly was wrapped up in an old hand-crocheted afghan, sitting upright on the couch, staring at the flame. She looked up at us when we entered, her face expressionless.

"Oh, Sey," she said, "come in. Thanks, you know," she said, nodding toward the back hall. She spoke in an odd monotone.

"Hey, no big deal. Molly, this is my friend, B. J. Moana. B. J., Molly Pontus."

Molly scooted over and patted the couch next to her. B. J. obliged and sat down. I'd been hoping we wouldn't stay long, so I remained standing, edging a little closer to the door each time I shifted my weight from one foot to the other.

"So how was he today?"

She had directed the question to B. J.

"About as good as you could expect for a kid going through this, but he had some tough moments. He's feeling typical survivor's guilt."

"Ha!" she said, but it wasn't a laugh. "Tell me about it."

"It's a normal part of the grieving process—as is the crying. He needs to cry, and you shouldn't discourage him from it. On the other hand, he also needs to laugh, and he shouldn't feel guilty when he does."

"You seem to know what you're talking about."

B. J. shrugged. "I read a lot."

I wanted to tell her that she was sitting next to a walking library, that he had two college degrees in fancy stuff like Asian and Classical Studies, whatever the hell that was, but I kept quiet. I felt like I was on the outside again. Like way back with Molly and Pit. The two of them were already talking as if they were old friends. B. J. had that effect on people. They warmed to him instantly and often told him things they wouldn't tell their own families.

"It's so hard to know what you're supposed to do with yourself at a time like this," Molly said. "Someone you love is dead, and it's still true whether you ride in a car or sit on a couch. Nothing you do can make that fact go away." She hiked the afghan up around her shoulders and sighed. "This has been the longest day. Jeannie took me to the police station and they took my statement. That was pretty simple—we were back here by two, but I didn't know what to do then. I've just been sitting here, watching as it got dark. I lit the candle when I got cold."

"Have you eaten anything?" B. J. asked.

"I'm not hungry," Molly answered, shaking her head.

B. J. slapped his hands on his thighs. "That's it. You've got to eat. Do you mind if I make myself at home in your kitchen?"

She shook her head. "Feel free," she said.

After B. J. left the room, I stood there for a while, my hands snuggled deep into the pockets of my sweatshirt. It was clear I wasn't going to get him to make this a short visit. The silence in the room was like a black hole, sucking all my energy into it. It's hard to come up with small talk when you haven't spoken to someone for over thirteen years. I leaned against the wall in that darkened living room, trying to get up the nerve to talk to Molly, to make it like it was in the old days when it was effortless, when we didn't have to think of what to say. I opened my mouth but the words wouldn't come. It wasn't like she was making it any easier, either, just sitting there staring at that damn flame.

"She called me this afternoon." Molly spoke so softly, I wasn't sure I heard her right.

"What?"

"She didn't say anything, but I heard her breathing. I knew it was her," she said. Then she got up, rearranged the blanket wrapped around her shoulders, and mumbled something about checking on Zale before disappearing down the dark hall.

I walked into the kitchen, where B. J. had turned on the lights. He was chopping some onions on a wood board. Leaning my cheek against the cool steel of the refrigerator door, I wondered what the hell that was all about. She had to have been talking about Janet. I didn't want to think my old friend was losing her grip on reality, but it didn't make any sense to think that a new widow was making crank calls. I wondered if Molly needed more help than any of us could give her. I fought down the urge to unload on B. J., to complain about the ache I felt deep in my gut whenever I was around her. He would tell me to let it go, to forgive her and move on. He wouldn't understand me when I told him it wasn't that easy.

My stomach growled. I could smell the garlic sizzling in the frying pan on the stove next to another lidded pot. B. J. stepped over to me, slid his hand under my sweatshirt, and rubbed my belly with his free hand while he kissed me on the mouth. His tongue tasted of cool mint. "Hungry?" he asked when he stopped for a breath.

"Hmm, ummm, yeah," I mumbled, trying to get my brain back in gear. I always had to do that after one of his kisses. "Can I help?"

B. J. turned back to the counter, swept his onions into the pan with the garlic, handed me the chopping board and knife, and pointed to a pile of zucchini.

Now what kind of man gets romantic, then hands a woman a knife and a zucchini? I looked at the vegetables and then at B. J.'s back as he lifted the lid, stirred some rice in butter, then poured in water from a measuring cup. "Uh, B. J., what do I do with these? I mean, do I cut them this way, or like this?" I demonstrated with the knife over the squash.

He sighed and took the knife from me. "Why don't you find the cutlery and go set the table? Then maybe see if you can round up some wine somewhere. Red, preferably. I'm making ratatouille."

"Ummm," I said, rolling my eyes as I started opening drawers, not willing to show my ignorance and ask him what the hell that was. "Sounds yummy."

B. J. did an admirable job of keeping the conversation going during the meal. The more they talked, the more he and Molly found they had in common. They were both fish-eating vegetarians and both were really into all that Eastern religion stuff. Molly's voice had lost that deadpan tone, and she seemed to be enjoying herself. She leaned her chin on her palm and listened, fascinated, as B. J. told her about how the Samoan people eat taro cooked in a coconut sauce back in the islands. I didn't know how she was finding a description of eating roots so fascinating—or if it was really his gorgeous face that was keeping her so engrossed. All through our teenage years, every time I liked a guy, Molly wiggled her ass or batted her eyelashes in his direction, and he was drawn off to follow after her. Old habits, apparently, die hard.

As we were finishing up and B. J. was carrying plates out to the kitchen, loading them in the dishwasher and brewing some hot tea, I said under my breath to Zale, "Anytime you want to break out of here and go for a Big Mac, just call me."

He attempted a smile and gave me a thumbs-up, then asked his mother if he could be excused and disappeared back into his room.

Molly watched him go. "He's just sitting in there in the dark with his headphones on, blasting that music of his into his ears. He's going to go deaf."

"Be careful," I said. "You're beginning to sound like your mother."

"Yeah, right," she said disgustedly, turning her head away.

B. J. set down the mugs of steaming tea and honey and was about to sit down while I remained standing, my arms straight, hands pressing down on the back of my chair. "I hate to be the party pooper here, but I really need to be getting back. Think you could just take a couple of swigs of that and we could get moving?"

B. J. gave me a quizzical look that reminded me of Abaco when I talk to her. "Okay, if you're in a hurry, we can do that," he said. "I'll just go finish straightening things up in the kitchen."

"Please, B. J., you've done enough," Molly said. "Really. I can take it from here. If Seychelle has to leave, I understand." She took his hand in both of hers. "Thanks so much for dinner and for the good company. I needed it tonight, but I'll be fine now."

We didn't say much on the drive to the boatyard, where I was to drop him off to pick up his truck. The zippered side windows did little to keep out the cold night air, but there were other reasons the atmosphere in the Jeep was so chilled.

When I pulled into the parking spot next to his El Camino, I didn't shut off the engine. The noise made conversation more difficult, and I hoped B. J. would get the hint.

"What's bothering you, Sey? You hardly said a word tonight, and that's not like you."

I took in a deep breath and blew it out, staring at the Jeep's overhead as though I might find the answer to his question written on the inside of the canvas there. "B. J., I think I just need time. You don't know the whole story. Hell, I don't even know what really happened. There's still a mountain of hurt there between me and Molly. For eleven years—basically my whole childhood—we were the best of friends, more like sisters." I turned and looked out the Jeep's window. He sat there, knowing I wasn't finished, waiting for the rest of it. "Then one day," I said, turning to face him, "she just disappeared. She'd moved out of her parents' house and got married to some guy I thought she didn't even like. I'd been under the impression that we told each other everything, and yeah, she talked about him, but to me she'd always kind of made fun of him. She never even told me she liked him." But even as I said it, I wasn't sure a man could ever comprehend the immensity of that. "She never called, never made the slightest effort to reach out to me. I know I'm older now, and I should be able to get beyond this, but I just can't. The way it ended back then, so abruptly, with no explanation, no communication, and now we're just supposed to start up again as though the last thirteen years never happened? I can't do that. There's a whole lot that needs saying right now, and it's not about tofu and taro."

VIII.

I HAD several jobs lined up over the next couple of days. February is the busy season in Fort Lauderdale's luxury yacht world. Hundreds of huge power yachts from all over the world converge on this little corner of South Florida, and, boats being boats, they always need work done. The parade of yachts headed up and down the New River, into the Dania Cut-off Canal, or down to the Miami River, appeared endless. In the winter there was always more business than I could handle, but I needed to work every minute in order to make it through the slow months from May through October, when the yacht crowd headed off to Europe or up to Newport. They left us here in the heat and humidity, swatting mosquitoes and trying to stretch our savings until the next season.

By Wednesday morning the weather had warmed considerably after Monday's cold front, and I was back in shorts and a T-shirt as I scrubbed down the boat from stem to stern. The wheelhouse VHF was squawking with the usual traffic, though these days it seemed I was just as likely to get calls from boaters' cell phones, so I had my portable phone sitting on the bench outside the cottage door.

I'd come back late the night before, after midnight, from a job that involved towing in a sailboat with en-

gine trouble that had sailed over from the Exumas. They
were able to get to the harbor mouth with no problem,
but they needed a tow up the New River to the dock behind their house in the Citrus Isles. They were worried
that the wind would quit once they got in the lee of the
condos on the north side of the channel, and since they
didn't fancy wallowing out of control in the channel off
the rock jetties, they'd called me on their cell phone after
nine o'clock to pick them up outside the breakwaters.
Trying to get the towlines rigged outside the harbor entrance in the seaway left over from the previous day's
norther, I'd gotten salty spray all over the deck and wheelhouse. When I'd come out late this morning, the tug glis-
tened like a sugary Easter egg with the thousands of tiny
salt crystals that clung to her topsides.

I picked up the hose and sprayed the soapy suds off
the windshield and the top of the wheelhouse. Abaco
barked and I squirted her with the hose. This was the
game she loved to play, barking and sticking her rump in
the air, daring me to catch her with the stream of water
before she darted off behind the cottage. Water dog that
she was, she loved getting wet so much, she'd been known
to leap off the dock to chase me in the dinghy when I left
without her.

I was trying everything I could to keep myself busy
and avoid thinking about Molly and Zale. That morning I'd wandered out in my sweats to get the paper, still
half asleep from the late night's work, and there on the
front page of the *Sun-Sentinel* was another story about
the shooting and the subsequent investigation. A photo
of Nick, Molly, and Zale, all smiling, was centered above
the fold on the front page. I'd refolded the paper and
thrown it on the couch, unread. Then I'd fixed myself
coffee and a bagel, dabbled with my paints for a bit, and
come out here to wash down the boat—anything just to

try to keep myself from thinking about it, from reading that story.

Maybe I wasn't rich, and maybe they didn't write stories about *me* in the paper, but I liked my life, dammit. And I liked it when I just went to work and did my thing and everyone out there left me alone. In Sullivan Towing and Salvage, I owned my own business, and what I did mattered to the people I worked for. Back when I was a lifeguard for the city, I saved lives on a regular basis, and I put in ten years at that. I'd paid some dues—more than most folks. And now, while my job often involved just helping rich folks move their toys around, it paid well and kept me in the business so that I could be there for the other times when I pulled people off wrecks, when boats would have sunk or people would have died if *Gorda* and I had not been there.

Now, though, I needed to get back to that place in my mind where I realized my job stopped when we reached the dock. Lately I'd gotten involved in a couple of incidents that stretched way beyond just salvaging boats. But I'd had enough. Things had been quiet for me ever since last spring, and I wanted it to stay that way. I'd had enough of getting involved with other people's problems, enough of police and intrigue, enough of trying to salvage lives as well as boats. In the past year I'd seen more dead bodies than I had in ten years of lifeguarding on Fort Lauderdale Beach. I wanted no more of that.

Still, I couldn't help wondering how Molly and Zale were holding up. I remembered all too well the decisions that had to be made in the wake of a death in a family. I wondered if the new wife would be handling all the funeral arrangements, if she was letting Molly take part in the service, or if she was continuing to ostracize her as Molly claimed. She couldn't leave the man's son out of the picture, for Pete's sake. And that got me started thinking about the way Molly had talked about the new Mrs. Pontus and Jeannie's reaction to her comments. I reminded myself to ask Jeannie about her take on Nick's widow.

After I washed down *Gorda,* I opened all the ports, doors, and hatches and aired out the interior. I spent some time in the engine room, cleaned out the strainer on the raw water pump, and checked my hoses and fittings with the visual I tried to do once every three months or so. There was a thick sheen of oil on the bilgewater that didn't make me very happy, and I went through some service records to figure out when I should block out some time to get Archie, my mechanic, in to take a look.

It was when I was standing in the wheelhouse wondering whether to go get the Brasso to polish the ship's bell that I decided I was being ridiculous. Enough of this "make work." Might as well just go in and read the goddamn article.

I rushed into the cottage, saw that it was just past noon, grabbed a beer out of the fridge, and sat down at the table to read the story under the photo.

The beer was still untouched when I got to the end on an inside page. The author had written all about "maverick businessman Nick Pontus" and what he had done throughout the years to create his empire of restaurants, resorts, and casino gambling boats. There was some lurid stuff in there about how he and this Russian guy Ari Kagan had apparently tried to outsmart each other in the *screw you* department, and when Kagan seemed to be winning, Nick went to a grand jury and spilled his guts on some of the dirt he knew about Kagan's misdeeds. The reporter had quotes in there from various Pontus Enterprises employees—including Leon Quinn, who had released an official statement. The paper said the bridge tender got a pretty good look at the car, and he said it was definitely a black Mustang, an older classic model, but he had been too high up to see the driver. He didn't know if the driver had stepped out of the car—he didn't see it. All of that, though, was not what made me forget about the St. Pauli Girl beading up at my elbow. It was when I saw Molly and Zale mentioned that I lost track of the world around me. The article stated that Molly had produced Nick's will from a safe deposit box they still shared, and it named Zale as Nick's primary heir to the millions in stock, real estate, boats, restaurants, and companies. In other words, this thirteen-year-old kid was soon to become the second-richest individual in Broward County.

I was still sitting there staring into space when the phone rang. I only have one portable phone in my cottage, and I tend to put it down wherever and whenever I finish using it. It was on the fourth ring and the machine was just about to kick in when I found the damn thing on the bench outside the front door.

"Hello. Sullivan Towing and Salvage. What do you want?" I said, breathing hard from the cursing I'd been doing during the search.

"You sound like you're in a charming mood today," Jeannie said, and I could hear the grin in her voice.

"Don't start with me," I said.

"What? What did I do?"

"I know what you're up to. Forget it. You want me to do something for Molly Pontus, and I'm telling you forget it."

"Molly? I didn't say anything about Molly."

"You didn't have to. I know you. I know how you think. You think that I just can't resist helping people who are in trouble. Well, let me tell you something. This time I *can* resist. After what she did to me and my brother, this time, it's different."

"You finished?"

"I guess."

"Actually, the purpose of my call is to invite you and the ever-charming Mr. Moana over to my house for barbecue this evening."

"Oh," I said. When I'd thought about it for a couple of seconds, I added, "Jeannie, it's February and it gets cold and dark by 5:30."

"I didn't say 'a barbecue' like I was going to be doing the barbecuing myself, did I? See, I'm in the mood for some of those good Tom Jenkins Barbecue ribs, and since the place is on the way from your house over here to mine, I thought maybe I could talk you into running by and picking up dinner on your way over here."

"That's low, my friend."

"Is that a yes?"

"Are you sure this is not about Molly?"

"This is about ribs and that great tangy sauce of Tom's."

"How does 6:30 sound?"

"Excellent. And don't forget the collard greens."

By the time B. J. and I drove into the yard in front of Jeannie's place, it was dark and the temperature was back down into the fifties. I had spent the remainder of my afternoon doing odd jobs on *Gorda*, then taking the Larsens' kayak on a long paddle upriver, and finally working on the business's books and paying off some bills. There was nothing I hated more than that kind of paperwork, and I knew when I resorted to that, I was desperate to fill my time.

Jeannie lived upriver from me in a neighborhood called Sailboat Bend. In the early twentieth century, when the

New River was the trading grounds for Seminole Indians and pioneer families, the S-shaped bend that passed through this part of town was particularly difficult for sailors to navigate. Today the area was home to some of the city's oldest houses, as well as some of the ugliest. In between the cute little rehabbed gingerbready wood cottages built by Bahamians and shipwrights were these cheap concrete block buildings that had gone up in the sixties. The one Jeannie lived in wasn't as bad as some of the government-subsidized housing. Her place was one of the four fairly large apartments into which her building was divided, and the surrounding grounds were beautifully landscaped with large old oaks, bromeliads, and ferns.

I had my arms full of warm white paper bags, and as B. J. held out the corn bread bag and raised an eyebrow, asking if I could carry that, too, I heard Jeannie's voice from up on the landing.

"Ummm, um. I smell that heavenly smell. And you're late."

"Hold on. We're on our way up," I said, as I balanced the pile of bags and navigated the concrete stairs. "Seems the upper crust has discovered your favorite barbecue place. Parking lot was full of SUVs the size of tanks."

When I reached the top of the stairs, I heard the sound of the television coming through the open screen door. The screeching laughter from a sitcom was drowned out by one of her son's *yeowls*.

She stood at the door wearing purple stretch leggings and a huge tropical print tunic with flowers the size and color of eggplants. I looked at her in alarm as the hollering in the house continued.

She shrugged. "I leave them alone, they work it out. I go in there, and it will just get worse." Her eyes flicked past me, then her whole face lit up with a wide grin. "Ah, here's that man of yours. I don't know which is yummier-looking—him or the ribs."

B. J. kissed her on the cheek, and we went into the kitchen to get the food onto plates. I wasn't sure how I felt about Jeannie referring to B. J. as "that man of yours."

As a lawyer who worked out of her home and was raising her twin sons alone, Jeannie had a thirst for adult conversation. She set her boys up in the playroom to eat on TV trays in front of the tube while the three of us ate at the table that was in a corner of her living room—after I had stacked the table's piles of file folders and books on the floor. I pulled three bottles of Corona out of her refrigerator, opened them on the bottle opener permanently affixed beneath her kitchen counter, and set the bottles on the table.

Throughout the meal we talked about my recent jobs, a good book B. J. had just read, and a divorce case that Jeannie was working that involved a Hollywood Beach restaurateur and his wife, who had once worked for him as a prostitute. We laughed and the conversation would have sounded comfortable and contented had we not all three known that we were talking around the one thing we really wanted to discuss.

It was B. J. who finally brought it up. He had made us tea, and we were sitting in the living room in front of Jeannie's television, which was usually on and competing in volume with the kids' set in the back room. Tonight, what with her having company, it was dark. I checked out the clock over the kitchen sink. I was thinking that in fifteen minutes the local news would be on, and I was wondering if the cops had any leads or suspects when B. J. asked the question I had been wanting to ask all night.

"So Jeannie, how's Molly handling everything? Is she doing all right?"

Jeannie raised her eyebrows, drew a deep breath, and stared into the bottom of her empty mug. "Depends on what you call 'all right,' I guess."

B. J. nodded. "Yeah. I see your point."

"I don't know that you do." She looked directly at me. "Either of you. Every time she leaves the house, some reporter accosts her somewhere—outside her door, at the grocery store, or when she goes to take care of business at Pontus Enterprises. The cops have been back twice to go over her Mustang." She shook her head. "And she gave them permission to search the garage without consulting me."

"The police suspect her?" B. J. asked, setting his mug down, and then sliding his hand over the top of his hair. "What are they, nuts?"

"B. J., don't be naïve. It's standard procedure," Jeannie said. "They always look at the family first."

"But Molly Pontus? I don't think I've ever met a woman who exudes such a strong sense of virtue. She has an inner beauty that—"

He paused to try to find the right word. B. J. *never* had trouble finding words, I thought. Obviously, Molly had made quite an impression on him.

"And the new merry widow Pontus, according to Molly, is acting like a bitch extraordinaire," Jeannie continued.

"Jeannie," I said, "what's going on there?" I hadn't shared Molly's odd comments about the phone call with anyone, but I wanted to get Jeannie's take on her state of mind. "Molly seems to be a little over the top when she talks about her."

"A little, ha! Molly's usually an exceptionally bright and sensible woman—except when it comes to Janet Pontus."

"So what's the deal? Have you met Janet?"

"Yeah, she's young, beautiful, self-centered, and not too bright. But I don't see her as the hard-bitten, conniving, evil bitch Molly makes her out to be."

"But Molly wouldn't lie," I said.

"See, I don't think it is a lie—exactly. It's like when there's a car accident and all the witnesses describe something different. It's a perspective thing. For example, yesterday Zale wanted to get some things out of his room in his father's house, and according to Molly, Janet told her everything inside the house belongs to her, Janet—including the contents of the boy's room. Molly said Janet threatened to call the police and have Molly arrested if she tried to go in and get her son's things."

"Wow, that's brutal."

"Wait a minute. When *I* called Janet late yesterday, she told me they were just doing an inventory of the contents of the house for the estate, and Zale could come get his things as soon as they were through. I asked her straight out if she had threatened Molly, and she sounded genuinely surprised by the question." Jeannie shook her head. "I'm sorry, but I believed Janet. Molly has always looked at that beautiful woman and seen a train wreck. She sees what she wants to see. Look, Molly and Nick were married for what, eleven years— and he and Janet had been married just over a year, yet because she is the widow, Janet's making all the decisions about the funeral service. And of course, Molly feels left out and stressed over that. She's realizing she's going to have to raise her son all alone now, too. But this story she told me last night has me really worried."

"What story?" B. J. asked, scooting his chair closer to the table.

"She called last night, woke me up around two in the morning. She said Janet was creeping around outside her house, in the bushes outside her bedroom window making spooky noises and trying to scare her."

I'd been tipping back the dregs of my beer, and I nearly sprayed the room. I choked it down, then said, "What?"

"Yeah, that's what I said."

"Did you go over there?"

"No. I asked her if she'd actually seen anything, and she admitted she hadn't. But she said she had heard strange rustlings in the bushes, and then this moaning sound. The more I asked her about it, the weirder the story got. Listen you two, Molly's trying to deal with this all alone, and I'm afraid she's not handling it real well. She feels completely abandoned since nobody has called or stopped by or said boo. Aside from all that, though," she said, looking up with a tight smile, "Molly's doing just skippy."

"Jeannie, I had no idea," B. J. said. "If you think it would help her out, I'd be glad to stop over, spend some time with her."

Yeah, I thought, I'll bet you would. Aloud I said, "B. J., the one Jeannie's trying to point the finger at here is me."

Jeannie pushed forward with a grunt and grabbed the remote off the coffee table. "I'm not trying to point fingers, Seychelle. I'm just answering the man's question." She aimed the remote at the television and the screen lit up with the face of a local newscaster. There was a small photo of Nick in a corner of the screen, and she was telling us that the story about Nick Pontus would be coming up right after the commercial break. Jeannie pointed the remote at the TV again and muted the sound.

I looked from the TV to her. "Do you think that means there's been some kind of break in the case?"

"What? Just because they're talking about it on TV?

They've been talking about it every hour. Seychelle, what have you got a TV for if you never turn it on?"

"Poor Molly," B. J. said. "I wasn't even thinking. I mean, I *had* been thinking about her—often actually—but I didn't want to intrude. I thought she needed time alone. I didn't realize that she was being hounded by the press and this other business with Janet. She could probably use a shoulder to lean on. Tomorrow. I'll go over there first thing."

"Well, tomorrow I'm expecting both of you to come with me to Nick's funeral."

Before she could say any more, the newscaster came back on the screen, and Jeannie turned off the muting. "And here at home, while the Fort Lauderdale police are reporting no new leads in Monday's gangland-style shooting death of maverick businessman Nikolas Pontus, a one-hundred-thousand-dollar reward has been established with the Crime Stoppers of Broward County for information leading to the arrest and conviction of those responsible for Pontus's death."

When they flashed the Crime Stoppers number on the screen, Jeannie said, "Boy, that's gonna bring the wackos out of the woodwork now."

The reporter continued, "Pontus had recently been involved in a series of lawsuits involving, among other things, his sale of the TropiCruz Casino gambling boat empire, a hotel and condo development project in Fort Lauderdale, and the alimony and child support in his messy divorce."

"Low blow!" Jeannie shouted as the announcer read the information that was displayed on the screen about the date and time of the funeral. She raised the remote and clicked off the tube. "That wasn't recent. His divorce was like over two years ago."

"I didn't know you'd had to sue him," I said.

"Oh yeah. Cheap bastard didn't want to give her anything. He claims to be worth over forty million! Course, Molly didn't want to ask for anything, either. I eventually got it all sorted out, but it took a while. She didn't get big bucks, but she doesn't have to go to work, either. She can stay home and work on her art, and the old family homestead is paid off. What we did get from Nick, however, was an agreed-upon prenuptial agreement that guaranteed that the remainder of his estate would eventually go to Zale instead of the new wife. The fiancée wasn't thrilled, but that's what they get for negotiating a divorce during their engagement. Molly didn't mind giving up most of her portion of that dough, but she didn't feel she could make that decision for Zale."

"I hope the reward they mentioned brings in some new information," B. J. said. "It must be hard hanging in limbo, knowing somebody killed him, but not knowing who. Molly and her son will need closure. I can't believe I've let her get to this point of feeling so alone." He turned to me and continued. "I can see why the two of you would have been such good friends. Even though you appear very different, there is something at the core that is similar. Something I haven't found in very many people."

Jeannie was smiling. "Yeah," she said, "the two of them can't even see it. Keep insisting that after all these years they got nothing in common. All the rest of us can see they're more like sisters."

"Not anymore," I said, although I was barely listening to what they were saying. I was still trying to comprehend the figure Jeannie had mentioned. Forty million dollars! Holy shit. Now *that's* an amount to kill for. And according to what Jeannie meant about the prenup and Molly wanting to protect the kid's interests, what the newspapers had reported was true—Zale was now the owner of that fortune.

"Whatever," Jeannie said. "The main point is, I expect to see the two of you at St. George's down in Hollywood tomorrow for the funeral."

I caught that last comment of hers and I had to object. "Ah, come on, Jeannie. You know how I feel about funerals. And in a Greek Orthodox church? I don't think so."

Jeannie ignored me, faced B. J., looked him square on, and raised her eyebrows.

"No problem," he said. "And I'll make sure she's there, too. Don't worry."

WHEN B. J. pulled his El Camino into the driveway at the Larsens' place, I could tell he was trying to gauge my mood, to see if there was a chance he would be invited to stay. When we had first started our relationship, it was intense, and we were together so continuously that after several months I started to back away. I was afraid of losing my independence, my sense of who I was, my comfortable life alone. After trying to swear off sex and relationships, which didn't work for me at all, I finally found this compromise that I could live with. B. J. had his place and I had mine, and when we felt like it, one or the other of us slept over. One day at a time. So far it was working.

So tonight B. J. was trying to figure out if an invitation was coming his way. He was well aware of how I usually reacted when he promised he would get me to do something like he had tonight with the funeral. And there was a part of me that was angry—angry with Molly for abandoning me years ago and with Jeannie for making me get involved now. Tonight I had started directing some of that anger and frustration at B. J. every time he spoke about how great Molly was. That part of me that was angry wanted to pick a fight with him and make him feel hurt like I did. Luckily, there was another part of me that knew that passionate, athletic, sweaty sex was another great cure for the kind of frustration I felt. I walked around to the driver's side door and leaned down as though to say good night. Instead, I opened the car door, took his hand, and without a word led him back to my cottage.

IX.

I WAS standing in my tiny bedroom wearing only panties and bra, my hair still wet from the shower, staring with unfocused eyes at the clothes hanging in my closet when I heard a familiar double rap on the door, the sound of the front door opening, and B. J.'s voice calling out, "Hey, you ready to go?"

I didn't answer him. I'm not really big on dressing up—I don't have much occasion in my life when I need to. Most of the time I wear jeans or shorts and T-shirts or tank tops. I had a couple of bright, tropical-print pareus that I sometimes tied around me Polynesian-style if I wanted to dress up and look more like a girl. I owned only one regular dress, a simple black shift with a short-sleeved jacket, and I had worn it only once before—to my father's memorial service at the Neptune Society.

"I guess not," he said. I turned and saw him leaning against the doorjamb, looking unbelievably sexy in his dark slacks, white shirt, and tie, his sleek hair pulled back into a ponytail. "Unless, of course, you're planning on going like that. That would cheer up most of the male mourners, I guess."

After we'd made love the night before, B. J. had spent the night and then disappeared early in the morning, leaving me to sleep in for another hour or so. I'd spent the day puttering around the estate, willing the clock to slow, to postpone the moment when I would have to go into that church.

"I don't know what to wear. I hate funerals. I—" My voice quit on me as my throat closed up.

B. J. walked over to the closet and pulled out the black dress. "What's wrong with this one?"

"That one's the one I wore, you know." He had been there that day in that small room filled with flowers as the hundreds of people who'd known Red filed through and wished me well. That was back before B. J. and I were lovers, before he knew me better than I know myself.

"Seychelle, it's only a dress." He held it up to his own body as though modeling it for me. It was an effort to make me smile, and I worked hard to keep the corners of my mouth from pulling down and giving me away. I felt stupid for making such a big deal out of this, but the loss of my father still felt so raw sometimes that I didn't have control over it.

He sighed, shaking his head. "Arms up," he said, and he slid the dress over my head. After he'd zipped it up, he turned me around and pulled me to him, wrapping me in his arms and pressing my wet head against his neck.

I could hear the low thudding of his pulse and I felt like I could have stood there like that all day. I inhaled his familiar clean smell and felt my breath hitch a few times in my chest. Forget the funeral, I wanted to say. Let's crawl back into my bed.

"It's okay," he whispered, stroking my hair. "I know this is going to be tough for you, but because you remember what it's like, you know how important it is for you to be there today. For Molly."

Much as I didn't want it to be so, I knew he was right.

*   *   *

WE ended up having to park over two blocks away from
the little church located in an older, struggling neighborhood down in Hollywood. There were hundreds of cars
parked along the swale, in the median, and on a weedy
lot across the street from the church. St. George's was
built on a pie-shaped lot just off a traffic circle, and the
iron fence that surrounded the round-shaped sanctuary
was lined with groups of people stopping to talk and
greet one another before entering the black gates along
the side of the church.

Parked on the median just opposite the front door of
the church was Detective Rich Amoretti's bright red
Corvette. Both he and Mabry were leaning against the
car, arms crossed, eyes hidden behind identical shades. I
wondered if the glasses were police-issue. I nodded to
them, but only Mabry showed any indication that he had
seen me when he dipped his head and said, "Ma'am."

Unlike me, B. J. was one of those people who is never
late to anything. In spite of his having to help me dress,
we arrived fifteen minutes before the 3:00 p.m. service
was set to start. I didn't know what to expect as we
threaded our way through the crowd, and I reached for
the iron handle on the heavy wood door. My experi-
ences in church had been few and far between. Red had
been indifferent about religion, but my mother had complained loud and long about what she considered to
be the evil ways of the Methodist church she had been
forced to attend with her mother. When I was little, I'd
heard her rants from the point of view of a ten-year-old,
and I'd believed all she said. Now, looking back, I think
she never escaped that adolescent rebellion that turned
her against anything her mother valued. My mother's
mother had died before I was born, when my mom was
still in college—about the time she met Red—and I think

her feelings about her mother got kind of frozen. I never
heard her utter a single positive word about my grandmother. The end result, however, was that the first time
I entered a church was a few months after my mother's
memorial service at the funeral home. I sneaked into a
church on a Saturday morning just out of curiosity. I'd
ridden my bicycle over the Davie Bridge, and when I saw
all the people flowing into the Seventh-Day Adventist
church, I parked my bike and followed them inside.

I tried to make sense of what the guy in front was saying, but I didn't really understand a word. So I squirmed
and fidgeted and played with the fringe on my cutoff
jeans. Finally, the lady sitting next to me in her fancy
dress and hat shot me one more look of disgust, and I
got up and ran out of there wondering what on earth
could make anybody *want* to go to church.

Even fifteen minutes before the service was due to
start, St. George's was crowded with people milling about
wearing muted-colored clothing, speaking to one another in low voices. The way Nick had been killed, the
way he had so clearly been targeted, had made many of
these people afraid. You could see it in their faces, the
way they looked around to see who was listening before
they spoke. This funeral would be bringing out all the
players, and no one really knew who was friend and
who was foe.

St. George's was nothing like the ultramodern chapel I
had visited as a kid. I felt inside this Greek Orthodox
church that we had been transported across oceans and
back in time. The domed ceiling featured a round painting of bearded saints in flowing blue-and-gold robes and
rustic Greek lettering that looked as though it had been
painted by a child's hand. A small choir of about a
dozen women stood on a raised platform at the back of
the round room, half singing, half chanting in a lan-

guage I guessed was either Greek or Latin. The open coffin, I could see through the crowd, was resting in front
of the ornately carved wood screen that was across the
hall, in what seemed to be the front of the church. I
couldn't help thinking about the makeup job that Nick
must have required to make the open casket possible.
What did they use, putty?

People were carrying candles in red glass jars and
placing them on the tables on either side of the church
front. You couldn't really call it an altar. The wide carved
screen had three doorways, and through the open center
doorway, we could see an elderly priest in white robes
standing next to a high table. He bent down and spoke
to a young boy wearing a pale blue robe. The bearded
priest would have been a hands-down winner in the An-
nual Key West Hemingway Look-Alike Contest.

B. J. reached back and took my hand and began
threading his way through the crowd to a spot down
front and off to the right, where Jeannie was waving
with what appeared to be rather inappropriate enthusiasm. Given the fact that she was wearing another of her
tropical print muumuus, it would have been difficult to
miss her in that somber crowd.

"I saved you two seats," she said, scooping up her
large handbag and sweater and sliding across the wood
pew to make room for us. "I wanted to be able to see
what was going on." She was in the third row, right side,
and once we'd settled ourselves, we had a perfect line of
sight to the coffin. And to the family in the front row.

My stomach tensed when I realized I was looking at
the backs of Molly and Zale's heads. The boy was seated
at the end of the pew, perched on the edge, back stiff and
poised as if he were ready to flee at any moment. He
looked uncomfortable in the suit jacket that was clearly
a size too small in the shoulders. His head was bowed as

though he couldn't look at the coffin, which rested on a stand barely ten feet in front of him. Next to him, Molly's dark hair was piled high on her head, showing her slender white neck. Her head kept bobbing as she nodded to the people parading past in front of them, murmuring condolences as they carried little red candles to the corners of the church. On the far side of Molly was a group of people standing. I recognized Leon Quinn. I figured the woman beside him in the expensive-looking jeweled earrings must be Janet Pontus. Her white-blond hair was cut in a perfect pageboy that just screamed expensive hair salon. I leaned in close to Jeannie's ear.

"I'm guessing that's the missus."

"Yup. Could you picture her rummaging in the bushes outside Molly's window?"

"I see what you mean." The black suit she was wearing hugged her curves, accentuating her tiny waist, which flared into a heart-shaped ass. She probably never lifted a finger to do anything for herself as long as there were men around slobbering for her attention.

"Who's the guy next to her?" The man I was referring to looked odd, even from the rear. He was tall and had an extraordinarily large head. His hairstyle really didn't help the matter much, either, as his wiry gray tight curls were longish and looked almost like an afro. The narrow shoulders and thin neck didn't look strong enough to support that huge Brillo Pad head. When he turned to shake hands with an elderly man, I saw that the suit he was wearing had a Western cut, complete with string tie.

"That's Janet's brother, Richard Hunter. The one Nick gave a job to as captain of the *TropiCruz IV*. He stayed with the new owners when the company was sold. He's like ten years older than Janet, but they're very close. It seems he raised her after their parents died, or something like that. Since Nick married Janet, he's over at the house too much. Molly doesn't like it."

A sort of reception line was passing along the front row and Janet was the center of all the attention. Leon Quinn's obsequious mannerisms toward her went unrewarded, as she smiled and nodded at all the passing mourners. God, she *looked* like a queen accepting the attention of her court. Her brother attempted to put his arm around her, and when his fingers touched the back of that elegant white neck, she reached back and flicked them off as though an insect had just landed on her skin.

"It must have been so hard on Molly to get dumped for that," I whispered to Jeannie.

When Janet turned her head aside to accept the cheek-to-cheek kiss from a gray-haired gentleman, the brilliance of her red shiny lip-gloss looked out of place for a funeral.

"Nick was a prick," Jeannie said, a little too loudly under the circumstances. "Molly should have felt lucky to be rid of him." I slid a little lower in my seat and hoped none of the folks around us had heard her.

I watched Janet greet the mourners and I tried to see what Molly saw. I consider myself a pretty good judge of character, and I watched how Janet interacted with the people around her. She thanked those who offered condolences, presented her cheek to close friends, and genuinely seemed to be struggling to put on a good front. It all looked like normal funeral stuff. But the more I watched her, the more I began to notice the little gestures from Leon Quinn. He kept touching her, and it probably wasn't something he was conscious of doing. He touched her elbow, the small of her back, her shoulder. It was more than just a touchy Greek thing. He even moved his body closer to hers whenever other men approached. It's a thing men do when they feel possessive about a woman. I'd be willing to bet that Leon Quinn and Janet were lovers, I thought.

Most of the mourners, when passing by Molly and Zale, nodded politely or shook hands. Their coolness toward the ex-wife was apparent. There was one woman, though, an artsy type in a shawl and long skirt, for whom Molly stood. The two women embraced with a familiarity I had once enjoyed. It had never occurred to me before that Molly might have a new best friend.

At that moment the priest came out and started chanting, and most of the crowd realized the service had begun. They either found a seat or pressed back against the walls in the rear of the church. The family settled into the front pew. I looked around and saw a few people I recognized. The mayor of the city of Hollywood was there, along with many of the corporate kings of Broward County. Standing next to political and financial bigwigs were several boat captains and bartenders I recognized from around town. The majority of the crowd, though, looked like this was their home church. There were families with dark-moustached men and well-made-up women, people who looked like they would have fit in just as well during the 1960s. They looked like working people, and some of the men still wore dark pants and white shirts with company names sewn over the pockets, shirts they had worn to work that morning.

It was difficult to judge when the service actually started. People continued to light candles and walk down in front near the coffin. But at some point a couple of guys dressed in suits got up and began their strange chanting at a raised platform over on our side of the church. There was a microphone there for them, and their tenor voices echoed in the church as the talking and movement ceased.

I had been raised without reverence, and yet in that

simple little church, watching these people perform rituals that dated back hundreds of years, I could not help but think of Zale's questions. Where was Nick? What did I believe? In a way, I envied these people who seemed so sure in their beliefs. They reminded me of the Haitian voodooists I had met the year before. They didn't seem to live with my unanswered questions.

About fifteen minutes after the service started, three very large men entered through the main door at the rear of the sanctuary and many heads turned to stare, then bent to the side as they whispered to their neighbors. The men crossed to the far wall and stood with their feet spread shoulder-width apart, their hands clasped in front of them. There was something decidedly military about their bearing. I looked at Jeannie, my eyes asking the question.

"Russians," she whispered.

"Kagan?" I asked quietly.

She shook her head. "His henchmen. Kagan's out of the country. Conveniently."

After what seemed like hours of singing, standing, sitting, and standing some more, and nothing being said or sung in English, the priest stepped forward and began talking about Nick. In English. He went on about what a great father, entrepreneur, and humanitarian he had been. After the priest's eulogy, Leon Quinn got up and, with his large gestures, bouncing moustache, and tears he dabbed with a handkerchief, he described what a fine friend Nick Pontus had been, and how he seemed to have a golden touch when it came to business. At a certain point I wanted to gag. The Nick Pontus I knew had been no saint.

Next, though, one of the fellows in work clothes with a broad handlebar moustache came forward and told a story of how Nick had loaned him money when he wasn't sure how he was going to feed his family. Nick had even set him up with a franchise sandwich place and made it possible for him to own his own business and be his own boss. A woman went to the front and told us how Nick had paid off the mortgage on her house when her husband, a cook in one of Nick's restaurants, had died of cancer. She wept as she explained how he had helped her keep her children in their familiar home. Others came forward with similar stories, and I began to realize that there had been a side of Nick Pontus that I had never known. Maybe that was what Molly had seen. Maybe that was how she had been able to leave Pit and choose Nick for a husband.

The priest came back out again with a brass incense burner on the end of a bunch of chains, and he clanked it all around the coffin, all the while chanting in that foreign language. The air—which was close already, with what must have been over three hundred people jammed into that tiny church—became doubly difficult to breathe. I was looking around the chapel, trying to figure out some excuse to leave, when I saw Molly's head turn. Our eyes met. She tipped her head forward ever so slightly. We'd always been able to say more to each other with a glance than most people can say with words, and in that moment, I was glad I'd come.

When it was finally over, Leon Quinn led a group of men in dark suits who came forward and carried the coffin out, the family following behind in a procession. As we stood and inched our way to the back door, I saw that we were going to have to pass by Molly and Zale and Leon and Janet, who were thanking the mourners as they left the church. I looked all around.

"Isn't there another way out?" I asked Jeannie, looking longingly across the church at a door on the far side.

"Hush," Jeannie said, and she gave me a shove in the small of my back.

But when I got there, I found I needn't have worried about what to say to Molly. B. J. was the first of us to reach her, and he enveloped her in a hug that was so powerful and lasted so long that a big gap opened up in the exit line ahead of him. I knew the people behind us were probably as anxious to leave as I was, so I walked around him, stepped up to Zale, and shook his hand.

"If there's anything I can do for you guys, just call me. I mean it, okay?"

He nodded solemnly. His eyes were unfocused, and I remembered what it was like as a kid having to stand there while adults told you that everything was going to be okay and you knew they were lying.

At that moment, B. J. released Molly and she looked at me. I reached out and our fingers touched and intertwined. I could not speak. I nodded to her and she nodded back, her eyes filled with the first tears that I'd seen her cry that afternoon. I released her hand and turned, hurried past Quinn, mumbling how sorry I was, and then I was standing in front of Janet. When she saw me, her face went flat and slack. For a moment she looked like some horrible wax imitation of a beautiful woman. Then she turned to B. J. and her face lit up like some Disney mechanical mannequin, and she looked beautiful and alive again. Finally, I found myself outside, squeezing through the crowd, dodging around the hearse, desperate to be alone, running.

I was standing in the late afternoon sunlight, leaning against a tree not far from the El Camino, trying to catch my breath, when B. J. walked up.

"Jeannie said to say bye."

I bounced the toe of my shoe against a root that protruded from the dirt. "It was all that incense. It was making me sick. I couldn't breathe in there."

"That's what it was, huh? The incense?"

I nodded, still focused on scraping the dust off my shoe.

He put his hands on either side of my face and kissed me softly on the lips. "I think what you need is some food in your belly."

WHEN we walked through the doors of the Downtowner, the TV over the corner of the bar was showing the intro for the six o'clock news, and the lead story was—surprise—the Pontus funeral. Pete was behind the bar and Nestor and several of the other charter boat captains turned to greet us as we walked in. I nodded and turned away from them, headed instead for a booth in the back where we would be able to avoid the regulars who would want to chew on the gossip. They'd know we'd been to the funeral and, especially since I'd been an eyewitness to the murder, I knew they'd be eager to pump me for details.

Tonight I wanted to talk about anything *but* the Pontus family. Especially after that long and tight clinch B. J. had delivered to Molly on our way out of the church. What was that about?

I ordered a half pound of peel-and-eat shrimp and asked Terry, the waitress, to bring me extra garlic bread along with a draft beer. B. J. went for the New River Salad and ordered his tuna rare. I shivered at the thought.

"How can you eat that fish all pink and raw like that? It's disgusting."

He smiled at me and didn't take the bait. We'd been friends long before we became lovers, and he knew when I was fishing for an argument.

"You still haven't told me what you want to do for your birthday," he said.

Five days. In five days, on Monday, I was going to turn thirty. At times it felt like a big deal, but really, it was just a number. Three. Zero. The world out there had certain expectations for a woman my age, but I had decided a while ago that I wasn't going to let that rule my life.

"I don't know, B. J. The only thing I know I *don't* want is a surprise party. I do want to do something to make the day memorable, though. I mean it's halfway to sixty. And when I turn sixty, I'd like to be able to look back and remember exactly what I did on the day I turned thirty."

I took a welcome drink of the beer the waitress had just brought, and when I looked back at him, B. J. was staring across the room. I followed his line of sight. There, on the TV screen, was a close-up of Molly. She was standing outdoors and, from what little I could see of the background, it must have been at the cemetery. Long wisps of her dark hair had escaped the mound on top of her head, and instead of it making her look disheveled, the tousled, gaunt look only made her look more beautiful. It was so late in the evening that the TV people had their camera lights on and she was shielding her eyes from the brightness. Quinn stepped in front of the camera then and motioned for the press to move back. He opened the door to a limousine. Molly's lips moved as she climbed in, then Zale got in after his mother. Quinn shut the door and climbed into the front, by the driver. If the sound on the TV was not muted, it wasn't loud enough to be heard over the bar music and laughter. I wondered what she had said.

I looked back at B. J. He still hadn't taken his eyes off the TV screen.

When I first met B. J., and during those early years we were friends, I had watched from the sidelines as he dated a string of the most gorgeous women I had ever seen. I was working as a lifeguard on Fort Lauderdale Beach and helping Red out sometimes on jobs aboard *Gorda*. B. J. and I, we'd run into each other around town from time to time. He'd be with some tall, lithe thing in a tube top, miniskirt, and little strappy high-heeled sandals while I'd be standing there in my flip-flops and gray sweats with *Fort Lauderdale Lifeguard* stenciled across the front, my nose peeling and my salty hair in wind tangles.

I was attracted to him from the very first, but I was determined never to be one of those flings of his. Even if he did always seem to part on friendly terms with them, the problem was he always *did* part with them. No relationship lasted longer than six months. And not only that, B. J. was an amazing, sexy, smart, attractive man, and I'd learned early on that men who looked like B. J. were not interested in women who looked like me. Flash attracted flash, and flashy I'm not. I'd started that education back in high school as Molly's best friend. The only time the good-looking guys ever talked to me was to ask me if I knew where Molly was.

The TV went to a commercial, but B. J. was still someplace far, far away, his eyes unfocused, staring at something across the bar and yet not seeing. How had it happened? How had this man come to want me? And with women like Molly in the world, how much longer could it possibly last?

WHEN our food arrived, I was glad to get busy with shelling the shrimp just to have something to do. Soon my fingernails were stained red from the Old Bay Seasoning, and I was concentrating on getting the last little bit of shrimp out of each tail. B. J. had been right about one thing—I had needed to get some food in my belly. As I washed down the garlic bread with a second beer and reached for another shrimp I felt the edge of my uneasiness evaporate.

B. J., who always ate with tiny methodical bites, still had another half hour to go before he would finish his raw fish salad, and between bites he had started telling me a story about the job he had begun that morning remodeling the galley cabinets on a Shannon 50. The owner was six-foot-six, and B. J. couldn't talk him out of having forty-five-inch-high countertops installed, in spite of the fact that it would seriously impact the resale value of the boat. The average woman would be chopping parsley under her chin.

"Not me," I said. At five-foot-ten, I usually found boat galleys far too small, the counters too low.

"No one ever called *you* average, Sey," he said.

"Damn right."

So, we were comfortable together, and if he could still look at me like he did at that moment when I was up to my elbows in shrimp shells, what did I have to worry about?

By the time B. J. had ordered hot tea for both of us, I reckoned I smelled like I'd spent a week working on board a Gulf Coast shrimper. I was sliding out of the booth, ready to head back to the washroom, when I saw Jeannie step into the bar and look around, the worry lines etched deep in her forehead. I waved my hand and she hurried over to our booth.

"I hoped I'd find you here," she said, panting, leaning on the table with one hand, the other holding her side.

"What's the matter?" As a single mom, Jeannie almost never went out in the evening. I knew that something serious must have happened to bring her out searching for me. I immediately thought of her kids. "Are the boys okay?"

"Yeah, I called my mother. She came right over as soon as I heard."

"Heard what? What are you talking about?"

"It's Molly."

"Molly?" I asked. "Oh my God, is she all right?"

"She's not hurt," she said.

"We saw some of the footage from the cemetery on the tube. Couldn't hear what they were saying, though."

B. J. put his hand on my forearm. "Sey, let her talk. What's happened, Jeannie?"

Jeannie pulled a chair over and sat on the outside of our booth. She was panting, but then a brisk walk could make her short of breath. "When she and Zale got back to the house, the cops were there. They asked her to go down to the station with them for more questions. They both went. And like some other people I know," she said, looking directly at me, "she didn't have the good sense to call me first. When they got there, they put Molly in an interrogation room, asked a few more questions, and then arrested her. For Nick's murder."

"What? Molly?"

B. J. said, "They really think Molly did it?"

Jeannie dipped her head in a fast nod. "Yup. That's when she finally called me. Told me to bring you, too, Seychelle. She didn't sound good—kind of like she was out of it. I told her it might take me a while to find you, but she said it didn't matter. She insisted. So that's why I'm here. Let's go."

"I've got to go wash up," I said, holding up my reddish, greasy, smelly hands.

"There's no time," she said, tossing me a paper napkin and picking my purse up off the booth.

I looked at B. J. and shrugged as I wiped my fingers. "I guess I'll see you later."

"Go on," he said. "She needs you. Tell her that if I can do anything for her, anything, she just needs to call."

"Yeah," I said as I chased Jeannie out the door, wondering just how far that meant he would go.

X.

At the Fort Lauderdale police station, Jeannie spoke to the lady in the glass booth, explaining that we were there to see Detectives Amoretti and Mabry, and she told us to sit on the plastic chairs and wait. Finally, the door next to the booth opened, and a young, dark-haired, uniformed policewoman told us to follow her.

I expected her to lead us up to the detectives' office cubicles on the second floor, but instead we wound around on the ground floor until she came to a door, where she motioned for us to go inside.

Molly was there, sitting at a table in the center of the small room, still wearing her dark funeral clothes. Mabry was sitting on the only other chair in the room, and Amoretti was slouching against the wall looking like he'd just come in off the golf course in snug-fitting khaki Dockers and a lime-green Polo shirt.

"D'ya mind if we speak to your friends outside for a minute, Miz Pontus?" Mabry asked.

Molly nodded without making eye contact with us. She had her head turned to face the far wall. She looked as though she had been slapped, but I knew that wasn't possible. Was it?

Detective Mabry braced his hands on his knees to help lift his body to a stand in a way that reminded me of Jeannie. He led us to what looked like the police briefing room, a big hall with lots of chairs and bulletin boards covered with notices bearing sketches of unsmiling, mean-looking men. Mabry wore a wrinkled piss-colored short-sleeved shirt and a Looney Tunes tie that he had pulled loose at the knot. I assumed that it was the same tie he'd worn at the funeral that afternoon, but he'd been too far away for me to notice. Odd choice for a funeral, I thought.

"Ladies, this'll just take a minute, so I guess this is as good a spot as any." Mabry stopped alongside the last row of chairs and attempted to tighten his tie. "Pardon my lack of manners. How are you ladies doing this evening?"

Amoretti rolled his eyes and smirked as Mabry attempted to pull back a chair for Jeannie, and she yanked it out of his hand.

"This isn't a social call, Detective," she said. "I'm not looking to settle in for a visit. We're here to find out what the hell's going on and to talk to Molly Pontus. What's this bullshit about your charging her with murder?"

Mabry ducked his head a little when Jeannie let the curse words fly. But he examined her, hungry-looking, as though he were looking at a sumptuous banquet. "Well, Ms. Black, I'm sorry to see you're so upset, but I'm afraid things aren't looking too good for your friend. The evidence is there. We didn't have to do any fancy footwork to get the arrest warrant. Prosecutor told us to bring her in for questioning, and that was that."

"What evidence?" Jeannie asked.

"Well, ma'am, right now I'm not at liberty to say. That's up to the D.A. But suffice it to say you'll need to get busy 'cuz the case against her is pretty tight. I wish it wadn't. I like the lady, but it's not up to us, you see, to decide who's guilty and who iddn't."

I wanted to bury my fist in that globe-sized gut of his. "Mabry, you are out of your friggin' mind if you think Molly could have killed anybody. This is insane."

Jeannie put her hand on my forearm. "Seychelle, enough. They're just doing their jobs."

He looked at Jeannie and his face split into a broad smile. "Glad you see it that way, ma'am." He reached back and pulled a box of Good & Plenty out of his back pants pocket, shook a couple of candies into his open palm, and then held up the crushed box, offering us some. I shook my head, but Jeannie refused to acknowledge him. That surprised me. It was the first time I'd ever seen her turn down sweets.

Mabry continued. "I wanted to let you know that we're going to be transferring her over to county in a little bit. Already told me they're going for no bail. Her boy is down in the break room with a service aide. Gonna need to figure out what to do with him."

"Can I see my client now?" Jeannie asked.

Mabry swung his fleshy hand and pointed to the door with a flourish. "After you, ma'am."

Back in the interrogation room, I let Jeannie take the only chair, and I rested my shoulder against the wall, trying to look nonchalant and unconcerned, as though getting arrested for murder wasn't any big deal, happened all the time. Mabry closed the door, leaving the three of us alone in the room.

"How are you doing?" Jeannie asked.

Molly coughed out what was supposed to be a laugh. "About as well as can be expected after burying my ex-husband and then getting arrested for his murder."

Jeannie nodded once. "So tell me what happened."

Molly sighed, and when she started to speak her voice sounded more tired than scared. I admired her for that. I would have been scared to death.

"Leon drove us home from the cemetery. I guess the cops were outside waiting then, but they were parked down the street, and we didn't notice the car. Zale and I weren't inside two minutes before the doorbell rang. It was that big one, by himself. He said they had some more questions to ask us and they wanted us to look at some photos. He wanted to see if we could identify them or something. Said it wouldn't take long. I don't know. I was barely listening. I asked him if it couldn't wait until tomorrow, and he said no, we really needed to go now." She looked up at Jeannie and the dark hollows under her eyes looked sharp and deep, as though carved in white stone. "I don't know how to explain it, Jeannie, but I feel as though I have lost all will. I'm just floating. I'm going through the motions, doing what people tell me to do, but it doesn't feel real."

"Molly, you listen to me. This is very real," Jeannie said. "If you keep talking to the cops without a lawyer, you could really be hurting yourself. They wouldn't have charged you unless they thought they could make it stick."

She nodded and waved her hand in the air as though to ward off a bad odor. "When they asked me to go, I said yes because I just didn't have the energy to say no. I brought Zale with me, too. I don't want to leave him alone right now. He's too fragile." Her hands fiddled with the gold chain that disappeared into the neckline of her dress. "Last night I fell asleep in the hammock in the backyard. I've been doing a lot of that the last couple of days. Sleeping. Zale looked for me all over the house and by the time he found me in the hammock, he was crying. He said he was afraid he was going to lose me, too." She bit her lower lip. "And now this."

"Hey, we're going to deal with things one at a time," Jeannie said. She glanced over at me as though to ask me to chime in anytime, to help her out, but Molly had not even so much as glanced at me since we'd walked in. I didn't know why she had asked for me to be there.

Jeannie continued. "He's a strong kid. He'll be all right. This is not going to stick. This is just temporary. So what happened when they brought you in?"

"A nice young woman offered to take Zale to go get a Coke. I didn't even tell her he doesn't drink soda."

"And they brought you here?" Jeannie prodded her, trying to keep her on subject.

"Yeah. When we got here, the short one joined the fat one—I can't seem to remember their names—and they both came in here and started asking me questions about guns." She tried to laugh again, and it sounded more strangled than it had the first time. "As if I know anything about guns. I told them that, and that Nick had been a collector. No matter how much I had protested. I'd never wanted those guns in the house, and I insisted that he keep them locked up. I was always afraid Zale would get into them. When he was little, he was fascinated. I think Nick and I argued over those guns more than anything else over the years. And that's saying something."

"Can you be more specific? What exactly were they asking you?"

"Huh?" She looked up as though she was surprised to find Jeannie there. "I'm sorry, Jeannie." She rubbed her eyes with the heels of both hands. "They went on and on about my car and the garage, but mostly it was about guns. They were asking me about a bunch of different makes of guns. It's all Greek to me. Ha!" Her face started to crumple and she put her head down on her arms on the table.

Jeannie looked over at me. I shrugged. I wanted to help her, but she didn't seem to want my help. I kept thinking that we were over it, beyond the hurt of all those years, and then the wall would go right back up again, and I didn't know how to bring it down.

"Molly." Jeannie reached over and rubbed her shoulder. "We can talk about this later. I'm not a criminal attorney, and right now you need one. I've got a friend who is excellent at this kind of thing. If you give the okay, I'm going to call him, and we are going to try to get you released on bail. It's late, though, and I think you have to prepare yourself to spend at least tonight in jail."

She nodded without lifting her head.

"If you have any jewelry or anything of value on you right now, I want you to give it to Seychelle."

Slowly, she sat up and turned to look at me. She reached behind her neck and undid the clasp on the gold chain that hung inside her dress. When she lifted the necklace, I saw hanging from the chain the tiny gold dolphin I had given her for her sixteenth birthday. I'd bought it with money I'd saved from my summer job lifeguarding at the city pool. She held it out. When I stepped forward to take it, she spoke to me at last.

"Sey, I need to ask you for another favor. That's why I asked Jeannie to bring you." She rubbed at her nose with the back of her hand. "I was pretty sure they weren't going to cut me loose once Jeannie got here. It's Zale. I don't want my son to be scared. I don't want him to be here watching this on the news and having to fend off reporters. Remember my grandmother? Gramma Tigertail? You met her at my house when she came by sometimes."

"Yeah, sure. I remember her. Zale was just talking about her the other day."

"Okay. She still lives out on the reservation at Big Cypress. Zale knows the family out there. He's spent weekends and holidays out there before. He needs to be away from all this, among people who love him."

"Hey, no problem. I'll take him out there. He can spend the night tonight with me in the cottage, and we'll go out first thing in the morning."

"And you'll make it fun for him, okay? Make him laugh?"

"I'll do my best," I said, remembering the somber boy who had sat in front of his father's coffin that afternoon, and who now sat with a policewoman while they arrested his mother for murder. The kid didn't have much to laugh about these days.

Molly stood up and shook my hand like we had just concluded some kind of business arrangement.

At that moment the door opened and Detective Mabry's bulk filled the frame. "Ladies, I'm afraid we are going to have to ask you to leave now."

I tucked the necklace in a side pocket of my shoulder bag and followed Jeannie out of the room.

XI.

ZALE sat straight-backed in a plastic chair, holding a can of Hawaiian Punch and watching the latest incarnation of the TV show *Survivor* with the young woman who had greeted us and shown us back to the interrogation room. Her blue uniform looked very much like those of the other officers, but she didn't wear a gun. Jeannie and Mabry waited out in the hall as I went in.

"Hey, Zale," I started, not knowing what words were going to come out of my mouth, but knowing that if I just kept talking I would at some point figure out how to tell him that his mother was going to jail. I nodded at the can in his hand. "Hawaiian Punch, huh? I can just hear what your mom would say about all the chemicals in that. Right?"

His mouth stretched wide and thin, but the corners turned down. "Where *is* my mom? Did you talk to her?"

"Yeah, yeah, I did." I pulled back a chair, scraping it across the linoleum, and sat down next to him. "And she asked a favor of me. See, the cops have really got this screwed up." The young woman looked at me with raised eyebrows. "Sorry, miss, but it's true. See, Zale, they've got it in their heads that your mom is somehow involved with your dad's murder. You and I both know they're nuts, but Jeannie is going to have to go through all kinds of red tape here to get her released, and your mom really doesn't want you sitting here all night drinking Hawaiian Punch, so I'm going to take you over to spend the night at my place."

"They've arrested her?"

Damn. The kid was sharp. Young as he was, he knew exactly what was going on. "Yeah, they have. There's no way they can make it stick, though."

"Is she going to jail?"

"Yeah, I'm afraid she is. Just for a little while, though." I watched the people on the television earnestly discussing one another's fate by candlelight. "They are going to take her over to the jail for the night. There will be a hearing first thing in the morning and hopefully they'll let her out then."

"Can I see her before we leave?"

I glanced back over my shoulder at the door. Detective Mabry was leaning on the doorjamb and he shook his head.

"I'm afraid not. Not tonight. We need to get you back to my place and into bed. It's late. Abaco will sure be glad to see you."

"Okay," he said, his voice a monotone. He stood and handed me the can of punch, which, by the feel of it, he had not touched.

Jeannie drove us by Molly's house so Zale could pack some clothes and things in a bag, then back to my place in Rio Vista. The night was not as cold as it had been the night before, as the Gulf Stream was once again carrying up the warm water and air from southern climes. The kid sat in the back of her van, his sweatshirt hood pulled up on his head, and didn't say a word the entire trip. When I asked him a question, he'd nod or shake his head, but that was all I could get out of him. When Jeannie pulled up to the curb, I jumped out first and slid the

side door open for him. He slung his backpack over his
shoulder before I dragged him around to the driver's
side so he could say good-bye to Jeannie with me.

She reached out her window, got his head in the crook
of her arm, and pulled him to her. The peak of his sweatshirt hood poked out above her ample biceps, and it
looked a little like she'd captured herself a lawn gnome.
"Son, I am not going to insult your intelligence by telling
you not to worry," she said. "We're all worried. But
notice I said *we*. You and your momma are not alone.
You've got friends. Lots of 'em. We are gonna fight this
thing with a fierceness like they've never seen. You
hear me?"

Zale tried to nod, but his head was clenched in the
mass of pink flesh.

"Okay," she said, releasing him. He stumbled back
and his hood slid down his back. I could see he was
fighting the urge to reach up and massage the back of his
neck. "I'll call you two soon as I hear anything," she
said, then put the van in gear and drove off up the dark
street.

Zale put a hand to the side of his neck and said, "Man,
she's strong."

I patted him on the back and directed him toward the
path along the side of the Larsens' house. "Yup. And
that's just the kind of woman you want fighting for you
when you go to battle."

WE were halfway across the Larsens' backyard before I
realized there were lights on in my cottage where there
shouldn't have been. B. J. knew where I hid the spare
key, but he'd never just let himself into my place on his
own. That would imply a level of what? Connectedness?
Some level that we hadn't reached, anyway. Abaco was
nowhere to be seen, either. Was she inside?

"Wait here a minute." I put my hand on the center of Zale's chest and pushed him into the shadows along the path. "I want to check something." I crossed to the window behind the bougainvillea bush on the side of the cottage and peered through gaps in the miniblinds. I couldn't see anyone in the middle of the living room, but my rustling the bushes set Abaco to barking inside. I heard a man's voice say, "What the heck are you barking at?" That was a very familiar voice.

The door swung inward just as I reached for the knob, and there stood my brother wearing my Fort Lauderdale Lifeguard sweatshirt.

"Pit!" I yelled and threw my arms around his neck.

"Hey, Sis."

I let go and looked up at him. "It is great to see you."

"Yeah," he said, rubbing at the spot where I'd planted a kiss on his cheek. "Hasn't even been a year. I seem to be making this visiting thing into a regular habit."

I stepped back outside the door and called into the darkness. "Come on, Zale. It's okay." When the boy got to the doorway, he stood there blinking at the interior lights through his wire-rimmed glasses, the straps of his backpack making his shoulders look even more thin and narrow. "Hey, come here. I want you to meet my brother. Pitcairn Sullivan, I'd like you to meet Zale Pontus."

Pit's eyes widened at the name, and he glanced at me with a look so quick our eyes never really connected. Then he stepped up to the boy and with a broad smile shook his hand. "Man, and I thought I had it bad in the name department. What excuse does your mom give for saddling you with Zale?"

"She says it means 'sea strength' in Greek."

Pit cocked his head to the side as though tasting the idea. "That's cool. That sounds like Molly. I'd rather have that than be named after some island in *Mutiny on the Bounty*."

"You know my mom?"

"*Know* her?" He spun the boy around and started helping him take the backpack off. "Man, once upon a time we were practically like family. We grew up together, me, Sey, and your mom. I could tell you some stories about her that she's probably never told you. Like about the time we let loose all the baby hopper frogs in Mrs. Vannostrand's fourth-grade class? Remember that, Sis? All the girls went screaming out of the room, and Miz V was running around trying to collect the little guys by sticking them in her coffee mug." He laughed, and I could see the hint of a smile on Zale's face.

"Molly's going to be furious with you, Pit, if you tell him all those old stories."

Pit threw the kid's backpack on the couch and motioned for him to sit. "Well, hell, I'd guess after all these years of her not talking to me, I really have to be careful not to get her mad."

Zale was still standing in the middle of what passed for a combined living room and dining room in my cottage. He was staring at Pit, slack-jawed, as though he were looking at some exotic creature he had never seen before. Pit walked around the bar into the tiny kitchen and opened the refrigerator door. "The first thing you've got to learn about my sister over there is that you can't expect to eat much at her house." He bent lower and peered onto the bottom shelf of the refrigerator. "Well, I can offer you a Coke, a glass of milk, or a cold beer." He stood up. "What'll it be?"

"Pit! He's a kid," I said.

Pit squinted across the room. "Looks old enough to drink beer to me."

"Milk," Zale blurted out. "I'd like milk."

Pit winked at him as he reached for a glass, and I figured I was happy to be the butt of their teasing if it made Zale feel better. Abaco hopped up on the couch and began to nuzzle at Zale's hand.

"She likes you," I told him.

That earned me a look that might have been a smile on another day. Zale scratched the dog's ears. "I'm always asking my mom if we can have a dog. I'd like one just like Abaco."

"Good choice, kid. Labs are great," Pit said, pouring the milk into a frosted beer mug.

"So, Bro," I asked, "what brings you to Lauderdale this time?"

"Got a delivery on a very cool go-fast sailboat. They're taking it down to Antigua for Race Week. Got an appointment in the morning to meet the owner and the captain over at the Marriott where they're tied up." He handed Zale his milk, flopped down on the opposite end of the couch, and chinked his bottle against the boy's mug. "After that I should be able to bunk on the boat."

"Zale's got dibs on the couch for tonight, but you can bunk out on *Gorda* if you want."

"That'll be great."

After a long drink that left him with a little white moustache, Zale said, "Are you talking about that red hull named *Firestorm*?"

Pit grinned at the boy. "That's right, you're a sailor, aren't you? Optimists at the Lauderdale Yacht Club, right?"

"Yeah," Zale said and shrugged. "Saturday I was racing with the Lasers, though. I'm trying to move up. Anyway, I watched as they brought that boat in and docked over there. She sure looks fast."

"You ever do much big-boat sailing?"

He shook his head. "My dad was into fishing."

I noticed that he had started using the past tense when referring to Nick.

"Yeah, I remember that," Pit said. "Even back before your old man could afford the fancy boats and gear, he always used to win the local tournaments. Heck, I bet they've got a whole room dedicated to him over at that new game-fishing museum."

Zale shrugged again, but I could see that he was pleased to hear his dad complimented. Probably didn't hear it very often.

"Hey," Pit said, "we're going to be doing some sea trials to check out the new sails the owner's buying here. I'm sure I could convince them to let you come along."

Zale's face looked more alive than I had ever seen it. "That would be awesome. What kind of sail inventory has she got?"

While I went about getting out the spare sheets and towels for the two of them, I marveled at the instant ease they had found. They spoke the same language, shared the same passion. I was always happy to see my brother Pit, but tonight his being here was an exceptionally lucky break.

I was only half listening to their conversation, but I heard the rhythm change when Pit asked, "So, where's your mom tonight?"

"Hey, Pit," I butted in as though I had not heard his question. "What time did you get in?"

"Round eight. Flew in from Baja, you know, Cabo? Been working at a resort down there, Los Frailes, all winter. I don't mind teaching windsurfing when the client has some kind of athletic ability, but I get so many of these yahoos who take lessons all week and still can't even stand up on the board. That gets boring. I was glad to get out of there, even if I did leave them in the middle of the season."

I threw a towel at Zale and pointed to the bathroom. "There's three of us and only one bathroom. You go first. Grab your PJs and do what you gotta do, 'cuz my brother here is next."

After the bathroom door had closed and the water started running, I sat down on the couch next to Pit and Abaco. The dog had moved her head into my brother's lap and he was scratching the top of her head.

He said, "So tell me what's going on. How did Molly's kid end up in your living room?"

"You haven't heard about Nick?"

"Nick?"

I sighed and tried to collect my thoughts so I could explain it as briefly as possible.

"You saw him get shot?" Pit asked when I had described the scene on the river that morning.

"Yeah. You know, over the last ten, twelve years, I've wasted a lot of time and energy hating that guy for what he did to us, for getting in the middle and destroying the best friendship I ever had. But I never wished him dead. Anyway, without going into all the details, Molly and I have started talking again. I had to be the one to break the news to her that morning, and I was there when she had to tell him," I nodded toward the bathroom, "that his father was dead. We all went to the funeral this afternoon."

"Holy shit," he said, shaking his head.

"B. J. and I were eating at the Downtowner tonight when Jeannie came and told us that Molly'd been arrested for murder."

"What?" Pit shouted as the bathroom door opened and Zale came out wearing Spiderman pajamas. With his hair wet and tousled, he looked even younger—far too young to have to face this kind of a loss of innocence. Kids were supposed to be able to go on believing that they and their parents were immortal. At least that's what I'd heard.

"Yup," I said. "So Zale's going to be bunking here on the couch, and I have to scoot you into the bathroom so I can make up his bed."

After all his recent experience with brief boat showers, Pit emerged, wet-headed and wearing my sweats, about the time we finished making up the sheets and blankets on the couch. I grabbed a sleeping bag and pillow out of my room and said, "Zale, I'm going to go unlock the boat for Pit. I'll be right back." Then I slapped the side of my leg. "Come on, Abaco. Time for you to go outside, too." She'd been sitting on the couch next to Zale, and she gave him a nudge with her nose, then jumped down to follow me.

As I punched in the combination on the keypad, Pit asked, "So what's this about Molly getting arrested?"

I slid open the side door and entered the wheelhouse. "Yeah, it surprised the hell out of me, too. Jeannie and I went to see her at the police station earlier tonight. We don't really know what kind of evidence they have yet, but Jeannie'll find out tomorrow. There's supposed to be some kind of hearing. They were about to transport her over to the county jail when we left. God, I hate to think of her in there." I handed him the sleeping bag, and he shook it out and smoothed it across the narrow bunk.

He boosted himself up and sat on the bunk, then kicked off his ratty-looking boat shoes. "What reason could they possibly have for thinking she did it?"

"It seems she got mad at him and threatened to kill him. Outside, in front of the neighbors. You know, she was just saying it. She didn't mean it. But then tonight the cops were questioning her about a gun and about who had access to her garage. I don't know what that means. The bridge tender said the shooter was in a black Mustang, and Molly drives a black Mustang. Whoever did this knew what they were doing. Molly must think she's going to be in there for a while because she asked me to take Zale out to Big Cypress to stay with Gramma Josie."

"She's still alive?"

"Seems so."

"I thought she was really old when we were kids."

"She was. She's got to be close to ninety now."

"Too bad I've got to go for my interview and start work tomorrow. I'd really like to see her again."

"Yeah. Our adopted grandmother, right?"

"That's how it was when we were kids, eh? We shared everything. We didn't have any grandparents, so Molly shared hers." He sat on the high bunk in the back of the wheelhouse and ran his hands over the sleeping bag next to him. "Hey, Sis, you know, if there's anything I can do to help Molly . . ." He left the sentence unfinished, but I knew what he was trying to say. "And if you want to let her know I'm in town. Since you're talking to her again. If she wanted to see me, I'd go wherever, do whatever. Will you let her know that?"

"Sure, Pit. I'll do that."

THE lights were out in the living room when I opened the door to my cottage, but if Zale was about to drop off to sleep, the front paws Abaco planted on his chest put a stop to that. In the light that came from the crack around my bedroom door, I saw the boy's hand reach out to scratch the dog's ears.

I was about to slip into my room when I heard his voice. "Seychelle? Do you think my mom's okay?"

At the age of thirteen, his voice had not yet changed,

and with the fear and the anxiety, his voice was even higher pitched. He was so smart it was sometimes hard to remember that he was really just a little kid. I crossed the room, perched on the edge of the couch, and scratched Abaco's back end while Zale worked on her ears. The dog was in heaven.

"I think your mom is fine, and she's probably more worried about you right now than she is about herself. She doesn't want you to be scared. Just spending a night or two in jail, heck, that's nothing for her. Molly's tough. She can handle that. But what would really bother her is thinking that all of this is hurting you. Just the same way I'm telling you she's fine, I need to be able to tell her that you're handling all this okay, too."

"Yeah." He nodded. One minute he seemed so young, and the next he seemed to have a wisdom outside the bounds of age. "You said 'a night or two.' Do you think it will be more than one night?"

"That's possible, Zale. When I talked to your mom at the police station, she asked me to drive you out to your Gramma Josie's place in the morning. What with all the stuff in the news about your mom's arrest and your dad's will, she doesn't want reporters or anybody bothering you."

"Okay," he said, but I could hear the tremor in his voice.

"Hey, I can't wait to see Gramma Josie." I glanced at him and raised my brows. "Think she'll still scare me?"

He shook his head. "Naw. She's pretty cool. She always gives me these little hard candies. She has 'em in some, like, secret pocket in those big old skirts she always wears."

Josie Tigertail still wore traditional Seminole Indian skirts, though she often wore them with T-shirts when I was a kid. She never gave us candy, I thought, but then I wasn't her real granddaughter.

"You know, I was always jealous of Molly for having grandparents. All my grandparents were dead by the time I came along. I wish I could have known them. You're lucky. Gramma Josie is your great-grandmother. That's four living generations. What about Molly's parents, your grandparents? Where are they?"

"Gramps moved up to New Smyrna Beach and Gram moved out to Arizona. She's living somewhere out there with her new husband."

I wanted to ask if they were still drinking, but I didn't know how much the boy knew about the situation. "How's their health?"

"It's all right. They got divorced because Gramps quit drinking. But Gram just found somebody else to get drunk with."

"I guess your mom has told you what it was like for her growing up with them."

"Yeah," he said.

"When we were kids, your mom used to tell me that she was gonna be a much better mom than her mom was."

He snuggled down under the blanket, handed me his glasses, and rolled onto his side, turning his back to the dog and me. "Yeah," he said, the oncoming sleep making his voice barely audible. "She was right."

XII.

By nine in the morning on Friday, we were loaded into my Jeep "Lightnin'" and headed west on I-75. I remember when I was a little kid and Alligator Alley was just a two-lane road across the Glades, there were frequent reports of terrible head-on collisions from impatient people trying to pass slower cars. Folks were always hurrying through, afraid of getting stuck out there with the gators and panthers and snakes. Even with the ultramodern six-lane toll road that crosses the state today, the Sea of Grass remains a place most folks just hurry across.

But I was in no hurry to cover the fifty or so miles west out to the northbound exit to the reservation. The weather on that February morning was about as close to perfect as a place can get, and a good example of why so much of the Glades has been drained and dredged to make room for the migrating masses who now called this state home. As Zale and I drove out of the tollbooth and started across the most desolate stretch, my eyes spent less time staring at the straight black path and more time looking out the window across the miles of sawgrass, at the clusters of clouds crouching on the horizon, and the sparklers dancing on the wind-ruffled canal that ran along the side of the highway. Almost all evidence of the week's earlier cold front was now gone, as the temperature was already in the upper sixties and headed for the seventies by afternoon. The cooler air had driven the humidity down and the air was so clear that from the height of the interstate, every blade of grass, every white egret stood out with crisp clarity.

We didn't say much for the first forty-five minutes. I'd rolled up all the zippered windows to let the wind blow through, so the fluttering canvas top and roaring engine made conversation difficult. I kept the speed as close to sixty as she'd go, trying in vain to hold my own in the herd of luxury cars and SUVs charging across the Alley. I had my hair tucked into a baseball cap so it didn't whip into my face, and I was wearing my dark Polaroid glasses to cut the glare. When you're prepared for the wind and sun, there's little more exhilarating than driving Ol' Lightnin' out into the Glades. I hoped Zale felt the same, but as he spent most of the trip with his body angled toward his open window, I had no idea if he was enjoying the drive as much as I was.

My mind, however, kept returning to what, if anything, I could do to help Molly. I was well aware that the police looked at family members first in this kind of thing, but clearly they were totally off-base on this one. What would she stand to gain by this? Yeah, her son might benefit financially, but she would never touch anything that belonged to her son. Surely it was business dealings that got Nick Pontus killed, and I wondered if the cops were continuing to look at that now that they had a suspect in custody.

The question in my mind was, what did Kagan and his associates stand to gain by killing Nick? And even there, I wasn't sure I understood the financial situation. To me, the business pages of The Miami Herald might as well have been written in another language. I had a difficult enough time deciphering my own bank statements. But if I understood correctly, Kagan had essentially defaulted on paying for TropiCruz, so whether Nick was alive or not, the courts would find that Kagan would lose the company. Did he expect that the reputation of his Russian mafia connections would make Nick too afraid to press him for payment? And then when Nick did, Kagan got pissed and decided to use him as an example? Or was it just personal on Kagan's part?

It wasn't until we turned off at the exit by the huge billboard for Swamp Billie Safaris that I slowed down enough to make conversation possible.

"So, are you going to join B. J. in maligning my poor car, or are you a fan now?"

He turned to face me. "What?"

I could see he'd been off somewhere far away from here.

"Nothing. Are you okay?" As soon as the words were out of my mouth, I remembered all the people asking me that after my mother's funeral. I saw on Zale's face now a look that must have mirrored my own from back then. It was a look that said, "My father's dead, my mother's in jail. What do *you* think, stupid?"

"Zale, did your father ever talk to you about his business?"

"Yeah."

"Did he talk about TropiCruz? The gambling boats?"

"Sometimes."

Ah, the one-word language of teenagers.

"Can you give me *a little* more than that?" I said, casting a quick look away from the windshield to see if he caught the sarcasm.

"He used to talk about it all the time. Especially when I was little. I didn't understand any of it. Sometimes, he didn't get that I was a little kid."

"Do you remember any of the stuff he used to talk

about? You know—names, specific stories? I'm asking you this because I'm going to try to help Jeannie help your mom, Zale. If she didn't do this, and we know she didn't, then maybe we can figure out who did."

"I don't know. He talked about stuff he did with Uncle Leon at the office."

"What about on the boats? Did he ever go out on the boats himself?"

"Yeah, all the time. Course when Janet was still working, he talked about her sometimes. And Captain Hunter, Janet's brother—my dad used to talk about him a lot. He made fun of his music, and he was upset that he sometimes showed up at work drunk. Dad said he was sloppy, that he wouldn't have kept him on if he wasn't his brother-in-law. He even hit the Dania Bridge going through there once. Did some damage to the ship. The only other person he ever used to talk about on the boats was Thompson."

"Who's that?"

"I don't know. I heard that name a few times, but I wasn't really listening."

"Think back. Can't you remember anything or anyone else? What about after the sale of TropiCruz?"

"I remember him saying that most of the people who worked on the ships were staying with the company, and he was glad to get rid of Uncle Richard. And the way he talked about Thompson, it was like he had some kind of spy after the company got sold. He used to say he could always trust Thompson to give him the inside poop."

"Knowing your dad, I don't think he said it quite that way."

He nodded and looked at me with the start of a twinkle in his eye. "You *did* know my dad."

*　*　*

THE road curved back and forth through green pasture-land and golden prairie with only the occasional pond or small lake. I'd never been out to the Big Cypress reservation, but I knew from the map that the road would continue like this for the next twenty miles. Off in the distance, cattle huddled under the clumps of trees, what had once been the cypress dome islands when all this was swamp. When we came around one bend, we frightened four turkey vultures fighting over the carcass of a black snake that had been unlucky enough to meet one of the few vehicles to travel this road. The big black birds lifted their wings and flew up in tight circles. In the rearview mirror, I saw them alight and renew their fight not ten seconds after the Jeep had passed.

"Did you hear about my dad's will?" Zale asked, as he twisted in his seat to watch the vultures behind us.

"Yeah. I guess you're the new owner of a pretty big company."

He nodded and chewed on his lower lip.

"How do you feel about that?" I asked.

He lifted his shoulders and released a long breath. "I'm just a kid. How am I supposed to know how to run a company like Pontus?"

"Well, I don't think they'll expect you to do too much until you finish eighth grade."

His brow wrinkled and I worried that he was going to draw blood from that lip.

"That was a joke, kid. I don't think you have to worry about running the company right now. With all that money, you hire people to do that for you."

"Yeah, but my dad always used to say that *he* was the one who made the important decisions. That's why he was so successful. The hardest part is knowing what to do."

Once again, I was struck by how mature this little boy could be.

"When your time comes, I know you're going to make good decisions just like your dad did."

He turned to me and opened his mouth as though he wanted to say something else on the matter, then he bit his lip and turned away. Something was bothering him, but I knew better than to try to hurry him. I'd just have to wait until he was ready to talk about it.

We passed the Big Cypress Rodeo Arena and finally crossed the small bridge over the L-28 canal, one of the canals that had turned this area from a swamp into agricultural land, then we entered the settled area of the Seminole Indian reservation. Zale told me to be sure to slow to the thirty-mile-per-hour speed limit as kids in the area raced around on their three- and four-wheeled ATVs. Since the old Indian bingo had grown into the modern casinos with poker and thousands of slot machines, every member of the tribe received a guaranteed monthly income from the tribe's gambling proceeds. The signs of newfound wealth jumped out everywhere, from the huge, shiny pickups and boats parked in front of many of the houses to the sandy stucco and green copper roof of the newly constructed Ahfachkee School. Just past the school, Zale instructed me to turn right off the main road onto a residential loop where there was a mix of modern homes, all of which had a traditional chickee somewhere on the property along with a compact satellite dish sprouting from the eaves.

Zale directed me to turn onto a dirt track that led back away from the main road, and as we bounced over the dried ruts I was glad Ol' Lightnin' could offer the choice of four-wheel drive if we needed it. Gramma Josie's house stood several hundred yards apart from the other homes, at the dead end where the concrete block home nestled under several large old trees. In the distance, across a large, bare field with scrubby-looking grass, I could see the pale blue of water through a stand of trees, probably a pond or lake out there.

The house made no effort at pretension. It was a simple rectangular house with an Old Florida–style porch running across the front that looked as though it had been screened in only recently. Three good-sized oak trees shaded the front yard, their branches filled with the spiky fronds of air plants. An enormous black Dodge pickup was parked on the dirt alongside the house, and I pulled in and parked next to it. Through the Jeep's windshield, I could see a wood frame shed out back with gardening tools, coils of rope, life jackets, and several helmets hanging on the walls. Two mud-splattered all-terrain vehicles faced outward in the center of the dirt floor.

As we climbed out of the Jeep and walked around the black truck, we were dwarfed by the size of the tires alone. Zale pointed up at the cab. "This means my uncles are here." He didn't look too happy about it.

Crossing the well-tended lawn to the screen door on the side of the porch, I looked around at the house and yard, and realized that there was little here that distinguished it as a Native American home. A rope swing hung from one of the old oaks, and a white cooler and a pair of oars leaned against the side of the house. A couple of orchid plants, their roots reaching out of their latticed wooden boxes, hung in a small gumbo-limbo tree closer to the house.

Zale rapped his knuckles on the wood screen door frame. "Gramma? It's me, Zale."

A large man wearing a black cowboy hat and mirrored sunglasses swung the door open. He reached out and tousled Zale's hair. "Look who's here, Mama. It's

Molly's boy." His voice was deep, but he spoke in a monotone. He stepped aside so Zale could pass, but it wasn't a welcoming gesture.

He continued to hold the door for me, so I followed Zale across the porch and into the shadowed house. The shades were drawn across the inside windows, and I could barely see anything at first after coming inside from the bright sunlight. Zale crossed the room, his outline blurring in the dark recesses. I wasn't sure whether I should follow him or not. Then I made him out, and I realized he was bending down to kiss a small form sitting in a large wingback chair.

When he stood up, I crossed the room and started to say, "I don't know if you'll remember me—" but she cut me off before I could finish.

"Seychelle? Give Gramma a kiss."

Her eyes, as I closed the gap between us, looked milky white and her smile showed big gaps where teeth should have been. Her gray hair was braided and wrapped round her head, and though she seemed to be smaller, either because I had grown or because she was shrinking, her ears remained the most remarkable aspect of her appearance. She'd always had these huge brown ears that looked like withered pancakes of Indian flatbread, and as I closed in to kiss her on the cheek, she turned her head aside when her son made a comment. I accidentally kissed her right on that dangling leathery lobe.

Zale was making the introductions, but I wasn't really listening. I was certain I was turning every shade of red imaginable. I could still taste that ear. The texture of it was imprinted on my lips, and I longed to wipe my mouth on my sleeve. The man who had opened the door for us, Josie's son Earl, was sitting on the other end of the couch, where they motioned me to sit. The younger man, who Zale said was Earl's son Jimmie, was smiling at my discomfort. As I recovered from my fit of embarrassment, I began to follow the conversation.

It seemed that Gramma Josie refused to get a satellite television dish, so the uncles had come over to tell her that they had seen Molly on TV—that she was in jail. They had just been discussing what they were going to do about it when we drove up. They were arguing over whether or not they should call Molly's mom, Ada Mae, out in Arizona.

"I don't think she'd want you to do that," I said. I knew that Molly and her mother had never been close, and the last thing Molly needed was the additional worry of having to deal with a frantic mother. Besides, according to Zale's report, she would be a drunk, frantic mother. And, though Gramma Josie herself had had a dalliance with a white man that had resulted in Ada Mae's birth, in general, Molly's white father was ignored by her mother's side of the family. These days, intermarriage was pretty common for Seminoles, but the old prejudices against marrying outside the tribe still ran fairly strong among the older folk.

"You think you know my niece better than me?" Earl asked. "I just saw her in Lauderdale a few days ago, and I been seeing her all these years."

I started to open my mouth to defend myself, then thought better of it. Surely, Molly's Uncle Earl didn't know about our long silence. I was probably reading too much into his comment.

He said, "You brought the boy here, but you are not family."

"Dad—enough." The younger of the two men, Jimmie, Molly's cousin, interrupted his father's next remark. He was dressed in Ralph Lauren chinos and a golf shirt, unlike his father, who wore faded black jeans and an Indian patchwork shirt beneath his black leather jacket. Jimmie looked like a South Beach businessman, and I imagined he was often mistaken for a Latino. Older than Molly, Jimmie had been in college, at FIU, when we were in high school. We'd thought of him as a real bore back then because he was studying business and marketing or something like that. Molly used to joke that when her cousin was a teenager, he used to take *Forbes* into the bathroom to jerk off. He was the one who, after expressing very brief condolences to Zale, brought up the will.

"Zale, I also heard on the news that your father left you the majority owner of Pontus Enterprises. Is this true?"

Zale turned to me. I gather it had not occurred to him before that it might possibly not be true. Or else he just didn't want to talk about it. "Yeah," I said. "It's true."

"So that son of a bitch finally did something right, eh?" Jimmie said with a smile that only played around his eyes.

This side of Molly's family pretty much agreed with me on her choice of husbands, but the question wasn't a fair one for Zale. I jumped in. "I talked to Molly last night at the Fort Lauderdale police station," I said. "She told me that, according to the will, Zale will be the owner of all the hotels and the restaurants and most likely the casino gambling boats. I don't know if you've been following the news story—"

"Miss, when it comes to the issue of gambling in this state, we follow it all very closely," Jimmie said.

"Right," I said, taking a deep breath. They sure weren't making any of this easy on me. "Well then, you know that Nick had sold TropiCruz to this guy, Ari Kagan, but now there are problems with the sale. It looks like Pontus will get the casino boats back, and it seems that Mr. Kagan isn't too happy about that."

"Nick was a fool for getting involved with them in the first place," Jimmie said. "The Italians, they had rules, you know? They didn't mess with your family. They had a gripe with you, they just took you out. These Russians, they've got no rules, no respect."

I glanced over at Zale to see if he was listening, if he understood the implication of Jimmie's words. The boy was staring down at his hands, his face hidden in the shadows. "Well, that was part of the reason why Molly asked me to bring Zale out here," I said. "To keep him safe and get him away from the press, who will now be salivating over Richie Rich here." I smiled at Zale, hoping he would take the nickname as a joke. He didn't look up.

Jimmie Tigertail stood and began pacing in the living room. "Zale, this is good news. This will eventually give the tribe control over the entire TropiCruz fleet of casino gambling boats. I tried for years to get Molly to talk to that idiot husband of hers, to get him to see the damage he was doing to the tribe's gambling revenues."

"I don't mean to be argumentative here, but Zale will be the owner, not the tribe."

Earl, who was sitting in a rocker next to his mother, still wearing the dark shades and hat, ignored me. He leaned forward and spoke to the boy for the first time. "But he will certainly do what is best for us, won't you, son?"

Zale lifted his head, and the look on his face was that of a good kid who liked to make grown-ups happy, and now he was uncomfortable not knowing the right answer. He looked at me, then swung back to face his great-uncle.

"Son," Earl Tigertail said, and there was an undercurrent of command in his voice. He leaned forward, his hands clenched in fists, the tendons in his forearms stretched taut under the skin. "You do realize that these gambling ships are a direct threat to Indian casinos? The casinos are our livelihood. They put food on our tables."

Yeah, I thought, and put the ATVs in your garages and the sixty-inch televisions in your living rooms. Last I heard, every member of the tribe got an income of several thousand dollars a month.

"Come on. Even once Zale inherits the company," I said, "it's not like he'll really be running it."

Jimmie walked over and clamped a hand on the boy's shoulder. "Less than five years and you'll be eighteen. Then they won't be able to stop you. In the meantime, Pontus is not publicly owned. The court will appoint managers, and they will know that if they don't do as you want, you'll can them as soon as you take over. You could make it happen, Zale. You could get rid of those damn ships for us."

Earl leaned forward and grabbed his wrist. "I know you wouldn't do anything to hurt the tribe, would you?"

Before Zale had a chance to answer, Gramma Josie pushed herself to a stand. Her son and grandson rushed to her side, but she waved them off and reached out for Zale. He stood and offered her his arm.

"We go outside, talk." She pointed her finger at me, and I took that as meaning that I was supposed to follow.

As we passed through the kitchen, a younger Seminole woman was standing at the counter stirring something that looked like batter in a large ceramic bowl. Josie said something to her in Creek, and she nodded her assent, then the old woman waved Zale on toward the back door.

Outside, the sun's glare was brutal, the sky now cloudless, but the Florida winter air was not going to climb to the punishing temperatures we would see come spring. She led us to the farther of two chickee huts behind the house. I hadn't seen them when we'd first driven up, as the house hid them from view. When we passed the first hut, I saw the blackened logs in a fire ring in the center of the round of dirt. Various cooking utensils hung from the cypress poles that supported the palmetto roof, and I wondered if Josie still liked to cook out there sometimes.

The shade afforded by the palmetto fronds was far easier on the eyes, and when Josie settled herself on a wood bench and then pointed to a second bench, we dragged it across the dirt and sat opposite her.

What I knew about Gramma Josie's life came from the stories I'd picked up from Ada, Molly's mom, when we were kids. She told us once that Josie had been born in 1915 in an Indian camp on the North Fork of the New River, near where the river goes under Broward Boulevard today, and not far from where we had grown up. That had so amazed me and Molly that we took the skiff that afternoon and motored up the North Fork to try to look for Indian arrowheads, not realizing that our TV view of Indians was less than accurate. By 1915 the Seminoles had been using guns for more than a century. Molly's mom once told us that when Josie was a little girl, her family brought her along when they conducted business at the Stranahan's trading post in the growing town of Fort Lauderdale. She was one of the first Seminole children to start to learn English. Josie had to leave Fort Lauderdale when her family moved to the Hollywood Reservation, and it was there that Josie was married. Later, widowed, with a son almost grown, Josie gave birth to a daughter, Ada Mae, Molly's mom, who was half white. It had been Seminole custom for many years to kill half-breed babies. Josie had to fight the tribal elder who came to take the baby from her arms in order to drown the child in the Dania Canal. Ada Mae, who knew this story, told it often to show others why she hated all things Indian. But at that time, just after the Second World War, half-breed children didn't fit entirely into either world, and the white world she chose to embrace didn't exactly welcome her, either.

Molly's mother would tell us these stories, swaying in the kitchen, a highball glass in one hand, a cigarette in the other, and she'd curse the Indians and their way of life. Ada Mae left the reservation as soon as she graduated from high school. She married a white man, and other than when her mother occasionally visited the family, or demanded that her granddaughter be brought out to visit her, Ada had little to do with Seminole life from then on. Josie's son Earl had married and gone to live with his wife's clan out at Big Cypress, and Josie followed him out there in the 1970s when she decided that she wanted to continue to cook and sleep in a chickee as she had done for the first fifty years of her life. Molly had only ever known her grandmother as a resident of "B.C.," as Ada used to call the Big Cypress.

Josie slapped her brown craggy hand on the bench next to her and Zale obeyed, moving across to sit next to his great-grandmother. She took his hand in hers and drew it onto the folds of her skirt. The contrast between his long white fingers and her brown gnarled ones made me remember how Molly had held his hand in exactly the same way, and how I had marveled then, too, at this sunny, fair boy in this Indian family.

"Your mother gone be fine. You stay wid me. Don' you worry about Uncle Earl."

"He scares me, Gramma," Zale said. He spoke very loudly. I guessed that Josie's deafness could only have worsened over the past decade.

She laughed a wheezy, almost girlish chuckle. "Earl remember the old Indian way. He don' like the white way."

I was going to point out that casinos were not exactly the old Indian way, but I decided that Josie was really talking about something else. I suspected she meant that Earl didn't like white people. And who could blame him? He was her firstborn, and that would make him about seventy years old and the first in his line to be born on a reservation. Josie had been born in an Indian camp back when the last of the free Seminoles still considered the land theirs.

"We losin' the old Indian way. Young people don' wan learn. We lose the last canoe builder. Henry John Billie. He die last month. Nobody leff to make canoe."

The young woman we had passed in the kitchen came out the back door and brought us a tray of iced glasses of limeade. I sipped mine slowly, as she'd been so heavy-handed with the sugar that I'd nearly gagged on my first big gulp.

"My children Ada Mae and Earl, they hold hate here." She hit her chest with her fist. "Don't let go."

Gramma Josie swung her head around and faced me. Her head continued to swivel just slightly from side to side as her cloudy eyes tried to make out my shape. She hummed softly to herself. I imagined her massive ears were working a little like radar.

"I'm here," I said.

"Yeah, you are here. Mean you and Molly talk again?"

I was shocked that this old Indian woman would know about my relationship with her granddaughter. This was her world out here in the Everglades. How could she possibly understand life back in Lauderdale? "We're starting to," I said.

"What?" She cupped her hand behind one of her ears.

"Yeah, we're starting to talk again," I said, louder this time.

"Good. You learn—let go." She nodded and rolled her lips over her teeth a few times. "Seychelle, you a smart girl. When I was lil' girl, I have white girlfriend like you. Good friend."

"Fort Lauderdale must have been so different when you were a little girl," I said.

She laughed and patted Zale's hand again. He was watching her face intently, as though trying to memorize it. The boy knew death now. He knew that he and his loved ones were not immortal.

"Oh yeah. When my family go trade, I go Miz Stranahan's house. My friend teach me English. We stay friend. So many years."

"You stayed in contact with this white woman?" I said. I saw her lean her head in to me, so I repeated, "You stayed friends as adults, too?"

She nodded vigorously. "Yeah. When I go Lauderdale, I see my friend. We talk. Not like Molly and you."

"Well, there were reasons for that, Gramma. Reasons you probably don't know anything about."

"No good reason to end friend." She turned to Zale. "Molly smart girl send you here. You need sun, sky, canoe on lake. Go hunt pig. No tink about father, mother."

"Thanks, Gramma. But you know, it's hard to stop thinking about everything that's happened."

It was also hard for the boy to shout his feelings on that subject. His voice was fading.

"Yeah, yeah," she said, nodding, not needing to hear it all to know what Zale was feeling. "Seychelle know. I care for you like I care for your mudder."

"That's what I told him," I said. "He's really lucky to have a grandmother like you."

"You have gramma," she said.

"No, all my grandparents died before I was born," I said, shaking my head.

"Seychelle, you talk when you need listen."

"I don't understand, Gramma Josie."

She laughed again in that high-pitched cackle, and the laugh ended with a fit of coughing. I crossed over and sat next to her, patting her softly on the back. Zale and I exchanged worried looks as she seemed to struggle to breathe. I lifted the limeade glass next to her and she took a sip. After several long seconds of quiet, she said, "Seychelle. You go home now. Zale, he safe here."

XIII.

O N the return trip to Lauderdale, I didn't scan the canals for gators or admire the various herons and egrets nesting in the trees along the sides of the highway. I was driving on autopilot, staying in the slow lane and ignoring the impatient drivers who zoomed past me. I kept thinking about Earl Tigertail and the sense of menace I felt in the man. He didn't like Zale or me, that was clear, but it was more than that. I sensed a deep well of suppressed rage in the man. Was it just us he hated, or was it all white people? And how far did that rage extend? Josie had mentioned that Zale could go hunting while he was out there. All the Seminole men hunted. Undoubtedly, old Earl was a pretty good shot.

My first stop back in town was at the Pontus Enterprises offices across the Seventeenth Street Bridge. The crowd of protesters was twice the size it had been two days before. I parked my Jeep at the far end of the parking lot as though I planned to visit one of the shops on the east side of the little shopping center. Strolling down the sidewalk, peering into windows, I made my way slowly toward the Pontus office. While I walked, I checked out the crowd. Most of them looked like well-turned-out housewives and their older children. Was it possible that someone in this crowd would have been angry enough about this development project to murder

Nick? There were a couple of men in the crowd, but they looked like retirees in their pastel high-wader pants, and I somehow couldn't see either one of them perched on a bridge looking through a gun's scope. Standing a little apart from the chanting masses was a middle-aged woman, her auburn hair cut in a neat pageboy. She was holding a clipboard and issuing commands like a general at the front. I stood on the perimeter of the group, looking for the strange older woman with the icy eyes I had seen before. I'd been scanning the crowd for no more than two minutes before Madame Generale was at my side.

"Hi," she said. "Have you signed the petition?"

"Uh, no, see I'm really—"

"Are you a resident of the city of Fort Lauderdale?"

"Yes, but—"

"Well, as a resident, I'm sure you've seen the number of these awful towers that have been shooting up all over town. Traffic is already unbearable, and we don't have the infrastructure to support this growth. We're all residents of the Harbor Isles circulating this petition to try to stop Pontus from building here. We want the city to seize the property under eminent domain."

"You sound like an attorney," I said.

"Ha!" she barked out, then said, "It's even worse. I'm married to one."

I didn't really want to get involved with these protesters, but her quick smile and dimpled cheeks were irresistible. I stuck out my hand. "My name's Seychelle Sullivan."

"Kathleen Ginestra," she said, sticking the pen in her mouth and her clipboard under her other arm. She then wiped her hand down the side of her jeans and finally took mine in a dry, firm grip.

"You know all these people?" I asked, indicating the crowd.

"Most of them."

A woman carrying a sign that read BUILD PARKS, NOT PENTHOUSES yelled, "Kathleen knows half of Fort Lauderdale!"

Kathleen turned her face aside, bunched up her features in a grimace, and then made a spitting sound. "I do not," she said.

"Maybe you could help me if you know someone I saw here the other day. She was an older woman— elderly, really—wearing a white blouse, white hair all piled up on top of her head." I motioned with my hands to show what I meant.

"You must mean Mrs. Wheeler. She comes around every once in a while to lend her support." She tucked her hair behind her ear and leaned in closer to me. Quietly, she said, "She's quite the character, you know."

"What do you mean?"

"Well," she said, pausing to look around to see who was listening, "Mrs. Wheeler is pretty well known around the city and the port commission. She's this really tenacious activist—been at it for about a hundred years. She fights all types of growth and development, and she's been known to bring down some pretty powerful politicians in this town. Remember that business when the port commissioners bought themselves gold and diamond rings with public money? She blew the whistle on that."

"Really? You seen her around here today?"

"As a matter of fact, she was here just before you walked up. I remember because she was saying something about next week's commission meeting." Kathleen was swiveling her head around as though counting her flock. "I don't think she drives. Nope, I'm afraid she's not here now, and I didn't see which way she went."

"Well, the name will help. You don't know her first name?"

"Oh God, no. You know how it is. Some of these old broads would just die if you didn't call them Mrs. Whatever. I'm sorry. I can't help you with that."

"The last name is more than I had. I don't even really know why I want to talk to her. It was just something about the way she looked at me. She looked like she had something she wanted to tell me." That wasn't a very clear explanation, but it was the best I could give the woman. I wanted to thank her, so I stuck out my hand. "You want me to sign that?"

Kathleen's eyebrows flew up in surprise. "Uh, sure!" She thrust the clipboard into my hands.

I'm not much of a political type, but I liked this woman, and if she could keep my town from becoming a concrete canyon, I was behind her 100 percent. After scrawling my name, I turned and headed for the doors to Pontus Enterprises. The look on Ms. Ginestra's face as I entered the building was priceless.

THE Pontus secretary, Roma, was at her station at the reception desk, and when she looked at me over the rims of her red glasses, I felt a little like a specimen pinned to a board.

"May I help you?"

"Yes, I'd like to see Leon Quinn."

"Do you have an appointment?"

"No, not exactly. But—"

"I'm afraid Mr. Quinn has appointments all day today."

"And *I'm* afraid *you're* going to have to figure out a way to get me in to see him." I hated it when secretaries got pissy with me. Just because I was standing there wearing jeans, boat shoes, a baseball cap, and a T-shirt commemorating the 1999 Blues Fest at the Downtowner didn't give her the right to treat me any differently than the women who walked in wearing polyester power suits and pumps.

She looked up at me and narrowed her eyes, trying to decide how to respond.

"Look," I said, realizing that force was probably not the way to get past this bouncer. "I came in here the other day with Zale Pontus. My name is Seychelle Sullivan. You might remember me—I'm a friend of the family. I figure if you've worked for Nick for all these years, you must know Molly pretty well, and that's what I want to see Mr. Quinn about." Actually, I also wanted to find out about the status of my salvage claim, but I didn't think that would get me in his door. "I assume you've heard she's been arrested."

She pressed her lips together in a thin line and sighed. I saw it in her face when she made the decision. Her eyes flicked to the clock on her desk and back to me. "Mr. Quinn has an appointment in twelve minutes." She reached for the phone. "Let me see if he will see you." She punched three numbers and swung away from me on her swivel chair so she could speak out of my earshot into the phone. I walked across the office and pretended to examine the model of the TropiTowers. A toy-sized version of the *TropiCruz IV* rested at the dock.

"Miss Sullivan," Roma called. "Please follow me." By the time I'd turned around, she had her back to me and was disappearing down the hallway. I hustled to catch up. As she opened her boss's door, she said in a husky whisper, "Ten minutes."

Leon Quinn did not bother to get up from behind his desk, but he did point with a flourish to one of the chairs opposite him. He had a cloth napkin tucked into his collar, and a large Styrofoam container rested on his desk blotter. He mopped at his moustache before he spoke. "Miss Sullivan," he said, the tightness evident in his voice. "How nice to see you again."

I ducked my chin and said, "Mr. Quinn."

"So, you're here about Molly? It's unbelievable." He pulled the napkin free and wiped his fingers one by one. "What kind of idiot cops think she shot Nick? Huh?"

"I don't know."

"First, they can't even enforce this restraining order and Nicky gets killed. Then they arrest Molly? *Blakas!*"

"I'm just worried that with Molly in jail, the cops will think it's over. They won't look for any other possibilities. I thought I'd nose around a little. See if I couldn't find something to give to the cops to make them consider another suspect."

"But it's so obvious," he said. He waved his arms as he talked. I knew the stereotype that Italians talk with their hands, but I was learning that Greeks did, too. "This was about the casino gambling boats. About money. And pride. *Perifania,* we say in Greek. Saving face. The last time Nick and Kagan met they called each other names, got into a shoving match. Nick filed a restraining order against Kagan." Quinn made his hand into the shape of a gun and pulled the thumb trigger. "Pow. The Russians had him killed."

"Why are you so sure it was them?"

He spread his hands wide. "Come on. A head shot like that? That was done by a pro. And the Russians? They're the only guys I know with connections like that."

"So you're saying that Ari Kagan *is* connected to the Russian mafia."

"Honey, after what just happened to Nicky? I'm not going on the record saying nothing."

"But the cops will say that wives have been known

to hire killers to knock off their husbands—and *ex-*husbands."

"Yeah, but not Molly."

"No," I said, "you're right, not Molly." I leaned forward and put my elbows on the desk. "So what can we do to convince the police of that? Is there anything you can think of that would steer the investigation that way?"

"I've already told that fat detective *everything* I know about Nicky." He swiveled around in his big leather chair and looked at the framed photos on the shelf behind him. "We had such good times, me and Nicky." He sighed. "I told that fat man all about Nick's relationship with Kagan, how they fought, how they tried to steal from us. I *told* him that son of a bitch Kagan did it. He killed him. They just write in their little notebooks and let them get away with it."

"What about some guy named Thompson who works on the ship? Do you know who that is?"

He waggled his hand in front of his face as though he were shooing away a fly. "We got more'n a hundred employees down there in Hollywood. I don't know them all. Hell, I don't even know half."

"This was somebody Nick knew."

"Nicky was a funny guy, miss. He's wearing fuckin' three-hundred-dollar shoes and designer pants and next thing you know he's laying sod in the planters around the dock or down in the engine room gettin' all greasy and sweaty with the engineer. Nicky knew *everybody* who worked for him. Me, I'm in the office all day. On the phone. Nick couldn't stand being cooped up like that. You could go down to the boat, ask them. Why you wanta know, anyways?"

"Just curious. Zale said his dad used to talk about this Thompson. I'm reaching for any answers here. I really don't want to have to call that kid in a couple of days and tell him his mom is still in jail."

The door to the office swung inward just then, almost hitting the chair where I sat, and Roma was shouting, "But you can't just go barging in" as Janet Pontus burst into the room. "Mr. Quinn, I'm sorry," Roma said, "but she refused to wait until you—" Janet stepped between Roma and her boss so that Roma was talking to the woman's back.

Janet Hunter Pontus was decked out in a candy apple–colored sweater with long sleeves and a deep V-neck that exposed her artificially tanned and swelled cleavage. She had blunt-cut bangs and shoulder-length platinum hair. Again, her pouty mouth was slicked over with lipstick the color of a divorcee's new Corvette with clear coat.

"It's all right," Quinn said.

Roma nodded and backed out of the room.

"I need to speak to you," Janet said in a soft, slow, deep voice, staring straight at Quinn. She was a petite woman with fine wrists and ankles, and the deep voice sounded like a ventriloquist's joke.

Quinn stood. "All right." He looked at me expectantly. I did not stand. "We were just finishing up here."

Janet took a small step backward as though noticing me for the first time. "I'm sorry. I didn't mean to interrupt," she said, and the voice was suddenly high-pitched, feminine, and soft. She smiled at me and the impact was so strong, I couldn't stop myself from smiling back. She reached out her hand. "I'm Janet Pontus."

Her grip was confident. "Seychelle Sullivan," I said. "I'm very sorry for your loss."

The light seemed to go out of her eyes and her chin began to tighten. "Thank you," she said in a near-whisper. Then she dug in her handbag until she produced a white tissue. "I get along fine for a few hours and the hurt almost goes away, and then it hits me again." A single tear spilled out of her right eye and she dabbed at it so expertly, she didn't even smear her makeup.

Quinn came around the desk and embraced her, kissing her lightly on the cheek. "There now. You've cried enough, honey." He eased her into the chair next to mine, then returned to his seat behind the desk, but not before trailing his fingers across the back of her neck.

Janet ignored him and spoke directly to me. "Sometimes I feel like I'm just never going to stop crying."

"I know what you mean," I said. "I know what it's like to lose loved ones."

She sat in the other chair and fastened those blue eyes on me, nodding. "You, too? Your parents?"

I nodded.

"I'm sorry," she said. "I never knew my daddy, and mama died when I was still in school. My brother was all I had left. And then I met Nick. It was like I was given another chance to start a family. We had our whole lives ahead of us. So many plans. None of it will be the same without him."

I watched her closely and tried to find any trace of the self-centered bitch that Molly claimed lived inside this body. I didn't see it. She seemed to be talking in Hallmark platitudes, but that was because it was what she knew. Jeannie had pegged her, pretty, not too bright, self-obsessed but not very self-aware.

I turned back to Quinn and made a show of glancing at my watch. "I promised Roma I wouldn't take more than ten minutes of your time. It's just that there's one more thing I wanted to discuss with you," I said and looked over at Janet. "I'm not sure now's the time . . ."

"Say what's bothering you," Quinn said. "Mrs. Pontus," he nodded at her, "is an amazing woman. She's stronger than she looks, and she has a good head for business. I'm very thankful for that given how things have turned out."

"I wanted to talk to you about the salvage claim on the *Mykonos*. Have you discussed it with the insurance company yet?"

He made a big show of slapping himself on the forehead. "I knew there was something I was forgetting."

"What about the boatyard? Have you been in touch with them? What kind of shape is she in?"

"I called over there this morning, and they said we were damn lucky. The water she was taking on was back around the shafts. The only other hull damage was cosmetic."

I could sense Janet fidgeting on the periphery of my vision. Clearly, like most beautiful women, she didn't like being ignored.

"Did the water reach the engines?" I asked.

"No, very little water damage. They said they might be able to put her back in the water tomorrow. I'll contact the insurance company first thing in the morning and authorize them—"

"*Leon,*" Janet said, then she turned to me and spoke in a quiet confidential voice. "It's going to take him a little time to start including me in decisions like this. You know how men are."

I looked at Leon, then back at Janet. "I'm afraid I don't understand what you're talking about. Mr. Quinn, I really do need to know the status of this claim. If you would like me to contact your insurance company directly, I'd be happy—"

"Miss Sullivan," Janet said, "we'll look into it and get back to you as soon as we can. I'm sure we'll be able to reach an agreement shortly."

"I'm a little confused here. I don't mean to be rude, but I don't see what you have to say about it."

She threw back her head and laughed a deep, throaty laugh. Her platinum hair swung around her face when she lowered her chin and fixed me with a big-eyed look I was certain she had practiced in front of the mirror. "You don't know? Don't you watch TV? I've been all over the news lately." She laughed that scratchy laugh again. "Go ahead, tell her, Leon."

Leon stared down at his desk and smoothed his moustache with the fingers of his right hand. Then he cleared his throat. "Miss Sullivan, after his second marriage to Janet here, Nick rewrote his will. We filed that will with the court yesterday afternoon, and in it Nick determined that all his assets are to be equally divided between his wife and his son. Mrs. Pontus here," he indicated Janet with his hand and a reverential nod of his head, "is now essentially my boss."

XIV.

BY the time I pulled into the drive back at the Larsens' place, it was after four and I was starved. No lunch and lots of driving can do that to me. But hungry as I was, I didn't jump out of the Jeep and head back to my cottage. I sat in the driver's seat and allowed myself time to think. I'd gone to Leon to ask him for help finding another suspect, and I walked out of there thinking that he looked the most suspicious of all. There was no doubt in my mind that Leon and Janet had slept together. Was it something that happened when the lawyer was consoling the grieving widow, or had it started while Nick was alive? If that was the case, the only thing that would have stood between him and his boss's wife was the boss. Beauty-wise, Janet was quite the prize, but now that it appeared that she was going to be worth millions, it looked even more believable that Leon Quinn could have murdered his best friend in order to grab the whole jackpot.

Then of course, there had been that bad gut feeling I'd gotten out at the reservation. Earl Tigertail was a man who carried a truckload of resentment and hatred. The way he talked to Zale about getting rid of the casino gambling ships made me think he had lost touch with reality. Zale was a Pontus heir, but he was still an eighth-grader who had just lost his dad. Was Earl so deep in his cloud of hate and blame that he would have killed Nick to try to seize the gambling boats? I found that idea less believable, but worthy of consideration nonetheless.

There were plenty of other possible suspects, but I had no evidence and no idea what more I could do to help Molly. Yet it made me sick to my stomach to think of her sitting in jail, suspected of murder while a woman she hated was taking over the company that rightfully belonged to her son. I was so far out of my league on this thing—I mean, what the hell did I know about the Russian mafia or contract hit men or how to investigate a murder? There was so much more that I needed to know, like what was the evidence the cops had against her, what were the details of the arguments between Nick and Kagan, and who was Kagan, anyway? Where did he come from? What was his background? I didn't know how to go about finding any of this information—and certainly couldn't do it tonight.

I swung open the Jeep's door when my stomach rumbled for the third time. Maybe I could rustle up a can of soup or something out of the kitchen in the cottage. The last dinner I'd eaten at home had consisted of bread and those plastic-wrapped orange slices of processed cheese. When I took out the cheddar cheese I'd meant to eat with the bread, it was all green and fuzzy. I'd lost track of when I'd bought it. I pitched it and reached for the processed cheese. That's the nice thing about those square slices. No matter how many years they're in the fridge, they never go moldy. B. J. would probably say that was because there wasn't enough organic material to grow mold on.

When I passed through the side gate, my dog wasn't standing on the other side waiting to greet me, so I suspected my brother was around somewhere. When I came out of the shadows of the path that led along the side of the house, I saw that not only was he there, he wasn't alone.

"Hey, guys," I called out across the lawn to the two figures sitting in deck chairs out on the dock, watching the last of the afternoon sunlight leak out of the winter sky.

"Hey Sis, c'mon over for a beer and some sausage."

Mike Beesting turned halfway around in his chair and waved. I hadn't recognized him at first because he was wearing his artificial leg, and with his jeans and Topsiders you'd never guess the leg was not his own. Mike was a good friend who had taken early retirement from the Lauderdale Police Department when some crazy city worker decided to get back at the boss who fired him by showing up with a shotgun and two pockets full of shells. Mike had just happened to be passing the scene, and he managed to save several lives—albeit at a mighty stiff personal cost. Mike never complained about it, though. He enjoyed his life aboard the Irwin 54 sailboat that was paid for by the compensation package he'd grabbed on his way out the door. The only thing he ever did complain about was the discomfort of wearing the prosthesis. Nine times out of ten, Mike was hopping around on his boat, with a rum drink in one hand and a grin on his face.

As I walked out to the dock, I saw that they had a Styrofoam beer cooler between them filled with cube ice and green bottles, and balanced on *Gorda*'s bucket was a piece of scrap plywood they must have scrounged from the Larsens' continuous remodeling lumber pile. On the plywood was a large brown sausage cut into fat slices with what looked to be the rigging knife I kept on board my tug. Abaco was sitting, trembling with anticipation, staring at the sausage and occasionally turning her eyes on one or the other of the two men. She was showing extraordinary restraint; somehow, the guys seemed not to notice.

I patted her on the head and told her what a good dog she was, then said, "Well, boys, looks like you've made yourselves mighty comfortable."

Mike pulled a beer out of the ice and offered it to me. "Have one," he said. "I'd offer you my chair, but I wouldn't want to offend an independent woman like you." He and Pit grinned like a couple of ten-year-olds. Judging from the number of empties lined up on the dock, the two of them had been at this for a while.

"No thanks, and I suggest you watch it with those wise-cracks." With my thumb and forefinger, I gave Mike a thump on the side of his head. "You can't afford to lose any other appendages." I turned to my brother. "I thought you were going to be bunking aboard the *Firestorm* from now on."

"Yeah, I am, but I needed to come back here to get my stuff. I didn't want to show up for the interview with my gear, like I knew I'd get the job. When I saw Mike go by in his dinghy, I hailed him, and he offered to bring me up here to get my stuff. And we were starved, so we stopped off at this little deli that just opened up by the Southport Raw Bar."

"And all you got was beer and a sausage."

Pit looked at Mike with a confused look. "Yeah. What's wrong with that?"

I shook my head, turned around, and crossed the yard to my cottage. And B. J. thought I was the one who had terrible taste in food. Inside, I threw my shoulder bag on the couch, washed up a little, then saw the red light blinking on my answering machine. I pushed the button for the message and got a two-word command in Jeannie's stern voice. "Call me."

"Hey, what's going on?" I said when she answered the phone.

"Seychelle, you have got to get a cell phone."

"Oh, come on. You know I hate those things. Most of the time the people who need me can reach me on the VHF."

"You're losing business, you know. People expect you to have a cell today."

"I know this is not why you wanted me to call you."

"No."

"What happened in court today? Is she coming home?"

"I'm afraid not. It's not totally unexpected, but I'm disappointed all the same. Listen, tell me about your day first, then I'll explain it to you."

My day, I thought, started out under the fresh clear sky of the Glades. I was free and Molly was sitting in a box, accused of murder. And I felt incredibly inadequate for the job of getting her out.

I told Jeannie the story about dropping Zale off at his great-grandmother's place, about the uncles, about Earl's attitude, and about Jimmie's comment about the Russian mafia as opposed to the Italians.

"He's right. The Russians are some nasty characters."

"After that, I went by Pontus Enterprises to check on my salvage claim and to nose around a little. Janet came by while I was there."

"So I assume you've heard the news."

"Yup. What a mess, huh? Jeannie, I thought you told me Nick had a prenup."

"Yeah, he did. That wouldn't stop him from changing his mind later, though."

"Hmm. There's something going on between Leon Quinn, Nick's attorney, and the grieving widow."

"Really?" Jeannie said. "How do you know?"

"You can see it in how he looks at her. How he touches her."

"Very interesting."

"Is it possible this second will is a fake?"

"Anything's possible, but I think there will be too much scrutiny on this one. They'd have to be crazy to think they could get away with that."

"Jeannie, I swear I don't know what to make of Janet. This afternoon, she seemed so sweet and sincere. I guess she's had a pretty rough life. But just about the time I was leaving, when she started to talk about inheriting the company, I saw a hint of what Molly claims to see."

"What do you mean?"

"I don't know. It sounds weird, but I could swear she has another, deeper voice. Her laugh is a part of it, too. It sounds different than the way she usually talks."

"And I suppose she handles serpents and speaks in tongues?"

"Come on, Jeannie. I know it sounds weird, but—"

"Like I said, you and Molly are more alike than either of you knows. Janet Pontus is just an ordinary woman who happened to win the lottery when Mother Nature was handing out looks and sex appeal. She's used it to her advantage, and that pisses some other women off. End of story. So what's happening with the salvage claim on the *Mykonos*?"

"Quinn says he hasn't done anything, and now Janet claims that she will handle it as Quinn's new boss. Maybe it would be best if we dealt directly with the insurance company on this one. Remember that insurance investigator we met when we were working on that trawler that caught fire right on the three-mile mark? What was his name?"

"Bill Casey?"

"Yeah, him. Why don't you call him? He knows or

can find out just about everything in the insurance business. Ask him who the insurers are and contact them directly. I'm sure they aren't going to want to pay the cost of us arguing this one in court. They'll see my claim is fair even if Janet and Quinn don't."

"Good idea."

"Okay, so tell me exactly what happened to Molly today."

"No surprises. They formally charged her and there's no bail. Until we can figure out what the hell is going on here, she has to stay in jail."

"I don't know if she's up to it, Jeannie. She was so thin when we saw her on Monday, and now, after all this, I'm afraid that spending too much time in there could make her really sick."

"I know. I'm worried, too, but it's not like we've got lots of choices here."

"Damn," I said, pacing the living room of my cottage, the portable phone held to my ear. "I feel so helpless, and I get really pissed when I feel helpless. I wish I knew what more I could do about it. I'll call Zale out at Big Cypress tomorrow. He gave me the number, and I promised I'd let him know what's happening with his mom. Poor kid. It's like he's lost both his parents in a couple of days."

Jeannie didn't say anything for several seconds, and I began to wonder if the line had gone dead. Then she said, "Sey, in spite of what they look like, those two detectives are *not* stupid. We just need to find something concrete, some kind of evidence that will point them in another direction. You know boats. Think about those boats—TropiCruz Casino gambling boats. Use what you know."

After I hung up the phone, I collected a half loaf of day-old French bread, some mustard, more orange cheese, and a very ripe tomato. I stuck a half can of peanuts under my chin and trotted back out to join the guys.

Sitting cross-legged on the wood dock beside the bucket table, I made myself a sandwich and accepted the cold beer Mike opened for me.

"Hey, Sis, I thought you might be interested to know that just about everybody I met down at the Marriott today eventually turned the subject around to Nick Pontus."

"Oh yeah? What were they saying?"

"I guess he was planning on building some big marina over on the other side of the Seventeenth Street Bridge from them."

I nodded.

"Well, most of the guys I was talking to either already work on big megayachts or are trying to find jobs on one. They're not exactly environmentalists, and they like the idea of having another marina for these gas-guzzling monsters. They see more jobs."

"I'm pretty sure I know most of the guys you were talking to, and, most of them, it doesn't matter how many megayachts come to town—they're still not going to find jobs."

Mike held his index finger in the air. "She's got a point."

"But that's not the point I'm trying to make. This morning, when I first got there, they were all worried because they'd heard that the kid was going to inherit Pontus, and they were afraid the development was going to be put on hold. Some of these guys knew Molly in high school, and they know her reputation. They figured the kid's like his mom—a real manatee-loving environmentalist. But then around one o'clock, after the midday news, word spread up and down the dock that there was a second will, leaving half of what he had to the new bimbo wife and putting her in charge of all of it. Is that true?"

I chewed my mouthful of sandwich, the spicy mustard mingling with the hot flavor of the sausage. It was so good I didn't want to hurry. I finally swallowed. "I guess so. That's what Nick's attorney Quinn said when I saw him today. And, by the way, the grieving widow was there, too."

"Word on the dock was that she's all about money and flash, and she'll certainly go through with the marina project."

"They're probably right—if she can get it approved by the city commission. I met a pretty together lady today who's doing everything she can to see that that doesn't happen."

"I wish your 'together lady' luck," Pit said.

"Me, too."

For the next several minutes I chewed my dinner too fast and finished my beer. About that time, the cross-legged position wasn't quite so comfortable anymore. My waistband was cutting off my air supply. I stretched out on my back on the sun-warmed planks, and though I was tempted to unbutton the top button of my jeans, my ladylike reserve prevented me.

After a particularly loud powerboat passed with blaring Latin hip-hop music, I opened one eye and looked up at my cop friend. "So, Mike, what's your theory? Who do you think shot Nick Pontus?"

"Well," he said, and then he belched loudly. "Excuse me. Well, it's hard to say, Seychelle. Nick had more enemies than Port Everglades has rats. From Key West to Jacksonville and even over in Tarpon Springs, that man was involved in more deals that went south—for one reason or another. Some folks made a ton of money off him—and others lost a ton. I'm talking folks who lost everything and were suing Nick to get it back. People have killed over lots less."

"Yeah, that's true," I said, and I thought for the first time in a long time about my old boyfriend, Neal Garrett. Greed was a powerful motive, and it had gotten Neal killed in the end. In this case, it looked as though both greed and revenge were part of the picture. I told the guys, "Leon Quinn is convinced that it was a professional hit by Ari Kagan's friends in the Russian mafia."

Mike set his empty bottle next to the three others on the dock by his chair and reached for another beer. "It does look like a pro job. I didn't know till just now, when your brother told me that you and Molly Pontus used to be friends."

"Yeah, what can I say? Life's complicated."

"Well, like I said, I didn't know you had anything to do with this, but a buddy of mine from the department called me today about chartering my boat for his anniversary. I'd been hearing all about the funeral and the arrest, and I asked him what he knew about the case. He told me they found the murder weapon in Molly Pontus's garage. It's an SKS rifle with a scope. Not your run-of-the-mill weapon."

I felt like I couldn't be hearing this right. What Mike was saying was so far out of the realm of possibility; I thought I must have slipped into some kind of dream. "What? Say that again."

"I said, they found the rifle that was used to shoot Nick in Molly's garage. That's a pretty damning piece of evidence."

"That's insane. If they really found it there, someone else put it there. Not Molly. She would have freaked if she even knew there was a gun somewhere on her property. What the hell's an SKS anyway?"

"It's a Russian-made semiautomatic rifle. What they

used in the military over there before the AK-47. They're not that common, but not *that* rare."

"Oh. It's Russian, huh? Well, duh. Haven't the police looked at what that might tell them?"

"They think that the shooter chose that weapon to throw suspicion on the Russians, that the shooter meant to take the gun somewhere and dump it so it would be found, but simply hadn't had the time. They think the shooter was either Molly herself or, more likely, someone she hired."

His face didn't have the usual merry cast, the twinkling eyes and the mouth that turned up in the corners. His skin looked as though it had grown heavy and was sagging on his face. It was so unusual to see sadness in Mike. "This is bad, isn't it? Really bad."

"Yeah, I'm afraid it is."

I didn't know what else to say. The world had gone haywire. The one person I knew who was least likely to ever hurt anybody was now sitting in a jail accused of murder.

"And what makes it worse," Mike said, "is how quickly Molly filed the will."

"But, Mike, today there's another will."

"Which Molly knew nothing about. She believed her son was going to inherit it all."

The three of us sat there in silence for the next ten minutes watching the last afternoon boats *putt-putting* their way up the river to their docks. Captain Courtney passed by on his tug *Cape Ann*, pulling a big Feadship, with Perry White on *Little Bitt* working the stern. I waved to them and didn't even have it in me to wonder why they got the job and I didn't. I had other things to worry about. More important things.

When we were kids, Molly was always littler than me. In a way, I protected her like she was my younger sister, while in truth she was a few months older. There was a time once, back when we were both about fourteen, when we took the bus down to Fort Lauderdale Beach over spring break. This was just before the city fathers decided to do a makeover of the beach, and the place was still jammed with college kids. We started talking to a couple of cute college boys from Georgia, and a while later we went out to sit on the empty lifeguard tower after the guards had packed up and left.

At first we were just talking, but then the guy sitting on the other side of Molly started trying to unbutton her shirt. She told him to cut it out, and he just laughed. When she told him again, and he still didn't stop, I reacted like a girl who had grown up with two older brothers. I reached back and punched him in the face with everything I had. The fierceness of that punch surprised even me. He wore glasses and they went flying as he toppled over, flat on his back on the wood floor of the lifeguard tower. His friend stared at me in horror, and I swear it was like a movie where everything just seemed to stop and hang frozen in time for several seconds. When time started back up again, I grabbed Molly's hand, yanked her to her feet, and we jumped off the side of the tower into the sand. We ran all the way to the bus stop, and it wasn't until we were on the bus, headed for home, that we looked at each other and started to laugh.

I wondered if we would ever be able to laugh over this whole mess, over her time spent in jail.

I supposed that story was another example of what B. J. called my tendency to act first and think later. Right now, thinking and worrying was all I could do, and it was driving me crazy. I needed to *do* something. I kept thinking about what Jeannie had said to me. Use what you know. Boats. Leon Quinn had said that this was all about the gambling boats.

"Mike," I said, sitting up fast and resting my hand on his good knee. "You ever been out on one of those TropiCruz Casino boats?"

"Can't say as I have, but you know, Sey, I enjoy doing a little gambling now and again." He rubbed his chin, pretending like he was deep in thought. "Haven't been to Vegas or Atlantic City in years."

Looking at the goofy expression on his face, I felt my spirits lift for the first time since I'd heard about Molly's arrest. Here was something we could do, some kind of action we could take. "You thinking what I'm thinking?"

He looked at his watch. "I've seen their ads on TV. They sail at 7:30." He slapped Pit on the shoulder with his open palm and said, "You better get moving, little brother. Grab your gear. The dinghy leaves in five minutes."

I cleaned up the sausage and packed a backpack with a camera, notebook, and wallet, while Mike loaded the cooler with the remaining beers back into his dinghy. I changed into a long-sleeved T-shirt and a navy blue zip-front sweatshirt. I knew how cold it could get out on the water. Pit boarded *Gorda* and threw his gear into Mike's dinghy from her afterdeck. In less than ten minutes we were pulling away from the dock and, for once, Abaco wasn't following us along the seawall to the property's edge. I'd rewarded her for her good behavior with a bowl of dry food mixed with chopped sausage bits. She was wolfing it down outside the cottage, her butt in the air and her tail wagging good-bye.

XV.

WE dropped Pit off at *Firestorm* about half an hour later. Even in the dark, thanks to the dock lights, I could see that the boat was every bit as spectacular as Zale had claimed. The night lights from the surrounding marinas reflected off her perfectly fair and fire-engine-red aluminum hull. I hoped Pit would be able to take the boy out for a sail before they left for the Caribbean.

Because it was manatee season, we were not allowed to put Mike's inflatable dinghy up onto a plane and speed our way south to Hollywood. These big marine mammals that weigh more than half a ton come to South Florida in the winter months to try to stay warm. They are bottom grazers, and when they come to the surface to take a breath, the propeller on a dinghy like ours could cause them a fatal injury. Even in daylight, boaters would never see them before they hit them. Now, with only our dim red and green running lights, we would never see them were it not for the lights on the docks at Port Everglades that lit the area bright as day.

When I was a kid, it didn't take all that long to pass through Port Everglades, even at less than five knots, a no-wake speed. The loading docks and piles of shipping containers ran only about a thousand yards south of the inlet and, after that, the wooded banks of the Intra-coastal Waterway were covered with mangroves and tall

Australian pines. Today, with the growth of Southport, the trees were almost all gone, and from the inlet all the way to the Dania Canal, the inland bank was now consumed by passenger terminals, cruise ship docks, and cargo dockage for container ships, all presided over by the looming 150-foot-high gantry cranes that looked to me like the giant walking armored vehicles out of the old *Star Wars* movies.

As we motored south on the Intracoastal, I did my best to fill Mike in on the little I had learned. Mike knew more than I did about the background of the whole Pontus operation—Fort Lauderdale police had been watching him even back when Mike was on the force, he told me. I told Mike about the Pontus family side of things—at least what I knew—and about my conversation with Zale, including his father's mention of this Thompson guy, his inside man.

"I'd really like to find Thompson and talk to him. See who he thinks might have killed Nick. Ask him what he thinks about the new bosses, too."

"Okay. That's the plan, then. Long as it leaves me time to hit the tables," Mike said.

When we got to the TropiCruz dock, I held the dinghy's cable and padlock while Mike walked over to talk to the kid who was handling the valet parking. Just beyond him, I saw a group of protesters standing on either side of the entrance to the parking lot. They were carrying signs and marching back and forth. A Hollywood cop had his cruiser parked on the side of A1A, his emergency lights flashing to slow the traffic as it entered the TropiCruz lot and passed the protesters. He walked over and shook Mike's hand, patting him on the shoulder. Apparently they were friends from the old days.

Mike came back and told me that it would be all right to lock the dinghy up at the end of the gambling boat's dock by the chain-link fence that separated it from Martha's Restaurant. He said the valet kid and the cop would keep an eye on it. When we went over to thank the kid, he asked, "You got coupons?" and he proceeded to tell us that nobody ever paid to go on these trips. The owners expected to make their money off the gambling.

I told Mike to wait a minute, I wanted to go over and see if someone I knew was among the protesters. He wandered over to shoot the breeze with his cop buddy while I walked out to the highway. I searched the group for Kathleen's amber pageboy cut, but she wasn't among the cluster of people shouting at the cars as they turned into the TropiCruz parking lot. In fact, as I neared the group, I saw that their signs were protesting the docking of the big casino gambling boat in their neighborhood. This was an entirely different group of protesters. Kathleen's group was against Pontus building the condo and dock facility, but Pontus didn't even own TropiCruz at this point. It was strange seeing two groups of protesters in my town, but just like the other group in Lauderdale, the common point was "Not in my backyard." Nobody wanted the casino gambling boats in their community.

Just as I was about to turn and leave, I saw her. Not Kathleen, but the older woman with the white hair pulled back on her head. She had already been watching me when I spotted her, and she didn't look away when our eyes met. There was still that strange element of anger or defiance in her face, and I felt there was something very familiar about her.

"Hello?" I said as I walked up to her. "Mrs. Wheeler?" She looked startled that I would know her name. "Did you want to tell me something?"

She swung her head, looking all around her, as though trying to gauge the best escape route. When she came back to face me, she said in a surprisingly strong voice, "You are the tugboat skipper. You were there."

That was when I remembered where I had seen her before. On the seawall, in front of the Downtowner Restaurant, the morning Nick had been shot. She had been there pushing a baby stroller full of clothes.

"Yeah, and you were there, too. I remember you."

"You are a very tall young woman."

"Listen, ma'am. I need to get on that casino boat. It's sailing soon and I don't have much time. If you saw something Monday morning, you've got to tell me."

"You want to talk about the black car."

"You saw the black car?"

"Seychelle!" Mike hollered. "Hurry up. Let's go!"

I turned to the ship and saw Mike standing at the base of the gangway. "Just a minute, Mike," I yelled.

"That boat?" she said. "You're getting on *that boat*?" Her long finger pointed behind me.

I turned to look where she was pointing, and I saw Mike waving his arm through the air motioning for me to come. "Yes," I told her. "I've got to go. But I want to talk to you about what you saw that morning."

When I turned back around, she was ten steps away from me, the crowd closing in around her. I saw her white bun over the tops of their heads, and I realized that she was rather tall, too, but age and probably osteoporosis had her stooped over slightly. "Mrs. Wheeler! I'll find you," I said. "We'll talk again." She didn't turn around.

I trotted across the blacktop parking lot and joined Mike at the base of the gangway. We were greeted by a couple of young twenty-somethings dressed identically in black slacks, white tuxedo shirts, and black bow ties. The woman was petite with straight black hair, and the guy looked like a frat boy. He was the one with the metal detector, and he joked with Mike about almost missing the boat as he wanded us. When he ran it over Mike's legs and the thing began to squeal, I was worried that Mike might be carrying a gun, but he just lifted his pant leg to show the artificial leg, and the young man laughed nervously and waved us through. Off to one side, and wearing a walkie-talkie on his belt and a wire to his ear, stood a tall, thin, once-blond and now balding guy. He looked like he was some kind of head honcho. He wore a blue oxford shirt and a beige tie that matched his pants, giving him an aging preppie look. He paced the dock, checking out all the passengers, and as his chest was almost concave and his posture so hunched forward, he looked like he had to keep moving or else he'd fall on his face. I wondered what his role was, and if he could be Thompson.

The gangway took us into the darkened casino located on the lowest of the three decks. We were directed to climb to the top deck, where the buffet was spread out. As we climbed the stairs, Mike started whistling the theme song from *Gilligan's Island,* and I punched him in the arm and said, "Don't forget why we're here, Gilligan. Remember, my friend Molly's sitting in the Broward County jail."

On the top deck, the crowd was bigger than I expected. The bar was doing excellent business, and the atmosphere was that of a party that hadn't quite started yet. A young guy at an electronic keyboard with a laptop computer on a stand just above it was playing a Jimmy Buffett tune. I wasn't sure which keyboard was producing most of the music. He had a habit that, after five minutes, I was already beginning to find quite annoying: winking, pointing to audience members, and shouting out "Who's yo daddy?" in the middle of a song.

The upper deck had a hardtop cover over the midships section, while aft were tables and chairs out under the stars. Roll-down curtains with cracked and scratched plastic window panels protected the midships area from rain and wind, but no longer provided any visibility. Over the bar and around the musician's stage, they'd hung little strings of Christmas lights, and with the Corona sign over the bar, the decor reminded me of a cheesy Mexican restaurant. If only the food looked that good.

I told Mike about my encounter with Mrs. Wheeler. "Now, I guess she thinks I'm in the enemy camp because I'm patronizing the casino gambling boats."

He'd heard of her. I guess most people who had worked for the county or the city knew about her activism.

"She was always a walker," Mike said. "I don't know how old she is, but I think she's lived in Fort Lauderdale all her life. You know, like back when it was really just a little pioneer town. She used to walk all over town then, and she still does today, some seventy or eighty years later. Now you see her mostly down along the Riverfront. She's always around, watching the river traffic. All the FLPD cops know her."

"She was there, Mike, the morning Nick was shot. I saw her in front of the Downtowner just before it happened. She said she saw the car with the shooter."

"Well, she shouldn't be hard to find. First thing tomorrow. I'll make some calls." Mike's eyes shifted focus and he began staring at something behind me with an amused look on his face.

I turned around to see what had caught his attention. The singer, Mr. "Who's yo daddy?" was in deep conversation with the ship's captain, Richard Hunter. There was no mistaking either that it was Janet's brother Richard—due to the steel wool–covered head—or that he was the captain, due to his dress whites and gold epaulettes. The thing that was making both me and Mike have to cover our mouths lest we burst out laughing was that perched atop that granite dome was an enormous black Stetson. And, Richard was just plugging in a cord to the tail end of a fat and gaudy twelve-string acoustic guitar.

"Ladies and gentlemen," the singer said into the microphone in his best imitation of a smooth-voiced DJ. "We have a treat for you tonight. Before piloting us out to the three-mile limit, Captain Richard Hunter would like to sing a special number just for you, 'You've Got to Fall to Learn to Fly.' Let's have a big round of applause for Captain Hunter!"

His voice actually wasn't half bad, but he tried so hard to get the country twang just right, it was impossible to understand what he was singing. The only words I could make out were "Jesus" and "Lord." Those got repeated pretty often, so I figured I got the gist of it.

The applause was much louder when he finished than when he had begun. The sad part was that Captain Richard didn't seem to get it. He really thought they liked his performance. Most of the folks onboard cared more about gambling than listening to music, especially if the music was reminding them that some considered gambling a sin. They were clapping for the captain to quit singing and take the boat out. It was past 7:45.

Mike and I stood at the rail sipping our beers and watched as the little ship finally pulled away from the dock and the captain spun her around 180 degrees in her own length. A couple of deckhands worked the lower deck fore and aft, and I figured if one of them was Thompson, I wouldn't really have access to him as a passenger. For all I knew, our Thompson could be the ship's engineer. I would definitely have to venture into some off-limits places if I wanted to meet everyone who worked aboard.

"**Hey,** I'm gonna get something to eat," Mike said.

He grabbed a Styrofoam plate and headed right into the buffet line. Now, I have never been on a cruise ship in my life, but I have heard stories, and I have seen cruise ships depicted on television, and this did not resemble anything remotely like those buffets. I didn't think there was anyone on earth less picky about food than me, but Mike, bachelor that he was, proved me wrong. He proceeded to pile on the crusty scalloped potatoes and dry ham, both of which looked as though they had been baking under the heat lamps since the ship's noon excursion. I decided that the sandwich I'd eaten back at the house would hold me over.

While Mike sat out at one of the tables under the stars on the top deck aft, I decided to explore and see if I could make my way to the bridge. I dropped my empty beer cup into a trash bin and headed up the starboard side of the ship. A glass door separated the forward wing decks from the gambling hordes. Stenciled on the glass were the words RESTRICTED AREA—CREW ONLY.

Hell, I figured, what were they going to do? Arrest me? I tried the door. It was unlocked, and I went on through.

I poked my head around the open door to the bridge and saw the familiar figure sitting in the helmsman's seat, a cigarette dangling out of the corner of his mouth, and this time only the cowboy hat was missing.

The boat was steaming straight north on the Intracoastal Waterway toward Port Everglades, and the captain was paying little attention to the helm. He was talking to the attractive woman we had seen earlier when she had been greeting passengers down on the gangplank. She was Asian, perhaps Filipino, and her long black hair flowed down her back to her size-six waist. He reached out and placed his hand on her tight black pants, just under the curve of her buttocks and squeezed. From where I was standing, I saw only her profile, but I could still make out the look of distaste that flitted across her face.

"How'd I do?" he asked her.

"Why do you always have to fish for compliments every time you play?"

He reached for her buttocks again. "Because I'm an artist." He leaned in and nuzzled her neck. "We're needy. Say something nice. Please."

"Excuse me," I said.

They jumped apart, like actors in a bad horror movie, and the captain nearly stumbled as he fell back in his seat, then tried to bounce back out of the chair. "Miss," he said. "This area is off-limits to our guests."

"Yeah, I'm sorry. I saw the sign. But I have a boat myself, and I really wanted to see the bridge." I widened my eyes in feigned delight as I looked at the instruments and gauges above the helm. "Wow, this is really cool. What kind of autopilot system do you have on here?"

"You can't just come barging up here like this," Richard said. When he looked straight at me, I saw the red streaks in the whites of his eyes. His pupils were like black sinkholes.

He might be singing about Jesus, but he had fallen off the straight and narrow tonight.

The stewardess placed a hand in the middle of his chest. "I'll take care of this," she said, turning to me. "Miss, I'll be happy to answer your questions, but," she said as she got a firm grip on my elbow and steered me back to the door to the guests' part of the ship, "our security measures will not permit nonemployees on the bridge, especially when the ship is under way." She was probably six inches shorter than me, her hand more like a child's, but she was solid, strong. I went along with her as she opened the door that led back to the buffet deck, and it was only when she let go of me so I could pass through that I twisted around and took the few steps back to the bridge door.

"Just one more question about your vessel, Captain." When I came around the corner this time, Richard was holding his cell phone to his ear.

He said quietly into the phone, "Hang on a minute, Sis." Then he looked up at me and gave me a look that was probably supposed to put the fear of God—or of not being allowed to gamble—in me. Somehow, though, since he looked like a bleary-eyed, bobblehead version of the father on *The Brady Bunch*, I just couldn't take him as a serious threat. "There is a police boat cruising the port twenty-four hours a day. If you don't get off this deck, I'll have you arrested for trespassing and removed from this vessel."

I didn't know if he could really do that, but clearly he was pissed. I decided it probably wouldn't be wise to test him. Besides, he was standing in front of me, his arms crossed on his chest, the phone under his armpit emitting a tinny-sounding, "Hello? Richard? Hello?"

"Jesus, I just wanted to look around a little. Okay." I lifted my hands in the universal sign of surrender, and when I backed out of the office, I stepped onto the toes of the stewardess, standing right behind me.

"You," he said, pointing a finger at my nose, "should not use the Lord's name in vain." He turned to the petite woman. "Anna, get her outta here."

"Okay, okay," I said. "I just wanted to ask if you knew Nick Pontus, that guy who got killed. I knew his wife when we were kids."

The captain took a step back and eased himself into the helmsman's seat as though he were moving in slow motion. He squinted at me and spoke slowly.

"What are you talking about?"

I tried to keep my voice light, dumb lost tourist that I was. "Yeah, I lived on the same street as his wife when we were kids. We were, like, best friends."

"I've never seen you before," he said. "My sister's never mentioned anyone like you."

"Molly's your sister?" I crinkled the skin between my eyebrows. "I didn't know she had a brother."

He dropped his head backward and sighed loudly up at the overhead. It occurred to me for a moment that his neck might not be strong enough to lift that big head back up again. When his face did rise back into view, his skin was tight and red. His voice seemed to burst out of his mouth.

"You moron! Molly was Nick's *ex*-wife. Now get out of here before I call the— Wait a minute. I know you. You're on that tugboat."

"By the way, Captain. I really liked that song you sang. Did you write that?"

He narrowed his eyes. "Yes," he said, dragging the word out almost like a question.

"So, that was original. The lyrics were very moving. You know, you have a real talent."

He nodded like that was a given. "I'm going to be cutting my first CD soon. Do you think I should include that one?"

Anna stepped around me and said, "Captain, it's getting late."

"Yeah, right. You need to get off the bridge," he said, like he'd just remembered who I was.

When Miss Size Six tried to grab my arm again, I

yanked it out of her grip and said, "I know my way out."

I was still laughing when I sat down next to Mike.

"What so funny?"

I told him my story about my encounter with the captain. "Guy doesn't seem too bright," I said.

Mike massaged his forehead with two fingers. "Remind me to give you a few pointers next time we go out undercover. Like, the first thing you should *not* do is walk into the heart of their operation and announce that you're there. Jumpin' Jehoshaphat, Seychelle, what made you think that was a good idea?"

"Uh, I don't know, Mike." I felt like an idiot. Of course, he was right. Now we had lost the advantage that anonymity might have given us.

"Well, do you think you could go over there to the bar and get us a couple of beers without telling the bartender who you grew up next door to?"

Glad of the chance to get up and do something, I said, "Sure."

WHEN we were passing alongside the Coast Guard station, I told Mike about the captain's eyes, about how Zale had said he was an intermittently reformed alcoholic. We were making our turn to head out through Port Everglades inlet when Mike said, "Thanks a lot. Thanks for waiting until we're on our way out into the Gulf Stream to tell me that the captain is an addict of some sort in addition to being an asshole." He still hadn't forgiven me for my stupidity. I hoped I could make up for it somehow before the night was over. I hated it when Mike was mad at me.

The musician finished playing his rendition of the song "Kung Fu Fighting" and announced, "Ladies and gentlemen, the casino will be opening in approximately twenty minutes." He punched at his computer keyboard then and launched into his version of the Commodores' "Brick House."

"What do you think about TropiCruz's customers?"

"I don't know. I haven't paid much attention."

"Change that," he said.

Mike was right again. I had been looking at the boat, memorizing the layout, mentally marking the doors that were labeled restricted so I could go back later and explore, but there was probably just as much to be learned from the people onboard.

Right off, I decided that the majority could be put into one of two groups—first-timers who had come to celebrate a birthday or an anniversary, and regulars. The first-timers were in couples or groups of couples, dressed in carefully chosen Florida tropical prints—what they thought of as cruising clothes. The regulars weren't dressed up or smiling. They could have been sitting on the train going to work. They sat slouched over, reading the paper or smoking a cigarette, and they were either singles or couples. Regulars did not travel in packs. Their only movement other than smoking or drinking was checking their watches. They knew the timing of the trip out. They knew how long it took to reach the three-mile limit and exactly when the casino would open.

The ship's decks started a slow roll when we cleared the breakwaters and began to feel the swell. Some of the first-timers giggled nervously at the motion, and the younger girls clutched at their boyfriends' or husbands' arms. Mike and I watched as the red and green lights of the pilot boat overtook our little ship and headed out toward an incoming freighter. Once clear of the land, there was a fairly brisk breeze out of the east-southeast, and although the night had seemed almost balmy for

February back at the dock, out here the wind was already trying to freeze-dry my nose.

The music man announced that it was only ten minutes until the casino would open, and all the regulars rose in unison and began shuffling toward the stairs.

"Shall we?" Mike asked, offering me his arm.

I hoped that meant we had made up. I linked my arm in his and we started after the herd. "So, you like gambling?" I asked him.

"Sure, don't you?"

"Never done it. It's never interested me."

"Why, Seychelle Sullivan, do you mean to tell me you're a casino virgin?"

"That I am, Officer."

"Well, we'll just have to bust your cherry on the dice tonight."

"Oh, you do have such a way with words, Mike."

XVI.

I STOOD at Mike's elbow nursing a plain Coke I'd ordered over half an hour ago, shaking my head when Mike ordered his second rum and Coke of the evening. This was going to be a five-hour cruise, and I wanted to stay clearheaded. I'd already goofed up once this evening, and Molly deserved better than that.

No matter how fascinated Mike was with these games, I could neither understand what was going on at the craps table nor enjoy it. Sometimes they gave him more chips and sometimes they took them away, and I think I could have figured it out if I had cared to, but that essential element—*interest*—was missing. My mind kept wandering, thinking about other things that seemed so much more important to me than the little numbers on the dice. I left Mike to his fascination with dice and wandered over to the blackjack table.

Now *this* was a game I could understand. Not that I wanted to play, but at least I could add up the cards and understand why somebody won. The table I was watching had six players sitting on high bar stools, and on the other side the dealer, a dark-skinned black woman nearly as tall as me, stood smiling, making it all look so easy. She stood with perfect posture, her long neck swooping up to the bun perched high on the back of her head. Her nametag read LaShon, and she filled out the white tux-

edo shirt beneath her black bow tie near to bursting.
That may have accounted for the fact that her table was
populated by five men and only one woman, but her
joking manner and helpful attitude made her the sort of
voluptuous woman that other women liked. A rarity, indeed.

All the blackjack dealers had their backs to the center
of the room, and in the middle, the tall thin man with
the walkie-talkie—the one I'd seen earlier on the dock—
wandered from dealer to dealer, watching them. He
glanced upward a couple of times, and I noticed that the
ceiling was polka-dotted with little smoke-colored domes:
the eyes in the sky—video security.

I didn't know if his interest in me stemmed from the
fact that I was watching him and not gambling, or if he
had heard from Captain Richard that I was a person of
interest. But his eyes kept darting my way, then moving
on so that we never really stared into each other's eyes. I
felt like I was always just catching him looking away.

There were only six blackjack tables and one roulette
wheel in the center of that little casino. The two craps
tables were against the outside walls. Windows ran the
length of the port side of the casino, but it was difficult
to see out at night. Through the slats in the miniblinds,
with my face pressed close to the glass, I could see a deck
walkway outside that was off-limits to passengers. The
aft bulkhead inside the casino was lined with slot machines, and in the center of the room, rows of machines
covered all the space not taken up by the gaming tables.
I wandered the floor, checking out the other dealers as
well as LaShon, and I calculated that she was making
about twice as much in tips as the others. I saw over a
hundred dollars in chips go into her kitty in the time I
stood by her table.

After I'd been standing there about forty-five minutes,

observing the game and learning as LaShon gently taught a neophyte lady how to play, one of the players got up and left the table. LaShon invited me to play with a look and a nod toward the empty chair. I shook my head to decline. She shrugged her shoulders, and a man with a belly that reminded me of Maddy's slid into the seat.

My oldest brother is four years older than me, and he would have been in his element on that ship. Maddy *loved* to gamble. Unfortunately, he didn't often win, and his wife, Jane, had grown adamant that if he didn't go to Gamblers Anonymous meetings and stay away from the track, she would divorce him and take their son and daughter with her. I must admit, though—having baby-sat my niece and nephew several times through the years, I tended to think that that might not be such a bad deal.

"Thompson, take a break." I heard a man's deep voice say the name, and it jerked me out of my memories. I swung my head around the room, trying to figure out who had spoken. What with the dinging and clanging of the slots and the strains of pop Muzak on the PA system, it was difficult to tell where the voice had come from. From the corner of my vision I noticed an unusual movement back at the blackjack table, and I turned to look. Dealers don't usually make big movements with their arms. It's all in their hands. LaShon was balancing a covered chip tray on her hip and patting the back of a stocky man with African-American features and skin as light as mine. His white shirt was pulled so tight at the shoulders, I feared LaShon's pats might tear it open. When the man greeted the players at the table, his voice was the same deep bass I had heard earlier. It took several seconds for me to put it together. I'd had my mind so fixed on the Thompson I thought I was looking for, that I had a little trouble shifting gears at first. LaShon *was* Thompson.

She was standing on the far side of the pit area, exchanging a few words with the skinny security chief. They were both tall, so I had little trouble watching them as I wormed my way through the crowd. I wanted to cut LaShon off before she disappeared through one of the off-limits doors. The security chief's shoulders bowed forward and his chest was so concave, his tie seemed to dangle and swing in midair as he stepped from one foot to the other in a nervous little dance. He was clearly talking to LaShon, since no one else was around, but he never once looked right at her. His eyes constantly flitted all over the floor, jumping from one dealer to the next.

"Excuse me, pardon me," I said as I pushed my way around through the onlookers. Though I was on the receiving end of several harsh glances and whispered curse words, I made it to her just as the security man moved off to take up his post by the blackjack tables.

"Miss Thompson?"

She turned round and smiled, and it was genuine. She was in a plastic business, but her friendliness was real. I didn't even know her and I liked her already.

"I'm a friend of Molly Pontus. I'd like to talk to you if you have a minute."

She glanced over my shoulder to where the security guy with his walkie-talkie was, but the look on her face never flickered with concern. Suddenly she laughed and reached out and patted me on the back as though congratulating me on something. As she leaned in close, she said in a barely audible whisper, "Meet me in the top deck ladies' room in five minutes." Then she pulled back, saying aloud, "Nice seeing you again. You take care now," and she turned and disappeared through the door.

I squeezed my way through the crowds back over to where Mike was still standing at the craps table. I felt the eyes of the security chief following me, and when I looked his way once, I saw that he was holding the black walkie-talkie to his mouth and speaking into it. I nudged Mike in the side with my elbow. "Hey, how you doing?"

"Great. I'm up by two hundred."

I tried unsuccessfully to whistle. "Wow, I'm impressed," I said, and I was. I didn't think anybody ever won on these gambling ships.

"Umm-hmm," he said as he watched the dice roll down the felt.

"Mike?"

"Umm-hmm," he said again. He wasn't even really aware that I was standing next to him.

I grabbed hold of his upper arm. "Mike. You've got to listen to me for a minute." He swung his head around, blinked a couple of times, and made a concentrated effort to focus. I got closer and put my mouth next to his ear. "Listen, I've found Thompson."

"Where is he?"

My lips were nearly touching his ear. "Actually, he's a she. I'm going up to the top deck to meet her in a couple of minutes. I just thought you should know."

He made a surprised face, then nodded. "Got it," he said, turning back to his game.

The women's restroom was at the top of the stairs on the left. Before entering, I walked up to the glass door that led to the "off-limits" bridge deck. I cupped my hands to the glass and looked through to see if anyone was outside on the wing decks. Though I could see the glow of the instrument lights around the doorway to the bridge, there was no one in sight on the deck.

I was standing at the sink washing my hands when she came in. There were four stalls and when she glanced at them, I said, "I already checked. There's nobody here."

"Yeah, that's why I chose this head. Top deck's usually empty as long as the casino is open. There are restrooms down there and the gamblers don't want to get too far away from Lady Luck."

"Yeah, it's weird. It's like they're possessed."

"We don't often see people on this ship who aren't afflicted. I notice you haven't played a single nickel."

"Might as well come in here and flush my money down the toilet."

Her laughter danced up and down the musical scale, and it popped into my head that she might do better singing in real casinos than working the tables here. I noticed then that she wore almost no makeup, only a touch of lipstick, and no jewelry save for tiny gold balls in her earlobes. The gold contrasted beautifully with her dark skin. Not that she needed makeup or jewelry. There was a cleanness to her beauty, something that all the cigarette smoke and alcohol and general seediness of the ship could not touch. That was undoubtedly part of what made her so successful at the tables.

"What did you want to see me about?" she asked.

Again, she'd cut clean to the point. I leaned on the sink and looked at her in the mirror. "I've known Molly Pontus since we were kids. Last night they arrested her for Nick's murder."

"I saw that on the news," she said. "I didn't know Molly well, but she always struck me as a decent woman."

I thought that was a good way to put it. Decent. That described Molly, and decent folks weren't guilty of murder.

"Miss Thompson," I started.

"Oh, please, call me LaShon." She waved a hand in the air with a dancer's elegance.

"Okay. I was talking to Molly and Nick's son today, and he told me that you and Nick were good friends, that you really knew the operation on this ship."

She shrugged her shoulders, and the hint of a smile played around her mouth, tucking in the skin beneath her high cheekbones. "Nick found out that I'm a bit of a techie. A geek, really. I grew up messing with computers. I've always got to know how things work."

"Computers? What does that have to do with this ship?"

She threw back her head and sang out that lilting laughter again.

"Are you kidding? Everything, my friend—everything, from the engine room to the bridge, but especially in the casino. This ship runs on computers. What do you think those slots are? They're nothing but video games."

"I guess I hadn't really thought about it. Yeah. I was still thinking of the old one-armed bandits. But they're all electronic now. So what did you do for Nick with your geek skills?"

"He wanted me to give up dealing and work in maintenance. I said to him, 'Are you nuts? For what pittance you pay those guys?' "

"Sounds like Nick would have paid you well as a computer consultant if he wanted you that bad."

"You know, much as I admired him in some ways, Nick Pontus was a cheap SOB. Not like these guys who come aboard, get all liquored up, and then start winning. I can make more in tips than most computer consultants make on salary. And I don't have to worry about getting caught poking around in something somebody don't want known."

I started to ask "Like what?" when we heard footsteps along the outside corridor. We both turned to the sink and started washing our hands as the door to the bathroom swung inward and Miss Size Six from the bridge walked in. She nodded at LaShon before she entered the stall, and LaShon smiled back saying, "Hi,

Anna." The woman's eyes passed right over me as though I did not exist.

LaShon finished drying her hands and left first. I walked out no more than ten seconds after her, but the upper deck was empty. I needed to think without all the noise and smoke from the casino below, but I didn't really want to be standing out there when Anna exited the head so that she could quiz me about what I was doing in there with LaShon. I headed down the stairs.

Two decks down, Mike was still at the craps table. The crowd around the table was three people deep in most places. There was no way I was going to have a quiet conversation with him about my meeting with Thompson. I wandered the casino floor for a while, checking out all the people sitting mesmerized in front of their machines. I watched one guy feed a hundred-dollar bill into a dollar slot machine, and he played it away in a matter of minutes by betting on seven lines at a time. Then he stood up and headed for the cage to get more money.

Similar scenes were being repeated all over the place. For every one person I saw getting a payout, there were a half dozen reaching into their wallets for more money to feed the machines. It did not matter whether they played the nickel machines or the five-dollar machines, the slots ate the money and gave the player a certain number of credits. When people won, the machines played happy music and dinged as credits were added to the readout. Only when someone decided to cash out on a machine did one hear the familiar sound of coins dropping into the pan.

No wonder Nick and Kagan had been fighting over ownership of this casino gambling boat business. It must make millions. And, as with other offshore businesses, there was little if any government regulation or oversight.

Several of the machines up against the wall were dark, broken down. No flashing lights or catchy tunes. I sat on a stool in front of one of the broken slots and looked it over. Buttons and a video screen, just like Thompson said. The thing was a computer. I noticed that the base had a locked access door. That must be for maintenance, to get at its brain.

As I wandered around some more, I noticed one guy playing a quarter machine and he was really up. His credits numbered over six thousand, which by my rough calculation meant he had more than fifteen hundred dollars coming his way. And he was still winning. I sat next to him and watched for a while. After several minutes he turned to look at me.

"Whatcha' lookin' at?" he asked.

I shrugged. "Sorry. Didn't mean to bother you. I'd say good luck, but it looks like you've already got plenty." I hiked my bag up on my shoulder, stood, and moved toward the crowd. I felt him looking at me as I walked away, and I shook my head. The gambling thing was supposed to be entertainment, but people seemed to be uptight both about winning *and* losing. Where was the fun in that?

When I wandered aft, I saw that LaShon was back at her blackjack table, and there was an open seat. She didn't move her head, but her eyes flicked from me to the seat. I sat down, pulled out a twenty-dollar bill for her to change, and unzipped my sweatshirt. It had been so cool out on the upper deck, but down here it was too hot. And stuffy. I wondered if there was something symbolic there, and I smiled. A couple of the men at the other end of the table smiled back at me. Oh boy. This was going to get ugly. I didn't know how to do all the cute little hand signals or what the right lingo was. Everyone at the table would soon know this was my first time.

LaShon was doing something fancy with a stack of chips, counting them by stacking and restacking them, then she slid them across the felt to me. I picked up the stack to look at them and felt something stuck to the bottom of the last chip. I set the chips back down on the table, well aware of the cameras in the ceiling, and began to play, taking the chips off the top of the stack. With help from LaShon and the others at the table, I actually won a couple of hands, but after fifteen minutes, when I was down to my last five chips, I pushed back my chair and said, "I guess I'm not much of a gambler. I'd better cash in or I won't have any lunch money tomorrow." I slid the chips into my sweatshirt pocket and headed over to the craps table.

Mike was throwing the dice. The crowd was thick as ever, and each time Mike threw, they broke out in a chorus of oohs and aahs and, sometimes, boos. The superheated air was thick with cigarette smoke, and I decided to head back up to the top deck. One added benefit of being up there was the scarcity of surveillance cameras.

Once on the upper deck, I walked to the stern and pulled out the tiny circle of paper that had been taped to the bottom of the last chip LaShon had given me. It read "11a.m.—under 17th bridge east." She must have felt nervous about talking to me on the ship. Going any further tonight would probably put her job in jeopardy. I wondered what it was she wanted to tell me.

The wind had picked up since we had first left harbor. I zipped my sweatshirt tight under my chin and pulled the hood up, both to keep my ears warm and to keep those pesky wisps of hair from whipping around my eyes and mouth. There still weren't any swells big enough to rock the little ship, but from where I stood at the corner of the stern, I could look forward along the windward side and there was chop breaking against the hull. We were probably making only two to three knots through the water, headed due south, taking the southeasterly winds on our forward quarter. My guess was that the captain just steamed south for a while, barely making headway into the Gulf Stream, and then when it was nearly time to head in he would turn around and steam north, making it back in a quarter of the time it had taken us to head out. We must be nearing the time to turn around.

I glanced at my watch and saw that we had been out at sea only three hours. It seemed like years. The lights of the buildings along the coast were lovely, but the view was entertaining for only so long. I never would have thought that I could be bored on any boat, but here, if you didn't enjoy the gambling bit, there was nothing else to do. The food was lousy, and I didn't feel like drinking anymore. It was too cold and windy out here and too hot and smoky down below.

I heard a crewman come up the CREW ONLY stairs from the lower deck, and he headed over to the side of the bar, where he helped himself to a cup of coffee from a machine along the side deck. When he had disappeared back below, I walked over to investigate. A warm beverage sounded pretty good about now.

The port-side deck was sectioned off with a rope that held another little CREW ONLY sign. I unsnapped the rope and draped it over the steel bulwark as I'd seen the crewman do. A stack of cardboard coffee cups was wedged in next to the machine, and I helped myself to a paper cup and then to some of the hot black liquid.

The coffee was weak, but the taste mattered less than the heat. There wasn't any sign of cream or sugar, but I didn't care. I stepped to the bulwark and leaned my elbows on the rail. That side of the ship was taking the brunt of the growing southeasterly winds, and I pulled my sleeves down over my hands so that only my fingers poked out and wrapped around the cup.

Far out on the horizon, a white light appeared and then disappeared as a far-off freighter made its way north in the Gulf Stream. The seas were probably higher out there, but I noticed that our ship was beginning to roll more in the swells as well. I wondered how long it would be before some of the gamblers below started feeling the effects and rushing to the bathrooms. Although I almost never got seasick, I imagined it could happen to me down there with all that noise and the smells of smoke and liquor.

I stretched my neck out a little to see if I could see into the windows of the casino below, but the side decks where the crew worked were too wide, and the casino windows were set too far back from the lower deck's railings. While I was extended out there, I heard the sound of footsteps below. Someone was in a hurry, running from somewhere forward and headed aft. Whoever was running was not close enough to the rail for me to see, but when he passed nearly beneath me, I heard a whoosh as though he had got the air knocked out of him, and then I heard a voice say, "What the hell?" I tried to balance on my tiptoes and lean way out over the railing. Another voice, lower and older-sounding, made a shushing noise and then began whispering in sharp, urgent tones. I couldn't make out the whispered words, but I could see a blue-clad arm occasionally gesture outward, and I heard the static crackle of the walkie-talkie.

I set my coffee cup down on the deck, braced my hands on the top of the gunwale, and leaned out as far as I could, trying to see who the security chief was talking to. Though I couldn't recognize the voice from those whispers, it had to be him. I wondered why he had punched the runner. After hearing nothing for several seconds, I wasn't even sure they were still there. They weren't speaking anymore. I held onto the CREW ONLY rope for balance and lifted one foot in an awkward arabesque, stretching out, trying to see what the hell was going on down below.

One minute I had a grin on my face, thinking how foolish I would look if anyone came onto the upper deck and saw me like that, and the next minute the one foot that was on the ground was lifted up and somebody pitched my body over the side.

I didn't have time to react. I remember thinking that it was going to hurt, like when I used to try to do forward flips into the pool, and I would hit my head or shoulders on the concrete coping around the edge. My head was too close to the ship's metal deck that extended out beneath the bulwark, and it was going to crack on that metal, for sure. But it was when my body did that forward flip over the side, when the weight of it hit the end of that rope, that I must have dislocated my shoulder. *That* was what hurt. Somehow, some survival mechanism in my brain made my left hand hold onto that rope with a death grip. Had I fallen overboard straight down the hull into the sea, I probably would have been sucked into the ship's props and been made into bite-sized fish food. I knew that whoever had tipped me over the side had had that in mind. Lucky for me, he didn't stick around to make sure I splashed down.

And now the ship was rolling. The captain must have been making his turn to head back toward the port. I hung with my back against the ship, trying not to look down at the churning black water beneath me. The ship was beam on to the swells, and I found myself alternately dangling out over the sea, and then slamming my back into the ship as she rolled in the other direction. I tried to reach up with my right hand to get another hand on the rope, but the movement made something grind in my shoulder, and I cried out in pain.

My head was at deck level on the upper deck while my feet dangled in the opening over the lower bulwarks on the next deck down. I didn't know if the men whose voices I'd heard were still down there, astonished at the sight of the dangling legs that had just appeared, or if they had gone before I'd been attacked. Maybe someone from inside the casino would see my legs and call for help. There were windows that I'd looked out from inside the casino down there, but I'd had to part the blinds that stretched across the glass. Besides, it was brightly lit in there and dark out here—and the slots zombies never looked out the windows.

The pain in my shoulder was so intense I was whimpering. Although the ship had turned so that I was no longer on the windward side, she had picked up speed and I could feel the wind blow the tears back from my eyes across the tight skin of my cheeks.

I was going to fall. I couldn't hold on much longer. Maybe, just maybe, if I timed it right and let go when the ship was rolling to starboard, maybe I would slide inside the bulwark and fall to the deck. I knew I couldn't risk it. Most of my body was too high up, on the outside of the ship. If only I could get lower so that I could get my feet and legs inside the bulwark. And I wasn't sure how long that silly rope was going to hold out supporting all my weight.

The next time the ship rolled, I used my free arm to shift my position, turning me around so that my body faced the ship. The sides of the upper deck had a big pipe welded along the outside, and the large round edge was impossible to grip. I reached out for something to grab onto aft. There was nothing. Not on the bulwark or the deck, nothing small enough for me to get a good grip on, nothing that I could use to pull myself up. Then I noticed about three feet aft a long rectangle of steel plate sticking out about eight inches from the underside of the top deck. The plate was a half inch thick, and in the end was a hole with a shackle attached. I remembered it was what they had used as a derrick back at the dock when they had attached a block and tackle to it to hoist the gangway off the ship. If I could get my right hand on that, it was lower than the rope, and I could probably ease myself down onto the next deck below. I reached my right arm out and the beam was at least a foot from the end of my fingers.

Damn.

I felt the rope slip a fraction of an inch through my fist. I tried to tighten my grip, but the pain from the shoulder was making me wonder if that arm and hand were even attached to my body. It felt as though I no longer had control of my left arm, and since it was the only thing that was keeping me out of the ship's wake, the thought sent a wave of nausea through my gut.

Great, I thought. Never been seasick in my life, and now I'm feeling queasy.

The ship rolled again and my body banged against the side, my chest and face now swinging into the steel deck and bulwarks. The half round of the pipe welded onto the edge of the deck hit my sternum. Now that I was facing the ship, I could use my free arm to try to slow my body as it swung against the topsides. But I was quickly tiring that arm and using up what little strength I had left.

I looked back at the piece of steel plate protruding just below the deck, a little over three feet aft of where I was hanging. I might be able to reach it if I could swing, get up some momentum, then let go of the rope and hope that my good right arm could grab hold of that piece of steel. With each roll of the boat, I wasted more energy just trying not to get hurt. If I was going to go, it better be now.

I swung my legs to the left, then threw them back to the right, and my body started to swing. The rope slipped through my hand another inch, and I could feel the cold steel of the snatch hook against my palm. I thought, *I'm at the end of my rope.* Then: Right, Sullivan, great comedic timing.

I grunted with effort as, once more, I swung my legs up toward the bow and then back toward the stern. Momentum started to build, and the zipper on the front of my sweatshirt screeched as my chest scraped across the metal pipe. When the ship rolled and my torso swung free over the water, the arc of my swing increased, free of the resistance of the ship.

The time to go for it was when the ship was starting to roll back to starboard, when my body was dangling free of the ship, but the momentum of the ship's roll was carrying me back toward the ship, not throwing me free. I heard my own voice making an animal-like sound, and as the ship rolled again and I threw my legs into the aft swing, I let go of the rope.

My fingers hit the metal post, and I felt the cold round bar of the shackle, the hard curves of the welded corners, and the slick wet surface of the metal as my fingers slipped across the steel plate, unable to get a grip. I was falling.

XVII.

MY mother was slapping my face. Not hard, mind you, she was just trying to bring me around, out of the near-unconscious state I was in after my belly flop into the New River. I was seven years old, and my mother had taken Molly and me upriver from our Shady Banks neighborhood to a spot she remembered from her own childhood. My mother went first, jumping out of the tree and swinging out from the bank of the river, clutching the knotted brown rope, screeching with joyous laughter, and I wanted to show her that I, too, could be that brave and beautiful. My fear made me hold onto the rope too long. My legs swung out until my body was parallel to the water, and I fell flat. The wind whooshed out of me and I inhaled water and sank like the skinny seven-year-old I was. The next thing I knew I was in the dinghy coughing up water and my mother was gently slapping my cheeks on either side, saying, "Honey, you're okay. Just breathe."

I shook my head to try to get her to stop slapping at my cheeks like that.

"Seychelle, wake up, darlin'," said a voice that definitely wasn't my mother's.

With effort, I pulled my eyelids apart and saw Mike's face leaning over me. My head exploded with bright white pain, and I closed my eyes again. At least he'd stopped patting my cheeks.

"Shit." I felt my forehead and my fingers came away sticky with blood. "What happened?"

"That's what I'm asking *you*. I was on a hell of a winning streak in there when I heard a thud, looked out through the blinds, and saw you crumpled in a heap on the deck out here."

One of my legs was bent under me, and I tried to straighten it out so I could sit up. The movement fired up a wave of pain down the right side of my body. I slid my T-shirt up and saw the makings of a whopper bruise on my side, just below my ribs. That explained where I hit the bulwark.

I remembered my hand on that iron post, how I had tried with all my strength to get a grip, to hold on, and how it had stopped my fall long enough for my legs to swing inboard. But as my fingers slid free, I fell and must have caught the upper rail right at my waist. The cut on my head was a mystery to me. I didn't remember anything past the moment where I knew my legs were inboard and I wasn't going over. I must have cracked my head a good one on the bulwarks or a stanchion. Under the cut, a nice lump was rising.

"You don't remember anything, Sey?"

"No. I mean, yeah, I do, but I don't know much."

"Well, spit it out, girl."

"There's not much to tell." I readjusted my legs, feeling the length of them with my hands and wiggling my toes, making sure nothing was broken. It was when I tried to lift my left arm that the pain in my shoulder tripled, causing me to cry out.

Mike seemed to care more about the story than my health. "Let me decide that. Talk."

"I was on the deck up there," I said, pointing with my good arm overhead, "and I heard someone running down here on this deck. Then I heard an argument. I think it was that guy in the blue shirt, the security guy with the walkie-talkie. I remember leaning over the rail, trying to hear what was going on, and the next thing I knew I was being pushed ass over teakettle."

"Why the hell would somebody try to push you overboard? What the hell you been doing while I was at the tables?"

"Nothing. Just talking to people."

"Whatever it was you said appears to be something somebody thinks is worth killing for."

I shrugged and then whimpered a little.

"You're damn lucky you didn't end up in the drink. How'd that happen, anyways?"

I tried to laugh but it came out more like a cough. "Just lucky."

Mike stood up, walked around behind me, and felt my shoulder. "Looks like this might need a bit of help." He placed one hand on the back of my shoulder and grabbed the top of my shoulder with the other. "This might hurt a bit," he said, and then he did something that caused another explosion in my head.

"Shit!" I cried out.

"Try moving it now," he said. To my amazement, it hardly hurt. Mike reached down for my good arm and helped me stand. "Let's get you inside, in plain view of a crowd of people until this friggin' ship gets back to port. You've probably got a concussion, a dislocated shoulder, and maybe a couple of broken ribs. You hungry?"

Only Mike, a guy who is missing one leg from the knee down, could make my injuries seem so slight. In fact, food sounded good to me, not only because I really hadn't eaten much all day, but because I had this hollow, shaky feeling in my gut, and I hoped food would settle me down.

We retraced Mike's steps to the empty top deck and then down the interior staircase into the casino, so that no one would see us passing through doors we didn't have permission to use. I stopped in the ladies' room, cleaned the blood off my face, and had a good look at my bruises. My waist, hip, and upper thigh were going to show some serious black and blue. My body was so sore down the right side that I walked with a faint limp as I joined Mike, and we went back inside. The face of the security chief as he turned to look at us registered neither shock nor surprise. He either didn't know anything about what had happened to me or he was very good at not showing it.

WHEN the *TropiCruz IV* returned to the dock in Dania, Mike's dinghy was just as we had left it. We didn't talk much as we untied it and climbed in for the ride back to my place. It was only when we made the turn at the mouth of the New River that Mike asked me, "So, other than nearly getting yourself killed, what else happened on the boat tonight?"

I sighed and shoved my hands deeper in the pockets of my sweatshirt. Sitting on the pontoon side of the boat, the cold bow wave licking dangerously close to my backside, I felt a bone-deep chill inside me. "I screwed up tonight," I said.

"Well, you could say that. Then again, *almost* getting yourself killed is way better than *getting* yourself killed. It's one of those cup half full or half empty things."

"Yeah, but I'm not sure I'm any closer to knowing who killed Nick."

"Tell me about this Thompson person."

I told him about discovering that Thompson was the gorgeous blackjack dealer, about meeting her in the women's head and then getting interrupted.

"Mike, what am I gonna do? I'm not a cop. I don't know what the hell I'm doing. It seems all I do is make things worse. Molly is sitting over there in that stinking jail, and the cops have stopped trying to find out who really killed Nick. I'm all she's got right now, and I'm out here screwing up."

"Hey, you and Molly aren't alone. And you're not the only one in the screw-up department, either. I was supposed to be helping you, and instead, once I started winning, I forgot all about you. I've got my own apologies to make."

I tried to laugh and it came out more like a snort. "Listen to us."

"We sound like a couple of whiners."

"Yup," I said.

"So what should I do about what happened out there tonight? Should I tell these detectives?"

"You can tell 'em, but don't expect them to do anything about it."

"What do you mean?"

"Sey, you've got no evidence. Why the hell do you think I didn't call the cops back there when the boat got to the dock? It's a pretty wild story, you've got to admit. Somebody tried to push you overboard? And you don't even know why?"

After that, I didn't tell him about my appointment to meet Thompson the next day. At that point in the conversation we had just pulled up to the dock in front of *Gorda* and my cottage. I kissed Mike on the cheek and thanked him for going with me, told him I didn't need any doctors to check me over. In some ways it felt like he was being too easy on me—making excuses for me. And I wasn't even sure *he* believed my story. I really needed to do something right to show him that I wasn't a total bumbling idiot.

XVIII.

THOMPSON'S note had said 11:00 a.m. It was now 11:15—and there was still no sign of her. I was sitting on a concrete bench under a white gazebo-style roof beneath the high ramparts of the Seventeenth Street Bridge. The bench was hard and the cold passed through my jeans with little problem. It was warm out in the sunlight, but here in the shade, my ass was freezing.

Numbness could be a good thing considering the way my body had felt when I had rolled out of bed this morning. I hadn't slept much at all, both from the pain and from my jumpiness. Every time the wind blew a branch against my cottage or I heard some noise I couldn't identify, I jumped. That happens when somebody tries to kill you. And every time my body tensed, the pain increased. The bump on the head wasn't bothering me nearly as much as the bruising down my right side and my sore ribs. I thought about lying down on the bench and pressing the cold concrete against my side.

This little park had been put up when they built the new, higher Seventeenth Street Bridge with a fifty-foot clearance, thinking this would allow more yachts to pass under the closed drawbridge and decrease the number of times it had to open. What the city fathers hadn't planned on was the way the yachts would grow—bigger masts, higher decks, greater numbers. Today the citizenry seemed to spend just as much time sitting in their over-heating cars waiting for the yachts of the rich and famous to pass through the open span.

Across the way, one of the bigger harbor tugs nudged a freighter into her berth in Port Everglades, and the small VHF radio I wore in a holster on my belt crackled to life as a fisherman hailed his buddy on the hailing frequency. Most of the big freighter traffic now went down to Southport, where they off-loaded the containers, but ships with bulk loads of concrete or the like still berthed in Midport, between the two cruise ship docks. Many of the smaller container ships that serviced the Caribbean Islands also still docked there, too. These weren't the gigantic boxy-looking steel monstrosities that had given up all pretense of maritime beauty. They were smaller, older ships with exotic names like *El Morro* and *El Junke,* and some of them had been docking at this port since those days, way back when, when my father used to lift me in his arms, pointing out the offices of Port Everglades Towing as we motored past in *Gorda.*

Small-boat traffic was heavy even for a Saturday morning, mostly small open fishing boats loaded with guys playing hooky from wives and weekend chores. I figured the weather made them do it. It was one of those clear February mornings where the sunlight prettied up the port and made Lauderdale look like she was wearing a blue sequined dress.

It was the weekend—already. Nick was shot on Monday morning, and here it was Saturday, and whoever *really* shot Nick was growing safer and safer with each passing day. Molly, meanwhile, was starting day number three in the county jail.

Along the seawall in front of where I sat, a bright yellow Water Bus pulled up and disgorged a young tourist couple who had apparently taken the best form of public transportation down to Bahia Mar and walked across to the beach for a morning swim. As they walked past me, towels draped over their shoulders, I heard them speaking German—and then it made sense. European tourists and French Canadians were about the only ones who would go in the water here in winter.

"Good morning."

I turned around and saw Thompson climbing the steps to the gazebo. "Sorry I'm late." She squinted her eyes in the bright morning sunlight. "I get lazy on my days off. Got on the computer this morning and lost track of time. When I realized how late it was, I dropped everything and trotted right over." When she'd settled on the concrete bench, she took a closer look at the lump on my head just at my hairline. "What happened to you?"

"It's a long story," I said. She was wearing loose-fitting gray stretch pants and a simple black long-sleeved top. The thin straps of a tiny backpack looped over her shoulders. The clothes were not meant to be provocative, but there was nothing this girl could do to hide her curves. The fur-lined moccasins on her feet looked more like slippers. "You live close by?"

She nodded and pointed behind the little park to the slightly run-down three-story brick-and-glass hotel overlooking the small marina and the port. "Right there. A couple of years ago when my gramma died, Nick offered to rent me a room there for a really good price. It suits me and I've just stayed. I like watching the ships out my window, the sea air." The corners of her mouth turned up, and those huge brown eyes sparkled with humor. "Even us geeks like to get outside, sometimes."

I patted the bench next to me. "Have a seat."

"Do you mind if we head over to the other side of the park?"

"No, I don't care," I said, although in truth, I didn't feel like getting up and walking anywhere.

"Good. The Pontus offices are right over there," she said, indicating the large parking lot behind us, "and I don't think we should be seen talking together."

She led the way to the matching gazebo at the opposite end of the deserted park. On the other side of the chain-link fence that bordered the park, I could see the maintenance facilities for the Pier Sixty-six Hotel and Marina. If her goal was to find a secluded place where we wouldn't be seen or heard, she'd picked a pretty good spot.

I turned off the radio on my waistband as I sat down. For people who don't live in the world of boats, it's too difficult to hold a conversation over the constant chatter on channel 16. I tried to monitor the radio most of the time on the odd chance I'd pick up a job, but right now Molly took priority.

"So you live in the hotel that the company plans to tear down?"

"Yeah. This place is about the cheapest thing you'll find on this side of the Intracoastal, and it's still never full. Well, look at it." She lifted her hands palms up as though offering me the hotel. "It's a place not even a mama could love. And the marina?" She exhaled with disgust.

LaShon was right. The marina was even worse than the hotel. The concrete walkways were riddled with wide cracks, and weedy grass grew out of most of them. Rust stains trailed down the seawall where iron fittings had turned to corroded knobs of flaking metal. Some of the pilings had been replaced, but others were so eaten away at the waterline that they narrowed to half their original diameter. I'd picked up tows in that marina before, and I was always leery of tying my tug up to their docks. None of it looked very secure. The current marina tenants were typical of their clientele. There was a rust-bucket schooner that belonged to some missionary group, a research vessel of dubious origins whose owners were probably more interested in treasure hunting than in any real research, and somebody's brilliant idea of a new and faster way to get tourists to the Bahamas—a hydroplane vessel that broke down on its third trip, rolled so badly in the Gulf Stream that all the passengers puked their guts out, and it hadn't moved since.

"How's Molly doing?" she asked.

"I don't really know. I haven't been to see her. I do plan on going this afternoon, though."

"She's no killer."

"Of course not. But *who* then? It's just too easy to laugh and say the guy was an asshole and everybody wanted him dead. Somebody must know something, but the cops have stopped looking, stopped asking. That's why I wanted to talk to you. I'm trying to come up with something I can take to them. I thought if I talked to people Nick was close to, I might come up with something that would interest them."

She tucked her hands under her thighs and rocked back and forth for several seconds, staring up at the huge concrete buttresses on the underside of the bridge.

"This can't get back to anybody at TropiCruz. Not what I'm about to tell you, not even that we talked."

"I understand."

"No, that's not good enough," she said. "You've got to promise me."

I tried to suppress my smile. It reminded me of something Molly and I might have said as kids. There was something about LaShon Thompson that was at the same time both streetwise and sweet. "I promise, then. Not a word to anyone."

"Okay." She slapped her palms on her thighs and exhaled. "I started working on the boat about three years ago. I keep my eyes open, but I don't say much. Around a year ago, I noticed that they changed maintenance companies for the machines. The tech guys come in all the time and fix the ones that have broken down. Like I was telling you last night, they're all computers. I got on the Internet and did a little research. Have you ever heard the term 'loose slots'?"

"Yeah. My brother Maddy has said that. I don't really know what it means, though."

"Gamblers use that term to mean a machine that pays off more often. Some people will tell you that it's purely gamblers' superstition, but it isn't. The casinos can and do program their machines to pay off a given percentage of the time. They can even set how often it will pay off the big jackpots. Video slots have chips in them that are programmed to select what will appear in the window. They're called random number generators, and they basically use an algorithm to select a series of numbers in a fraction of a second, and these numbers are used to designate—"

"Whoa. You can stop with that kind of stuff right there. I'll take your word for it that they can do it. The *why* part I'm not going to understand. Math and computers are not my thing."

"All right. Well, on top of the new tech guys, I also noticed that some of our regulars started winning on the slots. Now, we've got lots of regulars. They don't dress up or make a party out of going out on the boat. They're just there to gamble. A lot of them are older people, retirees, and some are just addicts. I'm used to watching these people gamble away everything they've got. When they do win, they just stay at it until they throw it all away again. Some of these folks have been getting lucky lately. I'm talking big-time lucky. Like a couple of thirty-thousand-dollar jackpots a week. Lots of smaller ones, too, where they might be going home with ten grand or so."

"When did this start?"

"It's hard to say, exactly. I might not have noticed it right off. I know it's been happening for about six months, probably longer. I'd say it's a group of maybe ten regulars who are winning way more than average. You do the math and these folks have made several hundred grand each, and yet they aren't dressing any better, they aren't driving flashy cars. But here's the thing that makes me sure it's a fix. I told you that Nick had hired this new tech crew. Well, sometimes I'd get to the boat early for my shift and I'd notice them working on certain machines. Then those were the machines that paid off that night. They must be swapping out the computer chips on certain machines, switching it around like, so it doesn't look like the same machines are paying out all the time.

"Everybody who works in casinos knows that really the only way to cheat them is to work with a customer. We get searched at the end of every shift. We can't take any money out with us. And to tell you the truth, I think security's got to be in on this, too. If I noticed it, they've got to have noticed it."

"That skinny guy with the walkie-talkie. Is he the head of security?"

"Yeah, that's Sarnov."

"That sounds Russian."

"Yeah, he is—a nasty, mean Russian."

"How so?"

"He's a sadist. He really likes to hurt people—I mean *really* likes it. Sometimes he just hits people for the fun of it."

"I think I saw—or heard that last night." I told her about what I'd witnessed from the top deck.

"Yeah. Sounds like Sarnov," she said.

I wanted to ask her if she thought he was capable of tossing someone overboard, but I really didn't think he would have had time to get from the lower to the upper deck in time to lift me over.

"LaShon, back to this slots thing. How long ago did Nick sell TropiCruz? Was it before or after this business with the slot machines started?"

"Like I said, I can only tell you when I noticed it. That was after Nick sold the business. It could have been going on before, I'm not sure."

"Okay, so the security chief is part of the Russian group. Why would the Russians be stealing from themselves? That doesn't make any sense."

"It might. When Nick sold out to them, he remained a partner. He was supposed to be getting ten percent of the business."

"So he wouldn't be getting his ten percent of what's going out the door through this little scam. How much do you think it is? You mentioned hundreds of thousands?"

She nodded. "Altogether? It's been more than a million since I started noticing it. Maybe two. There are lots of people involved in the scam, lots of partners, but the payoff has been pretty good, too."

"Maybe Nick found out that Kagan was ripping him off. Maybe he was threatening to do something about it and they had him killed."

She nodded. "That's what I was thinking. That's why I wanted to talk to you."

"LaShon, you've got to tell this to the police."

She put her hands up in front of her like she was trying to ward off evil spirits. "Oh no. Not me. I said that's why I wanted to talk to you. You can tell the police."

"But it's not the same if I tell them that I heard this from somebody. They are going to want to know who said what, and who saw what. They'll want to talk to you."

"Un-uhn. No cops."

The constant low hum of the outboard traffic on the Intracoastal Waterway was interrupted by the deep rumbling of a larger ship's engines. LaShon had been sitting with her back to the port, but now she turned as she saw the look on my face. The *TropiCruz IV* was about a thousand yards from us, using her bow thrusters to pivot the ship in front of the hotel's marina. The way the ship was angled now, beam on to the Seventeenth Street Bridge, I could see the captain through the open door to the bridge. The big head with its crown of tightly curled hair was unmistakable.

LaShon whipped around and ducked her head into her hands. She slid sideways so one of the concrete pillars that held up the gazebo would shield her from the ship's view. "This can't be happening," she said. "Do you think they can see us?"

I didn't see any reason why I should hide, so I watched the boat as she turned. "I don't see anybody looking this way," I said. The keyboard man on the upper deck was talking to the crowd, but I couldn't quite make out the words. He was probably telling them about the new facility Pontus Enterprises planned to build on the site, and that someday the ship would be docking there. "I think we're okay. They're looking at the site of the new TropiCruz docks—not at us."

The ship had made her turn and was lined up to head back toward the harbor entrance, her stern facing us. LaShon slid sideways and peered around the concrete column, and at that moment, a familiar figure stepped out onto the wing deck and lifted binoculars to his eyes. The glasses were pointed aft, trained on us.

She didn't notice him right away. "LaShon, I think I spoke too soon. Look up at the bridge deck."

She slid back behind her column with a soft moan and leaned her head back against the concrete, eyes closed.

Richard Hunter had stepped back to the helm, and the water at the stern of the ship began to foam and churn as her screws bit hard. Within a couple of minutes, during which we did not speak, the *TropiCruz IV* disappeared around the corner, out the harbor entrance, cruising to her post at the three-mile limit, where the casino would open.

LaShon was the first to speak. "It was good while it lasted."

"What do you mean?"

"I can't go back to the ship. Not now."

"You're sure he saw you?"

"No, but I can't take a chance. Not with these guys— these new owners. They don't play well with others."

"But the captain, he's Nick's brother-in-law. Are you sure he'd tell them?"

" 'Bout the only thing I am sure of concerning Captain Hunter is that the man'd do just about anything for cash. He has this crazy idea that he's gonna cut a CD with those wack country songs of his and get famous. If he thinks this information can be sold, he'll do it. In a heartbeat."

"If that's the case, you may not even be safe back in your room. Captain Hunter could be on his cell phone right now."

LaShon peeled off her backpack purse, unzipped the top, and pulled out her own cell phone. Her hands were shaking as she started to dial a number.

I put my hand on hers to stop her dialing. "These guys really scare you, don't they?"

"I haven't told you the half of it," she said.

"Who are you calling?"

"My sister. I figure I can stay there for a few days till I figure out what to do next."

"And how hard would it be to find you there? Do you really want to put her in danger?"

She snapped the phone closed and looked away from me. A large catamaran with a tall mast was circling on the south side, waiting for the bridge to open on the hour. "I grew up in a kinda' rough neighborhood," she said. "But nobody I ever met back home was near as cold-hearted as these guys. There isn't much that scares me." She lifted her head and met my eyes. "But these guys do."

I took the phone from her hands and dug around in the side pocket of my shoulder bag for the card Detective Amoretti had given to me. "Like it or not, LaShon, we're calling the cops."

AMORETTI pulled up in his red Corvette, parked in one of the metered spots, but didn't put any money into the machine. I revised my mental list of cop characteristics—cops speed and they park illegally. Today his outfit looked more like yachts than golf—navy Dockers, crisp white linen shirt, and soft Timberland boat shoes.

"What happened to you?" he asked when he saw the lump on my head.

"On the TropiCruz boat last night—I took the phrase 'hit the deck' a little too seriously."

LaShon stood up to shake his hand when I introduced her to the detective, and with her back defiantly straight and her impressive breasts thrust forward, Amoretti was flashing his too-perfect teeth and stammering incoherently as he pumped her hand. What was it about short men that they were always attracted to tall women? Was it something about nipples at eye level? Wanting to bury their heads at their mothers' breasts?

"Detective Amoretti," I said, interrupting him, trying to save him from making an idiot of himself, but as usual I was too late. "We want to talk to you about the TropiCruz gambling boats."

He swung his head around and fixed those pale blue eyes on me. "I'm listening."

"LaShon here works on the *TropiCruz IV*. Blackjack dealer."

He nodded. "Hey, look. There's nothing I would like more than to figure out a way to nail those bastards for something. But we can't touch them. We don't license or regulate them. The Coast Guard inspects the boats for safety, and they have to tell the Feds how much money they make—they're supposed to report any cash over ten thousand dollars they bring back into our waters—and that's it." He laughed. "It's the fucking honor system."

"What if we could come up with the details about how they're rigging the slots," I said.

"It still does me no good, sweetheart. I'm not allowed to investigate what goes on offshore in international waters."

"But you are allowed to investigate a local murder, right?"

He nodded.

"And what if we could show you that it was this particular scheme that got Nick Pontus killed?"

"Now you've got my attention."

As LaShon started explaining what I found to be mind-numbing details about chips and random number generators, Detective Amoretti sat down on the stone bench next to her and asked her pointed questions, as though he understood what the hell she was talking about. I stood, walked to the far side of the gazebo, and watched the boat traffic on the Intracoastal. Sitting too long had made my body stiffen up. I pressed the knot on my head to see if it still hurt. It did. Then I raised my arms over my head and tried to swing from side to side, stretching all those knotted, hurting places. I might not have broken any ribs, but bruised ribs hurt almost as much.

The more I tried to help, the more I seemed to screw things up. What had I done to LaShon? I'd asked her help and ended up by causing her to lose her job at the very least. Worse, I may have put her life in danger. What could I do to salvage this situation, I wondered.

In spite of the noise from the various engines, I could make out the sound of shouting and chanting coming from the direction of the Pontus offices. I figured Kathleen and her cohorts must be at it again. I looked back at Amoretti and LaShon. It was as though they were foreigners, people who spoke a rare language, and they had each just found a new compatriot.

"Hey, guys, seeing as I really don't have anything to add to this conversation at this point, I think I'm going to take off. Detective Amoretti, there's something you need to know. The captain of the *TropiCruz IV* saw us talking here earlier. I guess he brought the ship up here to show the location of their planned new docks and condo towers to his passengers. Anyway, the guy's a rat-bag, and while I don't really think he's dangerous, he would sell his grandmother for cash if he could. I don't think she should go back to her place alone."

"Don't worry. It sounds like this could be a break in the Pontus case. We don't want anything to happen to our new witness here. She'll be safe in my hands," he said.

Now, I expected the leer on Amoretti's face, but I hadn't expected to see LaShon return the look.

XIX.

B EFORE heading back to the dock where I'd tied up the Whaler, I walked over to check out the group making the racket in front of Pontus Enterprises. I needed to see a woman about a car. As I crossed the asphalt parking lot, I pulled a baseball cap out of my shoulder bag. I was tired of the questions about my head. I scanned the crowd, looking for her white hair. The protesters looked as though they were better organized this morning. Their signs were no longer hand-painted, but rather printed, and they were marching around in a circle chanting singsong rhymes about the evil developers. Something was missing, though. They lacked enthusiasm. As I approached, I noticed Kathleen standing off to one side, one foot slightly ahead of the other, her arms crossed over her chest. She leaned back and watched the group through slitted eyes.

"Morning," I said.

She glanced at me and bobbed her head in reply.

"They just don't seem very threatening," I said. This morning's group was made up of a majority of elderly women.

Kathleen opened her mouth, held her hands up in front of her face, then dropped them, crossed her arms, and closed her mouth.

"I don't know what it is, either," I said.

"I do."

"What is it?"

"It's Mrs. Wheeler."

"What do you mean?"

"See that blue minivan over there? She's sitting in a beach chair on the other side, in the shade of that little tree, resting. When she's here with them, she pumps them up, she makes them care. Walter," she said, pointing to an elderly man wearing white pants, a pink golf shirt, and white shoes and walking around the perimeter with the aid of a wood-and-brass cane, "is doing the best he can, but he yells at them. They're afraid of him. He's got a bit of a temper problem."

I looked at the man, his body bent in the shape of a letter C, and tried to imagine how anyone could be afraid of him. "What happened to Mrs. Wheeler?"

"This morning she was here, getting them all worked up, then she stumbled. I caught her before she hit the ground, thank God. The woman's almost ninety. We're all worried about her."

"I really need to speak to her."

She bit her lower lip. "Be careful. Please. She's an incredibly tough old bird, but," she paused, "well, just watch her. We need her, too."

When I came around the back end of the minivan, I saw her sitting upright, eyes closed, in a beach chair set up on a small patch of weedy grass. Her hair was pulled back in a bun, as usual, and she was wearing her white blouse and red shawl. The outline of her bony knees showed through the dark fabric of her skirt, and I noticed that what I once thought was dirt on her ankles was really skin darkened by masses of spidery blue veins beneath the thin, papery surface.

Just as I was about to speak, her eyes opened. "It's you," she said.

I sat on the curb next to her chair. "Hi. Are you feeling all right?"

She raised a hand and waved it in the air as though she were shooing away mosquitoes. "Child, do you know how old I am?"

"Not exactly."

"I was born in Lemon City in 1915." She closed her eyes and her whole body seemed to soften like melting butter as she looked at whatever she was seeing behind those lidded eyes. "Daddy brought us up here to Fort Lauderdale in '20." Her eyelids slid up slowly, and she looked past me out toward the Intracoastal, where the rumbling engines of several big Cigarette-style speedboats echoed beneath the concrete ramparts of the Seventeenth Street Bridge. One corner of her mouth turned up a little. "Wish you could have seen our river back then, dear. My best friend and I would sometimes swim in the evenings, then sit outside on the porch and watch the manatees."

I could picture them in my mind, two little girls playing on the river. That wasn't much of a stretch for me. It was something I could easily dredge up out of my own memories.

"I been through hurricanes, floods, drought, buried a husband, and lost a daughter. A little stumble isn't going to hurt me."

"Yes, ma'am, I can see that. I really came over here because I wanted to ask you about what you said the other night, by the boat. You told me you saw a car that morning, down by the river."

She nodded and rubbed a heavily veined hand across her forehead as though erasing the old pictures of the river and making room for the new scene called up from more recent times.

"Front of the courthouse and jail," she said, "on that

road runs along the river. Black car. A man just sitting there with his automobile engine running. Then that fishing boat come round the bend and he took off, passed right by me."

"You saw him? The driver?"

She closed her eyes again and bobbed her head once in assent. "I saw him, but I was mostly watching you. I've been watching you on that river for years. Since you worked with your daddy. You always reminded me of her."

I opened my mouth to say something, but nothing came out. What was she saying?

That was when all hell broke loose. I heard the shouting first. Standing to try to see beyond the minivan, I was nearly bowled over when Kathleen Ginestra came careening around the vehicle.

"Come on. I need help," she said between panting breaths.

I followed her around the van and was surprised to see the white-haired ladies now in a tight knot, like kids round a schoolyard fight. We shoved our way through the cheering crowd and there in the middle were Walter and Leon Quinn. Leon was doubled over at the waist, taking quite a beating from the brass-tipped end of the old guy's cane.

Reaching into the mess, I tried to grab the cane, but the old guy was quick and I took a good blow across the back of my knuckles. It stung like hell, and I wasn't about to get any more bruises on my poor body.

Walter must have been in his eighties, but the filthy language coming out of his mouth was enough to make a sailor like me blush.

"Hold it!" I shouted with all the lung power I could muster, and I took another glancing blow across my forearm. This guy was really making me mad.

Leon Quinn was twice the man's size and half his age. I could see from the look in his eyes that the big Greek was afraid of hurting the older man if he did anything more than just defend himself. Clearly he was thinking what the headlines would look like if he gave the old geezer what he deserved.

I heard the *swoop, swoop* sound of a siren as two FLPD squad cars pulled into the parking lot. Roma must have called 911 when she saw her boss getting caned by one of the protesters. When I heard the screech of tires and the sound of the doors popping open on the cars, I started to back out of the crowd.

Leon escaped Walter's grasp and hurried to my side. "What is wrong with these Americans? They get old and they go crazy! Did you see him? He was trying to kill me."

"Leon, what Pontus wants to do here is threatening their homes. They don't want to see Fort Lauderdale change."

"It is going to change," he said.

"I know."

"Youth! That is the future. Like Zale. I need to speak to Zale. His mother is in jail—we need to appoint a guardian. Where is the boy?"

"He's staying at his great-grandmother's now. His mom is going to get out. I'm sure of that. He won't need a guardian."

A uniformed Fort Lauderdale police officer walked up to Leon and asked to speak to him. "Excuse me," Leon said. "We will talk again, yes?"

"Okay," I said, and then I hurried back around the minivan.

The chair was empty. I spun around, checking out the crowd, the waterfront park where I'd sat with LaShon, the street leading up to the bridge. She was nowhere.

Once again, it was like she had just vanished. If she had been watching me on Monday, why was she avoiding me now?

BACK in the Whaler, heading upriver, I thought about what Mrs. Wheeler had said. The old woman couldn't seem to stay on topic for more than ten seconds before wandering off—literally. I reminded her of someone? Probably her childhood friend, I thought. The important thing was that she saw the face of the person driving the black car that was waiting for Nick's boat to show on his trip upriver. And it was a man. I'd need to pass that on to Detective Amoretti as soon as possible. Maybe they could get Mrs. Wheeler to go down to the police station and work with a sketch artist to get a drawing of what the driver might look like. And maybe, once she said it was a guy, maybe they would let Molly go.

Molly. I had no idea what she was going through there in the county jail. I told LaShon I was going to go visit her. I'd better make good on that promise, I thought, as I motored alongside *Gorda* and tied up my dink at the dock.

Jeannie answered her phone on the second ring, and I told her about the night Mike and I had had aboard the *TropiCruz IV.*

"They wouldn't have worried about you if they didn't think you were getting close to something," she said. "The fact that they tried to make you go for a midnight swim is a good sign."

"Yeah, well, it didn't feel all that good hanging out there in the freezing wind knowing that if I dropped I'd be ground fish food."

"Thankfully that didn't happen. So move on. Why do you think they feel threatened enough to want to kill you?"

"I don't know, Jeannie. I don't feel like I've done enough or learned enough to threaten anybody. Maybe they just don't like people snooping around. There is something funny going on, but I didn't discover what it is until this morning. I met again with Thompson," I told her, and went on to explain about LaShon's theory that a slot machine rip-off scheme was in place. "According to LaShon, she thinks they've netted over a million, maybe several. I guess there's no regulation of this offshore gambling stuff, and the boats are run so sloppy they don't know what they should be making. We did have a little problem with our meeting this morning, though."

"Yeah? What?"

"While I was talking to her, the *TropiCruz IV* came into view and the captain, Richard Hunter, you know, Janet's brother? He saw us talking. LaShon got pretty worked up about it. I guess these Russians are pretty scary guys. I called Detective Amoretti, and he came over and took her under his wing. He said he'd find a safe place for her to stay for a while. So I guess, thanks to me, she's finished with TropiCruz and may have to go into hiding for a while."

"Just so long as she's safe. Listen, don't try to take the blame for everything. You didn't make that girl meet you. I'll get hold of the detectives and make sure they follow through."

"Thanks, Jeannie. I also think I might have found another witness to Nick's shooting." I went on to tell her about my conversations with the elusive Mrs. Wheeler. Jeannie had heard of her, too. I guess everybody in the legal or law enforcement community knew about the local activist. Jeannie promised to pass on that information to the detectives as well. She'd ask them to pick her up, bring her in for questioning.

"I'll call that Mabry fella," she said. "I think he'd be more successful with a mature woman than that other detective. So what do you plan to do now?"

"I was thinking that I need to see Molly. I have some questions I want to ask her."

"It just so happens you're in luck."

"What do you mean?"

"Seychelle, you can't just go walking into the jail and visit people whenever the hell you feel like it."

"You can't?"

"I consider it a good sign that you don't know that. The inmates in the county jail system only get one visiting day per week. Used to be all female inmates were kept up at the North Broward Bureau, but they just opened a unit for female offenders here at the main jail. As long as she's still going in and out of court, they're holding her down here. Today happens to be Molly's day. From 2:00 to 4:00 this afternoon."

"It's already 1:30."

"Yes'm. You'd better get your butt in gear if you expect to see her."

BACK in the early eighties, when downtown Fort Lauderdale had fallen into disrepair and disrepute, like many city centers, there were more closed stores than open and more homeless people than customers. The city fathers decided it would be a good idea to build the new jail next door to the county courthouse in the heart of the old downtown.

Fast-forward to the twenty-first century and urban renewal, and today inmates in the jail, located just behind the Downtowner, look across the river into the condo tower windows of units that start at half a million dollars. Frequently, when walking from the parking lot into my favorite watering hole, I would hear strange pounding and clicking sounds from the jail and turn around to see the black silhouettes of figures in the slitted windows, waving their hands or holding papers with messages I couldn't read. It sounded as though they were pounding on the glass with keys or some other metallic object, and I've wondered what they're allowed to keep in their cells that's metal. In all my nearly thirty years of living in this town, I had never before had occasion to visit this local landmark. Today would be a first.

After locking the Whaler to a piling in front of the Downtowner, I ran inside to tell Pete that I'd left my dinghy out front. I asked him to keep an eye on it. Pete nodded while drawing a draft beer. I didn't dare tell him where I was going. Pete had a thing against cops and law enforcement of all kinds. Years ago, as a singlehander, he'd driven his boat right up onto Miami Beach after sleeping through his alarm, and when the local cops just stood by and watched as a horde of local bums swarmed aboard and stripped the boat, Pete developed a lifelong hatred of the boys in blue.

I followed the signs to the stairs that led up to the jail entrance, but stopped in my tracks when I saw the metal detector. I hadn't really been thinking about all the ramifications of visiting a jail, and I realized I still had my rigging knife in my shoulder bag, my radio on my waistband. The sheriff's deputy on duty saw my consternation and pointed me in the direction of the lockers. Once my gear was safely locked away, I merely had to drop the little key into one of the plastic bins, and then I breezed through security.

I would not have thought a person could change as much as Molly had in the past few days. She was wearing a drab brown outfit, square-cut cotton top and bottoms that looked like the scrubs hospital orderlies wear. At the neckline, the fabric hung from her angular collarbones, and her once shiny dark hair fell in strings around her face.

She attempted a smile when the guard brought her into the room. We sat on opposite sides of a long table. There were other women prisoners on either side of us meeting with relatives and friends. No one had any privacy. I found it interesting that all of the visitors were women, and I wondered if there was some legal or social convention that prevented men from visiting women in jail.

"How are you doing?" I asked, knowing as soon as the words were out of my mouth that it was a stupid question.

She pursed her lips and rolled her eyes toward the ceiling. "I'm getting by."

"Is there anything I can do for you, get for you?"

"Can you get me out of here?" She spoke slowly, her dark eyes looking straight at me, shining.

"I'm trying. God, I'm trying. But—"

"I know." She lowered her head and looked at her hands, at the handcuffs around her wrists. "I didn't mean to say that you weren't."

"I may have found out a few things. I can't really talk about it yet, though." I looked at the women around us and the guards standing at the perimeter of the room. "And not here."

"Tell me about Zale. You got him out to B.C.?"

"Yeah. I turned him over to Gramma Josie. She'll take care of him. But, Molly, I don't trust your uncles. Here the kid just lost his dad, and already they're putting pressure on him to close down the gambling boats. As if he even could."

"Sounds like Jimmie. He thinks of himself as the tribe's financial whiz kid."

"Molly, don't take this wrong, but you don't think it's

possible they killed Nick, do you? To get control of the boats through Zale?"

In the old days, when we disagreed, Molly was a fiery fighter. But the jail had taken all the fight out of her. She merely shook her head, sighed, and said, "No way."

"I'm just trying to explore all possibilities."

She nodded.

"I met somebody who was there, at the river Monday morning. I think she may have seen the shooter in his car before he went up on the bridge."

"Yeah?" She sat up a little straighter, the hope so bald in her eyes.

"Yeah. I'm working on it. I'm hoping that if I can get her to swear it was a man, they might spring you."

She slumped over again. "In court," she said, "the prosecutor told the judge that he doubted I did it myself. They're claiming I hired someone to kill Nick so that my son and I would inherit all his money. I would never touch that money, though. I have all the money I need."

Molly never had been into stuff. Her room, even as a teenager, had been much more minimalist than the rooms of most teenage girls. She didn't like clutter, and there were no dust-collecting gadgets on her dresser or posters of teen heartthrobs on her walls.

"Yeah," I said, "I remember that about you."

A smile danced on her lips all too briefly. I was ready to do just about anything to bring it back.

"Remember that time I slept over at your place and we dragged the phone on its long extension cord into your room? We had a flashlight and that phone inside the tent we'd made of your bedcovers. God, we stayed up all night trying to be the fourth caller or something like that into HOT 105."

There it was again. Her eyes creased and her mouth

stretched wide. "You wanted to win tickets on a cruise or something? What was it?"

"The Bahamas. It was a three-day cruise to the Bahamas, and I thought if we won, our parents would let us go. How old were we?"

"Maybe thirteen?" she said.

I shook my head and we both fell silent. We could hear the conversations going on along both sides of us, but my mind filtered them out. I was back there when we were young and hopeful.

"Pit's in town," I said, but I was looking at my hands, pretending interest in my own thumb. "He met your son before I took Zale out to Big Cypress. They were cute together, you know, talking boats. They seemed to hit it off." I glanced up to see how she was taking it. She was leaning back in her chair, her fists clenched so tight the tendons made deep ridges in her forearms, her face contorted with an emotion that looked like fear. "Molly, Pit still cares about you. He said to tell you that if you need anything, all you have to do is ask."

She didn't move. It was as though she had turned to stone.

"Why?" I asked her finally, after several minutes of silence.

She knew what I meant. She knew I was not talking about the events of the last couple of days, the shooting, or any of that.

"I can't—" she began, but her voice faltered. She coughed and began again in a voice barely more than a whisper. "I can't explain it to you, Sey. I couldn't back then, and I can't now."

"I just don't get it. That's what hurts so much. We always said we could tell each other *everything*, that we were best friends. And when I said it, *I* meant it. How could you just walk away like that? What did I do to deserve that?"

Her voice was so low, I could barely hear her over the conversations going on around us. "*You* didn't do anything."

"Did you love him? I mean, I could almost understand you throwing our friendship aside if you loved him that much, but I can't see that. Nick Pontus?"

"Sey, stop, *please*?"

"I mean, you used to laugh about him. You used to say things about him behind his back. Don't tell me you were cheating on my brother with Nick back then. You know some of the kids said that back in school, but I always stuck up for you. Molly, you had Pit, and we both loved you, and then, then, you just threw us away."

She signaled for the guard, stood, and turned her back to me.

"Molly? *Molly?*" I called out as the guard led her through the door and out of the room.

XX.

BEFORE I'd fully rounded the curve in the river, I could hear Abaco's joyous yelps echoing across the water. When the Larsens' yard finally came into view, I saw B. J. running across the grass, followed by a leaping Lab. He twisted sideways and sent a Frisbee spinning for the dog. Abaco jumped into the air like a hooked marlin and snagged the plastic disk. You'd think she was totally attention-starved the way she wiggled and squirmed with joy when he patted her and told her she was a good dog for catching the thing. Hell, speaking of attention-starved, I wondered if he would pet me if I jumped out of the dinghy and caught the damn thing in my teeth.

When he noticed the Whaler cruising toward the dock, he trotted over to help me crank the dinghy up in the davits. Handing me the lines, he said, "That kid Zale has called twice. He won't tell me what's bothering him, but he seems pretty worked up. He sounds scared, actually. I'll take care of the boat if you want to go on inside and call him."

"Thanks, B. J.," I said, stepping onto the dock and hurrying past him.

The young woman who worked for Gramma Josie picked up the phone, but by the sound of it, Zale must have been standing right next to her when it rang. He came on just seconds after I identified myself.

"Hang on a minute," he said. I heard footsteps, then the sound of a door closing in the background. His voice was low and secretive when he spoke again. "You've got to come get me," he said.

"Zale, your mom thinks—"

"No, listen. I'm scared. Somebody tried to kill me today."

B. J. offered to drive Lightnin', and I gladly took him up on it. I preferred to take my Jeep for going out to Big Cypress, but I'd already driven out to the Glades once that week and, besides, I wanted his company. My phone conversation with the boy had been cut short when someone on his end wandered into the room. He didn't want to say any more. It was clear he no longer trusted anyone out there. Concerned as I was about Zale's safety, I really wanted to talk to B. J. about Molly. I was worried about her health, both physical and mental. The way she had just walked away from that visiting table scared me. It was possible that whatever chance we had of reconciliation had already died.

I was climbing into the Jeep's passenger seat out in the Larsens' driveway when I heard the rumble of a powerful engine driving too fast on the quiet Rio Vista street. When I turned around, I saw Amoretti pull his Corvette to the curb with a flashy spray of gravel. I closed the door to the Jeep and walked out to meet him.

"Hey, Amoretti, what's up?"

The door flew open and he leaped out. "What the devil did you send that lawyer of yours downtown for?"

To my surprise, LaShon climbed out of the passenger-side door. I would not have thought it possible for anyone to have teeth whiter than Amoretti's, but the smile on that girl's face definitely put her in the running.

"What are you talking about?"

"Rich took me down to the station," LaShon said, "and your friend Jeannie was there. She was kinda hard on him." Again she laughed up and down the scale.

"Rich?" I said to LaShon. "Well, well."

"That woman's a menace," Amoretti said. "She's got no taste in men, either."

"That's just because she likes that other detective more than you," LaShon said. "I think he's kinda cute, too."

"That hippo? That uncouth, uncultured behemoth?"

"Come on, guys," I said. They were obviously having a good time playing these little verbal jousts that had become part of whatever relationship was starting up here, but I had to get out to the Big Cypress to get Zale. "I know you didn't come out here to discuss Detective Mabry's social skills."

"No," Amoretti said, "you're right. After talking to LaShon here, and hearing from your lawyer friend, I realized you've been running around playing Nancy Drew. I'm here to tell you to stop."

"I'd be more than happy to stop if you guys would start looking at some other suspect besides Molly Pontus. There's no way she killed Nick."

"Give us cops a little more credit than that, Ms. Sullivan. We never stopped looking. I never liked that woman for the crime in the first place. But we gotta go through the motions, do the job. Now, based on the information from Ms. Thompson here, we've set up an appointment this afternoon to meet with Kagan over at TropiCruz. We're going to use this slots information. He may or may not be aware of this enterprise, and we don't know what repercussions our conversation will create. One thing I do know, and it's why I came over here personally. I don't want you going anywhere near those ships or anyone involved with TropiCruz. Do you understand?"

"Sure. No problem, Detective. My friend and I are just on our way out to the Everglades—about as far from the ocean as you can get in Florida." At that point I realized I hadn't even introduced B. J. He'd been patiently sitting in the driver's seat of the Jeep. "B. J., I'd like to introduce you to these friends of mine."

He climbed out and shook hands with the detective and LaShon. "We need to get moving," he said to me.

"Yeah, I know. If there's nothing more, Detective, we need to get out there before dark."

LaShon said, "Can I talk to you for a minute?" She motioned for me to walk aside onto the grass in front of the Larsens' house.

"LaShon, I'm so sorry that I dragged you into all this."

She wasn't even looking at me. Her eyes were focused on B. J., where he was leaning against the side of the Jeep. "He is so hot," she said.

I grabbed my head. "LaShon, we don't have time."

"I know. I just didn't know if I'd ever see you again, and I wanted to thank you."

"Why?"

"I'd been wanting to leave TropiCruz for a long time. It had started to feel dirty working there. But to tell the truth, I was afraid to leave. Rich assures me that he'll keep me safe over the next few days, and once things blow over, maybe I will go find a job consulting. Maybe it's time to try that out."

"That's a really good idea, LaShon. And, hey, what's this about you and *Rich*?"

She glanced over her shoulder. "Him? I just like to

flirt. Day may come when I find the one man, but until then, flirting's all I do."

I embraced her. "Listen, you be safe," I said.

"You, too."

AS we drove out the interstate through the western suburbs, I kept replaying my conversation with Molly at the jail. I wanted to rewind time and take back the words I'd said. I didn't know why I'd pushed her like that. She'd been married to the man for over ten years, he'd just died, and there I was questioning her love for him. Way to go, Miss Sensitivity. I went there to try to help her, cheer her up, console her, and I ended up insulting her.

Right after we'd exited onto I-75, when the strip malls and look-alike subdivisions were starting to retreat behind us, B. J. spoke for the first time. He startled me.

"What?"

"I asked you how Molly was doing. You said you went by the jail, but you didn't really say much about it."

A chain-link fence separated the mown berm along the side of the road from the canal running parallel to the highway. I watched as a blue heron came gliding in over the sawgrass, his legs dropping behind him like landing gear as he neared the shallows.

"What's to say? She's in jail."

"Right. So you guys had an argument?"

"What do you mean? Why do you say that?"

"Listen, I know you. When a topic makes you uncomfortable, you avoid talking about it."

I stared out the windshield at the long asphalt path that stretched ahead through the endless green grasses. "I pushed her. I don't really understand why. I pushed her to explain to me how she could have just walked away like that back in high school. And in the process I may have pushed her away for good."

"No, I don't think so. Give her more credit than that. Molly's a pretty amazing woman."

I turned to look at him. His profile was so familiar. The straight line of the bridge of his nose, the swell of the cheekbones below his eyes, the strong jaw. Just looking at his smooth brown skin made me long to reach over, touch him, caress him. And often it made me terrified of losing him.

"How do you know? You haven't really known her very long," I said.

"No, but there are some people with whom we are naturally in tune. I feel that with Molly. We don't have to know each other well to feel the harmony. She has a strong spirit and an inner beauty. Losing her freedom must be incredibly painful for a person like her, but she'll survive it. Probably better than most."

"Huh," I said, but I was thinking *inner beauty, my ass*. "You and Molly really seem to have hit it off."

He took his eyes off the road for a moment and flicked them in my direction. "Yeah. And is that a problem?"

"No, no, of course not."

THE rest of the drive up Snake Road toward the reservation passed in silence, or at least with no conversation. No trip in my Jeep was ever silent. As we roared through the cattle pastures, past the lakes and the distant stands of cypress trees, I tried to put the visions of Molly and B. J. together out of my mind. I tried to think about Nick's murder and his frightened son. I wasn't terribly successful.

When we pulled into the dirt drive at Gramma Josie's house, Zale burst out of the door as soon as we turned off the engine. He had been watching for us. He ran around to my side of the Jeep and said, "Let's go. I've gotta get out of here."

"Zale, you can't just leave like that," I said.

"Why not?"

"Well, it's not polite, for one thing. We have to go inside and say good-bye to Gramma Josie, at least."

"I don't want to go back in there. I just want to leave."

I put my hand on his shoulder and walked him out into the middle of the front lawn, away from earshot of the house. "What happened, Zale? Why are you so spooked?"

"I *told* you. Someone tried to kill me."

I shook my head. "I need a few more details. What exactly happened?"

He jerked his head, indicating that I should follow him. We walked to the far side of the yard and he pointed back behind the house. "See the lake back there?"

The thicket of trees was dense, but in one spot a glint of blue water was showing through. "Yeah."

"I got bored. Gramma Josie suggested I go riding on the ATV. I did that for a while, but that was boring, too. Gramma had mentioned a canoe, so I came back here and asked her if I could take it out, paddle around a little. While I was out there on the lake, somebody tried to shoot me."

I stopped breathing for several seconds. I was picturing Molly's face while I tried to explain that her son had been shot. Only when I started to feel light-headed did I remember that I needed to breathe.

"Are you sure?"

"Yeah. It's kinda hard to make a mistake about something like that."

"Maybe it was an accident or something."

"Yeah, right. Two bullets came this close." He held up his fingers only inches apart.

"This happened a while ago, right?"

He nodded. "This morning."

"And did you tell anybody else about it?"

"No," he said, kicking a toe of his sneaker at the ground, digging a hole in Gramma Josie's lawn. When he looked up at me, I saw the panic that was just below the surface. In a matter of days this boy had lost his father and his mother, and now he believed someone was trying to kill him.

I put my arm around his shoulder and gave it a squeeze. "Show me where it happened," I said.

I motioned to B. J. that we were going out behind the house. He nodded and gave me the okay sign. I followed Zale across the mowed grass of the back lawn and off onto a path through the scrub to the trees by the lake.

When we reached the edge of the trees, Zale turned and looked back at me, his eyes questioning whether or not we should be doing this.

"Whoever was around here this morning is long gone. I'm with you now. It's okay." I hoped I was right.

The stand of cypress trees did an excellent job of hiding the lake from the house. The Seminoles called these cypress domes. Years ago, most of the dry land on which we were standing was once Everglades marshland. Hammocks were the high, dry places where slash pines and mahogany trees grew in the drier soil. Those mounds were like tree islands in the river of grass. Cypress trees, on the other hand, thrive in water. They grew in depressions where the soil would stay soaked, even in the drought years. In the middle of the depression, where the water was deepest, the trees would grow tall and thick, while at the outer edges of the dome, where the water was scarcer, the trees would be shorter, hence the appearance on the horizon of a dome-shaped stand of trees. The earth under this canopy was drier than most, leading me to believe that the lake had been dredged, draining some of the water out of the swamp.

It was much cooler in the shade of the trees, and if someone hadn't cleared the trail we were on, the brush would have been impenetrable. The faint breeze rustling the palmetto fronds smelled like damp, rotting vegetation. Patches of white lichen on the trunks of the thin cypress trees looked like snow, and in the golden evening light, with the greens of palmettos and ferns growing among the bushy shrubs, tall grasses, and mossy pools, I thought, this is a place where myth and magic are born, where the imagination can invent almost anything—even murderous gunmen. I hadn't realized how big the lake was until we broke out into the sunlight on the far side of the woods.

I was expecting the boy to take me to a canoe that looked something like the old hunter-green aluminum model Red had bought me at Sears when I was a kid. Instead, the boat he led me to was nearly invisible, drawn up onto the knobby beach of cypress knees: a handmade dugout canoe. A ten-foot-long wood pole, knotted where the branches had been lopped off, rested in the bottom of the canoe. I ran my hand over the boat's rough surface. You could still feel the cut marks from the small axe the canoe carver, probably Henry John Billie, had used to shape the canoe out of a tree.

Zale walked up into the trees, near the boat's bow. "See here?" He pointed to two splintered holes in the wood. One bullet had entered up near the bow where the boat builder had hardly dug out any of the tree's center core. The wood was probably ten inches thick there. The other bullet had entered about three feet aft, and an exit hole showed where it had gone clean through the side of the boat.

Zale pointed out to the center of the lake. "I had poled out there, in the middle. The sun felt good and I

lay down to watch the hawks and just drift for a while.
I heard—"

From the direction of the path came a sharp crack,
like the sound of someone stepping on a piece of wood.
Zale stopped talking, and we both turned to look through
the sunlight-dappled woods in the direction of the sound.
I couldn't see anyone, but the trees were so thick it
would be easy to hide. My heart rate doubled and I motioned Zale to get around behind the canoe and crouch
down. The old canoe had stopped one bullet. Maybe it
could do it again.

The seconds dragged past and I was almost ready to
stand up when we heard a distinct crunching sound, like
a person stepping on a pile of limestone rock and crum-
bling it underfoot. That was followed by another snap
of breaking twigs. Definitely footsteps. I found myself
thinking that these modern Indians had certainly lost
some of that tracking ability their forefathers were known
for. This guy was making a hell of a racket.

XXI.

I **PEEKED** my head up over the side of the canoe to see if I could spot movement back there. I could see only twenty-five feet or so into the thick clusters of lichen-covered tree trunks.

"Seychelle?"

I thought I was going to have a heart attack. It was B. J. leaning against a tree, watching us. He'd come up behind us.

"What're you guys doing?"

"Shit, B. J. You scared the hell out of me." I rolled onto my back on the ground and tried to catch my breath.

"Sey, watch your language in front of the kid."

"We thought . . ." I sat up and began pulling twigs out of my ponytail. Zale looked at me, and I understood for the first time just how frightened he really was. "Oh, never mind, B. J. Come here and look at these bullet holes."

B. J. ran his hand over the holes much the same as I had. "Wow. I've never seen one of these made by Seminoles. They are like the ones my ancestors made. I once saw a Samoan canoe at my uncle's in California. Only the wood is different."

"B. J., I wasn't telling you to look at the canoe. Geez, these are bullet holes. Zale was in the canoe today when somebody shot at him." I turned to the boy. "You were starting to tell me about it. You heard the shots?"

He nodded. "They sounded far away. You know, I've spent time out here before, and it's not that unusual to hear shots. They hunt pig and wild turkeys, and the kids mess around with target practice. There were three shots. I heard the third one hit the water. The ones that hit the boat made these loud *thunks*."

"When did this happen, Zale?" B. J. asked.

"This morning, after eleven, probably."

I looked at my watch. It was almost five o'clock. At this time of year, it would be dark by six. The warmth from the sun had already abandoned the day, and the evening chill was taking over. "What did you do after you heard the shots?"

"I was too scared to do anything. I was just lying there in the canoe, afraid to sit up. After what seemed like about two hours, but probably wasn't that long, the canoe grounded over there." He pointed to the shore about one hundred feet from us. "Then I sat up and paddled over here, ran to the house, and called you. I stayed in the house until you got here."

"That was good, Zale. It probably was just an accident. Somebody was hunting or something and didn't realize you were in here on the lake," B. J. said.

"I was scared that it was the same person who shot my dad."

"That's not likely," I said, thinking about Molly's comments about Jimmie and how much he cared about the financial welfare of the tribe and himself. "When you asked Gramma Josie if you could go out in the canoe on the lake, was anybody else around? Did anybody else hear you say that?"

He shrugged his shoulders. "I don't think so."

"What about Earl and Jimmie? Had they been around at all?"

"They left yesterday right after you did. Uncle Earl's truck is really loud. I'd have heard it if he was around."

Yeah, I thought, *if* he came in his truck. But every family out here has several all-terrain vehicles. Kids ride their ATVs to school, and adults take them out hunting and just to go visit a neighbor.

"You did the right thing to call. I don't think you should spend another night out here. Come on, let's go tell Gramma Josie we're taking you back to town."

THERE was simply no polite way to escape staying for dinner. Gramma Josie didn't ask us, she just assumed. When we walked into the house, the table was already set for four, and when I introduced her to B. J., she asked him to come close to her so she could see him better.

"You look like Earl when he a boy," she said, stroking the side of his head, running her hand across his slick black hair, back to his ponytail.

She had a point. Put one of those patchwork Seminole shirts and a cowboy hat on B. J., and anyone would take him for a Native American.

"What clan?" she asked.

"My family is from islands in the South Pacific," he said. "A place called Samoa. It is very far from here."

She nodded her head, smiling, and patted him on the cheek. "Okay. Okay. You not white man."

B. J. laughed. "I think you mean that as a compliment, and I'll take it as such."

Gramma Josie told me to go to the kitchen and pour iced tea for everyone. It seemed crazy, but I swear she wanted me out of the way so she could flirt with B. J. The young girl who worked for Josie during the day had left a plate of pan-fried fish and a macaroni and cheese casserole in the oven. After a while, B. J. came into the kitchen. He rummaged in the refrigerator and added a side of steamed green beans after a raised-eyebrow look at the crusty pasta dish.

Zale helped his great-grandmother serve herself. As I watched her eat, I wondered how much those clouded eyes were still able to see. Did she really know what B. J. or Zale looked like, or did she only see shadows?

I went out to the kitchen to find some catsup for my fish, and when I returned, B. J. and the old lady were deep in conversation as though they had known each other for years.

"When I girl, no TV, no car. Live in chickee, eat turtle, garfish, sell eggs and skins. All this place *i:laponi* land. They Seminoles who talk Mikasuki. My people talk Creek."

"My people in the islands? It was the same story. They lived in huts, too, just like chickees. They also hunted and fished. That all changed when the white man came. Now, I don't speak my people's language."

"You Indian."

"In a way, you could say that."

I pushed my catsup-soaked fish around my plate. "So I guess I'm one of the bad guys, huh?"

Gramma Josie cackled at that. "Not *all* white people bad."

"Ah, well, that's good to know," I said, looking at Zale and wondering just where he fit into the picture.

"You like her," Gramma Josie said.

"Like who? What are you talking about?"

"I say I have white friend. You talk like her. Now she old like me."

I turned to B. J. "Gramma Josie was telling us about this girl she knew when she was very young. She said she met her at the Stranahans' house when her family used to come to town to trade."

Frank Stranahan and his bride Ivy were considered by many to be the founders of modern Fort Lauderdale. A real pioneer, Frank had opened the first trading post on the banks of the New River in the late 1890s, ran the ferry for crossing the river, started the first bank in town, and married the town's first schoolteacher. What local history I knew came from Mrs. Cross, who taught me that mandatory month of Florida history in fourth grade at Croissant Park Elementary School, as well as the many tales Red used to tell me as we chugged up and down the river on *Gorda*. My father had been something of a local history buff.

B. J. pushed his plate out of the way. As usual, his food had disappeared without my being aware that he was eating. He was so precise, cutting his food into these tiny bites and downing them without a sound. I, on the other hand, ate with loads of mess and noise. He placed his forearms on the table and leaned closer to Josie.

"Tell me about those days."

"We live in Annie Tommie's camp on de New River. I help my mother. Fish. Cook *sofki*."

"What's that?"

"Seminoles eat corn *sofki*. Cook de corn in water, add *cappie*. Taste real good."

"So, you were friends with a white girl?" B. J. asked.

"Mizz Stranahan teach English. I see her dere. White kids throw rocks. Call us 'dirty Indian.' "

B. J. shook his head. "Kids. They act out what they hear from their parents."

"My grandmother on my mom's side lived in those early days of Fort Lauderdale," I said. "I hope she wasn't one of those kind of kids."

"Dis girl nice," Josie continued as though I hadn't spoken. "No rocks. She teach Josie English, too."

"She must have been a very special girl," B. J. said.

"De whole family good," she said, and then she started her cackling again, which turned into coughing, and finally B. J. got up from his seat and went over and began to massage her back. The coughing quieted and the wheeze left her breathing. She cocked her head back and looked at him over her shoulder. "You strong medicine."

When B. J. sat back down, Josie turned to me. "You see Molly," she said. It wasn't a question. She knew.

"I visited her this afternoon."

"You saw Mom?" Zale said. "How was she?"

"She's okay." I didn't want anybody to ask me any more questions about her, so I tried to shift the subject from that disastrous visit. "I think I might have found someone who could help her. There's an old woman who was there, walking along the river the morning it happened. She witnessed something, and it might help get Molly off. The police are looking for her now."

Josie sighed and shook her head. "She got to let go."

At the time, I thought she was talking about Molly.

AFTER dinner, when we were cleaning up in the kitchen, I pulled out the white trash bag from the corner can and was tying the red ties when I looked up to ask what to do with it. B. J. was standing at the sink in front of a window that looked out across the back of the house. It was dark outside now, and his face was reflected in the glass. I still felt my heart go pitter-pat when I caught him unawares and had the chance to study him. Though his face had a classic beauty, a huge part of his allure was the serenity in him. Even without her eyes, Gramma Josie had "seen" it. Like B. J., she saw things most of the rest of us could not see. Maybe it was some kind of special radar built into those mammoth ears of hers. Molly used to say that the kids around here on the reservation called Josie an old medicine woman and said she had magic powers. She recognized similar qualities in B. J.

"So, your power as a ladies' man continues to amaze me. Even ninety-year-old Indian ladies go ga-ga for you."

His eyes flicked up to the glass and connected with my reflection. He shrugged and said deadpan, "Oh yeah, baby, it's that Moana magic."

"Right," I said, rolling my eyes at Zale. "You know, though, listening to your grandmother tell those stories, it makes me wish I knew more about my own grandmother. My mother hardly ever talked about her. Do you think it's possible to miss someone you never knew?"

Zale was sitting on a stool in the middle of the kitchen. "Yeah, in a way, that's kinda how I felt about you."

"Me? What do you mean?"

"My mom used to tell me about you. She used to talk about how much fun she had with you when you guys were kids. She always used to say she was sorry she had hurt you."

"Molly said that?"

"Yeah. Those stories made me wish I knew you."

I stood there, stunned. Zale's words were forcing me to rewrite our history, and I didn't know if I was ready for that.

B. J. put his fist under my chin and angled my face up toward his. "You and Molly need to sit down and talk. Sort all this out. Start new," he said.

I didn't know what to say. I felt like they were both watching me, and I just wanted to get off somewhere by myself. "Anybody know where the trash goes around here?" I asked, holding up the white plastic bag.

"Come on," Zale said. "It's outside. I'll show you." He walked over and put his hand on the doorknob.

"That's okay, I'll find it," I said, hoping he would understand that I wanted to go out alone.

He looked from my face to the bag, and then over to B. J. When he looked back at me, he opened his eyes very wide and jerked his head toward the back door. "It's out in the shed," he said. *"Come on."*

Okay, so sometimes I'm kinda slow, but I finally got it. The kid wanted me to go outside with *him.*

"All right. Just let me go grab my sweatshirt. It must be ten degrees colder out there already."

When we were halfway across the yard, I pulled on the sleeve of Zale's sweatshirt. "Hey, hold on a minute," I said. "I just want to stand here and look at these stars."

The sky on a moonless, clear night out in the Everglades is a sight not easily forgotten. The only other times in my life I could remember ever seeing the sky look like that was once years ago when I'd sailed down to the Dry Tortugas with Neal, my last boyfriend, or lover, or whatever we almost thirty-year-old women were supposed to call the men in our lives. And the time I'd once been left dog-paddling in the Gulf Stream. That night, I'd said good-bye to the stars, and now, like then, the Milky Way looked like a solid mass of light. There were so many stars you couldn't distinguish them as separate spots of light. No wonder someone named it the Milky Way. It really did look like someone had splashed milk across the sky.

I draped my arm across Zale's shoulder. "Isn't it amazing?' I whispered.

"Yeah," he said, "it's great, but I want to talk to you. Come on."

We walked back to the shed at the back corner of the mowed section of Gramma Josie's yard. It was dark inside the structure, but Zale had obviously made earlier trips out to the trash cans and he knew how to thread his way around the two parked vehicles to the back of the shed where the big garbage can resided. I lifted the lid and he swung the heavy white bag into the can, then turned to face me.

"There's something I need to do," he said, "and I've got to talk to somebody about it."

"Okay. Go ahead."

"I hope I'm doing the right thing. Ever since I got the news that Dad had," he paused and I heard him swallow, struggling against the emotion that was backing up in his throat, "that Dad had been shot, I've been trying to figure out what to do. It seemed easy enough when my dad first told me about it because it didn't seem like it would ever happen. I mean, I had even forgotten all about it."

"Slow down, Zale. What did your dad tell you?"

I could barely see the outline of the hood of his sweatshirt. Only the lights from the house reflected off his eyes as he blinked at me. "I don't know what to do."

"Come on. What are you talking about?"

"You were once Mom's best friend and I know she trusted you."

I nodded.

"I was gonna tell Gramma Josie 'cuz she's family, but after what happened out here this afternoon, I got scared. I don't think that was an accident."

"I've been thinking about it, Zale, and I don't think so, either."

He was still for a minute, and then he exhaled a long breath. "Okay. About two or three months ago, when I was over at my dad's, he came in my room and said he wanted to talk to me. He closed the door and everything. He told me he didn't like what was going on with the business, and he was worried that something might happen to him."

"Wow," I said. So Nick had known, or at least suspected. Had he voiced his suspicions to the kid? Was that why someone was after him?

"Yeah," he continued. "This was right after he'd hired the bodyguards. I didn't know about the bodyguards until he told me that night, and then he said it bothered him to always have these guys hanging out with him like they were his babysitters. It all really scared me. It was like something out of the movies or a video game."

"Yeah, it's hard to believe that someone wants to kill your father."

"Like, I was scared, but I also couldn't totally believe it. I mean, I still went to school and went to his house on weekends, and I forgot all about it after a while."

"That's normal, Zale."

"But that night he made me promise."

"Promise what?"

"He said there was a safe onboard the *Mykonos*, and that he had put something important in there."

"Did he tell you what it was?"

He shook his head. "He said that if something were to happen to him, though, I was supposed to tell my mom about it, and we were supposed to go get it. He made me promise."

"So did you tell her?"

"Well, when I first heard about him, you know, getting shot and all, I didn't even think about it. It was hard enough to believe my dad was really dead. I didn't remember about what he'd told me to do until the day of his funeral. I was gonna talk to my mom about it that night, but I never got a chance to."

"So what you're saying is your dad knew he was in

danger and he left some kind of documents or something on his boat."

"I guess. I don't know what it is. I was thinking at first
that I just wouldn't say anything to anyone except my
mom, because that was what I'd promised. But then I
kept thinking that whatever is there could maybe *help*
my mom, and I didn't know what to do. The Tigertail
family out here is more worried about what's gonna
happen to TropiCruz than they are about my mom." He
sniffed and rubbed his nose with the back of his hand.
"So, I decided to tell you."

I reached over and rested a hand on his shoulder. "I
appreciate that. I'll make good on it, I promise. Now,
let's get back inside and get on the road home before we
freeze our asses off out here."

With a little pressure on his shoulder, I guided him to
start walking around the parked ATVs. Just as we neared
the mouth of the structure, I thought I saw some movement out in the front yard, and I gripped his shoulder
hard. He stopped and turned to look at me. I held my
finger to my lips and eased us back into the shadows.
Maybe it was just Jimmie and Earl coming back over to
talk to their mother, but I decided to wait and see if I
could identify them before we crossed the open yard.

I could see the outlines of what looked like two
men standing on the far side of my Jeep, keeping the vehicle between them and the house. Both were dressed in
black—black jackets, black pants, and their heads looked
misshapen, as though they were wearing some kind of
hats. They seemed to be talking to each other, although
I couldn't hear even a whisper. One of them was shaking
his head and waving his arms in the air, as though in vi-
olent disagreement with the other.

I was trying to see if the larger of the two had a ponytail, to see if it was Earl, but they had their backs to me

and I couldn't tell. Finally the larger one waved his finger to signal them to get going, and they reached up and pulled what I had thought were hats down over their faces: ski masks. Then they ran, hunched over, out from behind the car. It was when they passed the open space between the car and the house that I saw that the one in the lead was carrying a gun.

XXII.

I PULLED Zale down into a crouch. We were hunched between the two all-terrain vehicles, and I hoped that we would just blend in with the dark outline of the machinery.

The two men were working their way down the side of the house with their backs to the wall, the larger one in the lead, his rifle or whatever held at an angle across his chest. The second one was very small and, as near as I could tell, he wasn't carrying any weapon. When they made it to the corner, they would be about a dozen feet from the back door.

I glanced over to the kitchen window. B. J. was no longer standing at the sink, so I guessed that he and Gramma Josie were finished with the dishes and sitting in the living room waiting for us to come back inside. If those men entered through the kitchen door, B. J. and Gramma Josie would be only one room away from that gun.

I couldn't let that happen. But if I attracted their attention, we were probably dead. Unless.

I reached up and felt around on the ATV. Hallelujah! The keys were in the ignition. I'd never driven one of these things, but I figured they must be just like jet skis with wheels.

I put my mouth close to Zale's ear and whispered, "Which one did you ride today?"

He pointed to the one on our left.

"Did it start right up?"

He nodded.

I looked back at the two men. They had rounded the corner of the house and were now inching their way toward the back door. They peeked in the window on the kitchen door and passed by, crawling beneath the window. They were heading, instead, for the sliding glass doors on the far side of the kitchen window. If Josie and B. J. were sitting in there, they'd be easy targets.

The good news was that the men were traveling farther away from the mouth of the garage. We would need that distance to give us the time to get around the corner and behind the shelter of the building before they realized what was going on and shot us in the back.

I jerked my head to indicate that Zale should get on. I grabbed two helmets off the wall and plunked one on the boy's head, slid the other on mine. They were the kind of big motorcycle helmets that have dark faceplates that slide up and down, but the faceplate on mine was missing. I climbed on behind him. I wasn't crazy about the idea that it would be my back they'd be shooting at, but I had to keep Zale safe.

"Once you get it started," I whispered under his helmet, "swing around to the side of the garage and try to keep the garage between us and them. If they start shooting, do zigzags and head for the trees, okay?"

The big plastic helmet bobbed up and down. I could feel how fast his chest was expanding and contracting. He was hyperventilating.

"Hey, Zale? I'm scared, too, but we can do this. I won't let them hurt you. And we can't let them hurt Josie and B. J."

We pushed the vehicle out to the garage opening. We could see the two intruders standing next to the sliding glass doors, starting to peer around the edge.

"I got your back," I said, and put my arms around his waist. "Let's do it."

The kid was quick. It must have been the reflexes from all those hours spent sailing dinghies. The ignition had barely caught when he cranked the throttle and the ATV leaped forward. I clutched hard at his waist, nearly sliding off the back of the seat, my bruised body screaming at the new assault. Then we were careening on two of four wheels as we made the turn around the corner of the garage. We'd crossed the grass and were into the scrub and I hadn't heard a single shot. The terrain was so bumpy, I felt like I'd got whiplash, and I bit my tongue twice in the first few yards. Zale didn't let up on the throttle and somehow we didn't tip over. I felt like my back must have a big red target on it, but I still didn't hear any shots. Then we were in the cover of the trees, and forced to slow down as the bushes and dead undergrowth clutched at the wheels and tangled round our legs.

The fact that they hadn't shot at us worried me. I suddenly pictured B. J. and Josie sitting on the couch, their arms in the air, two masked men holding a gun on them, but seconds later I heard the powerful roar of a big engine. It sounded like a monster truck, one of those swamp buggies Earl drove, with the big mud tires and heightened suspension.

Zale kept us in the fringes of the wood, where the ATV could make it through the shrubbery. The night had seemed cold enough when we were standing in that shed, but now, as the wind whipped at my bare hands and face, I thought I would freeze solid. Without headlights, we couldn't see where we were going or what we were likely to encounter on the ground. Zale continually gunned the engine and then overcorrected when the vines and shrubs let go of the frame and we shot forward or up or down, depending on the terrain. We crossed limestone boulders and downed trees, but the knobby tires just climbed over it all. I couldn't hear the roar of the truck over the sound of our vehicle's engine, so I had no idea if they were following us or not.

Then suddenly, like magic, a dark hole appeared in front of us. It was a dirt path made by kids on ATVs just like ours and it seemed to stretch, arrow-straight, right through the woods. Not a real dirt road, it was only a path, and definitely not something designed for trucks. When we hit the smooth dirt, the back end of the ATV fishtailed a bit, and then we took off, our speed climbing. Water streamed from my eyes as the cold air bit at every inch of bare flesh.

I've had vertigo on a boat at night before, but it was nothing like this. Shooting down this forest trail at forty miles per hour, I began to lose track of up and down. I had the sensation that we were climbing a mountain, but my rational mind kept telling me that there were no mountains in the Everglades.

And then we shot out of the woods, the tree canopy was gone, and we were on a dirt road. We barreled forward toward a crossroads and only at the last minute did both Zale and I realize that the road we were traveling dead-ended in a T, and the dirt road we were crossing ran parallel to a canal. The kid's body stiffened as he hit the brakes, hard.

By the time Zale stopped the ATV, the front two tires were in the water, we were engulfed in a cloud of dust, and the engine had stalled. We both sat there, shaking, trying to catch our breath, realizing just how close we had come to launching that vehicle into the middle of the canal. Zale climbed off, tore off his helmet, and bent over, his hands on his knees, his face parallel to the ground. "I think I'm gonna throw up," he said, and then he did.

In the absence of the engine's roar, the night sounds filled in. I'd always been under the impression that the birds out there were day creatures, and I was startled at the cawing, chirping, and peeping going on around us.

And I was completely turned around. I thought this must be the L-28 canal that we normally passed over on Snake Road when arriving at the reservation, but I wasn't certain. And if it was, which way should we turn to get back to the settlement? I wanted to get somewhere where there were other cars on the roads and streetlights, and the occasional law enforcement officer patrolling around.

"You okay?" I asked.

He stood up straight and looked at me. He shook his head and then lifted his arm and pointed down the dirt road behind me. I turned. The road stretched along the canal to the horizon, growing nearly invisible, but the canal reflected the starlight as far as we could see. About halfway down, I saw a pair of headlights coming our way.

"Shit," I said, climbing on the ATV and backing it off the canal bank by hand and onto the dirt road.

"I can't," Zale said. "My hands. I don't have any strength left."

"Climb on back and hold on to me," I said as I turned the key. The ATV roared to life again, and though I winced and thought I might vomit when he squeezed my ribs, once I felt his arms around me, I twisted the throttle.

The machine seemed to have lots more power than any water bike I'd ever ridden. We were up to forty in a matter of seconds and bouncing over the uneven terrain on the open road. I understood why Zale said his hands were tired. The icy wind made mine ache unbearably. My fingers felt like frozen claws, and even on that smooth dirt road, it took nearly all my strength to maintain control. Dark shadows, the clumps of cypress trees, flew by on the right. I glanced over my shoulder. I was going as fast as I dared without risking a rollover, and they were still gaining on me. I had to get out of the open.

Just then another dirt road opened up, ahead on the right, and I swerved wildly, trying not to hit the brakes that would light up the taillights, but I just couldn't help it. Even using the brakes, we lifted two wheels making the turn. As we slowed, I could hear the increased RPMs of the vehicle following us. If it were just some Seminole headed home after a long day at work, he wouldn't have reacted like that to the sight of our lights.

The road we'd turned onto dead-ended in less than a quarter mile in a clearing between two cypress domes. An old chickee hut with half the roof missing stood abandoned in the center of the dirt clearing. I could hear the engine growing louder behind us and I knew I had no choice. I turned toward the woods and gassed it.

We were barely into the tree line before we hit water. No matter where you are in the Everglades, there's always water underfoot. In many places it's just a foot or two underground, flowing through the aquifer. Anyplace where you find a low-lying area, the water will fill in. This particular clump of cypress trees was old and wet, the hollow here deep. These trees had been around for a while and their trunks were broader than any others I'd seen. I dodged the ATV in and out between the trees, and the bottom switched from a little water over mud to water up to the height of the engine. I was afraid the engine was going to suck water and stall. I tried to turn around and head back the way we'd come, but the trees all looked alike, and I couldn't tell which way would lead us to drier ground.

"Which way?" I hollered, hoping the boy would have a better sense of direction than I did. He lifted a hand from my midsection and pointed straight ahead.

The front tires threw mud and water all over us. My jeans and sweatshirt were soaked through, and my hands felt like they were encased in ice. The swamp seemed to continue on and on forever. Finally the trees started to thin and the ground changed from water to pure mud. Spatter off the front tires hit me right under the chin. My eyes burned.

And then we were out, and the same old canal was now off to our left. I had to assume that we hadn't crossed over Snake Road, that we were still on the east side, so I headed in the direction I assumed would be west—if that was indeed the L-28 canal. We'd traveled about a mile on the dirt road, taking it fairly slow so the wind wasn't too bad, when a man stepped out into the road just yards ahead of me. He was walking into the road and, in profile, I saw the ponytail.

I swerved and started to crank the throttle when I recognized the face. It was B. J.

I overshot by about fifty feet, circled around, and pulled up next to him. I turned the key to switch off the steaming engine. Past his shoulders, I saw where he had parked Lightnin' away from the canal bank road.

"Did you see them?" I asked him.

"See who, Seychelle?" His voice sounded tight.

"The guys, back at Gramma Josie's. We saw them. There were these two guys with ski masks and guns . . ."

"Ski masks and guns?"

"Yeah!" I swung my leg over the front of the bike and climbed off. I pointed to the boy still sitting on the back of the bike. His glasses were completely caked with mud. It was only when I saw him that I realized how mud-covered we *both* were. "He can tell you. We saw two men creeping around the house, ready to break in."

"Sey, I ran out as soon as I heard the ATV start up. There wasn't anybody out there."

"And there was this truck that they were in. Surely you heard that? You heard their truck start up?"

"After you guys took off like bats out of hell, I went back into the house, got your keys out of your purse, got into your Jeep, and started looking for you."

He must have been in the house when the truck started up. He wouldn't have heard it from inside. They'd obviously parked it some distance from the house.

"There were two guys, B. J. They had a truck."

"I was driving along the canal here looking for you when I noticed something running dark ahead of me on the canal road. No headlights. Then I saw brake lights. I thought it was you and I tried to catch up to see what the heck you were doing joyriding in the middle of the night on an ATV."

"Joyriding? Dammit, B. J." I stomped around in several circles trying to work off the anger. And to generate a little warmth. I stopped in front of him. "That was you?"

He nodded.

"We went into that friggin' swamp running from you?"

He smiled and ran his finger through the mud on my cheek. "It is a rather fetching look, though. Very earthy."

B. J. Moana might never know how close he came to getting decked then and there. I was cold, I was in serious pain, and I grew up with two older brothers. The only thing that prevented me from taking a swing at him at that moment was the fact that I knew he was something like a third-degree black belt in Aikido.

"You want to go back to Gramma Josie's and try to change?" B. J. asked.

"No," I said. "I just want to get Zale the hell out of here."

The boy spoke up for the first time. "We could probably leave the ATV at Sadie's store by the bridge."

I looked at him, trying to remember a store in the settlement.

"That place called Big Cypress Arts and Crafts," he said.

I nodded.

B. J. and Zale led the way in the Jeep, and I followed them down the couple of miles of dirt road until we arrived back at Snake Road. I insisted on writing a note on a fast-food napkin wedged under the Jeep's seat—"This ATV is the property of Josie Tigertail"—and I stuck it under a strap on the vinyl seat.

Jeep Wranglers with zippered windows are not best known for their airtight qualities, but the canvas on Ol' Lightnin' was especially stretched out and ill fitting. Wet and cold as we were, I knew that the ride on I-75 back across the Everglades was going to be brutal. I scrounged up an old green army blanket that I kept in the car for spur-of-the-moment beach excursions, and Zale and I crawled into the backseat and huddled under it, hoping to find some protection from the wind.

Somehow, Zale slept. I guess that comes under the heading of "the resilience of youth." Me, I was awake for every freezing minute of that hour and a half it took us to get home. I thought about the fact that I was about to turn thirty and the youth thing didn't really apply to me anymore, and then that made me think about the alternative. Death. Nick Pontus—that guy who I had seen on the beach and thought was so cute, that guy my dearest friend had married, that guy who had fathered the boy sleeping here in the backseat with me—was dead. Up until that moment I had been so self-involved, only thinking about how Nick's death had impacted me and forced me to reconnect with Molly, I hadn't really thought about Nick. He had been so full of energy and arrogant and determined to change the world and slap the Pontus mark on it. I'd probably stopped liking him that very first afternoon we met when he acted like every other boy I knew and chose Molly over me. The only reason I disliked him so much was because I had liked him in the first place. He'd been so full of life with his broad shoulders, olive skin, and thick brown hair. I found myself smiling at those days long ago, and while I rode through the night with my lover at the wheel, the first and only tears I would ever shed for Nick washed a tiny bit of the mud off my face.

XXIII.

I ASKED B. J. not to bother coming in with us. I insisted that we were fine, that all we wanted to do was get clean and dry and go to sleep. He had pulled Lightnin' into the Larsens' driveway and parked next to his El Camino, so he just stepped out of one vehicle and into the other.

Zale and I said little as we took turns in the shower. I sent him in first while I made myself a hot cup of tea, and it was nearly midnight by the time I came out in the living room dressed in black jeans and a navy turtleneck. Zale was lacing up his shoes, and he looked up at me.

"You sure you want to do this tonight?" I asked him.

"Yeah. If it'll help my mom, the sooner the better. Besides, now that I slept in the car, I'm wide awake."

"Okay, then let's go."

We decided to take the Whaler because the boatyard gate would be locked this late, and I didn't feel up to trying to talk our way in or climbing over the gate and getting busted by the night watchman. We'd had enough excitement for one night. As Nick's heir and son, Zale basically owned the *Mykonos*, so it wasn't like we were doing anything illegal by going aboard. The kid said he had a key to the boat on his key ring, so we might as well go look. Once we knew what was in the safe, we'd be able to sleep. Or so I hoped.

I didn't have running lights on my dink like Mike did, so I had Zale sit up in the bow with a flashlight to keep us legal. We took it slow. Even though it was after midnight, it was a Saturday night and the restaurants downtown were crowded with couples. Every other home was still well-lit within, and we felt a little like voyeurs as we admired their furniture, watched people moving inside, and checked out what they were watching on their big-screen TVs.

I'd listened to the weather on my handheld VHF before leaving it behind on the dining table, and the Coast Guard robot voice had told us that another cold front was headed our way overnight. After being so cold out there in the Everglades we'd both overdone it a bit, and we were wearing layers on top of our layers.

When we arrived off River Bend and I made my turn, I looked down the row of boats propped up on the hard ground on the right side of the basin. The hulls looked like fat bugs, the prop stands supporting them like spidery legs. I didn't see the *Mykonos*. Zale was the one who pointed out that I'd missed her, that she was tied up on the end tie, afloat.

"Well I'll be damned," I said, turning the Whaler around. "I guess the name Pontus really gets the boat-yard boys hopping. I'd never have guessed she'd be back in the water this soon."

I tied the Whaler up in almost exactly the same spot I'd left *Gorda* on Monday. The boatyard was shaped like a U around the small marina basin, with the two little peninsulas of land covered with boats high and dry on the hard ground. At that time of night it was quiet, and very few boats had lights on inside. The handful of live-aboards were already tucked tight in their beds. Out by the main gate there was probably a night watchman, but likely as not he was asleep, too, at this hour.

We crossed the wood dock and jumped down into the *Mykonos*'s cockpit aft. Zale's key opened the sliding door and we entered and turned on the lights. The galley and the salon couches were off to starboard while a small dinette was to port. White shag carpet and black leather combined with some kind of purplish modern art gave me the sense that if this was Janet's redecorating taste, I would hate to see their house. All that was missing was a black-velvet painting of Elvis. White curtains were drawn across all the windows, a trick often used by workmen when they wanted to take a break on the salon couch beyond the prying eyes of the yard foreman.

Zale stood in the center of the main cabin and I saw his shoulders lift with a brief shudder. "What?" he said.

"Hey, are you okay?" I asked.

"I thought I heard something," he said.

Zale passed through the main cabin and down a couple of steps forward to a companionway. I followed him. The master stateroom was to port. The black-and-white motif translated here into a comforter with the wildest geometric pattern and black satin covers on the pillows. When Zale lifted the mattress on the queen-sized berth, I saw a plywood hatch. Under it was a large built-in safe.

"I assume you know the combination."

"I think so."

"You think so? We came all the way over here at this time of night on an 'I think so'?"

"I know it as long as he didn't change it. It's a variation on my birthday," he said as he meticulously dialed, then pulled the lever. To my amazement, he lifted the door open.

Only one item was inside: a silver case. While Zale held the door, I reached past him and pulled it out.

It was one of those aluminum photographer's cases,

like a little suitcase, about a foot and a half long and maybe five inches thick. I handed it to Zale and he carried it up into the main salon. When he tried to open the two latches, they wouldn't budge. Each latch had a keyhole, and the thing was clearly locked.

"I don't suppose you have the key to that thing on your ring, do you?" I asked.

"Nope. Dad never said anything about what was in the safe." He peered at me through those glasses of his. He looked like such a little boy. "Why put a locked box in a safe?"

"A lot of people on boats use those boxes for their important documents. There's a rubber gasket inside so they're waterproof, and well, you know—on a boat, there's always that chance. I guess safes are safe, but they're not waterproof."

"Do you think we can break the lock?"

"Yeah, I'm pretty sure we can. I've got stuff back at the house. Why don't you close up that safe and make the bunk look like nobody's been here?"

"Okay." He tucked the case under his arm and went down the stairs into the forward stateroom. I could see he didn't want to entrust that case to anyone. It was a part of his father, and he was going to hang on to it.

Zale had just disappeared into that forward cabin when I felt the boat lurch. There is a distinctive feel to a boat when someone steps aboard and the deck tips slightly with the added outboard weight. I turned to look at the sliding door aft leading to the cockpit, and before I could react, two black-clad figures rushed into the salon and knocked me to the ground.

No one said a thing. I heard Zale let out a little cry, but then he was quiet. A hand on the back of my head smashed my face into the white shag carpet while they yanked my arms behind my back and bound my wrists with heavy, rough rope. Then some sort of cloth hood was slipped over my head just before they yanked me to a standing position.

Part of me felt like I should be yelling and struggling, but we'd been caught by surprise and were so clearly outmanned that I figured if I did scream, I'd just get hurt. Even a big, strong woman like me is no match for a couple of men. Especially when my hands are bound behind my back and I can't even see my assailants. Someone lifted my hands and propelled me forward. I nearly stumbled when I got to the stairs, but whoever was holding my hands prevented me from falling by grabbing the shoulder of my sweatshirt. He shoved me into the guest stateroom on the starboard side. I was barely through the door before my knees collided with the lower berth and I started to fall. I tried to duck, knowing that there must be an upper berth, too, but I still caught the top of my head on the underside of it. Knocks on the head hurt like hell, and I cried out for the first time, but I had little time to feel sorry for myself. Seconds later another body landed on top of me with a grunt, and I knew Zale had arrived. The door closed with a soft *click*, then a *clack*. They'd locked the stateroom door.

I rolled out from under him and shifted around so I was lying on my side, and so my bruised ribs and arms didn't hurt quite so much. There was nothing to be done about my head. I was probably headed for goose egg number two. "You okay?" I asked.

"Yeah," he said, so softly I could barely hear him.

I moved my head so that my cheek slid against the fabric of my hood. It was soft, silky, and I figured they had just thrown a couple of Nick's pillowcases over our heads.

"Did you get a look at them?" I asked him.

"Uhn-uhn," he said.

"Me neither. It happened too quick."

I heard him sniffling then. After I heard a couple of sharp breaths and felt his body shudder, I wished like hell my hands weren't bound so that I could wrap my arms around him.

The hull around us began to vibrate as the big boat's twin diesels started up and reverberated throughout the boat. They didn't wait around long enough for the engines to warm up. I could tell from the change in RPMs that we were pulling away from the dock, leaving River Bend.

"Hey, kid. I know it seems pretty bad right now, but we need to hold it together."

"It's them," he said.

"Yeah, but I don't know who the hell 'them' is, what they want, or where they're taking us."

"They're gonna kill us, aren't they?"

"Not if I can help it," I said, trying to sound surer than I felt.

WE eventually squirmed around enough so that we were able to pull the hoods off each other's heads by using our teeth. It didn't make a whole lot of difference since there were no lights on in the stateroom, and there was no porthole to see outside. And I didn't need to see outside to know we were headed down the river. It was too noisy down there in the hull to hear the chimes as the bridge tenders lowered the traffic gates, but I could feel the engines idle down as we waited for each of the bridges to open for the Hatteras's high hardtop. I stood up and tried to feel my way around the cabin with my bound hands, looking for a sharp edge that might cut through the rope. I found a bunk light, but after doing a contortionist's trick to try to turn it on, it didn't even work. Zale lay on the bunk as I explored, and by the time I was through, he had fallen asleep on his side with his face to the hull. I thought that I would go to work on the ropes that bound him with my teeth, but I lay down next to him to rest up for the effort. Never in a million years did I believe that in those conditions, I would fall asleep.

I awoke to the clattering noise of the anchor chain rattling out. In that forward cabin, it sounded like the chain locker was right over our heads. I was painfully aware of our whereabouts from the moment I opened my eyes. The pain in my hands, wrists, ribs, and shoulders did not allow a gradual rise from the depths of sleep. The bindings around my wrists had loosened a little as I slept, but the rope had embedded itself in my flesh, and now as I moved, it felt as though it was tearing off a layer of skin. And as I was lying on top of one of my arms, the hand on that side had fallen asleep. I struggled to sit up, and when the blood started to flow back into that arm, the prickling pain intensified.

I sat on the edge of the bunk, waiting, assuming that now that we had anchored, they would come for us and something would happen. But no one appeared. For several minutes I heard the sound of their footsteps moving about on deck over our heads. When the footsteps stopped, they were followed by muffled voices outside the door to our cabin. There was a little *snick* as the master stateroom door closed, and then all went quiet.

I hadn't even been able to make out what language they were speaking. Creek? Russian? English?

"You awake?" I whispered.

There was no answer. I could hear Zale's rhythmic breathing.

Sleep was a great way to try to escape our predicament, but the problem was, now that I had slept, I was wide awake. I envied the boy his ability to sleep through this. It was his way of handing the reins over to me, saying, "Okay, you're the grown-up, you figure out how to get us out of this." And, yeah, I was supposed to be the adult here, but the problem was, I didn't feel like being the one in charge. Hell, look at my track record. Ever since I was eleven years old, it seemed all I had been doing was screwing up and losing people. I'd managed to save a few strangers through the years, both as a lifeguard and as a salver, but the important ones, the ones I loved, were all lost. My mother, my father, Neal. And Elysia, the one I came so close to saving.

I looked down at the shadowy form of the sleeping boy, and I thought about that other child, the only one I had saved, Solange. She and her mother, Celeste, were now set up in a small apartment of their own, not far from Jeannie's in Sailboat Bend. The little Haitian girl had started fifth grade and she was catching up fast. One out of five. Not much of a record. And now there were two more on my tally sheet. Molly and Zale. Onto which list would they fall?

I felt the sour taste of poisonous despair crawling up my throat, and I wanted to wail and tear at my hair and curl up in a ball and wait to die. That was what was going to happen to us, after all. It didn't matter who these people were, what language they spoke, or what they wanted. They had us, bound up, locked up, powerless, and they wouldn't do that unless they didn't think we were ever going to get away.

I'd faced it before. Just a few months earlier I had been stranded, dog-paddling in the middle of the Gulf Stream for a day and night, and I thought I was going to die for certain. I remembered both the terror and the peace that had come over me at some point when I had given myself up to it.

But this was different. This time I was not alone. Zale was just a kid. An amazing, great kid. This was a kid who knew how to pole a dugout canoe and sail a Laser. A kid who drove a mean ATV and who wanted a dog just like Abaco. This was Molly's kid.

And it wasn't like me to give up. It was time to stop whining and moaning and get serious about our situation. With my bound hands, I reached behind me and touched the fringe of hair that fell across the boy's forehead. I watched the way his lips moved as he breathed in through his open mouth. The cabin was growing lighter, and I saw the strip of light at the bottom of the door. Daylight had arrived, but there would be no cavalry. I'd been mad at B. J.—for what, I don't even really know, so I had sent him off, preferring not to tell him that Zale and I had other plans. Why did I keep making the same mistakes over and over? Why couldn't I learn to just let things go? Now, no one knew where we were.

First of all, I needed to figure out who and what we were up against. Were these the same guys I had seen out at Gramma Josie's? Both were outfitted in black right down to their ski masks, but it wasn't as though that was a terribly unique fashion statement for bad guys. I had assumed that those guys out at Big Cypress were Seminoles, but it didn't make any sense to imagine them following us back into town and driving off with the *Mykonos*. And what good would it do the Seminoles to kill Zale? That would probably leave Molly and Janet in court fighting for years over ownership of Pontus Enterprises. I couldn't see what they stood to gain. On the other hand, maybe all they'd wanted to do was scare the kid.

I was still trying to make all the different pieces fit into a coherent story when I heard people moving around out on the deck above us. Within the last hour or so, I had noticed that the chop slapping against the outer hull had increased. And we were doing a bit more dancing around on the hook. The front they'd predicted last night was likely passing over us, and that would make the wind swing around to the west. If the yahoos running this boat didn't know what they were doing, we'd likely wind up dragging anchor and running aground.

XXIV.

WHEN the door finally did open, I had dozed off again into a sort of half-awake, half-asleep state. I had finally concluded that everything pointed to the Russians having killed Nick—because of his discovering their slots scam or trying to take the cruise line back or any of a million other reasons, that was the only thing that made sense. But I couldn't see what the Russians would stand to gain by killing Zale. I couldn't see any logical reason why they would follow the kid out into the Everglades and try to shoot him. Besides, if the will that Janet had produced turned out to be the one that stood up in court, Zale wasn't even slated to become full owner of the company.

So when the door opened and this tall, good-looking blond guy was standing out there holding a pistol in his hand and telling us to get up, I just assumed he was a member of the Russian mob.

You can never really understand how hard it is to get around with your hands tied behind your back if you haven't done it. He told us to get up, but it wasn't that easy. First of all, we were both waking up out of a doze, and then we had to roll off the bunk because it wasn't really possible to just sit up and climb out the way you normally would. Blondie was losing patience with how long it was taking us, but I did my best to ignore him.

Once Zale got to his feet, he looked at me with sleepy eyes and whispered, "Do you think they'll let us use the head?"

"No whispering," the gunman said. He was trying very hard to sound mean and gruff, but the fact was, he looked entirely too preppy to be that scary. There was even something vaguely familiar about him that gave me a sort of friendly feeling. Okay, the gun in his hand? That was scary, but the guy was wearing new jeans, a Polo sweater with the little insignia over his breast, and very clean boat shoes.

"The kid says he needs to use the head," I told him. "I do, too. And it won't exactly be easy with our hands tied." I probably wouldn't have been that glib with him if he hadn't looked like a South Beach model.

He reached into his jeans pocket and pulled out a pocketknife. After he'd slit the ropes on Zale's wrists, he pointed to the bathroom. "You first," he told him.

I'd been aware of a heavenly smell since the cabin door first opened, but it was only now really starting to register in my foggy brain. "I smell coffee," I said.

He ignored me.

"Not even just a half a cup?"

He twitched a little, and I think I was supposed to take that for a shake of the head.

"Oh, man. That's cruel."

When we'd both finished with the head, he didn't bother tying us up again. He pointed the gun to indicate that we should go up the steps into the main salon. Then he gestured for us to continue out through the sliding door aft.

It only took me a few seconds of examining the horizon to figure out where we were. Off the boat's starboard beam, I could make out the hazy skyline of the city of Miami, the tall buildings seeming to touch the low gray clouds. The wind was blowing at a good fifteen to twenty out of the west-southwest, churning up wind chop across the wide bay that separated us from the mainland. I could see the brown scrub of an island off our port side and stern. I figured we were anchored in the cove off Sand Key at the north end of Elliot. Somewhere out in the waters off our stern were the remaining structures out in Stiltsville, the colony of houses that had existed out there in Biscayne Bay since the 1930s when old Crawfish Eddie Walker had built his first fishing shack. And beyond that? The lighthouse at Cape Florida on Key Biscayne.

If they were looking for an out-of-the-way place where they could do whatever they wanted, they'd certainly found it. On a warm spring day, Elliot Key would be crawling with boats and sunbathers, but in February weather like this, not a sane soul would venture out to this island.

Blondie grunted again and pointed with the gun at the stainless ladder that led up to the bridge deck. I looked over at Zale and I realized that he was thinking the same thing I was. That was where Nick, his father, had died. Neither of us stepped up to the ladder.

"Move it," Blondie said. He poked me in the arm with his gun.

As I pulled myself up onto the bridge deck, I saw two people sitting in the twin helmsman's seats on the bridge. Even with their backs to me, I recognized them, and it was not anybody I expected.

When Zale's face appeared over the ledge of that deck, he recognized that head of hair just as I had. Richard Hunter slowly swiveled around in his chair to face us.

"Good morning," he said. He held his guitar across his lap and he strummed a few chords. The woman sitting in the chair next to him glanced over her shoulder at us. Her long black hair disappeared down the crevice between her back and the chair, and though the upper bridge was encased on three sides with a plastic enclosure, the force of the wind swirling in from the back was making her hair fly around her face like a swarm of angry insects. Richard pointed to the bench seat that ran along the starboard side of the bridge. "Have a seat," he said.

I motioned for Zale to slide onto the seat ahead of me. Once we were both seated, we looked at him and waited for him to say something. Richard Hunter was dressed from head to foot in brown camouflage military clothes. He was even wearing the black lace-up boots. A web belt circled his waist with a whole array of paraphernalia, from gun to baton. A knife in a black sheath was strapped to the outside of his right leg. He spread his arms, elbows in, palms upward, and said, "Well?"

"Well, what?" I asked.

He snapped at me "Shut up." He spoke way too loud, and that's when I figured out that he was already drunk at whatever hour of the morning it was.

"Where is it?"

Zale turned to me with a look of total puzzlement on his face. "What's he talking about?" The kid was good.

I did, of course, have an inkling as to what it was, but I wasn't about to let on. I raised my shoulders. "Beats me."

Honestly, I hadn't thought any more about the silver case we'd found in the safe. Once we were bound up and thrown into that stateroom, it seemed like the least of my worries. If I'd had to guess, I would have assumed that it was now in our captors' possession. Apparently, I would have guessed wrong.

"Don't you mess with me," he shouted, pointing his finger at Zale's face. He turned to me. "I've got no time for this. I've been chasing you all over the Everglades and back. You *know* what I'm talking about. Nick told Quinn that the kid knew where it was."

Anna reached over and put a hand on his thigh. "It's okay, baby."

"Where *what* was?" I asked.

"If you think for a minute that I'm gonna let that kid get all that money—no way. Not after all my sister's been through."

Was that *it* then? The case was full of money? Why didn't they have it already? Or was it that they just didn't know they had it?

"I wouldn't say your sister's exactly had a hard life as Mrs. Nick Pontus."

He exploded. "You shut up about my sister! You don't know nothin' about her life or what she went through as a kid."

Anna reached over from the other helmsman's chair and patted him on the arm, trying to calm him down. "Sshhh. Richie, baby, it's okay."

He jerked his arm into the air, away from her touch, and glared through the plastic windows at the deserted island off our bow.

The wind was picking up as the day grew lighter. The big Hatteras, with all her windage, was sailing around on her anchor line. At times, when we'd sail up on the anchor, then turn sideways to the wind just as a gust hit, the boat would heel over at about a twenty-degree angle. And because I could see the black clouds and curtains of rain of at least two squalls on the horizon, I hoped the anchor was well set.

I wondered about the way Richard reacted to comments about his sister. He was definitely close to the edge there. I figured Anna for a pretty sensible person, and now that I thought about it, the preppy-looking guy down in the main salon was the guy who had wanded me and Mike before we'd boarded the *TropiCruz IV*. Those two seemed to have thrown their lots in with Richard, but maybe if they realized he was a total nutcase, which seemed obvious enough to me, I could inspire a little mutiny here.

"So, Richard, I don't get it. If the kid's the only one who knows where it is, why'd you try to shoot him out at the Big Cypress yesterday? That was you, right?"

"I didn't try to shoot him."

"So that wasn't you out at Big Cypress last night? Sure it was." I turned to the woman, remembering the smaller figure in black. "You were there, too."

She turned away from me and sucked her teeth, as though she couldn't believe I was so stupid I hadn't figured all this out yet. But I hadn't.

"We weren't trying to kill him," Richard said. "I'd wanted him dead, he'd be dead. I don't miss. We were trying to grab him."

"Why? Anna, did you know this guy was getting you involved in this? Kidnapping, at the very least. Something tells me he doesn't really plan to let us go, either. So that's murder. Did he tell you that's what he was planning?"

She wouldn't look at me. She'd pulled her long hair into her hands and was twisting it in a coil so the wind wouldn't whip it into knots.

Richard sighed and plucked a little riff on the guitar. "I *told* you. Leon says the kid knows where Nick hid it. Janet asked me to find out. You tell us that and you can go."

So, Jeannie and I both were so very wrong about Janet. Molly had known all along. And she'd tried to tell us. And now we were on this boat with this lunatic.

Anna had to see that he was planning to kill us and perhaps she wouldn't be willing to go that far.

"Okay, but then why out here? Why take us all the way down here to deserted Elliot Key just to ask us some questions? You could have done this back at the dock."

"That's enough. You don't ask the questions. I decide when or where I want to go or stay. I am the captain."

Anna rubbed her fingers along the side of his head. He ignored her and continued to fiddle with the strings of the guitar, tuning the instrument, trying out chords.

"Did you know gambling's a sin?" he asked without looking up from the instrument.

"No, I'm not real up on religious stuff."

"Preacher says so. I can't find the place in the Bible where it says so, but I'll keep looking. The scripture does say 'Thou shalt not covet,' and I figure gambling's coveting. All them Russians, they're going to hell. And now that Janet's gonna get her money, I'm done with them. I figured it was time to get out of that sinful business."

"So were you the one who was running the slots scam? Stealing from the Russians? That wasn't too smart."

He threw back his head and laughed. "You know about that, too? How does everybody know about that all of a sudden? Jesus Christ." He glanced heavenward, then said, "Forgive me, Lord."

A bigger-than-average gust heeled the boat over, and when we hit the end of the anchor rode, I could feel the rumble of the chain over the anchor bed through the deck.

"Jason!" he yelled. "Jason, go let out some more scope," he yelled. The younger man ran up onto the foredeck and went forward to the windlass. In order to walk, he had to bend his body into the wind. I figured we probably had almost thirty knots sustained, and if one of those squalls hit us, it was going to get much worse.

He strummed a chord and sang, "I walk through this valley on my knees, and I pray till I feel Him close to me." He stopped and put his hand across the strings to quiet the instrument. "Were you lying when you said you thought I had talent?"

"No. I like your voice. And, while I'm no expert, your guitar-picking sounds pretty good to me."

"I picked that up overseas. We didn't have much else to do most of the time. Buddy who taught me? He drove over a mine a week before he was due to ship back home." He threw back his head and shouted, "The Lord works in mysterious ways!"

"Richard, why is your sister making you do all the dirty work? She's the one who's coveting this money, not you."

He jumped to his feet, handed Anna the guitar, and pulled the knife from the sheath on his leg. He grabbed my ponytail and held the knife under my chin. "I told you not to talk about her. I came back from Kuwait sick as a dog, coughing up all that black shit from the stinkin' oil well fires, and my baby sister took care of me. She held me through all the night tremors. You have no idea what that baby angel did for me. You don't even say her name, you hear me?"

He pulled my head so far back, all I could see was the white canvas of the overhead. I felt the tip of the knife pressing hard against my throat. I opened my mouth and tried to speak, but my chin shook with spasms. I knew he was crazy enough to kill me, and all I could see was an image of the knife slicing through the skin of my throat. I couldn't speak. Even if I had been able to dredge up the courage or could figure out what to say at that moment, I physically could not speak.

"Uncle Richard," Zale said. "Please, Uncle Richard, don't hurt her."

The pressure against my throat eased, and I rasped air into my lungs.

He let go of my hair, slid the knife back into the sheath, and flopped back down into the helmsman's seat. I stared down at my knees, tears streaming from my eyes, not wanting him to see how frightened I was.

"Kid, I'm gonna write a song about my life someday. 'Bout how I found Jesus. It wasn't easy. None of it. You have no idea what it's like to grow up with an old lady who's a crackhead whore. We had to find our own food, get our own selves to school. She made us get her cigarettes, cook her food, change her filthy sheets with the cum and condoms from all them johns. Soon as I turned eighteen, I got out. Joined the Marines. Baby sister was only eight, but she was already good at steering clear of the old lady and stealing enough food and money to stay alive."

He pointed his finger in my face. "Don't you say she's coveting something that ain't hers. She deserves every penny after all she's been through. All those dirty hands on her—coveting her body. God wants her to have the peace all that money can buy." He looked at Anna. "And if she wants to put up the dough for me to cut a CD, then it was the least I could do for her, right, baby?" He laughed.

Zale was staring at his clenched hands, and I could feel the tension in every muscle of his body. I knew we were both thinking it, and one of us was going to have to say it aloud. It was too much to ask of the boy.

"It was you, wasn't it?" I said. "You shot Nick."

He pantomimed holding a rifle, closing one eye, and sighting through the scope, and then he made these popping sounds with his lips and jerked with the imaginary recoil, "Powp, powp, powp." Then he threw back that big head and laughed again.

Zale leaped up with an animal cry and swung and beat at him with mostly ineffectual punches. Richard never stopped smiling, but he got his hands around the boy's wrists and lifted him up until his feet left the deck.

"You gotta learn to fight better than *that,* boy. You're looking at a trained U.S. Marine scout sniper. When Janet told me what your mama yelled out so's everybody could hear—about wanting to kill your daddy? That was an opportunity the Lord had provided, and I just couldn't pass it up. I'd been wanting to put a bullet in your daddy's head since the first time he fucked my sister on a blackjack table on the *TropiCruz IV.* I watched the whole thing, thanks to the eye in the sky. She only did it so's we could get enough money to get ourselves some peace. That's what she says. I'm gonna cut my CD and she's gonna run a business where she can get some peace from all those dirty hands. My sister's smart. It was her idea to use a Russian gun. And she put it in your mama's garage. Those cops didn't know what to think. Now, once you tell me what your daddy told you, then Janet will be through with all these other men. This time it'll be enough for her."

Zale hung from Richard's grip like a limp marionette, his head slumped forward on his chest. He had been sobbing when he first struck out at the man, but he was quiet now—too quiet. Richard shook him hard. "Your daddy told you where he hid it," he yelled, and he pushed him away. The boy collapsed against me as though all the life had been wrung from his body. "It won't do you any good. I'll find out eventually. No food, no mama, and if it comes to it, I'll start working on her with my blade. You'll tell me. Janet's been tearing up the house for days looking everywhere, but I don't think it's there. Doesn't matter. You'll tell me."

There is a difference between a regular strong gust of wind and the first heavy gust of a squall. The squall's wind carries with it a colder chill and the clean smell of rain. It was at that moment that I felt the first gust, and only seconds later fat raindrops began to burst against the plastic windows. When I turned and looked behind me, it was like something out of *The Wizard of Oz*. Not a waterspout, thankfully, but the meanest, blackest-looking squall I'd ever seen was swallowing up the south tip of the island and heading our way.

"Jason!" Richard yelled. Then he turned to us. "You. Both of you. Down below."

I helped Zale down the ladder, but he was listless and unseeing. When Richard yelled for him to hurry up, Jason reached up and pulled the boy off the ladder. I scrambled down and put my arm around the child's waist. Jason, still carrying his gun, pointed the way inside.

In the main salon, I turned to him. "Jason, he's nuts. What are you and Anna doing here?"

"Move," he said, poking me in the ribs with the gun. Just before he closed the stateroom door, he said, "It's just about the money. Nothing personal." And then he locked the door.

Rain was now hammering the deck overhead, and the motion of the boat had become so rough that it was difficult to stand as she hobbyhorsed in the wind chop kicked up by the squall. Just before the engine growled to life, I heard the anchor chain rumbling across the coral pan bottom, and I knew we had broken free and were dragging at a fast clip. I heard their feet pounding overhead and the grinding of the windlass trying to bring in the anchor rode against the force of that wind.

I wished I could see, wished they'd let me help. But since there was nothing I could do to help with the wild anchor drill on deck, I sat on the bunk, put a pillow on my lap, and rested Zale's head on the pillow. I stroked his hair and told him that everything was going to be okay, that I was going to figure out how to get us out of that place, that he didn't have to worry. In other words, I lied.

XXV.

It was only after the squall had passed and Richard and his gang had managed to re-anchor the boat that I slipped out from under the pillow and stood and stretched. Residual chop from the high winds still rocked the boat, but I was accustomed to moving around with that kind of motion. I switched on the reading light in the top bunk and found that it worked.

I started with a thorough search of the stateroom, including crawling up into the top bunk, checking out the types of screws on the dome lights, examining the twelve-volt bunk fans, and seeing if there wasn't some way I could pull out the bar in the hanging locker. I tried to pull the decorative mirror off the bulkhead, but decided it must have been stuck on there with 5200 adhesive, and nothing was going to pull that damn thing down.

Although I didn't come up with a whole lot of great ideas, the fact was, it felt good just to be doing something. I don't take well to confinement, and after all those hours, I was beginning to *feel* as nuts as Richard Hunter. I wondered how Molly was handling it. Better than me, probably. Now if I could just get out of here in one piece, I could clear her, too.

Of course, Richard would not have told me so much if he had thought I was going to survive our little Keys trip. Nor Zale. I'm sure he intended to go a ways off-shore and dump both our bodies. Right now it was three against two, and those weren't the worst odds ever. I had no doubt that I could take care of skinny little Anna, but the other two? As if it weren't bad enough that they were bigger and stronger and my partner was a seem-ingly catatonic thirteen-year-old boy, they were the ones who had all the guns.

But we had something they wanted. I figured there had to be some way we could use that.

IT had been quiet for a couple of hours, and I had man-aged to take apart one of the bunk fans and extract the wooden bar out of the hanging locker. I now had a bat and had fashioned a nasty device out of the stainless steel cage that had covered the bunk fan. When I held it in my fist, steel prongs protruded between my fingers.

The quiet ended when somebody turned on the boat's stereo full blast and Richard Hunter began singing along with the Oak Ridge Boys' tune "Put Your Arms Around Me Blessed Jesus." The music pounded from the speak-ers. I had no idea what time it was, but my guess was mid- to late afternoon. The sustained wind had not let up after the squall, and judging from the whistling and flapping noises as well as the motion of the boat, I fig-ured this nasty norther was going to blow like stink all night long. They lowered the volume on the music just enough so that I could hear their voices, but I could not understand what they were saying. In between songs I heard the microwave running, and I began to smell food. The generator wasn't going, so I figured they were running stuff off an inverter, and from the sound of the laughter out there, they were starting to party. Maybe they'd get too drunk, flatten their batteries, and we'd all die out here.

My stomach grumbled and my mouth felt dry all of a sudden. It smelled like pizza and fried chicken out there. And beer. And I thought that coffee had been bad hours ago. I had to get out of here.

I sat on the edge of the bunk and tried to rouse Zale. He moaned and jerked away, a perturbed look on his face.

"Look, Zale, we've got to do something to get out of here. I'm not willing to sit here until they decide to come and start cutting my fingers off one by one. You saw how crazy he is. He'd do something like that."

The kid grabbed the pillow and pulled it over his head. I yanked it off. "Stop that. You've got to get up. You've got to help me."

"Go away," he said, his voice muffled as his face was pressed to the mattress.

"What would your mother think of me if I just lay down on this bunk and let them kill both of us? What would she think of you? Do you want her to stay in that jail for the rest of her life?" He rolled over so that I could see his face in profile. "That's right. What about your mom? We know who *really* killed your dad. That means they'll let her go home. But we've got to get out of here so we can tell them."

He sighed and pushed himself up to a sitting position. "But what can we do? We're never gonna get out of here."

The sounds of the party in the main salon were growing louder and more raucous. They were nuts to get bombed in this kind of weather. Especially with two very angry prisoners in the bow. The drunker they got, the better our chances got.

I showed Zale my weaponry, such as it was, and we began to hatch our plan.

Twenty minutes later when we thought we were ready

to try it, we were interrupted by the sound of large marine engines. Even with their music, we could hear the engine noise transmitted through the water and then through the hull. It's hard to tell direction from down in the hull, but it sounded like a big go-fast boat like a Donzi or a Cigarette. They were probably going to ask if we needed help. There was no good reason for anyone to anchor out at Elliot on an afternoon like this.

When Richard and the others realized we were being approached, the music shut down abruptly and, in the quiet, all I could hear was cursing and the sound of panic. Somebody went scrambling into the cabin across the hall and began throwing things around. Anna was crying and cursing at Richard for what he'd brought her to. I wasn't sure where it started or who started it, but just before the first shots were fired I heard an amplified voice from the other boat, and then Richard yelled, "Go straight to hell, Kagan!"

I was standing by the cabin door with my ear to the wood when it sounded like World War III broke out. I pulled Zale off the bunk and we landed with me half on top of him on the little bit of cabin sole. I reached up and pulled the mattress off the bunk and down on top of us. It wasn't as though I really believed that foam could stop bullets, but there is no such thing as rational thinking when your world explodes in a storm of gunfire. I squeezed my eyes shut, grabbed hold of the dolphin charm around my neck with one hand, and wrapped my other arm around the boy's back.

I know that it couldn't have taken that long, but when we were there, huddled under that cushion, hearing the nonstop blasts from those guns, the crashing noise of the breaking windows, and the splintering of the interior woodwork, the screams of the others as they were hit and wounded and dying, it seemed to go on for hours. I didn't even know I was screaming until the shooting stopped.

And that was when I felt the first shock of cold water as it started to seep up through the floorboards. The engines of the other boat roared to life, grew less and less audible, and soon were gone.

Aside from the sound of lapping water, it was quiet for a moment before I heard the moaning start.

I pushed the cushion off us, and Zale and I rose warily to our feet. The water was up over the tops of my boat shoes already. Scared as I was of getting shot, I wasn't real keen on the idea of being locked in a stateroom on a sinking boat, either. I banged on the door with my fist. "Hey, hello! Open the door!"

Someone out there coughed and spit. I wasn't sure it was the same voice that had been moaning.

"Anna? Is that you? Open this door. We can help you."

The moaning changed. It was definitely a woman's voice. She started saying, "Oh, oh, oh."

I grabbed hold of the doorknob and shook and rattled it senselessly. I stopped to listen.

Then a different voice, a lower voice, the one that had been coughing and spitting earlier, started choking out the word, "Help. Help me," he said.

I picked up the bar we'd taken out of the closet and began banging on the door. "Richard, Anna, Jason, unlock this door and I can help you."

"Help, help me," he said again, and I attacked that door, beating on it with everything I had, cursing and spewing every curse word I knew. I threw my shoulder at the wood, oblivious to the pain in my ribs, until finally, tears streaming down my cheeks, I pounded my head against the door as the moaning and crying faded.

When I stopped, exhausted, there was no sound but

the lapping of the waves against the hull. The water was already up to my midcalf. "Hello? Are you there?"

No moaning. No coughing. No answer.

I looked at Zale's wide eyes and saw that he was hyperventilating. I knew I had to pull myself together, calm down, think this through.

"Come on. We can do this together." There were only about three to four feet from the cabin door to the edge of the lower bunk. I pulled Zale next to me and said, "On three. One, two, three," and we both slammed our shoulders into the door. Nothing moved.

I looked down at the door handle and saw below that water was pouring in around the edges of the door. This meant that the water level was much higher outside the door than it was inside our cabin. There was no way we were going to budge that door against that kind of water pressure. I knew what that meant, and I didn't like it at all.

"Zale, listen." I looked up at the top of the door. There were a good three inches between the top of the door frame and the vinyl headliner. "See if you can use that metal cage off the fan to tear down some of that headliner. We're going to need every last inch of space in here. See that ventilation hole there? That's what's letting the air out so that the water can come in this fast."

Before I'd even stopped talking, the boy had seen what I was thinking. Whereas a few minutes ago he'd been willing to lie there and let death take him, now that he had something to do, he was attacking it with an enthusiasm that would have made Molly proud.

"I'm going to have to wait until the pressure on the outside of this door is equalized before I'll be able to bust it down. Once the water reaches the top of the door frame, there will still be a few inches of air left. I might have about four or five chances to try to bust through, then we'll take a breath and swim out." Standing as I was on the cabin sole, the water was already up to my armpits. It was achingly cold. Zale was pulling down the vinyl in long sheets, exposing the fiberglass underside of the deck. Once he saw that the hole for the ventilator was only about five inches across and nothing we could crawl out through, he began stuffing vinyl in the hole, trying to slow down the exiting air so we might be left with a little pocket.

I was standing on the lower bunk with my face up close to the overhead, trying to make myself take long calm breaths, oxygenating my blood, when the boat lurched aft and the bow rose, tilting everything in the cabin at a crazy angle. Zale and I both lost our balance and our heads went underwater. There was now a pocket of air in the bow big enough for us to breathe in, but the door to the cabin was about two feet underwater. Amazingly, the upper bunk light was still on.

I took three deep breaths and pulled myself underwater. I opened my eyes. I couldn't see a thing. I felt for the door, found it, then found the bunks opposite. It was amazing how just tilting the cabin on its side had disoriented me so. I braced my back against the bunk, holding on with both arms, and kicked with everything I had. The door didn't move. I resurfaced for air.

In the small remaining air space in the bow, it was difficult to get through to the surface. The bunk cushions and pillows had floated up to the top of the four-foot-square hole, where Zale kept pushing them aside. There was just enough space now for me to get my head above water, but the top of my head bumped against the overhead. Somehow, Zale's glasses were still on his face, but they were covered with droplets of saltwater and for some reason, as I took my next three deep breaths, I wondered how well he could see.

Another deep breath, and down I pulled my body. This time I didn't take as long getting lined up on the door, as the geography of the strangely canted boat had grown more familiar. I braced my back once again and kicked with both feet. Nothing. I paused to refocus and this time as I kicked, I screamed with all the rage and will to live I had inside me.

My right foot busted through the plywood as the bubbles floated up around my face. I was desperate for air. For a second, when I tried to withdraw my shoe, I thought my leg was stuck, but then I twisted right and pointed my toe and pulled free. I brought myself up for air, hoping there would still be some. Zale was holding aside the debris so I could get my head into the tiny air pocket. This time, I had to hold my head sideways, my mouth close to the overhead. I allowed myself four breaths before I spoke. "This time, you've got to come with me, okay? I'm almost through the door. Hold my hand. Don't let go. We're going to take three deep breaths. Okay? On the count of three. One, two, three."

We both took slow, long, deep breaths, our cheeks scraping against the scratchy underside of the fiberglass deck, and we dove.

XXVI.

I HELD tight to his hand as I felt again for the door and then lined my body up, my back against the bunk. That's when his hand slipped out of mine.

I opened my eyes and looked around in the darkness, feeling this moment of utter despair. Somewhere in my mind or my heart, Zale and Molly had become one, and I knew if I could only save him, I could save *us* and restore all that I had once lost. I wanted to rewrite that ending. I wanted to create a new beginning. I could not leave him behind.

And then, as I was just about ready to start for the surface, I felt his arm over my shoulder, his back, too, against the bunk, and together we kicked for our lives. Two kicks later and the hole was big enough to swim through.

Without a face mask, it's difficult to see underwater, and with all the chop the north wind was kicking up, the water was unusually murky as well. I didn't even try to open my eyes. My brain was screaming for air, but I tried to concentrate on the layout of the boat. I told myself to stay calm. Because of the way she was sinking stern first, we had to swim down to get out the companionway to get into the salon, and then we had to go deeper yet to reach the windows on the port side. I followed the overhead down, knowing that I would soon get to the windows that I was sure had been shot out.

I prefer free diving to scuba, always have. And I can normally hold my breath a very long time. But breath-holding is harder when you're exerting yourself, and even harder still when you're scared. I felt the blackness closing in. My eyes were closed, but even then you still see lights on the insides of your eyelids. This blackness was different. I'd been this close before and managed to hold on until I reached the surface, but I knew I had only seconds before I would black out.

Then I cut my hand on something—glass or splintered wood—and then I opened my eyes and saw brighter light. I pulled Zale with me and we swam through the window and began to rise toward the surface.

I inhaled a little water as I broke through into the air because in my hurry I didn't wait until my mouth was clear. Air. Sweet, sweet air. I was coughing, but it was air, and I was still clutching Zale's hand. We both floated on our backs, breathing in the sweet taste of air. We'd been so focused on trying to get out, I hadn't really cared how cold the water was. Now I felt the cold reaching into my body, leaching out the heat.

Then I heard a *whoosh* sound, and when I looked over at the boat, the sharp point of the bow disappeared under the waves and the flybridge canvas reared up out of the water as the boat settled on the bottom in what must have been eighteen to twenty feet of water.

"Come on," I said to Zale, and we both swam for the canvas. The day was nearly over, the overcast sky dark and low. The wind chop that had pushed us along as we floated now made it hard to swim back to the boat. My sweatshirt and jeans and layers of T-shirts and turtle-necks also made swimming more difficult, not to mention the debris covering the surface of the water. We had to push aside the bits of wood cabinetry and cushions and clothing that continued to rise to the surface downwind of the boat. When we finally reached the flybridge enclosure, I reached for what I thought was part of the canvas and found instead that I'd grabbed Richard Hunter's arm. His clothes had caught in the metal framework.

I was startled and I pulled back my hand as though I'd been burned. But I wasn't frightened. It wasn't the first time in my life I'd seen a dead body, and a part of me had known they must be around. Earlier that day I'd felt so angry and afraid. But seeing his open eyes, his lips pulled back, baring his teeth in a grimace of pain, his tattered camouflage shirt ripped with holes from dozens of bullets, I was surprised that I felt pity for the man. He may have been the one who pulled the trigger and shot Nick Pontus, but life had made him into a killing machine, and I suspected his sister had pointed him at the target.

I found we were able to stand on the bridge deck in water up to our thighs, though when we stood, the air felt far colder than the water. The forecast for this cold front was for an overnight low in the forties. I knew we would have to get dry somehow or we were going to face hypothermia.

I worked to disentangle the fragments of Richard's shirt from the metal frame that held the canvas around the bridge. After pushing his eyelids closed, I set him adrift. I supposed the other two had either drifted off or were trapped in the cabin below. I was glad we hadn't run into them on our way out of the boat. I might never have made it to the surface if that had happened.

"You know this boat," I shouted as I pushed the body away. "We're going to need to salvage some gear."

When I turned back to the helm, he ducked his head

underwater, only to resurface a few seconds later with a waterproof flashlight in one hand and an emergency flare kit in the other. His teeth were chattering when he handed them to me.

"Terrific," I said, taking the box from him. Once we opened it, though, the plastic case was full of water and the flare gun was useless. The cartridges were sodden and fell apart in our hands. There was a sealed packet of two handheld flares, though, and they looked clean and dry inside the plastic.

"Zale, look at the way you're shaking. Maybe we'll use one of these later to start a fire onshore. Where did your dad keep his life jackets?"

"I know of something better," he said, and he took about three deep breaths and dove off the flybridge. As a woman, at least I had a little—okay, *more* than a little— padding on my body to act as insulation against this cold. Zale was all skin and bones. How could he keep going back into that water like that? Had it been lighter, I would have been able to see him down there, but I could only make out the faint yellow glow of the flashlight. He surfaced a few seconds later with two mesh dive bags and two full-length wet suits.

"Kid, you are amazing. I was just starting to think about how the hell we were going to get dry and warm. These just may save our lives."

"That one's my dad's. We used to come down to the Keys during the lobster miniseason sometimes. It should fit you okay."

We stripped down to our underwear, turning our backs to each other with a modesty that, under the circumstances, seemed a little ridiculous. Then we pulled on the wet suits. Nick's suit fit me well enough, though it was a little tight round the hips and loose in the shoulders. Even though they weren't very heavy neoprene suits, we stopped losing heat at such a rapid rate as soon as we zipped them up. We threw our clothes and shoes up on the flybridge console.

"I think we'd better swim to the island," I said, "while there's still a little light left."

Across Biscayne Bay, the lights on the mainland were starting to wink on. The high-rises of the city of Miami were glowing in the evening haze, and while we could make out the lights of the Turkey Point Power Plant, most of the rest of the coast was dark. We'd need to get out of this water as soon as possible. Then we could build a fire, try to find some shelter from the wind.

"Zale, there's a ranger station a few miles south of here on Elliot. We could try to walk it tonight or wait until first light. Even closer, there are some buildings up on Boca Chita, about a mile away. I'm sure there wouldn't be any boats out there in this weather, but we'd find shelter."

Zale shook his head. "We've got to get back tonight. Like you said, we've got to get my mom out of jail."

"But there's no way we can do that, Zale. We can't swim across to the mainland," I said, pointing to the dark shape on the horizon speckled with scattered pricks of light. "It's five or six miles. We'd never make it."

"No, we can't swim," he said, and then he grinned at me for the first time ever. "But we could sail," he said. I'd met this boy by telling him that his father was dead, and other than a few halfhearted attempts at smiles, I'd never really seen him happy. This was a different kid.

"What are you talking about?"

"We've got a boat. My dad always wanted me to go on these summer trips down to the Keys with him and his friends. It was boring. A couple of years ago he bought me a Metzler inflatable sailing dinghy, so I could sail while he and his friends went fishing. It's pretty cool."

"You're telling me that onboard this boat there are all the parts for a sailing dinghy?"

"Yeah. There's a lot of stuff, but we could swim it ashore and put it together there."

"Let's do it then," I said. The top of the steering console was not underwater, and although the wind chop was breaking against the plastic windows, we were fairly protected there. Zale had set the dive bags up there earlier, and now we lifted them down and put on the fins and masks with snorkels. Following his directions, we retrieved two bags out of the cockpit deck box and the two-part aluminum mast that had been lashed to a stanchion on the floor of the cockpit. We piled everything up on the console.

"That's almost everything," Zale said. "I just need one more thing." He grabbed the flashlight, took three quick breaths, and dove. I watched the light disappear into the cabin.

I didn't like it. So far, we hadn't tried to go inside the cabin for anything. Everything we'd retrieved had been stored in lockers accessible from the deck area. I was worried that one of the other two bodies might still be in the cabin. We hadn't seen any sharks so far, but that didn't mean they weren't down where we couldn't see them. I pulled my mask down over my eyes and fit my snorkel into my teeth and started to take a deep breath, but Zale bobbed to the surface before I jumped.

"Here," he said, shoving the aluminum photographer's case across the surface of the water. It banged against my knees.

I lifted it out of the water. "Geez, Zale."

He spit out his snorkel. "Can't forget what we came for," he said.

I took the bag with the folded inflatable dinghy and the two pieces of mast. Zale took the bag with the floorboards, pump, leeboards, rudder, rigging, and sail. He tied one end of a piece of light line to the silver case, the other end to his wrist.

As we got ready to leave for shore, he lifted the case a couple of times. "I don't think it could be that much money," he said. "It's not heavy."

"Maybe it's some kind of stock certificates or bonds or something that's worth millions. You never know with Nick," I said.

"It's kinda cool guessing, huh?"

I returned his smile. "Yeah."

Although the swim to shore started out with difficulty, loaded as we were with gear, we'd not gone a hundred yards before the bottom came up under our feet and we found we could walk the rest of the way.

Wasn't much of a shore, though—just some rough coral rubble that went up about three feet from the water's edge. Then the brush started. Years of salt spray and strong winds had stunted the growth of most bushes on the island. Only a few were taller than my armpit.

We decided to inflate the dinghy afloat. With the foot pump right down at the water's edge, I stomped on the pump's bellows while Zale kept it from impaling itself on a sharp coral rock. Once inflated, we added the floorboards, the daggerboards, and all the sailing rigging.

It didn't look like much of a sailing boat. First of all, the thing was bright orange. It was really a typical twelve-foot inflatable sport boat with pointed pontoons aft and a little wooden transom for mounting an outboard motor. But she had a braced mast step on her floorboards and various pad-eyes for tying down her running rigging.

"She's not really designed to sail in this much wind," Zale explained. "The good thing is, there are two of us. We need the ballast."

"Always glad to be counted on as ballast."

"We're going to make lots of leeway, though. That's the bad part. Do you know what's over there?" He pointed across to the mainland.

"I've been thinking about that," I said. "I think we should head for just north of the power plant. That would put us in around the park there at Convoy Point. This whole area, including the island we're sitting on, is part of Biscayne National Park. The park is mostly water, but there's a visitors' center and a little marina on the mainland over there. We should be able to find somebody or walk our way out from there."

"Okay. We'd better aim farther north, though. Those daggerboards don't do much. That'll put us on a reach all the way. I just hope the rig can take it."

"If we lose the rig, we'll just get blown down into Card Sound and we'll end up on Key Largo. At least we won't be blown out to sea."

"True," he said. "But I need to get home."

"We'll get you there."

FIRST, we rowed out to deeper water so that we could inflate the keel. Then we started with just the jib. Zale was on the tiller while I raised the little sail. It flapped like crazy until he pulled the sheet in and got it under control. We started to move forward.

At first, it was great. This is going to be easy, I thought. We were moving on the water at about two knots, and I figured we'd be across in two to three hours. With each little gust, the pontoon on the windward side would lift just a little as we heeled over with the wind. We were taking the chop on the forward quarter, but the soft pontoons rose up easily over the little waves. Only a little water shipped aboard.

But the farther we traveled away from Sand Key, the

rougher the water grew. We'd been experiencing some protection from the north winds from Key Biscayne, but as we got out into the channel, the little wind waves grew to three to five feet in height, and they started curling and breaking into the dink.

We had nothing to bail with. Zale had his hands full with steering, so I cupped my hands and started trying to throw the water out of the boat. The water was a couple of inches above the dinghy's floorboards, and I couldn't seem to get it any lower than that.

"Can't you get the water out any faster?" Zale yelled. "It's slowing us down."

We had not yet dared to put up the mainsail, but we were wallowing in the troughs of the seas. Another good-sized swell shipped aboard, and I began to worry about the rig. Part of what keeps a sailboat's rig intact is the fact that the boat *can* heel over a little. The extra weight of the water in the boat wasn't allowing the mast to lean over. If it didn't get some relief soon, the rig would just snap off.

I looked around the dinghy. We had a paddle, the pump, dive bags with our snorkel gear, and tucked next to Zale was his silver case, the line still tied to his wrist. We had nothing to use as a bailer. Even with our wet suits, sitting in the cold water was taking a toll. My fingers and toes were numb, and the skin on my face ached from the salt and the freezing wind. The little rigging lines creaked and groaned as the waterlogged vessel was hit with another gust.

Of course! The face masks! The moment I thought of it, I couldn't understand why I hadn't seen it before. My brain must be frozen, I thought, as I dug into the dive bags and pulled out the clear silicone masks. I found a position where I could sit, leaning against the leeward pontoon, and scooped two-fisted, throwing the water over my shoulder back into the sea. I started to gain on it. Then, just when I thought I'd solved our biggest problem, I realized that the pontoon I was leaning against was going soft. We had a leak.

XXVII.

WE'D brought the foot pump with us, but there was no way I could stand up in the dinghy in that seaway. I wanted to get on my knees and push down with my arms on the pump, but I couldn't get far enough ahead of the water. The pump needed to rest on the floorboards, completely clear of water. Otherwise, the bellows couldn't draw in the air. Bailing with the face masks, I just couldn't get rid of that last couple of inches of water. Finally, I hooked up the air pump and held the bellows between my arms like an old sailor's squeeze box, only I wasn't playing a tune. I was trying to keep our boat afloat.

Though we were steering the boat toward a spot on the coastline about a mile north of Convoy Point, we continued to be shoved sideways by the strong northerly winds. I did not want to land on the grounds of the nuclear power plant for a couple of reasons. Given their security there, and their fear of a terrorist attack, they would be more likely to ship us off to jail first and ask questions later. The second problem with the power plant did not come from the human element. The plant was surrounded by cooling canals in the mangroves that worked like a giant radiator to disperse the heat created by the big turbines. These canals had become the nesting grounds for up to forty American crocodiles.

Normally, when people think of Florida and the Everglades, they think of gators, which are strictly freshwater creatures. Along the coast, where the environment is often a mix of fresh and saltwater, is where the crocs survive. Because American crocodiles are endangered, the nuclear power plant had scored some much-needed points with the environmental community when it had made the wetlands around the plant into a preserve for the endangered animals. I did not want to be trying to hike my way out of a mangrove preserve, waiting for the crocs to get me.

"How're you holding up?" I hollered at Zale, the wind whipping my voice off across the water.

"What?" he yelled back. He sat huddled at the stern of the boat like a little gnome, the tiller under his arm, held tight against his body. His wet suit was black with yellow stripes down the sides, making his body nearly invisible in the night. From time to time he took his index finger and wiped it across his glasses like an ineffectual little windshield wiper.

"I asked how you're doing. Are you okay?"

"Yeah. But I'm worried about leeway."

"Me, too," I shouted back, continuing to bail, scraping my raw hands across the floorboards as I scooped with the silicone masks. "I think the seas will let up a little, though, when we pass the halfway mark. We'll start to get a little protection from the mainland."

Zale had sheeted in the headsail, and we were sailing as hard on the wind as the little boat could manage, but we were still sliding past our destination. The worst part of the trip lasted for about an hour. If the whole voyage had been like that, neither the boat nor her crew would have held up. I kept alternating between bailing and pumping the bellows to keep the boat inflated.

The wind and the waves screamed straight down the

middle of the channel from some point north of Miami. Since the bay waters were relatively shallow, the waves built up to heights one normally wouldn't find with such a short fetch. In an inflatable dinghy, a three-foot curling wave looks like a monster. Just one of those could have completely swamped the boat. Zale seemed to have a sixth sense about how and where the waves were going to break and somehow he steered us through them. Waves would break and engulf us in white water that poured over the pontoons, but never did one of those curling monsters dump right on top of us.

To keep my bailing and pumping rhythm going, I sang songs. The only ones I knew all the words to were shanties like "My Father Was the Keeper of the Eddystone Light" and drinking songs like "Ninety-nine Bottles of Beer on the Wall." I'd made it down to twenty-nine bottles of beer when Zale interrupted my song.

"Hey," he said.

"Yeah?" I stopped bailing and slid closer to him. "What?"

"We're still headed for a landing at the power plant."

"We can't land there. If that's the case, we'll have to fall off and sail down to a landing somewhere to the south. Maybe another three miles down."

"No," he said. "I think I can do it if we raise the main. The wind and seas have let up a little."

I thought he was being a bit too optimistic, but after two hours in the dinghy watching the way the kid handled the boat, I decided to trust him. "Whatever you say, Captain."

He pointed the halyard out to me and, after untying the sail ties, I raised the small sail. The sail fluttered and flapped loose in the wind, making loud snapping and crackling noises. It sounded like the fabric was self-destructing. My frozen fingers had a time tying off the little lines on the baby cleats. Everything on the boat was so miniature, and my fingers felt like they had ballooned to three times their normal size. Finally, Zale sheeted it in and the flapping grew quiet.

When the wind first caught that sail, I thought we were going over for sure. I grabbed for my bag of snorkel gear and scrambled for the high side. But somehow that kid kept the boat upright, and all of a sudden we were flying.

At that point, if we both hadn't been so exhausted, we might have enjoyed ourselves. The seas flattened out and the wind eased off and that goofy-looking little inflatable sailboat sailed like a real rocket. I figured at times we were hitting four or five knots, and it felt as if she were trying to climb up out of the water and plane.

He never even had to tack. The closer we got to the coast, the better we were able to make out what was there along the shoreline. Because it was a national park, the mangroves along the coast had been well preserved. There were no beachfront mansions or high-rises here. From our viewpoint, that meant the coastline in the foreground was dark, a barely visible black line on the horizon, but the yellow phosphorus lights at the park marina could be seen from over a mile out. And he hit it bang on.

Most days you probably lose your wind as soon as you sail into the mangrove-lined system of canals and lagoons, but this night, with the norther blowing, we were able to sail that little boat right into the basin and over to the fuel dock. Several dive and snorkel tour boats were tied up there. Farther down the dock, I saw a glass-bottom boat, and just aft of that a stainless-steel ladder reached down to the water. I pointed it out to Zale.

We tied the dinghy painter to the ladder and climbed up, stretching and walking in circles for a bit, trying to get the kinks out of our bodies. It seemed like we'd been in that dinghy all night, but I had no concept of how much time had really passed. I went over to one of the dock lights and peeled back the wet suit sleeve to look at my watch. It was almost 1:00 a.m. I hoped there was a resident ranger at the park, but as we followed the road in our bare feet, we saw no one.

We left behind the boat and our snorkel gear, though Zale refused to let go of the silver case, and we began to explore the area around the little marina. There was a closed visitors' center, locked bathrooms, and a broken public telephone—not that we had any money on us anyway. I had thought we might be able to make a 911 call at least, but more and more cell phones were making pay phone repair a low priority.

Just behind the fuel dock buildings was the launch ramp and a huge parking area. I could imagine how, when the weather was fine, the whole lot would be filled with pickup trucks and boat trailers. Tonight there was one lone truck and trailer. The pickup was one of those huge dually trucks with a fancy paint job on the side with the boat name. I wondered who would be crazy enough to be out there on a night like this. Whoever it was had probably decided to hole up at another marina, call his wife, and go fetch the boat later.

There were no cars and no lights on in the small boat marina. The weather had turned the place into a ghost town, so we followed the road that looked like it headed out to the park entrance. The gate was a simple metal bar designed to stop cars, not pedestrians. We ducked under it and started to walk.

I regretted that I hadn't thought to toss our shoes into the dinghy. The road was covered with sharp little rocks, sticks, and prickly burrs from the dry underbrush that grew along the banks leading down to the mangrove marsh on either side of us. We took it slow, stopping to flick off the stones or burrs that got stuck in the flesh.

The wet suits did a pretty good job of keeping our bodies warm, but my feet and hands were freezing. I had no idea what the temperature was, but I guessed it had dropped into the forties. And it was often colder here in this more rural Homestead area because there was so much less concrete to hold the day's warmth. The cold felt worse now that we were out of the water. The water temperature had been around seventy degrees, but now this wind felt absolutely frigid.

We'd been walking for about forty-five minutes when we saw a set of headlights appear on the road from the direction in which we were headed. The lights were over a mile off, but coming our way fast.

"Thank goodness," I said. "My feet are killing me."

"Who do you think it is?"

"I don't care. As long as their car heater is on."

The lights were coming closer at a remarkable speed. "What if it's those guys. The ones who killed Uncle Richard?"

"Do you think?" I started to say, then I grabbed Zale and pulled him into the bushes along the side of the road. From the sound of that boat's engine, they had been on a high-performance racing boat, and the trailer and truck back there in the marina were for just such a boat.

The vehicle was on us in a matter of seconds, but neither of us saw it as we had our heads tucked down behind the shrubbery. It was marshy down there and our feet and knees were in the mud. I'd just stood and started to step out of the muck when I heard the whining sound of a vehicle traveling in reverse. I considered jumping back into the muck, but decided there was no escape. We'd been seen.

"Hola! Que paso?" called a voice from the interior of the pickup.

"Damn," I said, stepping out onto the asphalt "We stink."

"Are you okay?" The truck's passenger was hanging his head out the window, a beer can in his hand.

"We're trying to get to a phone," I said, then I gave them a heavily edited version of our story—that my nephew and I had gone snorkeling and hadn't realized the weather was going to get bad. I told them that we had lost our clothes and wallets and we needed to call the boy's mother. The guys were on their way out to pick up the truck and trailer we had seen, but they offered to turn around and drive us to Florida City first—to the police station if we wanted, but I told them no, just to a gas station would be great. I didn't want to get mixed up with the cops down here in Homestead. I wanted to talk to Jeannie first. I wanted to get some sleep.

Due to the mud and smell, they had us climb into the back of the pickup. We huddled together just behind the truck cab while they drove at ninety miles an hour through the dark night. Barely ten minutes later they dropped us off at a 7-Eleven store, where they bought us hot dogs and Cokes and the driver let me use his cell phone. I walked outside and dialed Jeannie. She sounded more like three-quarters asleep when she answered.

"Hey, it's me."

"Seychelle? Jesus!" She seemed to be waking up fast. I could hear the noise of her bed creaking and the covers rustling and the phone jostling against her ear. "Where are you? Is Zale with you? Are you okay?"

"Yeah, we're together and we're both okay. We're down in Homestead."

"Thank God, you're all right. Homestead?"

"Yeah, it's quite a story, but I'm too tired to tell it over the phone. I just want to get home and I don't know who else to ask."

"I'm on my way. I'll ask my neighbor to watch the boys."

"And one more thing. Could you bring some towels and blankets? And thick warm socks."

I gave her directions to the all-night convenience store and went back inside. I thanked the two guys for the ride and learned they were Mexicans who were racing a team boat here during the winter season. I told them to call me on the VHF if they were under in Lauderdale.

The store clerk was a car guy. I didn't want to have to go back outside into that cold wind, so I leaned on the counter and asked him a hundred questions about cars and engines and the Homestead Motor Speedway. Zale drifted over to the magazine rack and kept his nose buried in the pages of *Sail* and *Yachting* and the like. Jeannie must have broken all kinds of speed records, as she showed up outside the store—some sixty miles south of Fort Lauderdale—in just over an hour.

She climbed out of the driver's seat and hugged us both in suffocating Jeannie-style bear hugs. She was wearing some sort of enormous fringed poncho that both looked and smelled a little like a used horse blanket, but I didn't care. She didn't say a word about the fact that we were standing there barefoot and in wet suits, smelling like a swamp, at almost three in the morning on a night the citrus growers would be thinking about firing up their smudge pots. She just slid open the side door on her minivan and handed us both clean, cushy socks and two queen-sized comforters. She did pause when she noticed the silver case tied with a thin line to Zale's wrist and turned to me with raised brows, but she asked no questions right away. Knowing Jeannie, I thought she was showing incredible restraint. Inside the car she had the heater going, and it felt wonderful. I sat in front, Zale in back, and finally, as she sped up the ramp onto the Florida Turnpike, she turned to me and said, "Okay, so dish. What happened?"

I started by asking her if she had talked to B. J., and she told me that yes, he had gone to my house early on what was now yesterday morning and discovered that we had not spent the night there and the Whaler was gone. He'd called around and located my dinghy at River Bend. The yard guys also reported that the *Mykonos* had been taken out of the yard overnight, but that Leon Quinn assured them that his guys had just shown up very early to move the boat, and that the yard bill would be paid in full as soon as they processed the insurance claim. B. J. and Jeannie couldn't get any law enforcement help on hunting for the boat because they had no evidence that a crime had been committed.

"So, I take it you two were on the *Mykonos*? B. J. was sure of it."

"Yeah." I paused for a minute to think about where this story started, what she already knew. I told her about the story Nick had told his son, about the promise the boy had made, and about our belief that whatever was inside that case was going to help Molly.

Jeannie interrupted me. "I've good news for you on that count." She swiveled her head around and looked back at Zale in the backseat. There were hardly any other cars on the highway, but she made me so nervous when she drove like that. "Zale, we're taking you home to your house, tonight. Your mom's home."

"She's home?" Zale said as he leaned forward, sticking his head into the opening between the two bucket-style seats in the front of the van.

"How'd you do it, Jeannie?"

"I can't take the credit for it. You know that detective, that Mabry fella?"

"Yeah."

"Well, he's taken to sort of stopping by my house and letting me know what's going on with their end of things. Seems he chased down that Wheeler woman you told me about and, though she wouldn't talk to him at first, she called him back later and said a friend of hers had talked her into helping. They got a good description of the shooter from her and sent her to work with a police artist. Then that other guy, Detective Amoretti, was working with that Thompson woman, and the detectives paid a visit to Kagan over at TropiCruz to talk to him about some shady business with the slots. Turns out these guys at TropiCruz knew nothing about it, and they weren't at all happy about it, either. 'Bout that same time, three of their employees stopped showing up for work. After taking a good look at Mrs. Wheeler's police sketch of the guy she thought was the shooter, and noting that the frizzy, big head bore a remarkable resemblance to the missing TropiCruz skipper, the cops issued a warrant for Richard Hunter's arrest for the shooting of Nick Pontus and released Molly. She got home around five and she's been worried sick about Zale. I didn't even think to call her before I left home."

"Do you want to call her?" I asked Zale.

"No, she might be sleeping. Let's just surprise her. We'll get there pretty soon, right?"

"Listen kid, the way Jeannie drives, we'll get there almost as fast as you could dial."

Then Jeannie asked me to fill her in on what had happened out on the *Mykonos*.

"The cops might not have been willing or able to track down the *Mykonos* for you, but the Russians had no trouble."

"What happened?"

It took me the rest of the trip home to bring Jeannie up-to-date on all that had happened to us. She's a great listener, and when I got to the part about being in that stateroom with the water coming in and the trapped air space getting smaller and smaller, she rolled her eyes and clutched at her chest and finally reached over to grab me by the arm.

"That was too close. I almost lost you, didn't I?"

I was doing okay, holding it together and telling the story until she touched me like that. Then I just couldn't hold on anymore.

"Jeannie, we heard them. Jason and Anna. We heard them dying out there. We heard them and we couldn't get to them. We were locked in that cabin and we listened as they died right outside our door." Once the tears started, I couldn't stop the flood. "We couldn't—"

"Seychelle, you stop that right now. Those people are the ones who locked you in there. There was probably nothing you could have done to save them, anyway. You can't save everyone. You saved yourself, and you saved Zale."

My breath came in gulping gasps when I tried to talk. I just felt I had to make her understand. "But I'm— always gonna hear—their voices."

"I know, kid," she said. "I know."

XXVIII.

WHEN we pulled to the curb on the dark street where I had grown up, I thought Zale was asleep. But before Jeannie even shut off the ignition, the back door slid open and the kid leaped out and ran up the steps and into the house. There was some faint light in the living room windows, and I assumed Molly was burning her candles, standing watch, waiting for her boy to come home. I expected to find her dozing, wrapped in her comforter on the couch, waiting to hear that her boy was safe. At least there was that. At least I could bring her this child and maybe, somehow, whatever had happened between us could finally be finished.

When Jeannie and I walked through the front door, mother and son were still standing in the center of the living room, unmoving, locked in an embrace. When Molly looked up, I saw in her face the fierceness of her love for him and the depth of her gratitude for returning him safe to her arms.

And then I saw something else. Something I didn't understand. I saw fear.

I had thought it was all over. We were home and we were all safe. I'd let my guard down, and I wasn't paying attention. So when Janet walked out of the kitchen and started talking, I couldn't even comprehend at first what I was seeing. She'd asked me a question and I hadn't heard a word.

"What?" I said.

"What's the matter with you? Are you some kind of moron? I asked you to bring that fucking case over here. But I'm not asking now. Do it or I'll shoot the kid."

I was such an idiot, I hadn't even seen that she was holding a gun. Again, I noticed that she was speaking in that deep voice of hers. Maybe some men found it sexy, but it was so raspy I found it unsettling to listen to. It was as though this was a different Janet who was speaking.

She was leaning against the door frame, the gun dangling from her right hand, like an accessory to her outfit of black leather pants, pale blue sweater, and black leather jacket. Her too-red lips posed in a perfect little pout, but no one in the room found the look attractive.

"All right," I said. "Don't get excited. I just thought you might want to know what happened to your brother."

I saw in her eyes that she didn't know and she wanted to know. But she was afraid of what I was about to tell her. I knew that I could use that.

"He probably called you from the *Mykonos,* right? Yesterday afternoon? He told you he had the kid and he was going to get the kid to tell him where it was. He didn't know he was sleeping right on top of it. Poor Richard was too stupid to know that case was right under his bunk." I took a couple of steps to my right, away from Molly and Zale in the center of the living room.

"You shut up and bring me the case."

"Bet he hasn't answered his cell phone in the last few hours, though, has he? He's dead, Janet."

"I told you to shut up." I looked at her face. When our eyes met, I saw that there was a flatness to hers.

"It was Kagan," I said.

"You don't know what you're talking about."

I just kept talking right over her words.

"Kagan and his men came out to the *Mykonos* and shot Richard—"

"That's not true."

"So many times his shirt was in bloody tatters."

"Stop it," she kept yelling. "Stop it!"

"The last time I saw him, I pushed his body away to drift down Biscayne Bay."

She stepped away from the kitchen door frame, closer to Molly and Zale, and raised the gun. She pointed it at Zale. Her voice sounded even deeper and more masculine than it had before as she struggled to get her emotions under control. "I swear I'll shoot him."

Zale was hugging the case to his neoprene-covered chest, shaking his head. His glasses glinted in the candlelight.

Molly said, "Zale, honey, it doesn't matter. Whatever it is, just give it to her."

He shook his head. "Huh-uhn. It's Dad's and she killed him."

"Shut up!" Janet shouted, and the volume and pitch of her scream made everyone, Molly, Zale, and Jeannie, all take a step back. I attempted to move a little farther away from Molly, increasing the distance between us, making Janet have to choose a target. "You little monster. You and that fucking Pollyanna mother of yours." She waved the gun up and down Molly's body. "Look at you. What did he ever see in you? You kept calling yourself Mrs. Pontus, acting like *you* were his wife, not me. Kept coming over to the house and bringing that worthless, snotty kid. Kept meeting us at the yacht club after all the brat's races, and every time he saw you, all Nicky could talk about was 'Molly this or Zale that,' " she said, imitating a whining voice, "until I just wanted to puke. What the fuck did you have on him?"

Molly took a step toward Janet, pushing her son behind her. "The difference *was,* Janet, I loved him. Yeah, the sex with you was good at first, and that was why he left. But when he realized who you really were, that you were empty inside, he wanted out. He told me so not too long before he died."

I took a couple more steps to my right, circling around Janet, who was so focused on spewing her hatred for Molly and Zale, she didn't even notice me.

"You liar! Nicky never said no such thing," Janet screamed.

I wanted to get closer, close enough to use one of the fancy Aikido moves that B. J. had taught me to bat the weapon out of your attacker's hand. But when I saw the change in Janet's face, when I saw that perfect porcelain skin pull back into that snarl, teeth bared and the gun coming up, I knew she was going to shoot.

I didn't even think—I just leaped and tackled her. The gun went off and then clattered to the terrazzo when we landed in a heap next to the coffee table. I couldn't see if anyone had been hit because Janet and I were on the floor in what can only be described as a real catfight. I was used to fighting my brothers, who punched and kicked and struggled to get me into wrestling holds. And for the past several years I had been participating in the classic artful moves of Aikido fighting on the mats at the dojo. I'd never before fought against someone who bit and scratched and pulled hair and head-butted, all the while screaming at the top of her lungs.

We rolled around on the floor knocking over furniture and breaking lamps. She yanked so hard on my hair that I thought I was going to black out, and then her fingernails dug into my shoulder where the wet suit I was wearing hung too loose. She ripped at my skin. She was trying without much effect to bite me through the wet suit, and then I was doing my best to keep those frigging teeth away from my face. She wrapped her fingers in the gold chain around my neck, tightening it, trying to strangle me until, with a pop, the chain broke and the dolphin charm flew across the floor. That was it. That was when I decided I'd had enough. I saw my opening and went for it.

I pulled back my fist and nailed her jaw with every ounce of weight I could get behind it. We'd just rolled up onto our knees, face to face, and when I punched her, she fell on her side on the terrazzo floor. I crawled on top of her back, straddling her, and pulled her arms back and up until she squeaked a little, so I knew she wasn't unconscious. I lifted my head fast, trying to flip all the hair out of my eyes to see what was going on in the rest of the room.

"Is everybody okay?" I asked just as Detectives Mabry and Amoretti came through the front door, guns drawn.

XXIX.

THE cops seemed to outnumber us within a matter of seconds. I climbed off Janet, a uniformed officer got cuffs on her, and she was gone, out the front door of Molly's house. Thankfully, the one shot Janet fired had merely cut a hole in one of Molly's original oil paintings on the wall. It turned out that Jeannie, who had been surprisingly quiet while Janet was spitting her vile stuff at us, had actually reached into her pocket under that horse blanket of hers and pushed redial on her cell phone.

"Since Clay was the last one I called—right after you called from Homestead," she said, "I knew it would dial him."

"Clay?" I asked.

She looked over at Detective Mabry and stuck her chin out. "That one. Detective Mabry," but she wasn't quite able to pull it off without a little smile.

I'm certain I was standing there with my jaw dragging on Molly's terrazzo floors when Detective Amoretti asked Zale about the case he was holding.

"It was my dad's. It was on his boat, the *Mykonos*."

"Well, I guess that means it's yours now, son. What's in it?"

"I don't know." Zale hugged the case tighter to him.

"Do you want to tell us about what's happened here?" Mabry asked.

I gave him a grateful look. He understood that we shouldn't push Zale right now. He'd give up the case when he was ready. Jeannie jumped up and said she'd make some tea, and Molly was walking around her living room, trying to push the furniture back into place. Detective Amoretti took her arm and asked her to sit.

"Do you guys mind if Zale and I clean up a little before we get into this long story? This wet suit is giving me the worst goddamn case of chafe you've ever seen."

While Jeannie made the tea, Molly found me an extra-large T-shirt and a pair of overalls she used for painting, and Zale and I retreated to the two bathrooms for a little desalting. When I came out ten minutes later, Jeannie and Detective Mabry were sitting next to each other on Molly's dining room chairs chatting and laughing as though they were on a date. Molly and Zale came out of his room, and Detective Amoretti took up his usual position leaning against the wall, watching. A uniformed officer stood by the door, his pad at the ready, taking notes.

Through the front door, I could see the sky growing a pale pink. There were still clouds out there, but they were cumulous now, bulbous and blue, blowing fast across the horizon. The old Florida houses like Molly's were built without heat or air, and though her parents had installed air conditioning, they'd never added heat. Someone had started a fire in the fireplace, and it was making a big difference in the temperature in the room.

"Have a seat, everybody," Mabry said. "My partner's already spoken to Ms. Pontus while you were in the shower and taken her statement as to what occurred here between the time Ms. Black brought her home from the courthouse and when we arrived. Now, Ms. Sullivan, if you please."

"First, I don't get it. What was Janet doing here?"

Molly spoke first. "She was really acting crazy when she came to the door. She said she'd searched their whole house. Torn everything apart. She said there was no way it was over there, so it had to be here in my house. She said the cops were looking for her brother, and he wasn't answering his phone, and somehow all of that had gotten mixed up in her head to mean it was my fault. Everything that was happening to her was my fault, she said. She was just about to have me start tearing my house apart, when you guys showed up."

"Molly," I said, "you tried to tell us what a monster Janet was and we didn't believe you. I'm sorry about that. She was a hell of an actress. Janet played the part of a normal human being so well. She fooled me."

"Me, too," Jeannie said. "And not many people manage that."

So then it was my turn. I had a feeling they already knew what had happened to Richard Hunter and his two crew members, but I told the story and they took their notes. I noticed that Zale no longer had the line tied to his wrist, but he sat with the case on his lap, fingering the keyholes. Some details of the story—details Zale had already heard once and that I didn't think the kid needed to hear again—I omitted. Maybe it was history that explained who these Hunters were, but I decided to keep my mouth shut about it for now. Besides, I didn't have the stomach for it. So, I told them how Richard had kept asking us about "it," and we assumed "it" was in the case, but we really had no idea what "it" was. And I told them how they'd died, that we hadn't seen or heard anything, and how Zale had sailed us home. When I'd run out of story, everyone turned to Zale.

"Well, son," Mabry said. "Are you ready to see what it was your daddy wanted you to see?"

Zale nodded and held the case out to Detective Amoretti. He set it on the dining table, produced a set of picklocks out of his pocket, and opened the case in seconds. Amoretti lifted out a simple manila folder and opened it. "Interesting," he said, handing the open folder to Molly. Zale craned his neck and read over her shoulder.

After a few seconds' reading, she looked up from the document and stared out through the front windows. "It's a third will?" she asked.

"Looks like it," Amoretti said.

Molly flipped to the back of the document. "It's signed by Nick and witnessed by Leon Quinn. Why wouldn't he have said anything about this? He never told me."

Mabry motioned for the uniformed officer, and when he came, Mabry spoke at length in his ear. The officer then left through the front door and went out to the car.

"He may be long gone, but we would like to have a talk with Mr. Quinn, it appears."

"That's just reminded me of something Richard said yesterday. When he was trying to get Zale to tell him where it was, he said, 'Nick told Quinn that the kid knew where it was.' How would Richard know that unless Quinn told him?"

"Or told Janet," Mabry said. "I think it's likely Quinn was involved with the boss's wife. He probably thought *he'd* seduced *her*."

"So you're saying Nick rewrote his will to make Janet happy, then secretly had Quinn prepare a third will that made the second one null and void?"

"Apparently that was his plan," Mabry said. "Only Quinn then went and spilled the beans to Janet, setting the gears in motion that resulted in Nick's murder."

"And once Nick was dead, the only person who knew about the will besides Quinn and the Hunters—was Zale."

The front door opened and the policeman poked his head in. Bright sunshine was shining on the cars at the curb, and a group of people was standing behind the cop.

"Detectives, there are several individuals out here who insist on talking to these folks. They say they're family."

Molly had been moving her head from side to side, trying to see who was standing outside her door. Suddenly she called out, "Gramma Josie?"

B. J. accompanied Josie into the house, and behind them came my brother, Pit. We all hugged and carried on while the cops stood off to one side and watched, their hands scratching and fidgeting as though this display of affection made them nervous.

B. J. explained that he had been over at my cottage taking care of Abaco and waiting for me to return home when Pit arrived. The two of them were there at my cottage at something like two in the morning when Gramma Josie called, saying she'd had a dream about her great-grandson and needed to come to Fort Lauderdale.

"Pit and I got in my truck and went out to pick her up. We didn't know what else to do," he said. "She insisted we drive her here, and here you all are."

Pit and Molly were smiling shyly and talking, saying the "Hello, gee, you sure look good" stuff that people say when they haven't seen or spoken to each other in years. It sure looked like my brother was having an easier time of it than I had.

The detectives told us that they were leaving then, that they would probably be calling on us again for more statements and certainly later for testimony, but for now, they knew we needed some quiet time with family. Detective Mabry walked over and whispered something to Jeannie, and though it was hard to see past the two of them standing side by side, from the way he jumped a little and grinned at her, I swear, I think she grabbed his ass.

As all the adults hovered around the door, I helped Josie to a chair. I could have sworn she was staring at Zale across the room, sitting at the dining room table, but I didn't think she could really see that well. Her interest in the boy, though, made me look, and now that I had, I realized he was reading some other papers from his father's case. In one hand he held a stapled sheaf of papers that had been inside a manila envelope, and in the other hand he had what looked like a letter. He turned from the letter to the group of adults, and I realized he was staring at my brother.

"Zale," I said. "Are you okay?"

Molly looked at her son. "Honey? What is it?"

Pit walked over to the boy. "Hey, man, I hear you pulled off quite a feat of sailing skill last night."

Zale handed him the letter. Pit cocked his head, shrugged his shoulders, and started to read. As he read, he reached out for a dining room chair without taking his eyes off the page and lowered himself into the chair. When he got to the end of the document, he looked up at Molly.

Molly said, "Would somebody tell me what's going on here?"

Gramma Josie chuckled as though she already knew.

Molly glanced at Josie, puzzled, then said, "Pit, what is that?"

Pit looked back down at the document in his hand and started to read.

Dear son,

If you are reading this, it means I am gone. I want you to know how much I love you and how proud I

*am to be your father. You made me a better man
than I ever would have been without you. I always
told you I would never lie to you, so there is a final
truth I want you to know.*

*Last year when you had your physical for the
International Sailing Association, I asked our doctor
to run some other tests. The results of those tests are
in the report enclosed with this letter. I hope you will
always consider me your true father, but the tests
confirmed something I had suspected for several
years. You have another father. Your mother was in
love with another man when I first met her. I believe
he is your biological father. Now that I am gone, the
truth will come out, and I wanted you to learn about
this from me.*

*Some people will remember me as a real son of a
bitch, but others have always seen me as a generous
man. I want you to be happy, son, so always look on
my death as a time not when you a lost a father, but
when you gained a new one.*

> *Love always,*
> *Dad*

When Pit finished reading the letter, everyone in the
room turned to look at Molly. She stood with her head
lowered, staring down at her hands, rubbing the palm of
one hand as though there were some sort of stain she
could rub off.

"Mom?" Zale said. "Is that true?"

When she did look up finally, she didn't look at her
son or at my brother. She looked at me.

"Yes," she said. "It's true. When I found out I was
pregnant, I panicked. Pit," she said, turning to face him.
"You weren't ready to settle down with a baby and a

wife. You're too much of a free spirit. It would have killed you."

He opened his mouth to protest, but stopped. I knew it was true, and I think my brother was too honest with himself to say otherwise.

"Nick had been giving me the hard press for weeks," Molly said. "He knew I was going with Pit, but he always used to say I was the girl he was going to marry. So I went out with him once and we eloped the next day. I'm sorry about the lies. I'm sorry about all the hurt I caused. But I was young, and I did what I thought was best."

Pit dropped the letter and turned to Zale. "Hey, I don't know what to say. That's a lot to take in, isn't it?"

Zale nodded, looking at my brother as though afraid of what would come next.

"You've just lost your dad, and I know that still hurts. And I know that I couldn't ever presume to take Nick's place in your heart or in your life. But I just found out I've got a son." He paused at hearing the words come out of his mouth. "I've got a son."

It was impossible to say which one of them moved first, they just came together and hugged, my brother and his son, both of them laughing and crying at the same time.

I don't think anyone else noticed the tears on Molly's cheeks.

I stood up and crossed the room and took my friend in my arms. "I'm so sorry for all those years lost," I whispered.

"Me, too," she said.

We didn't have to say the rest of it. It was as though some muscle in my body that had been holding tight in a cramp for thirteen years just let go.

We looked across the room at Pit and Zale standing

next to each other talking. "Look at them," I said to her, knowing that she would know I was talking about the resemblance. "How did we not see it?"

"I don't know," she said. "I figured Nick knew."

Maybe if I had seen the kid as a baby and looked at his Greek father and part-Seminole mother, I would have realized this fair-haired boy was something strange. But meeting him as I had, and under these circumstances, I never guessed. Maybe that had been part of Molly's plan.

Jeannie was sitting on the couch, and she picked up the will that was resting on the coffee table. "Hey, Molly," she said as she read down the document. "This will is different than the first one Nick wrote right after your divorce. Significantly different."

"Really?" Molly said, though she didn't sound all that interested.

"Yeah, really. Like, for example, you and your son inherit Pontus jointly, and you are expected to run the company."

"What?"

"Yup, says so right here."

"No!" Molly said, and everyone laughed.

B. J. said, "You must be the only person in history who ever acted like that when told they were about to inherit millions." B. J. turned to me and draped his arm across my shoulders. "I knew I liked this friend of yours."

"But I'm not a businessperson," Molly said.

Zale laughed. "Mom, you sound like me when I complained that I was just a kid. It's like Seychelle told me. We'll hire people to do that."

AFTER that, B. J. and Molly went into the kitchen to make pancakes for everyone. I volunteered to go in B. J.'s place, but he made some comment about everybody having lived through enough life-threatening situations for one day, and he shooed me away.

When we'd eaten our fill, Gramma Josie called out my name and motioned for me to go sit next to her. I sat in the chair Molly had just vacated.

"What is it, Gramma Josie?"

"I need to show you something. You brother, too. You drive."

"I can't right this minute, Gramma Josie. I don't have my car here."

"I do," Jeannie said, and given the way she was smirking at B. J., I had the feeling this was something the two of them had planned. In the end, everybody wanted to go see what Gramma Josie wanted to show Pit and me, and we all piled into Jeannie's minivan.

Josie directed us to drive downtown, onto Las Olas, heading east. Just after the shopping district, she told Jeannie to turn into the neighborhood on the right. After a couple of blocks, past a large church, she pointed to an old vine-covered house I recognized. It was squeezed in between the larger, more luxurious estates, but on the other side of the house, it fronted on the river. I had motored past this house a hundred times in *Gorda*. Though I couldn't see it when we got out of the car, I knew there was a beautiful classic wooden sailboat moored on the other side.

Gramma Josie took Pit and me by the hands and led us through a side gate that led through a small courtyard and on to the back of the house. Everything was overgrown and unkempt. Whoever lived in this house had really let it get away from them.

When we walked into the backyard, we saw a group of several chairs, but there was only a single woman sitting alone. She rose and turned when she heard us approach, and I was astonished to see that it was Mrs.

Wheeler, who had tried to avoid me whenever I tried to speak to her, and now, she was frowning at the sight of us. Josie let go of us and walked up to the woman. She took her hand without saying a word. I thought maybe Josie had brought us there to thank her for her part in identifying Nick's killer, but when I saw the way the women held hands, the way they communicated without having to use words, I suddenly realized that Faith Wheeler was the little white girl who had taught Josie how to speak English at the trading post.

Josie turned to Pit and me and said, "Seychelle, Pit, meet your grandmother."

XXX.

O F all the things that I had been thinking on the drive over and the walk around the house, that didn't even come close to being something I'd considered.

"What?" Pit and I said in unison.

Mrs. Wheeler stepped forward and offered us her hands palms up. We grasped her hands and tried to look enthusiastic. I wasn't too sure about how Pit felt, but I felt like we had just fallen down the rabbit hole. She asked us to sit with her and listen, and it wasn't like we could say no. Besides, I thought, glancing at B. J.'s smug expression, I was waiting to hear the punch line.

We all sat out on the old wood deck chairs. Zale and Molly sat side by side cross-legged in the grass.

"I've been watching you all for a long time," she said. "All your lives, really. You lived just up the river, but it was always a distance I couldn't cross. My second husband thought maybe I should tell you all after Annie died, but I knew your father would never forgive me."

"I don't understand," I said. "We have a grandmother we've never met? Why? What happened?"

"It's a long story, and it's not one I'm particularly proud of." Her veined hands fidgeted in her lap. She looked over in Josie's direction. The old Indian woman was nodding and rubbing her lips over her teeth. "I've imagined this day so many times. Now it's here and I just don't know where to begin."

"We have so many questions," I said. "Who are you, and why haven't we ever met you before?"

"Okay," she said. "Well, my name was Faith Hitchings when my daughter Annie was born right here in this house," she began, and with those words, I suddenly realized it was true. This woman *was* my grandmother. "Your grandfather and I, we'd been trying to have a baby for years, but God does not always provide. When we finally did get pregnant, she was the most beautiful little baby girl you'd ever seen. But we soon learned that our Annie was a headstrong girl, too. We were so happy to have her, we indulged her. More often than not, she got her way. Her father died when she was in high school, and I spoiled her even more after that. When she was a grown girl and off in college down at the University of Miami, she came home one weekend and met a fella over at the Elbow Room. I thought he was a common boy, not good enough for her, and I told her so. We argued. She said she'd fallen in love with her sailor and wanted to marry him. I told her if she did that I would never speak to her again as long as she lived. They ran off to the Bahamas the next week and were married, and for once in my life, I kept my word to my child."

"Oh my God. Mom knew you lived right here and she never spoke to you? She never brought us to visit you?"

She'd taken a handkerchief out of her pocket and was twisting and pulling at it in her lap. She nodded. "Annie and Red lived in an apartment when you children were little, but I knew from Realtor friends of mine that they were looking for a house on a canal. I bought the house next door to Josie's daughter and had the Realtor offer it to them at a steal of a price. They never knew it was me—never would have bought it if they'd known, and from then on I'd get news about you all from Josie or from a few other friends I had who knew about my family. I've always watched you on the river ever since you were both such little things scrambling all over that boat of your daddy's. I knew the sound of *Gorda*'s engine, and whenever she passed, I'd watch from behind the curtains."

"Is this the house you grew up in?" I asked.

"Yes, my daddy had this house built for us in 1920. Josie wasn't allowed to come here when we were girls, but later, after mother died, Josie visited whenever her family came to town. It was after the war when your mother was born. Things were different then. Fort Lauderdale was booming. Your grandfather bought that boat," she indicated the little yawl with the varnished trunk cabin and teak decks, "and we used to go on lovely sails with Annie, when she was young. In fact, we named the boat for our daughter. Would you like to see her?"

"Sure," I said.

"You go on ahead," she said. Make yourself at home. I'm afraid I'm not as comfortable on deck as I once was."

As we walked across the grass, Pit said, "This is too much for one day."

"I know. But think about Mom. Think about her relationship with Dad. This explains a lot about her. I've certainly read enough about depression through the years to know that she didn't need to have a reason for her sadness. But it was always hard to *feel* that. I always felt we just hadn't done enough to make her happy. There's something about knowing this that makes me feel better. We weren't the ones making her so sad."

Pit climbed aboard first, but B. J. turned to me and wrapped his arms around me. He kissed me on the lips. "Happy birthday, Seychelle," he said.

I hadn't thought of it until that moment. It was Monday and I was thirty years old.

"It's not a surprise party," he said.

"You. You arranged this?"

"You said you wanted something memorable. It was Josie's idea. She told me that your grandmother was alive. She had promised Faith years ago that she would never tell you. Even so, lately, she tried to tell you a couple of times, but you weren't ready yet to hear it. She told me if I arranged it, she wouldn't feel like she had broken her promise to Faith."

"I still can't get used to it."

"None of us knew you were going to get kidnapped and nearly killed in the middle of it all, but somehow Josie always knew you were going to be ready for this day. She never lost faith."

XXXI.

WITH the helm lashed and the sails balanced, *Annie* sailed as true a course as any vessel with an autopilot. B. J. was out on deck, sitting with his back to the mast in the shadow of the mainsail, reading one of several fat philosophy books he had brought along on the trip. I was down in the galley, digging through the stores I'd carefully packed in the icebox, trying to find the shrimp that I knew I had bought. Tonight was going to be an evening to remember. I was going to cook B. J.'s dinner.

When I found the shrimp, I pulled out the package and closed the heavy lid to the box. I climbed two steps up the ladder to glance around the horizon and check for traffic, a habit I kept up even when B. J. was on deck. I knew he could get into a book and be lost for hours.

The wind was light out of the east-southeast, typical for late April, and we were sailing close-hauled just offshore from Key Biscayne. The Cape Florida Light was a couple of miles ahead off the starboard quarter. We'd turn at the light and sail through Stiltsville, heading for an anchorage off Elliot Key, our first night's anchorage on this trip down the Keys. We were allowing ourselves two weeks and hoping to get down as far as the Dry Tortugas, but in the way of sailors, we'd take each day as it came. Part of me felt a need to return to Elliot to seek some kind of closure, to probe at what was still an open wound. Janet was headed to trial, but I still heard the voices of the dying in my dreams.

In the months since my birthday, my brothers and I had begun to know our grandmother. She was not a warm woman, and as an old-time Methodist, she disapproved of much of what we did. Maddy had thought Pit and I were playing a joke on him when we went down to his house that week and sprang the news on him. But Faith invited the whole family over for dinner the next week, including Maddy's wife, Jane, and his kids, Freddie and Annie, and Zale came along with his mom and Gramma Josie. Faith tried to look like she enjoyed all the noise and bedlam, but I could tell she wasn't used to having people in her house.

After that, we all went over to visit her on our own. Pit worked on the *Annie* when he was in town, which tended to be lots more often these days. He always brought Zale with him. Maddy brought in a yard crew and relandscaped the house, which Faith said she appreciated, but she wrinkled her nose sometimes when we sat out on the deck at her house, me with my beer and her with a gin and tonic, and watched the boats go by.

It was on my second or third visit that Faith started insisting that I should take the *Annie* out on a cruise. She told me it hurt her to see the boat sit there growing barnacles all the time. Pit was down in Antigua and Maddy didn't know a thing about sailboats, she said, so it was up to me. So I'd talked to B. J. about it, we'd compared our calendars, gone for sea trials, bought our stores, and here we were.

I wanted to try to make shrimp scampi for dinner. B. J. had promised me he would bring several cookbooks on the trip, so I crossed to the main salon to look through the books he had stored in the bookshelf behind the settee. There were lots of fat tomes with unpronounceable authors' names, and several ratty paperback novels that looked like they dated back to the seventies. I didn't see anything that resembled a cookbook. I began to pull out books to see what was stored behind the front volumes, and stuck behind a copy of Slocum's *Sailing Alone Around the World,* I found a slim leather photo album.

I could tell from the mildew on the leather that the album had been on the boat for a while. I pulled it out and made my way to the companionway ladder. The light in the dark wood cabin was far too dim to examine this treasure. After another quick glance around the horizon, checking our relationship to the sportfisherman overtaking us on the seaward side, I settled in and opened the album.

At first I was disappointed. I didn't recognize any of the people in the black-and-white photos. I thought it was possible that some of them were photos of Faith, but she had changed so much through the years that I couldn't be sure. It was only at the very end of the album, where there were a few loose color snapshots, that I saw a face I recognized.

It was my mother, about ten years old, and in the first photo she was standing with a beautiful woman next to a tree. They were wearing very dated swimsuits from the late forties or early fifties, and they both had one hand raised grasping a rough, knotted rope suspended from the tree. They weren't looking at the camera. They were looking at each other and laughing as though one of them had just told a very good joke. In the next photo, my mother was flying through the air, her mouth open wide, her dark hair splayed in the wind. The photographer had caught her at just the moment when she'd let go of the rope and her legs and arms were spread wide. She was going to land in one heck of a belly flop.

"Hey, whatcha got there?" B. J. asked as he climbed down into the cockpit and sat next to me.

"It's an old album I found. Look at this one of my mom." I handed him the snapshot. "And this one. I think that's Faith with her."

"Yeah. These are great. Look at the swimsuits."

"Look how happy they were together. They were so young. So free. Is it getting old that changes us so much?"

"It does for some people."

"I know what that girl's feeling in this picture, swinging from that rope, being afraid to just let go."

A flock of pelicans flying in a perfect V formation glided past just a few feet above the swells.

"B. J., how does it happen that people who love each other *so much* can get mad over some stupid thing and never speak to each other again? How did my mother let that happen with her own mother?"

"The same way you and Molly did."

I sighed and looked at the photo of the girl screaming with joy as she flew through the air. "You know, sometimes it really scares me how much I'm like her."

"But you're also different. You are the age now that your mother was when she turned her back on her family. Instead of shrinking, your family is growing. Instead of holding on to hurt and allowing it to end your friendship, you're learning to let go."

I turned and tucked an arm around his bare chest and pulled him to me. Our kiss was long and deep. And like every time we touched, he fired up all the thousands of sparkly little nerves in my body. But there was an ease and a peace that I hadn't known before. Yeah, Molly Pontus had flirted with B. J., just like a hundred other beautiful women did each day, and for some crazy reason, here he was in the cockpit of this sailboat sailing with me to the Keys. Maybe, just maybe, I could begin to believe he would stay.

When we pulled apart, I saw we were abeam of the lighthouse. It was time to make our turn if we were going to make Elliot by nightfall. The sails were trimmed perfectly and we were making a good five knots through the water. The sky was starting to pale and the night promised to be warm and clear. There was nothing between us and the Dry Tortugas.

"I'd really hate to mess with these sails," I said. "What do you say we just let her go?"

Read on for an exciting sneak preview of

WRECKERS' KEY
by
Christine Kling

Now available in hardcover
from Ballantine Books

"WE hit the reef so hard, I'm surprised no one was killed," Nestor said. "I keep dreaming about it, you know? Hearing the sound of the hull crunching across the coral and then Kent's screams when his arm broke." He rubbed his hand across his eyes like he was trying to wipe away the vision. "This situation scares me, Seychelle. My whole career's on the line here."

I couldn't disagree with him. When you put a multi-million-dollar yacht on the reef on her maiden voyage, your reputation as a captain is toast. I was there to help with the salvage of the boat, but I wasn't sure what I could do to salvage Nestor's career.

Catalina Frias reached across the table, took her husband's hand, and focused her large brown eyes on his face. She didn't say anything for several seconds, but there was a sense of intimacy in that moment that was stronger than if she'd grabbed him and planted a wet one on him. "Hey, we are going to get through this, *mi amor*, okay?" Her soft voice was accented, but her English was perfect. She squeezed his hand, her other arm resting across the top of the belly that bulged beneath her pretty print maternity top.

I was sitting with the two of them at an outside table at the Two Friends Patio Restaurant on Front Street. I'd arrived in Key West late the afternoon before on my forty-foot aluminum tug *Gorda,* and when I called Nestor on the VHF, I told him I was too tired to come ashore after a four-day trip down from Lauderdale with only my dog as crew. I just wanted to drop the hook and collapse in my bunk, so we'd agreed to meet in the morning for Sunday brunch. Now, here I was sitting under a lush trellis of bougainvillea pushing scrambled eggs and sausage around my plate, my appetite gone.

"Nestor, this is the first time I've taken *Gorda* this far from home. I wouldn't do this for just anybody, you know."

When he smiled that boyish smile so full of gratitude, my heart ached for him. He was in a hell of a spot.

"*Gracias, amiga.* I can't lose this job," he said, the backs of his fingers caressing his wife's belly. "Not now, with the baby coming in just a few weeks."

I'd known Nestor much longer than his wife had and I loved him like a brother. There was a time when maybe that love could have gone another way, but the attraction that might have been had turned into an abiding friendship. He really was one of the good guys. He showed up on the docks just before Red died, and afterward, when I started running *Gorda* on my own and several of the captains were bad-mouthing the only female captain in the towing business, he always stood up for me. I'd watched him work his way up the waterfront, going from being a captain on the water taxi to running the charter fishing boat *My Way,* until now, finally, he'd gotten his big break about four months ago, and he was the captain of a luxury power yacht. The *Power Play* was a newly commissioned Sunseeker 94 owned by a local resident millionaire, Ted Berger. Berger had made his money in dot-com-related businesses, and when he'd sold out he'd bought several South Florida TV stations and sports teams.

"Do you think Berger's going to can you?"

"I don't know. Maybe. He hasn't said anything yet. Seychelle, this was the first passage I'd made as captain. Other than a couple of sea trials to work on the engines, we hadn't really taken her out yet. He told me when he hired me to commission the yacht that he wanted her down here in Key West for Race Week, but then he decided to install new flat-screen TVs in all the staterooms, then a new sound system, and we were late getting out of the yard. The festivities down here had already started, and the boss was itching to come down and party. Otherwise, we wouldn't have been going so fast in a squall."

"You hit that reef going almost twenty knots in a rain squall?"

"I know it sounds bad, Seychelle. Especially to someone like you. But let's face it—you've not exactly embraced the electronics age. Do you even *have* a GPS on that tugboat of yours?"

"Nestor, what I do is not the point here."

"Sey, you don't even own a cell phone."

"Okay, already."

"See, the *Power Play* is loaded with every bit of electronic equipment imaginable. Berger spared no expense. The man is really into toys, and there are backups for the backups. So what we were doing is running on instruments, the same way commercial pilots do with planes full of hundreds of passengers. The autopilot is tied into one of three separate GPS systems. We were in Hawk's Channel and everything had been working great up to that point. I was on the bridge myself because I knew we were nearing the entrance to Key West Harbor.

All the instruments showed us more than a half mile from any obstructions when *bam*! We ran right up onto these rocks off West Washerwoman Shoal. The impact knocked Kent off his feet, and when he tried to break his fall, the bone just snapped—came right out through his skin." Nestor shuddered at the memory. He'd already told me it had been a nasty compound fracture.

Nobody said anything for several long seconds while we all saw it happen in our minds, saw the big ninety-four-footer come to a grinding halt on the rocks, the men on the bridge thrown off their feet, the screams and the blood. Nestor grasped the Saint Christopher's medal he wore round his neck and kissed the face of the saint.

"So, Nestor," I said, "what do you think happened?"

My friend looked at his wife for a moment, as though unsure he should say what he was thinking. It was amazing to watch how the two of them communicated, saying so much in a glance or a touch.

"Seychelle," Nestor started, after a quick look around the dining patio to see if anyone was listening to our conversation. Satisfied, he leaned closer and lowered his voice. "I've spent a lot of time with Ted Berger these past weeks, and I wouldn't put anything past him. He calls himself The Other Ted, as though he's in the same league as Turner. But he'd do anything to get there. Ruthless is the word that comes to mind." Nestor lifted his shoulders and bobbed his head once, like a bow. "Okay, maybe you have to be that way to get the kind of money he has, but lately, with the start-up of this girls' hockey league and buying this boat, I think he's overextended himself. He wants out of this boat deal and now he seems more pissed over the fact that he's getting hit with a big salvage claim than over the business of wrecking her in the first place."

"Wait a minute. Are you saying you think Berger tried

to wreck his own boat?" I tried hard to keep the disbelief out of my voice.

"Jesus," he said, swiveling his head to look around the empty patio. "Not so loud, Sey. I don't have any proof—yet. But it just doesn't make sense otherwise. The only way this could have happened is if the equipment malfunctioned somehow. And I'm just saying that Ted Berger would have been better off with the insurance company cashing him out of an investment that had got out of hand."

"Nestor, I'm finding this kind of hard to believe."

"You'd understand if you could have heard him while we were in the boatyard. He was constantly complaining about how much things cost. He had no idea what he was getting into when he bought a yacht that size."

"I suppose it makes sense in a way. If he'd just put the boat up for sale, it would have signaled to people that he was in financial trouble."

"Exactly. And he has the background—he *made* his money in electronics. I'm going to have a buddy of mine check out the equipment on the boat and see if he can find evidence it's been tampered with. Get him to come down before we take off to head back up north. I don't intend to take the fall for Ted Berger's financial problems."

At that moment Nestor's eyes flicked to the right and focused on something outside the restaurant. The skin across his cheeks grew taut and his eyes narrowed for only a second before his face broke into a huge, forced grin. He lifted his hand and waved.

I twisted in my seat, glanced over my shoulder. A white-haired man wearing a loud red and blue Hawaiian shirt was standing on the sidewalk in front of the restaurant. He waved, and then went in the front door, clearly headed for us out on the patio. A moment later, he appeared in the side door, and his voice boomed, "Good morning," causing the other diners' heads to turn. When he reached our table, he placed both his hands on Catalina's shoulders, then bent and kissed her on the cheek. He said, "Our mommy-to-be looks more glowingly beautiful every time I see her."

Catalina's body had gone still at his touch, her only movement when she turned her face away as he kissed her, so his mouth wound up kissing her hair.

Nestor stood and shook hands with the man. Either he hadn't noticed or he was choosing to ignore his wife's discomfort. "Good morning," he said as he pumped the man's hand. Then he turned to me. "Seychelle, I'd like to introduce you to Ted Berger."

I started to stand, but Berger waved me back down. "So, you're the tugboat captain," he said as he seated himself in the fourth chair at the table and waggled a coffee mug at the waitress. "I kind of expected a hag with a corncob pipe." He cocked his head to one side and looked at me from head to as much as he could see under the table. "You're definitely not a hag."

The Tugboat Annie jokes had grown old about the second month after I inherited Sullivan Towing and Salvage from my father. That was more than three years ago.

"I'm just here to do the job you hired me for, Mr. Berger."

He threw his hands in the air in mock surrender. "Oh my, I've offended her. Very businesslike of you, Miss Sullivan. Or should I call you captain?"

"Seychelle is fine," I said. Up close, I realized that the man's white hair was deceiving. He wasn't as old as I'd originally thought. His face and neck looked like they belonged to a man not yet out of his forties. He was a couple of inches shorter than me, maybe five foot eight, and his forced joviality and loud clothes made him appear as though he was overcompensating for something.

"Okay. Seychelle, then. Interesting name."

I got ready to go into the usual explanation, but he beat me to it. "Named after the islands in the Indian Ocean, I assume."

"Pretty good. Not many people recognize the name."

"Trust me, Ted, Sey's a lot better off than her brothers," Nestor said.

"Oh?" Berger asked, his eyebrows lifting into the lock of white hair that had fallen on his forehead.

I nodded. "Madagascar and Pitcairn," I said.

"Oh dear," he said, laughing. "Parents *can* be cruel. So, Seychelle, Nestor tells me he would rather have you tow the boat up to Lauderdale than any of that scum over at Ocean Towing."

"Ted, I may have exchanged a few harsh words with those guys, but I didn't call them scum," Nestor said.

"Well, I'll call them that!" He turned to me. "Do you know what they are trying to charge me for getting the *Power Play* off that reef and into Robbie's Marina on Stock Island?"

"I can imagine. Nestor told me it took them almost twelve hours to get her free."

"They're goddamn pirates!"

"No, sir, actually, they probably saved the boat and saved the insurance company a bundle. They'd rather pay the yard bill and salvage than suffer a total loss."

He rolled his eyes and turned away from me.

Out in the street, a tall man with stringy shoulder-length hair, wearing nothing but swim trunks, was trying to untangle the leash of his mangy German shepherd from around his legs and the pedals of his beach bike. He was mumbling to himself. Our table was situated so close to the street that we could not help but overhear the string of obscenities and incomprehensible answers he was giving to the voices he apparently heard in his head.

When Berger spoke again, he continued staring out at the man on the street. I wasn't sure if he was talking to himself or to us. "I like things that are new and shiny. No matter what, *now* the *Power Play* is going to be a repaired vessel." He turned and focused his eyes on mine. "And I don't like patched-up shit."

I smiled, refusing to look away. "Well, welcome to boats, Mr. Berger. If you're not running them, you're working on them. As I understand it, the hull wasn't even holed. You've just got damage to rudders, stabilizers, props, and the like," I said. "You know, I wouldn't think of it as a patched-up boat. I'd say Nestor was just breaking her in."

He tightened one cheek in a half smile. "That's one way of looking at it." His tone told me it would not be his view. "So you're going to help our boy here get the boat back to Lauderdale where they can make proper repairs?"

I didn't like the way he called Nestor *our boy*. "Sure am."

Nestor said, "The guys at Robbie's have put a temporary epoxy patch on the deep scratches in the hull. It will have to be faired and painted later; they just didn't like the bare glass underwater. One prop was a total loss and the other is slightly damaged, but usable. Rudders were totaled. There was some structural damage to interior bulkheads and issues that will need to be addressed up in Lauderdale. I just want these guys to get her in shape for the trip north. It'll be close, but I'll bet we could launch tomorrow."

"That sounds good to me," I said. "The sooner the better."

Berger pushed back his chair and stood. He looked down at Catalina. "You gonna get this guy to show you around Key West, relax a little bit? Beautiful woman like you comes down to be with her man—he should show you off. Seems he spends all his time in that boat-yard."

"I told her I was going to be busy," Nestor said. "And I didn't like the idea of her riding the bus in her condition, but she insisted."

"My husband says *my condition* like pregnancy is an illness," Catalina said to me. She was ignoring Berger's comments. "Having babies is natural. Stop worrying." She reached for his hand again. "I've been trying to talk him into doing a little windsurfing," she said. "I'd like to see him relax, have a little fun. He's very good, you know. When he was in his teens, he was the National Windsurfing Champion in the Dominican Republic."

"Listen to your wife, Nestor. She's a smart, stand-by-your-man kind of woman. Makes me wonder what she sees in a guy like you." He punched Nestor in the arm hard enough to rock him back in his chair. "So, how soon do you two think the boat will be ready to head north?"

"We've got a good weather window coming up, and I'd like to leave as soon as possible," I said. "Nestor and I were just starting to discuss our departure plans when you arrived."

"Really?" he said. "You looked so serious. And secretive. Like my crew here was plotting a mutiny."

Nestor and I both must have shown our surprise. Berger laughed and punched Nestor in the arm again, harder. "Just kidding, buddy."